CONVENT GIRLS ON PARADE

Excitement had run high when the girls had been informed they would be receiving the eager bachelors of the town in the main parlor of the convent.

Now the moment had arrived. Charlotte sat in the large, whitewashed parlor with the rest of the girls, dressed in her bright blue woolen dress with a freshly whitened kerchief and cap, her eyes demurely fixed on the floorboards, awaiting the onslaught of suitors who had been clamoring outside the doors since noon.

Their entrance was greatly subdued, however, once they got past the sentries and were met by the stoic-faced nuns. Somewhat abashed, they followed the nuns into the main parlor and then stood sheepishly in the center of the room, blinking at the equally apprehensive girls lining its walls.

There was an awkward moment, and then the ice broke. The men began to move toward the girls of their liking. Some of the more forward women even rose to meet them, although they did try to remember to keep their eyes lowered with proper maidenly modesty, as they had been warned to do time and again by the ever-present nuns.

Like bees drawn to honey, at least a third of the fifty men swarmed down upon Charlotte, all talking at once, pushing and shoving to capture her attention. She pressed back against the wall, wishing it would open up and let her in, not knowing what to do—or say. . . .

THE LAST CASQUETTE GIRL

LORENA DUREAU

PINNACLE BOOKS   NEW YORK

THE LAST CASQUETTE GIRL

An original Pinnacle Books edition, published for the first time anywhere.

First printing, July 1981

Second printing, November 1983

ISBN: 0-523-41266-5

Cover illustration by John Solie

Printed in Canada

PINNACLE BOOKS, INC.
1430 Broadway
New York, New York 10018

To my three parents:
Aline, Henry and Josephine Dureau
without whose help—each in a different
but very important way—this book probably
never would have seen the light of day,

and

To the "godparents" of my Casquette Girl:
Marion Chesney and Harry Scott Gibbons

The Last Casquette Girl

Preface

The Casquette Girls are an integral part of New Orleans folklore. Those early eighteenth-century brides of the lower Mississippi Valley played as important a role in the development of America as the Pilgrim mothers of New England or the pioneer women of the West.

A distinction should be made, however, between the *filles à la cassette* and those random boatloads of women of rather questionable reputation who, prior to 1728, had been sent over from France to keep the predominantly male population of His Majesty's Louisiana colonies "content." It was because the officers and more educated men of New Orleans refused to accept such women as wives, protesting that they wanted the future mothers of their children to be of better caliber, that the Casquette Girls, or "maids with the little traveling chests," arrived on the scene. Distinguished from their predecessors by the fact that they were "good little girls" coming with dowries in their hands and the blessings of King and Church on their virginal brows, they were the hope for the future of that precarious little city set in the midst of the swamplands, struggling for survival and some semblance of stability.

Although the leading characters of this book are fictitious, the multifaceted world of colonial New Orleans in which they move, as well as most of the principal events and personages involved, are all based on historical fact. Actually, the "acorn" from which this novel eventually grew was a brief statement in a history book that referred to Gov. Perier's having intervened between two men on the verge of fighting a duel over one of the women in that famous bridal consignment. How the real-life Casquette Girl felt about the governor's suggestion that her rivals draw lots for her is not recorded, however, so our heroine has been permitted to react to that official intervention in her own singular manner.

Besides the usual sources of information consulted while researching material for such a book, the author wishes to give special acknowledgment to the invaluable information gleaned from Sister Jane Frances, former historian of the Ursuline Convent in New Orleans; Sidney Villere, well-known Louisiana historian; George Dureau, Sr., commander of the United States Power Squadron, and last but not least, Sister Marie Madeleine Hachard of St. Stanislas, whose charming collection of letters to her father, first published in Rouen in 1728, has left for posterity a detailed account of her long, perilous voyage from France to New Orleans, as well as her impressions of the ten-year-old settlement on her arrival there—impressions that have served to enlighten and inspire many a subsequent generation and most certainly this author.

Lorena Dureau
New Orleans
January 1981

x

Chapter I

"Charlotte, you naughty girl! Go to your room at once!"

Charlotte pushed a honey-colored curl back from her forehead with an exasperated sigh, as she rose reluctantly to the call. Even as she obeyed, the gold glints flashing in her hazel eyes betrayed the rebellion that welled up within her despite her efforts to control her annoyance.

There was always that same sharp-edged tone in her aunt's voice whenever the latter addressed her. Charlotte had been living with Germaine almost a year now, and her aunt's hostility toward her, if anything, was growing worse.

In the beginning it had been so disappointing to go to what she had hoped would be her first real home and encounter such a cool reception. After eleven years in the confines of the Ursuline convent, she had been looking forward to living a more relaxed, perhaps even exciting life with her still attractive, pleasure-loving aunt. Charlotte recalled how fascinated she had always been by Germaine when the latter would stop by the convent on one of those rare breathless visits of hers, enveloped in an aura of exotic perfume and clad in colorful hoop-skirted gowns and luxurious furs that contrasted so vividly with the drabness around her.

Orphaned at an early age, when her parents and three brothers had been wiped out by the plague, Charlotte had fallen under the guardianship of her *Tante* Germaine, her mother's younger sister, only fifteen years older than Charlotte herself. At the time, Germaine, who had a basically carefree but rather shallow nature, did her duty by her young niece obligingly enough, deciding that the best way

1

to see to it that the girl was properly educated would be to "turn the child over to the nuns."

Although Germaine's own marriage to a man thirty years her senior had been childless, she ignored the suggestions of well-meaning friends who advised her to keep the girl at home. Her husband was extremely active in the local politics of Marseilles, and a five-year-old youngster underfoot simply did not fit into the social life she led, which the wealthy young matron frankly enjoyed and had no desire to curtail.

When the time finally came, however, for the nuns to return Charlotte, a full-grown maid of seventeen summers, to the rather reluctant bosom of her aunt, Germaine found the presence of a pretty young girl just ripening into womanhood even less welcome than before. Recently widowed, the rather plump but still attractive Germaine, with her generous mass of dark brown hair and large blue eyes, was just beginning to enjoy her newly acquired riches and eligibility for remarriage. Most certainly the last person she wanted around her was a lovely niece, fifteen years her junior, to distract the attentions of prospective suitors from herself!

At first her aunt's belligerent attitude had bewildered Charlotte. It dampened the original joy she had felt at being free at last from the rigid routine of the convent. The girl soon realized she had simply exchanged one frustration for another. It was becoming increasingly obvious that, as long as she remained under her aunt's roof, she would be spending most of her time isolated in her room.

Although life was quite gay at the manor, with frequent *soirées* and a steady flow of visitors coming and going, Charlotte was kept in the background. She was expected to help with the preparations for a party, but was seldom allowed to attend one. Somehow Germaine would always manage to find some excuse to get her off the scene.

On two or three occasions her aunt, with unaccustomed concern, had suddenly noticed how "pallid" Charlotte looked and insisted she go straight to bed instead of joining the party downstairs, since she might be "catching something."

Other times, Germaine would embarrass her before the

2

guests by enumerating all her shortcomings, real or fancied, and then seize the slightest pretext to send her to her room.

Last night it started as soon as the presentations had begun. Despite the simple, almost inappropriate gown Charlotte had been given to wear for so elegant an occasion, several people had been gracious enough to approach her as she entered the room and exclaim over "what a lovely young niece Germaine had."

Feeling a little timid with s many eyes scrutinizing her, especially after having heard some of the disparaging remarks her aunt had made about her just before her entrance, Charlotte had curtsied self-consciously and murmured the usual acknowledgments, fearful of saying the wrong thing and bringing further criticism down on her head. Germaine, however, had been quick to pounce upon that failure to speak louder.

"Speak up, girl! Lift your head and speak plainly. You know it's impolite to mumble like that!"

Trying to articulate past the growing knot in her throat, Charlotte heard herself squeak out an *"Enchantée"* to the next guest in such a strained, high-pitched voice that not even she had recognized it as her own.

Already annoyed, her aunt had become even angrier.

"Don't be insolent!" she had chided. "There's no need to speak in that tone just because I corrected you!" Then the words Charlotte had been expecting came. "If you're going to behave so rudely, go to your room this minute!"

The guests in their immediate vicinity had shifted rather uneasily, as they had seen her dismay, and an elderly lady had put a calming hand on Germaine's arm in an effort to cut the tirade short. "Please, *chérie*, don't be too hard on the child. Can't you see the poor girl is frightened half out of her wits? I'm sure she doesn't mean to be discourteous."

With a start, Germaine had quickly regained her composure and turned to her guest with a placating smile. "Of course, you're right, my dear. The girl is a dunce, that's all! But don't let that innocent look fool you. She can be very impudent at times." Then she had turned back to where Charlotte stood trembling with mortification, and added sternly, "You heard me. Excuse yourself and go to your

3

room. It's best you don't attend any social functions until you've learned to conduct yourself properly."

For one tense moment Charlotte had clenched her hands beneath the folds of her flowered overskirt. Then, with a hasty "By your leave," to the guests, she had walked, almost run, from the room, wishing the polished floor would open up and swallow her on the spot. Even as she had made her way blindly up the stairs, her angry, frustrated tears stinging her hot, flushed cheeks, she could still hear her aunt lamenting, "I apologize for my niece. But what can I do, if even the nuns haven't been able to teach her manners! She's so stubborn and high-spirited! You don't know the cross I've had to bear since that child has come home."

Charlotte could feel the blood rushing to her face even now, as she recalled the humiliation and resentment of that moment. Since she had left the convent and come to live with Germaine, she had begun to discover things about herself she had never suspected before. Perhaps she was indeed, as her aunt had said, stubborn and high-spirited by nature.

In the convent she had always been a playful, relatively happy child. Although she might not have been quite as docile as the Ursulines would have liked her to be, and had been given to occasional lapses into romantic daydreaming when she should have been paying closer attention to her catechism, she had, nevertheless, been considered a fairly good student and never really gotten into any serious trouble.

Of course, there had always been her favorite nun, Sister Marie, to defend and counsel her, and dear sweet Madelón, her bosom companion, with whom to share her innermost secrets. How she missed those childhood friends now! It was difficult not to have a sympathetic ear to talk to or a comforting shoulder to cry on when sad and lonely, as she so often felt these days. More and more Charlotte found herself longing to be back in the convent. Those high stone walls seemed more protective now than confining. At least one thing was certain—every day she was becoming increasingly aware of new, often rebellious feelings awakening within her, and she wondered how long it would be

4

before they would come exploding to the surface. Amid all those emotions bubbling and churning inside of her, the naïve child of the convent seemed to be giving way to a strange, rebellious woman even she could not fully understand yet.

For the moment it was her awe of Germaine, as well as her complete lack of experience with life outside the convent, that made Charlotte hesitate to rebel completely against the disagreeable situation in which she found herself. Even during the relatively sheltered life she had continued to live during the year she had spent with her aunt, the brief glimpses she had had of the world had made Charlotte wary of trying to venture forth into it alone. On one hand she longed to break away and seek new horizons, but on the other, she knew that, despite the fact that this was the year of our Lord, 1728, a woman simply could not survive for long without the protection of a family or guardian and, later, a husband or the Church.

As she made her way down the hall to ask her aunt what she had done wrong this time, Charlotte found herself wondering whether she simply ought to ask Germaine to let her return to the convent to take the veil. It would be a pity to cut herself off from life before she had had an opportunity to know what it was all about, but at least she could find peace and security with the Ursulines. Sometimes she felt like a full-grown woman, but there were other moments when she suspected she was still very much a child. . . .

Germaine's voice suddenly interrupted her thoughts, as it came drifting out of the parlor a few steps farther down the hallway. Charlotte paused, hesitating to disturb her aunt now that she knew the latter had a visitor. Germaine never wanted her around when there were guests in the house.

Charlotte turned to mount the staircase, deciding it would be unwise to go in the parlor just then, but suddenly, as the words wafting out of the room began to make sense, she paused once more, her curiosity aroused. They were talking about *her*! As a rule, Charlotte would have had little desire to eavesdrop, knowing as she did that the theme would probably be just a repetition of the usual criticisms and complaints about her behavior, but she had caught the

5

phrase "what to do about Charlotte . . ." and she could not walk away from that! Besides, there was something in the tone of her aunt's voice . . .

Taking a few steps back down the hall toward the parlor, she stood near the doorway and listened quietly, even as a faint sense of foreboding began to stir inside her.

Chapter II

"I've been thinking things over carefully, Melanie," Germaine was saying, "and I've just about decided that what the child needs is a good stable husband before she gets into any mischief."

"*Vraiment*, perhaps that would be best," agreed her guest, a short, poodle-faced woman who was a frequent visitor at the manor. "And do you have anyone in mind?"

"Charlotte's a born coquette," continued her aunt. "What she needs is the stern hand of an older man."

"You're right, *chérie*, of course. The poor girl has been sadly lacking a father all these years. Perhaps a combination father-husband might be exactly what the child needs to give her more equilibrium. But do you know of such a man who is eligible?"

"It's occurred to me that someone like Monsieur Blégot, for example . . ."

"Blégot? But he's past sixty, Germaine! Wouldn't that be exaggerating things *un petit peu*?"

"He can still get around very well. I admit I'm probably partial to him because he reminds me so much of my own dear Gaspin—may he rest in peace—don't you think?"

And indeed he should, thought Charlotte, as her heart sank, for M. Blégot had been a schoolmate of her late uncle's. In fact, he was the same age as Germaine's deceased husband would have been, had the latter lived to reach sixty and then some.

"Oh, I know he has a fine position in society," acquiesced Melanie, "but that much age difference might be hard on the girl. She's still so young . . ."

"That's precisely the point. What would she know about such things? After all, a woman's first marriage should be for money and position. If she gets a chance for a second, then she can give herself the luxury of marrying for love—as I plan to do now myself. Oh, not that I didn't love my poor dear Gaspin," she hastily added, "but I didn't know what life was all about, either, when I was Charlotte's age and my marriage was arranged by my parents."

"*Oui,* I know too well what you mean," sighed Melanie. "After all, no marriage is perfect. Look at my Claude. He's near my own age, so what do I have? The problems of his whoring behind my back with that brazen hussy he's taken up with! At least Charlotte would be spared such humiliations. A man the age of Blégot would hardly have enough left over to be keeping a mistress along with a wife."

"I tell you, I know I'm right! After all, the girl is my only niece, and except for me, she's alone in the world. I'm aware of my duty toward her. I really have her best interests at heart."

"I know, *chérie,* but you must think of yourself, too. Remember that scandal a few years back when Madame Bernard caught her second husband playing around with her eldest daughter? I don't mean to imply anything like that could happen in your case, but such things do occur, you know. And if you say the girl is a coquette . . ."

There was a momentary rattle of china, as Germaine nervously poured another cup of tea. "I—I hadn't thought of that, but I suppose you're right to warn me," she replied. "Something similar could happen, perhaps, if I were to remarry and keep the girl around the house. She already loves to attract attention to herself."

"Then you've already made up your mind about Blégot? The old *roué* will probably jump at the prospect. I've heard he still likes to ride the young ones. Your niece might have her hands full with him, despite his years! He's the kind

7

who will probably be able to keep her going until he's well past seventy. He just might get a pregnancy or two out of her, who knows?"

"I really think he'll be ideal for Charlotte," agreed Germaine, warming up to the idea even more. "Perhaps he can quiet her down a bit and rule her with the iron hand she so sorely needs. I plan to go to the de Lesseps' ball the end of this month, and I know I'll see him there. It should be a good moment to broach the subject to him and see how he reacts."

"Oh, he'll go for it, rest assured!" laughed Melanie. "I wager he'll want to set the date immediately."

Charlotte had not waited to hear more. She dashed up the stairs to her room, desperately suppressing her sobs so Germaine would not hear and know she had overheard their conversation.

She wondered what her aunt would say if she knew her niece had already had the questionable honor of meeting the candidate being considered for her future husband!

It had been shortly after she had come to live at the chateau, when Blégot had stopped by for a brief visit to offer his excuses to Germaine for not being able to attend the dinner party she was planning to give that same night.

At the time Charlotte had been out in the large garden to one side of the house, where her aunt had sent her to gather a bouquet for the main table, and as Blégot had made his way back to his carriage parked just outside the gate, he had suddenly caught a fleeting glimpse of her—a splash of blue, as she had walked amid the colorful exuberance of the flowering garden, which was at its height at that time of year.

With a signal to his driver to wait, Blégot had quickly made his way down the shaded path that wound its way through the maze of trees and foliage until he had come to the spot where she stood.

"And what do we have here?" he had exclaimed, startling Charlotte so that she had nearly dropped the half-filled basket of freshly cut roses on her arm. "And who are you, *mon enfant?*"

"I'm Charlotte Montier, Monsieur, Madame Germaine's niece."

8

"Aha! And how well she's kept you hidden! Where have you been all these years?"

"In a convent, monsieur. I have only recently come to live here."

"I see," he smiled, his eyes hungrily following the outline of her firm young breasts where they pushed against the confines of her tightly laced bodice. "Well, I'm a close friend of the family's, child," he said, continuing to ease in closer to her, until the thorns of the rose bush behind her were snagging and clawing at her dress.

"I knew your late uncle well. There's nothing I wouldn't do for him, or his family . . ." He had worked her into a corner of the garden where the bushes were higher and thicker so they could not be seen from the house or the entrance gate. "You're a pretty little thing . . . *très jolie*. You may look upon me as if I were your uncle."

Suddenly, with an agility surprising for his years, he had pulled her to him by the waist and run a swift exploratory hand along the contours of her bodice, finally pausing at the bow of her lacings.

"Let's have a look at you, child," he purred, as he tugged at the ribbons with eager, misshapen fingers. "Your're growing fast, *n'est-ce pas*?"

"Monsieur . . . please . . . my aunt . . . the nuns . . ."

No man had ever been so close to her before, and the feel of that withered, gnarled body pressing so insistently against hers frightened and bewildered her.

"Don't be alarmed, child," he continued to whisper soothingly in her ear. "This can be our little secret, *non*? Yours and mine . . . no one need ever know, *vraiment*?"

Despite herself, Charlotte had begun to tremble uncontrollably, as he reached into her decolletage and cupped one of her breasts in his bony hand. Her first impulse had been to scream, but she feared what her aunt would say. The blame would probably be put on her, as usual, and she would be punished!

Although he reeked of perfume, the stench of his breath in her face nauseated her. She turned her head to one side and tried to break away, but his grip tightened on her breast.

9

"Come now, child, don't be frightened. I won't hurt you. I only want to see you, that's all."

The feel of her pulse racing wildly beneath the warm flesh trapped in his hand roused him all the more. "Just be nice to me," he begged. "I'm your elder—be obedient, child, I only want to take a little peek . . ."

At that moment Germaine's voice came floating across the rose-scented air from the back door of the house.

"Charlotte! What's keeping you so long? Charlotte! Now where is that lazy girl?"

Blégot froze with the terrified girl still caught in his tenacious grasp. The devil take that silly aunt of hers! Just when it seemed the snippet was going to let him go further! But his carriage was still by the gate, and he knew he would probably be discovered if Germaine were to come out of the house to look for her niece.

"Answer her!" he hissed in Charlotte's ear. "Tell her you're all right and will go there in a minute."

For a moment no words came to her paralyzed lips. Her fear of her aunt was almost as great as the fear she felt for this horrid old man. Germaine's voice came again, even more impatient than before.

"Do as I say!" Blégot ordered, digging his fingers deeper into her breast until the girl winced with pain.

"Yes, *ma tante*, I'll be there," she finally managed to call back. "In just a minute." Her voice sounded shrill and thin. She hoped Germaine would not notice.

"*Mon Dieu!* It's time you answered!" snorted her aunt. "Hurry up, you trifling girl, and stop daydreaming out there!"

"*Oui*, I—I'm coming."

They heard the door slam as Germaine reentered the house.

For one last moment Blégot continued to hold her pinned against him.

"If you say anything to your aunt about this, I'll tell her you enticed me," he warned her hoarsely, his foul breath bathing her cheek. "Do you hear what I'm saying? I'll tell everyone you bared yourself for me to see. Do you understand?" He twisted her breast until she nodded her head in feeble assent.

With that he pushed her back from him so hard that she fell against the rose bush, leaving her there disheveled and struggling to free herself from the thorns, as he dashed away down the path without so much as a backward look.

By the time Charlotte had managed to free herself, not without pricking her arms and hands badly in the process, she heard Blégot's carriage take off down the street. Thank God her aunt had called when she had, but thank God, too, she had been busy in the back of the house instructing the servants and had seen nothing! Her aunt always seemed so ready tó believe the worst of her. No matter what she would have said, Charlotte was certain Germaine would have believed Blégot's version over hers.

She had hastily rearranged her hair and clothing and gone back to the house, resigned to hear the long harangue her aunt was sure to give her for having loitered so long in the garden. For the first time she had bowed her head and accepted one of Germaine's scoldings as the lesser of the many evils that could have befallen her that afternoon.

Charlotte had never breathed a word to her aunt or anyone else about her encounter with Blégot. To this day it shamed her even to recall it. For months afterwards her breast had smarted and burned every time she remembered the feel of those horny fingers digging into her flesh. The nuns had warned her about men like Blégot, but they had never told her what to do when confronted by one of them.

She had only seen Blégot one other time after that, when he had come by with a group of people Germaine had invited for tea one afternoon. He had given no sign of recognition, however, when she was presented to him. There had only been a fraction of a second, as he murmured an appropriate compliment and bent over her hand, that she had caught a warning flicker in his dark smoldering eyes, but no one else seemed to sense that anything was amiss between them, despite the fact that the blood had drained from Charlotte's face and her knees were melting like butter beneath her skirts.

Charlotte had been only too glad when Germaine sent her to her room shortly afterwards and spared her any further contact with him. Just the sight of Blégot had left her physically ill for the rest of that day.

11

Fortunately Blégot was not too frequent a visitor at the manor. Germaine preferred to surround herself with younger men. Sometimes she even favored admirers who were five to ten years younger than herself. It was quite obvious she was not considering anyone as old as Blégot as a possible candidate for herself. After all, as she had said, her next marriage was going to be for love, and even Germaine, who had the knack of looking at things in whatever way she found most convenient at the moment, could not, by the wildest stretch of imagination, find any romantic qualities in M. Blégot!

The thought of a loveless marriage with a lecherous *vieillard* old enough to be her grandfather intensified the dilemma in which Charlotte found herself. As an orphan, she had no one to turn to except Germaine or the nuns. It seemed that, at only a few weeks short of eighteen, her future had narrowed down to a choice between being the plaything of someone like Blégot or taking the veil.

She had to act quickly now. Germaine had said she would talk to Blégot at the end of that month, which only left two and a half weeks to find an alternative . . . if there was one. As Charlotte's legal guardian, Germaine's word would be binding. The memory of Blégot's foul mouth and probing fingers filled her with such disgust that she knew she had no recourse except to seek the refuge of the convent. But she felt a little guilty about her attitude toward taking the veil. After all, the nuns had been kind to her, and she had nothing against them. But the rigidity of convent life had not appealed to her, and the prospect of spending the rest of her life behind cloistered walls saddened her. It would seem a little like a prison. Was she never to know more of life than a convent dormitory and the upstairs rooms of Germaine's manor?

Chapter III

Two days later Charlotte set out for the convent, on the pretext of wanting to visit her former friends and teachers.

It had been difficult to bite her tongue and say nothing to her aunt about having overheard that conversation in the parlor, but she had held herself in check, knowing it would have only antagonized Germaine all the more if she had tried to argue about the decision to marry her off to Blégot. Charlotte hoped that, with the nuns to back her up, she might at least succeed in returning to the convent and thus slip out of the trap being laid for her. Germaine could hardly raise too many objections against her choosing the veil. It would be like arguing against the Church.

Charlotte smiled sadly. There were occasions, it seemed, when one's wits could serve better than prayers! She had taken advantage of the fact that Germaine had been expecting guests that particular day and that among them would be her aunt's youngest admirer, a slim young man almost ten years the latter's junior. That meant Germaine would be only too glad to get her out of the house for a few hours.

Her aunt even accompanied her to the coach and saw her off with a loving peck on the cheek and a warning to the driver to look after her "most cherished niece's safety."

As soon as Charlotte arrived at her destination, she asked for Sister Marie, but the place was bustling with excitement. Everywhere there was talk of a new convent being built for the Ursulines in the Louisiana Colony and of a special shipment of young brides being sent to the settlers there. It seemed that three of the nuns who were to accompany the girls, as well as several of Charlotte's childhood companions, had been chosen to join the group and were even then busily preparing for their departure. She was especially taken aback when she learned that Sister Marie and her friend Madelón were among those who planned to make the voyage.

No sooner had she entered the convent gates than her friends descended upon her like a swarm of magpies.

"Isn't it romantic? Just like a storybook!" exclaimed one of the girls, swinging her skirts merrily as she danced about the courtyard.

"But how will you get there? Where will you get the money to go so far?" asked Charlotte, unable to comprehend the bombardment of excited phrases and shrieks that were coming at her from all sides.

"There is a company . . . *la Compagnie des Indes Occidentales* . . . our passages will be paid . . . the king . . . Louis XV himself is giving us a dowry . . . little chests . . . Casquette Girls . . . *filles à la cassette*, they are calling us!"

By the time Sister Marie came upon the scene to calm the young girls down and lead Charlotte to the peaceful shade of the convent garden, Charlotte was more confused than ever.

"Yes, my dear, it's true," the Ursuline was saying, as she smoothed her black woolen robes neatly beneath her and sat on the stone bench.

Dreamy-eyed Madelón, who had been invited to join them, sat timidly near the edge, but Charlotte remained standing for a while longer, too caught up in the bristling atmosphere around her and her own inner turmoil to be still.

"But it all seems so cold and businesslike!" observed Charlotte. Here she was trying to escape a loveless match, and there were her friends waxing enthusiastic over traveling halfway across the world to marry perfect strangers!

"Not really, *ma petite*," replied Sister Marie, her sweet, unlined face belying her fifty-some years, because she was at peace within herself. "You see, no one will tell a Casquette Girl whom she must marry. The choice will be hers."

14

"And we will stay at the convent in the capital city of *La Nouvelle Orléans* under the protection of the nuns until we make our selections," Madelón ventured to add, her delicate, porcelainlike features aglow with the hope shining in her soft grey eyes. She was only five months younger than Charlotte, so she, too, had been worried over what the future would hold for her, now that she was nearing womanhood. The opportunity to go to the new life that America offered seemed heaven-sent to her.

"The king has even promised to give each of us a dowry," she went on, her enthusiasm overriding her usual shyness. "Oh, Charlotte, how I wish you could come with us! We are each to be given a chest with clothing and linens . . ."

Her voice trailed off, and she cast an embarrassed glance at Sister Marie, but the nun smiled and patted the young girl's hand affectionately, as she took up the theme.

"It really is a wonderful opportunity for the girls," the latter agreed. "I'm sure they'll find fine new lives awaiting them in the colony."

"But I thought only *bad* women were being sent there!" exclaimed Charlotte. "One of my aunt's friends is a judge, and I heard him say once that most of the women he had sentenced to the Saltpêtriere had been deported to the colonies to console his majesty's troops and settlers there. I don't understand . . ."

"Those days are over now, thank God," sighed Sister Marie. "It was wrong of the dauphin to do that. Now they want only decent girls of marriageable age in Louisiana, who can settle down with the colonists and make good homes for them there. The former governor of the colony and founder of its capital had been asking the *Compagnie* for years to send him respectable women for his men, and now the new governor has pleaded directly to the king himself, so his majesty has finally stepped in and is not only giving his blessing to our group, but including dowries for the future brides, as well.

"What's more, each girl must be approved by the bishop himself. She must be of irreproachable character and well schooled in the womanly arts of sewing and cooking, as well as have an adequate knowledge of reading and writing. The requisites are quite exacting.

"Last year six of our nuns from Rouen went to New Orleans, and now they are asking for more of us to join them in their work. The good people of that city have already begun to build an Ursuline convent there, where we can set up a school for girls and help care for the sick. So you see, my children, how all this must end well? *Le bon Dieu* wants the mothers of the New World to be good, God-fearing women."

As Sister Marie explained in her soft, calm voice, the anxiety within Charlotte began to subside, and she instinctively knelt beside the nun, as if seeking to draw even closer to the warm glow that this woman of God always seemed to radiate.

"It sounds as if *le bon Dieu* does have a hand in it," the girl agreed. "But Louisiana is so far away . . ." A great loneliness suddenly overwhelmed her, as she realized her friends would no longer be at the convent when she took the veil.

"Ah, *ma petite!*" Sister Marie smiled down at the girl's golden brown head, as she caressed one of its curls tenderly. "We are all in God's kingdom. Besides, there are ships sailing now almost every month from France to the colonies, so we can keep in contact. Who knows, your aunt is a wealthy woman—it's not unlikely that you, too, will end up with a rich husband and have the means to visit us in New Orleans someday. But then we have been very selfish in taking up all your visit with talk of ourselves! You must have many new things to tell us, too, probably many exciting plans for a bright new future of your own, now that you have settled down in your lovely home with your aunt, *n'est-ce pas?*"

Charlotte's hazel eyes suddenly filled with tears and she buried her face in her hands, sobbing.

"But, child, what is this?" exclaimed Sister Marie, looking at her in surprise.

"Oh, Charlotte, whatever is the matter?" murmured Madelón helplessly, as her friend continued to weep uncontrollably. For the first time Charlotte was able to release some of the pent-up anguish she had been keeping within

16

her for so long, and now that she had let go, it seemed the tears would never stop flowing!

"Oh, *Soeur* Marie . . . Madelón . . . I'm so miserable! I really came here today to ask if I could come back to the convent!"

"*Mon Dieu!* But why, dear?" asked Sister Marie. "Aren't you happy with your aunt? The few times she came here, she seemed like such a nice person."

"I suppose she's nice sometimes," conceded Charlotte, dabbing her eyes with her kerchief and feeling a little ashamed of her sudden outburst of emotion. "But she doesn't want me around her very much. It's hard to explain . . . I always have the feeling she's angry with me for some reason."

"Perhaps you did something to displease her," suggested Sister Marie. "Think, my dear. You may not have meant to, but . . ."

"No . . . well . . . she's always saying I'm lazy and a coquette and . . . I don't know, perhaps . . . She makes me keep to my room most of the time, especially when there's company."

"Have you ever done anything to embarrass your aunt around other people?" insisted the nun.

"Not that I know of," replied Charlotte, "but that's not the only thing that makes me want to leave," she went on, and the tears welled up again, until she could hardly continue. "It's Monsieur Blégot!" she blurted out at last. "Oh, *Soeur* Marie, please help me! He's a horrible old man. One day he tried to undress me in the garden—he told me he'd tell my aunt I had enticed him, but I hadn't—I swear by the Holy Virgin!"

"My poor child!" Sister Marie drew the weeping girl into her arms, and the long flowing sleeves of her dark habit enveloped the slim, trembling figure. There was the faint odor of camphor, but at that moment, the warm circle of those homespun robes and that familiar aroma represented to Charlotte the only refuge she had ever known in those long, lonely years since she had lost her mother, a mother she could hardly remember now.

"Do you think that horrid man might have told your aunt something and that's why she's so angry with you?"

"Oh, no, I'm sure he hasn't. Besides, *Tante* Germaine has always been that way, since the first day I went to live with her." Charlotte sat up now, beginning to regain her composure. "No, it can't be that. To the contrary, she spoke about his being *good* for me, when I heard her telling Madame Melanie . . ."

"Charlotte! You should not have been eavesdropping! You know better than that!"

"I really didn't mean to. She'd called to me, and I was going down the hallway—she didn't know I was there."

"All right, child. Go on."

"Well, I heard her telling Madame Melanie she was planning to talk to M. Blégot about giving me to him in marriage."

"Are you sure you understood correctly, Charlotte? M. Blégot is well known here in Marseilles, and I'm sure he's over sixty!"

"That he is! But *Tante* Germaine says first marriages should be for money and position, that age doesn't really matter. Madame Melanie even said he might still make me pregnant! God forgive me, the very thought of it makes me puke! He reeks of rotten teeth and—and his hands . . . his hands . . ." She shuddered, as she tried to push the memory back into the darkest recesses of her mind.

"The marriage would certainly be an ill-matched one," agreed Sister Marie. "But remember, child, your aunt is your legal guardian and, if she arranges such a nuptial contract, it'll be almost impossible for you to refuse."

Suddenly Madelón, who had been listening with misty eyes as her friend told them of her desperate plight, could contain herself no longer. "Oh, Charlotte," she exclaimed, "why don't you come to America with us? You'd be free there!"

At Madelón's words, a glimmer of hope suddenly flashed across Charlotte's wan face, and she shot a questioning glance at Sister Marie, almost pleadingly, as she wondered whether such a possibility might indeed be open to her.

"It might be a good alternative," the nun agreed. "The idea occurred to me, too, while we were talking, but even so, you would need your aunt's consent to make the voyage. Do you think you could convince her to let you go?"

Charlotte was confused once more. "I don't know, perhaps she would. . . . As long as she'd be rid of me, she might consent."

"We'd love to have you, child, and I'll be glad to speak to your aunt about the details. But we'll be sailing on the first of August, so I'd have to talk to her right away, since there would be arrangements to be made with the *Compagnie,* as well as the approval to be gotten from the bishop," said Sister Marie. "There is a group going with us from Paris, too, and space is limited, so we must act quickly if you really want to go with us. You must pray to God for guidance in this matter, my dear."

"And I'll pray, too," declared Madelón. "How wonderful it would be if you could come along with us!"

The more Charlotte thought of the idea, the more it appealed to her. Going to a free new world to find a destiny all her own would be to her liking. It seemed the best way to get both Aunt Germaine and M. Blégot out of her life once and for all. Surely in that faroff land, carved from the wilderness by brave, bold pioneers, she could find someone to love. At least, Sister Marie had assured her that there the choice would be hers.

Chapter IV

When Charlotte suddenly announced her desire to join the group of Casquette Girls leaving for La Nouvelle Orléans in just a few weeks, Germaine was taken completely by surprise. She had already made up her mind to negotiate with Blégot for the girl's hand before the month was out, but what had occurred that very afternoon made her more determined than ever now to get the matter settled immediately.

The humiliation of it all! How could she have known Antoine had been referring to Charlotte when he had stayed behind after the other guests had left and begun to speak of his feelings and hint at matrimony! He had begun frequenting the house long before her niece had come home from the convent and, despite the fact that he was younger than she was, Germaine had always considered him to be one of her most ardent admirers. She was sure he had been seriously interested in her until he had laid eyes on Charlotte!

The whole episode that afternoon had been doubly embarrassing to her, since she had coyly encouraged him to go on speaking, not realizing until he had gotten halfway into his declaration that he was referring to Charlotte and not herself.

"*Mon Dieu*, Antoine!" she had exclaimed, trying to suppress the fury welling up within her. "But Charlotte is not for you! If and when she marries, it will be to a much older man who can give her the stability she so sorely needs. Meantime," here her large blue eyes narrowed almost to slits as she added. "I think it best you don't go near my niece. It would only disquiet her. She's really quite an addle-headed goose, you know. Frankly, I'm surprised you're interested in someone like her. I'd have thought you preferred a more mature woman."

After Antoine, somewhat abashed, had gone, Germaine sat down to try to compose an appropriate note to invite Blégot over for tea that very weekend. Charlotte was going to be eighteen on the last day of the month, so it would be a good time to hold a big party and formally announce her niece's engagement, as well. She would be glad to get the marriage contract settled and the girl finally out from underfoot. Although the Ursulines had educated Charlotte fairly well—actually *overly* educated her in such frivolities as reading and writing—the nuns had left the girl sadly lacking in worldly matters. Emotionally Charlotte was more a child than a woman, and a headstrong one at that. If only the girl were plainer and smiled less. She had a way

20

of attracting people to her that was exasperating. Once the girl was wed, however, things would be different.

Germaine was in the middle of writing her invitation to Blégot when Charlotte returned from the convent, bubbling over with her incredible request to go to the colonies to find a husband there. Germaine's first reaction had been that the whole project would be the height of folly, but as Charlotte had gone on to explain more of the details, the idea, ridiculous as it was, had begun to show redeeming features worthy of consideration.

Germaine was well aware of the fact that, although Blégot would probably jump at the prospect of having such a pretty young thing to warm his bed in his declining years, he was still an astute businessman, and would expect a generous dowry to be included in the offer. On the other hand, if she were to let the silly girl go with those *filles à la cassette,* her trousseau would be furnished by the king, and that would be an expense she would be relieved of, as well as the cost of the wedding itself, which would be another large financial commitment that would be expected of her if her niece were to marry in Marseilles. Then, too, there was still a third advantage to consider. With an ocean separating her from the charms of her provocative niece, she would finally be rid of such embarrassing situations as the one she had had to suffer that afternoon!

Germaine really bore the girl no ill will. After all, Charlotte was her dear dead sister's child, and it would not be difficult to love the girl once she were no longer her rival. A sudden wave of stifled affection toward her niece engulfed her. If the child wanted to go with the Ursulines to the New World, she would give her consent and, what's more, even add something to the girl's dowry herself. No one could say she couldn't be generous when it came to her own kin.

"But I still think the whole thing is foolhardy," declared Germaine, as Charlotte's face lit up with joy when her aunt promised to talk further with Sister Marie about signing the contract with the Company of the Indies for the voyage to Louisiana. "It's beyond me what you can find so attractive about going to such a godforsaken place! I still think you'd do better staying here and making a good match with someone of your social class. No one in our family has ever had to go looking for a husband like a common peasant wench! Remember, you're not an orphan like the majority of those who are going. You have a guardian to look out for your interests. I could arrange a fine marriage for you with a wealthy husband of good standing in the community, you know. As a matter of fact, I was in the middle of writing to Monsieur Blégot . . . perhaps you remember him? He was a very dear friend of your late uncle's. A man like Blégot could give you social standing and security for life. You see how I'm always thinking of your welfare?"

Now that she had the goal in sight, Charlotte thought it best to be discreet and choose her words with care.

"I thank you for all your efforts on my behalf, *ma tante*," she replied meekly, lowering her eyes a little so they would not betray those last vestiges of resentment she couldn't help feeling toward Germaine, "and I'm sure my dear mother in heaven who is looking down on us at this moment does too, but I'd still prefer to take my chances in the New World. There will probably be more opportunities for me there. They say the men outnumber the women twenty to one in the colonies."

"Perhaps, but what class of men are they? I doubt you'll find anyone of the category of M. Blégot in that half-civilized place. But I've always said you're a foolish girl, Charlotte, and stubborn, too, so I won't stand in your way, if that's what you really want. I dread to think, however, what will happen to you off on your own like that. My only consolation is that the nuns will be there to keep you from doing anything too foolhardy!"

Germaine dabbed at a large tear rolling down her delicately rouged cheek, and continued, "I only hope the pirates won't get you before you even get where you're going! The ocean is filled with them these days. And then there are the swamp monsters with thick, scaly hides and huge jaws lined with teeth, which they say can gulp a man down in one bite! And if those creatures don't get you, surely the Indians will! *Mon Dieu!* I won't sleep nights imagining you being drowned, raped, scalped or eaten alive! I'll have to offer up dozens of novenas for you—wretched child, to fret your poor aunt so!"

So it was settled, and with far greater ease than Charlotte had dared hope for. Germaine's ominous predictions did little to dampen her spirits. Actually, Charlotte felt so relieved to be escaping her fate with Blégot that she would have accepted passage to the end of the world to get away from him. Of course, there were some who said America *was* the end of the world, but at least there she might have an opportunity to find a better life and, at the same time, be with the only "family" she had ever really known and loved during her rather lonely life.

The fact that she was officially going to marry some stranger on the other side of the ocean was still too remote for her to visualize with clarity. The one thing that had stayed foremost in her mind was the phrase in the contract that she and her aunt had signed which had said "of her own choice."

Even as late as the afternoon before the embarkation, as she busily packed her few belongings and pretty "party gown" that Germaine had insisted on giving her at the last minute in the chest beside the linens and clothing that compromised her dowry from the king, there was an unreality about it all. She looked down at her trousseau lying there at the bottom of the small traveling trunk: four sheets, a blanket, two pairs of stockings, six headdresses, a pelisse. These were meant to be shared with some man far away in the New World . . . a man she had never seen who would be her husband and father her children. Would it be someone she could love?

It was hard to believe that tomorrow at this time she would be on the high seas, sailing away from France, perhaps never to see Marseilles again. Aunt Germaine had a way of exaggerating things, of course, but she wondered just how civilized the New World would be. Was she really going to be attacked by pirates, monsters and savages as her aunt had predicted? Perhaps she was jumping from the kettle into the fire in her haste to get away from her present situation?

It was midsummer and the bathing season, so she had

23

asked the maid to help her fill the large iron tub with water, deciding it was best to take what might be her last leisurely bath for several months. She was sure the accommodations aboard ship would be much too crowded to permit anything more than quick sponge-baths, and Sister Marie had warned them that the voyage might take anywhere from three to five months, depending upon how favorable the winds would be during the crossing.

As she stood in the large tub, with her abundant mass of honey-colored curls caught up high off her neck and held in place by a narrow ribbon, she soaped herself through the thin white shift that hung loosely about her. Although today—July 31, the Feast of St. Ignatius—marked her eighteenth *anniversaire*, she had never seen herself completely naked. The nuns said a decent woman should not look at her body like that. But, as the wet muslin molded itself to her slim young curves and she ran her hands curiously over the firm roundness of her breasts, past the gentle indentation of her waist and on down to the sweeping curve of her buttocks, Charlotte wondered what she really looked like. Would her husband be pleased with what he saw? Blégot had seemed to think she was pretty. So far he had been the only man who had ever touched her. The memory of his clawlike fingers probing her body still revolted her. Is that the way a man made love to a woman? She hoped not.

Sliding down into the tub, she lay back slowly, enjoying the feel of the warm water rising and caressing her body through the thin shift. Charlotte closed her eyes and tried to imagine what it would be like to be with a man—one she didn't find repulsive and perhaps even loved. It might be nice, after all, and might make her tingle inside, even as the feel of the soap slipping over her body had just now, or as the warm water lapping gently around her did at that very moment. In all the years she had bathed in her shift, obedient to the rules of the convent, she had never dared look upon her body, but tonight, with the awareness of her budding womanhood foremost in her thoughts, and the spirit of adventure high within her as she prepared to embark the next day on a new unknown life, Charlotte felt bold enough not only to peek, but to untie the drawstring around her neck and let the wet shift fall completely to the floor as she stepped out of the tub and reached for a towel.

The heat of the late July afternoon felt cool now on her bare flesh after the warm bath, so she wrapped the towel around her as she lit a candle in the semidarkened room.

Then, deliberately, slowly, her heart pounding at her daring, she stood before the candle and opened the towel. The glow of the soft candlelight gave a rosy tint to the whiteness of her body. Curiously she examined the pink nipples of her full young breasts and felt them harden at her touch. The sensation pleased her, but she quickly drew back her hand in a wave of guilt. Even as she did so, she caught sight of the patch of golden hairs below and was fascinated by its triangular shape. There had been times when she was soaping herself through her bathing garment when she had felt strange, not unpleasant sensations there, too, but she had never dared linger. Her finger explored for a moment, then, afraid of the feelings that were beginning to stir within her, she hastily folded the towel around herself again. Although alone, she could feel her cheeks burning hot with shame. God forgive her for being such a brazen hussy!

That night she said double the usual number of *décades* on her rosary and begged the blessed Virgin to forgive her sinful curiosity. Whatever had possessed her to look at herself like that? She was shocked and even a little frightened by her own daring. It seemed that, as the ship sailed out of the harbor tomorrow, she would be leaving behind not only her aunt and Monsieur Blégot, but Charlotte Montier, the shy little convent girl, as well!

Chapter V

Les Deux Frères sailed out of the port of Marseilles at noon on the first day of August, 1728. It was a typical summer afternoon with the sun shining brightly and a breeze gently blowing which everyone said was a good omen for the voyage.

Germaine accompanied Charlotte to the docks to say goodbye and make an impressive farewell speech to Sister Marie, begging her to look after her "dearly beloved niece" and to see to it that the girl married well. The solemnity of the occasion seemed to move her to genuine tears, and for a moment Charlotte felt her aunt might have really felt something for her after all, as Germaine held her close and pressed a tear-stained face against hers.

Then her aunt drew forth a small breast-pin with a heart-shaped locket dangling from it and opened it to reveal a pair of miniatures of herself and Charlotte's mother when the two sisters had been young girls.

"I thought you might like to have this, child, as a keepsake of the roots you are leaving behind in France," she continued, her blue eyes clouding again with tears. "Show it to people so they'll see you are not an orphan and know where you come from."

Even Charlotte was momentarily moved to tears, as she thanked her aunt for that final gesture of affection, and she bade her guardian a fond *adieu*. It was futile now to look back and wonder how different things might have been had Germaine opened her heart to her sooner.

"I'll always treasure the locket," Charlotte promised, pinning it to her bodice as she kissed her aunt again and,

26

thanking her for all her attentions over the years, promised to write as soon as she arrived in New Orleans.

From that day forth, Charlotte found herself thinking of Germaine with more pity than resentment. Although she recognized her guardian's shortcomings, she seemed to have suddenly developed a new perspective on things, now that she had cut herself free of her past and could look back at the world she had lived in with less emotional involvement. Perhaps all those negative qualities in her aunt might have never surfaced so dramatically had the latter only been ten years older or she ten years younger!

At first Charlotte and her friends, eight in all, were awed by the size of the ship towering so high above them and wondered how they would ever get aboard, for there were no gangplanks to be seen. They were afraid they might be hoisted up in sacks on a pulley in the same manner as the crew was doing with some barrels and bales that were being loaded on the vessel when they arrived. But the representative of the *Compagnie* soon came over to greet the nuns and assured them that Captain Hébert had arranged for the passengers to be lifted aboard, one by one, strapped comfortably in an upholstered armchair.

Besides Sister Marie and two other nuns, Sisters Anne and Ernestine, from the Ursuline convent in Marseilles, there were also three Sisters of Charity in their long grey habits who had journeyed from Paris to join the group, bringing with them a dozen girls, to make a total of twenty prospective brides and six nuns who would be sailing to the New World.

There was a festive air about the occasion, and after the delegation of Jesuit priests who had gone to see the group off had blessed them and their ship, the young girls laughed merrily as each was slowly lifted into the air and deposited high on the deck of the *Deux Frères*, holding her freshly starched organdy cap with one hand and her flying skirts with the other.

Once on board, the girls stood by the railing for a while, watching in fascination as the sailors noisily continued hoisting aboard the bleating sheep and cackling chickens that were to be their bill of fare during the long months to come.

27

Finally the nuns, who had been conversing with the captain and another ship's officer, called their charges together to say a final prayer, led by Sister Marie, for their safe voyage to America.

The hustle and bustle of that great vessel fell silent, as the captain and his crew bared their heads and everyone knelt beneath the blaze of the noonday sun. Charlotte bowed her white-capped head and, with her precious *cassete* bearing all her worldly belongings beside her, clutched her rosary a little tighter, as the full impact of what she was about to do suddenly began to creep over her.

The *Deux Frères* was typical of the crafts used by the *Compagnie*. Since such ships could not be convoyed by the navy and were obliged to stand alone against any pirates or enemy warships they might encounter during their long, perilous voyage across the ocean, each vessel was designed to be a combination fighter and cargo carrier, ready for any emergency. Every inch of space was at a premium, therefore, and no luxury accommodations were to be found aboard such a ship.

When the women saw the crammed quarters destined to be their home for the next few months, there was some disappointment, but their spirits were high, and they soon accepted the fact, once they realized there was nothing better to be had.

Since there was not enough room to hold more than seven double berths closely set together lengthwise, four on one side and three on the other of the long, narrow, low-beamed enclosure that had been improvised for them in the between-decks, it was decided that they should sleep in alternate shifts, rather than try to fit two to a bunk or overflow into the aisle. Even so, they were terribly crowded.

There were only two small portholes, which could not always be left open because of the waves that would come splashing in to douse their beds, so the place was often like an oven, especially during that first month when the hot August sun made the dark, unventilated quarters unbearable.

What little that was left of their festive mood had evaporated completely by the time they reached the open sea and the rock and pull of the boat had begun to take its toll. The vessel that had seemed so imposing when they boarded it was like a fragile toy now in the hands of a malicious giant as it was hurled hither and yon by the towering waves that sometimes even came crashing across its decks. The girls fell and bumped into one another so frequently, as they tried to make their way over the unpredictable flooring beneath their feet, that they finally began to make jokes about it and laugh at themselves.

But there were still greater challenges to be faced. Just keeping the food on the mess table and out of their laps required all the ingenuity and skill they could muster, but keeping it in their stomachs often proved to be the most difficult feat of all.

They were rocked and tossed so incessantly that Madelón and several of the women in the group immediately fell ill, and by the time they hit their first spell of inclement weather, after about a week out of port, Charlotte and many others who had held out that far finally had to take to their beds for a couple of days, as well.

They soon learned, however, that although one might wish for the blessed relief of death while in the grip of that horrendous malady known as *mal de mer*, no one really died of it, and sooner or later the unfortunate victims would appear on deck, a little the worse for the experience, but still alive and glad to be up and around again.

Fortunately the majority of the girls were young and healthy and able to snap back quickly, while the nuns who had chosen to accompany them were also a hardy lot. The long years of life in convents or public insitutions enabled them to take the rigors of such a voyage in their stride.

It was probably thanks to the scrupulous care of the nuns that, despite the conditions under which they traveled, the plague—that dreaded scourge of most extended sea voyages—did not break out among them. They were told it was quite rare in those days for a boatload of so many people to reach port without having lost at least a few of its passengers to dysentery or the pox along the way.

From the very beginning, however, the *religieuses* had imposed strict rules of cleanliness which, with few exceptions, were followed to the letter, no matter how adverse the circumstances. Once a week the living quarters were

29

scrubbed down and personal linens and bedding changed; sometimes more often, if necessary.

Then, too, there was Sister Marie, with a physical fortitude that was surpassed only by her indomitable spirit. She always seemed to be there when needed, with a consoling word and a cup of one of those special brews of hers, made from the ample selection of herbs which, thanks to her usual foresight, she had brought along. Night or day, there she would be, her slight, dark-robed figure making its way down the narrow lane between the bunks, ministering to the sick or calming the fears of those more timid souls who, as the days melted into weeks and the weeks into months, sometimes began to doubt that they would ever set foot on dry land again. Even Charlotte found herself wondering occasionally how many of them would have undertaken the voyage, had they known beforehand all the perils and hardships they would have to endure before ever reaching the shores of the New World.

Of course, all was not dark and dreary. With so many young girls, most in their late teens or early twenties, banded together with a mutual dream in their hearts, there would always be some lighter moments to temper even the most difficult times.

Often the high, almost childlike voices of those future brides of the New World could be heard wafting across the broad expanse of limitless ocean, as they sat on the upper deck on calmer days, singing the old familiar hymns and folksongs that reminded them of the land they were leaving farther and farther behind. Then, too, many a long hour was passed amid the lilting hum of whispered confidences, interspersed with a suppressed giggle or two, while deft fingers, keeping up with equally nimble tongues, flew over the daily mending or worked diligently on additional tidbits for their trousseaux.

Those hours of leisure on deck, where they could be free of the stuffy, dimly lighted atmosphere of their cabin and take in the fresh, salt-spiked air of the sea, were a welcome respite from the strict routine of daily chores that the nuns had set up for them, as well as the usual prayers four times a day, more on Sundays and special feast days. Exchanging their hopes and dreams with one another seemed to help keep them glowing in their hearts. They could compare secret yearnings and romantic fantasies, each trying to imagine how her future husband would be—handsome, prosperous, brave, tender. . . . It was still good to be young with all of one's life ahead.

The captain and his crew seemed a little awed by so many *religieuses* and "good little girls" on their ship, and there were moments when it was evident that those rough and ready seamen were as uncomfortable with their new style of living as their passengers were. On more than one occasion one of them would forget and let slip a bit of colorful vocabulary not meant for "delicate ears," whereupon the offender would hang his head sheepishly and, shifting his weight awkwardly from one foot to the other, murmur a feeble apology.

Of course, Charlotte suspected that there were times when the mariners were not nearly as respectful, once out of earshot, and often she had the feeling that she and her companions were the inspiration for many of those comments exchanged by the sailors amid loud guffaws, whenever the women went topside.

Captain Hébert, however, took the responsibility that had been placed on his shoulders very seriously. The safety of so many virtuous women weighed heavily on him. It made him go into a nervous sweat just to think of all the things that could go wrong before he deposited his precious cargo in Louisiana.

Although he had made a similar voyage to the colonies several years back with a group of females for the men there, that occasion could hardly be compared with this one. That first batch had been an assorted lot of "undesirables," scraped from the gutters and prisons of Paris—a far cry from this bevy of convent girls, handpicked by the Church and endorsed by King Louis himself. As if he didn't have enough problems just getting them all through the usual perils of pirates, storms and shipwrecks, without having to worry about some scatterbrained wench falling overboard or one of his men getting out of hand and causing a national scandal!

The first spell of bad weather, in which Charlotte had suffered her attack of seasickness, was nothing compared

31

to the raging storm they ran into during early September, right after they had stopped off at the Canaries to take on fresh water and supplies.

The women were forced to take to the questionable refuge of their cabin, tied two to a bunk to keep themselves from being hurled to the floor, while the ship twisted and trembled like a creature in the agonies of purgatory.

Charlotte and Madelón clung tenaciously to each other in one of the upper berths, desperately praying to the Blessed Virgin that the straining ropes would not give way. Their lofty niche swayed so precariously that they feared the whole structure was going to collapse beneath them at any moment. Since it had been necessary to extinguish the wildly swinging lantern above them, they lay in the impenetrable darkness, rosaries in hand, their spasmodic, terrified breathing and murmured prayers drowned out by the fury of the storm lashing out at them from all sides.

The luggage, jammed into a heap at the far end of the cabin, had also been made fast, but one piece had worked itself loose and was banging up and down the aisle every time the ship writhed in the throes of the storm, keeping them in constant fear that the whole pile of chests would soon give way and come crashing down on their heads, as they lay there tied helplessly to their beds.

Howling wind sent sheets of rain and mountainous waves pounding against the quivering vessel with such force that, although the portholes were tightly closed and the hatch battened down, huge droplets of rain still managed to find their way into the room, frightening reminders that the boat might burst at the seams at any moment and spew them out from its shattered belly into the watery inferno below.

"Ah, *mon Dieu!*" thought Charlotte, as she clung to the edge of her berth until her knuckles turned white. "Is this how we're going to end, buried with all our hopes and dreams at the bottom of the sea, churning and churning forever in a twilight world? Please, God, don't let it end like this, not yet . . ."

There was no way to tell how long they lay there enveloped in the storm, an integral part of it. Sometime before dawn, however, the winds finally subsided, leaving a steady downpour in its wake and a still turbulent ocean that took several hours more to calm down again. Only then did the weary women doze off, still tied in their bunks, but too exhausted to resist the steady rocking of the boat any longer.

Chapter VI

The storm had left them with damaged rigging and a broken yardarm, so the mariners set about making repairs as best they could. Unfortunately they had also lost a third of their chickens and sheep. The poor creatures had been thrown against one another so violently that they had suffocated and had to be thrown overboard. That meant tighter rationing of the food supply, and in the weeks that followed, less appetizing meals were served, often seasoned with salted beef or bacon too greasy and tough to get down one's throat.

After another three-day delay, however, while they anchored off an apparently deserted island to take on fresh water and make the more essential repairs, the *Deux Frères* finally got underway once more.

About a week later they crossed the Tropic, that invisible equinoctial line, which seemed to be an event for riotous celebration among the members of the crew. Despite the captain's request that the latter forego their usual tradition of throwing buckets of water on those who would not "pay the tithe," they persisted in what Sister Mathilde, the eldest of the Grey Sisters from Paris, termed "blackmail" and collected a goodly number of *pistoles* from the passengers who wished to be spared that ceremony of baptism, while Hébert looked discreetly the other way.

33

Although the captain later expressed his apologies for the behavior of his men, it was evident that he really felt the crew had deserved its few hours of fun and the opportunity to supplement their miserable wages with those few extra coins "donated" by the passengers.

With the exception of that one day, however, Charlotte and her friends settled down to the monotonous routine of life aboard ship once more, returning to their usual chores, the recitation of Angelus four times a day, and the welcome respite of their sewing circles every afternoon.

They had no sooner begun to feel it was not so bad just to be alive, despite the cut rations and miserable quarters, when they had their first encounter with pirates.

Captain Hébert certainly did not want to take any chances if he could help it—not with twenty-six virgins on his hands and all of France to answer to for their safety! But he was worried about the damaged yardarm, which had been only hastily repaired and might not hold out if they tried to run for it, so, cursing his rotten luck, he ordered the women to their quarters until further notice and piped his men to their battle stations.

Thus Charlotte and Madelón found themselves once more seated below in the same spot where, only a few weeks before, they had lain bound to their bunks, listening to the storm raging around them and expecting to be sent to the bottom of the sea at any moment. Now they were huddled together again in fear, discovering that there could be even greater perils than those they had already experienced.

The boards of the deck over their heads creaked and groaned beneath the scurrying feet of the sailors running hither and yon in urgent preparations for the coming battle, while the terrified women strained their ears, trying desperately to interpret the meaning of those unfamiliar sounds above them.

Sister Marie and the nuns began saying their beads softly and urged the girls to join them, but one or two were near hysteria at the thought of falling into the hands of the pirates.

"*Mon Dieu!* We'll all be killed!" came a moan from the berth beneath Charlotte's.

34

"Silly girl! How much you know!" quipped a pert little brunette, recently turned nineteen, who still held in her hands the doily she had been knitting for her trousseau when they had suddenly been ordered to their cabin. "Pirates don't kill girls like us. They rape them!"

"God forbid!" shuddered one of the Grey Sisters in horror, crossing herself fervently.

"*Chut*, Cecile, and say your prayers!" scolded Sister Marie.

Madelón, already suffering from one of her attacks of *mal de mer*, wondered whether death might not bring blessed relief from that whole dreadful nightmare, and whispered as much to her friend.

"Hush, dear, don't despair yet," Charlotte exclaimed, trying to console her friend with an optimism she really did not feel. "Captain Hébert and his crew are very able men. They'll save us, I'm sure."

But the captain wasn't all that sure himself. Despite the murmur of prayers that greeted him when he finally went below to see his terrified passengers, he was not anticipating any miracles. His furrowed brow was more creased than ever, as he mopped his face with a coarse, half-soiled handkerchief. The pirates, he told them hurriedly, were circling them like hawks sizing up their prey, trying to decide whether they should strike or not.

Although the *Deux Frères* was the larger of the two vessels, it was also the more cumbersome. From what he could see, the enemy had the same number of cannons they did, but equalled or outnumbered them man for man. He did not dare tell his passengers all his fears, however, for he did not wish to alarm them any more than they already were. But heaven help them if those renegades knew what cargo the *Deux Frères* was carrying! A boatload of females on the high seas was a booty almost as desirable as gold bullion. For a good tumble with a wench such ruffians would be more than willing to fight their way through hell.

"There's one gamble we might take to tip the scales in our favor," continued Hébert, venturing at last to put some of his thoughts into words, yet regretting that he had so little time in which to convince the *religieuses* of what he had come to ask them to do.

"It's only a slim chance," he continued hesitantly, "but considering the odds, I think it might be worth the risk. Your girls are so young, though—they'd have to keep their heads no matter what happened. The slightest slip would be our undoing."

"*Mon Dieu!* What are you proposing, *Capitaine?*" asked Sister Marie, her apprehension mounting.

"That we try a subterfuge on our pursuers, Madame," replied Hébert. Sucking in his breath, he dove in head first. "Perhaps if we dressed as many of the girls here as possible in men's clothing and sent them up top to swell our ranks, the enemy might think we outnumbered them."

"Holy Mother of God!" exclaimed Sister Marie. "But my poor girls are not fighting men!"

"I know, I know," nodded Hébert, taking another dab at his broad countenance with his crumpled handkerchief. "But they wouldn't have to fight. They'd just stand there so it'd *look* like we had more men aboard than we really do, that's all."

"I—I still don't understand," insisted Sister Marie. "How could you possibly pass off any of these young girls as seafaring men? Those villains would know they weren't members of your crew in a minute."

"Not necessarily so," argued Hébert. "I could scrape together about fifteen outfits," he went on, while the nuns' eyes grew wider by the second. "If your taller girls could put on our spare clothing and mingle among the crewmen, it might discourage the pirates from attacking us. We could scatter the young ladies in such a way that they wouldn't be seen too cleary from the other ship—just enough to let their heads be counted. That would be enough."

A few nuns, however, were beginning to raise their voices in dissent.

"Merciful heavens! Our girls up there with the crew? Never!"

"All I ask, ladies, is that they just stand there. They wouldn't have to lift a finger."

"But isn't there some other way?" asked Sister Marie, still reluctant to accept so hazardous a proposition.

"None that I know of, my lady," answered Hébert. "It's that or risk a lot worse if those scum board us."

The nuns broke out again in protest. "Women in the midst of fighting men! Preposterous!"

"Ladies, please!" pleaded Hébert, growing impatient. "This is no time to quibble over feminine niceties. The enemy is getting nearer by the minute."

"But if the pirates started shooting, the girls would be up there in the thick of it!" moaned Sister Mathilde, her round face as grey as her habit by now.

"Women in breeches? *Mon Dieu!* What a sacrilege!" exclaimed Sister Anne of the Ursulines.

"If our little masquerade doesn't work, they'll be learning a lot more about men's breeches than just wearing them!" grunted Hébert, his patience exhausted as precious minutes ticked away in such bickering.

Sister Mathilde shrieked in horror, and her plump figure fell back in a faint on top of two unfortunate girls seated on a bunk behind her.

"Really, Captain," chided Sister Marie, "such comments are uncalled for!"

"Begging your pardon, ladies, I don't mean to offend, but the sands are running low for us. It's a gamble any way you look at it, but there'll be no time to do anything at all if we don't act quickly."

Charlotte, swept up in the wave of urgency she had caught in the captain's voice, dared to speak up, hoping she would be forgiven for the intrusion under the circumstances.

"Please, *Soeur* Marie, don't be afraid for us," she ventured. "Anything is better than just sitting here and doing nothing. Besides, haven't you always said God is always with us, no matter where we are? Wouldn't He be up there on the deck just as much as down here?"

The clear young voice, calm in the midst of their own excited exclamations, seemed to bring the nuns back to their senses.

"You're right, of course!" agreed Sister Marie, taking Charlotte by the hand and drawing her closer into the group that had gathered around the captain. "Out of the mouths of babes! Let the courage and faith of this dear child be a lesson to all of us!"

So it was decided. Fifteen of the girls were chosen and rapidly dressed in random clothing sent down by the captain. Although Charlotte was far from being the tallest of the group, she was considered slightly above average height, so she was immediately included among those elected to go topside.

Madelón, however, did not qualify. Her frail figure would have never been convincing even from a distance. The poor girl and the sea, it seemed, were incompatible. Pale and hollow-eyed, she had hardly been able to hold down anything since the voyage had begun, and it was only because of Sister Marie's herb teas, which helped give her some nourishment, that she had managed to survive thus far. Her friend's deteriorating health worried Charlotte, but now it was Madelón's turn to be fearful for her.

Weak and terrified, the golden-haired girl wept uncontrollably while she watched the girls chosen to go topside change into their disguises.

"Don't fret, my dear," Charlotte laughed a little tremulously, as she strutted about clumsily in the oversized buckled shoes they had given her to go with her mariner's outfit. "Look at me, see how fierce I am? They'll think we're celebrating Mardi Gras, non?"

But Charlotte's attempt to make light of their masquerade in the hopes of calming Madelón's fears was shortlived. It was a solemn little group that gathered before Sister Marie, as the nun gave each of them her blessing and assured them she had made a special vow to the Blessed Virgin and St. Francis Xavier to have six masses said for the souls in Purgatory if the little group merited their protection during the coming encounter.

Captain Hébert returned to inspect them personally, making a criticism here and there and urging them to throw back their shoulders and stand as tall as they could. When Charlotte and one or two of her compaions obeyed him, however, the captain hastily added, somewhat sheepishly, that perhaps the slimmer ladies should give their jackets to their "more generously endowed" companions.

Finally, warning them to be silent and not to cry out no matter what happened, Hébert took them topside and assigned each girl to a group of sailors who could partially cover her from too close a scrutiny. At that moment it was the captain who was praying even more than the nuns.

Chapter VII

Charlotte found herself posted on the main deck near the forecastle, which was commanded by the second captain, a very serious-looking, clean-shaven young man in his mid-twenties, whose countenance betrayed some of his inner misgivings over mixing women with fighting men.

Charlotte knew she and her companions made a motley addition to that crew of fierce-looking mariners milling around them. The full sleeves of her coarsely woven white shirt hung limply over her shoulders and would have engulfed her hands, but for the wristbands that held them in place. The shirt fitted snugly only over her bust, but the sleeveless rawhide vest the captain had given her at the last minute helped hide the imperfect fit fairly well.

Her faded breeches, raveling around the bottom where they had once been shortened without benefit of needle and thread, hung equally limply. She had wrapped a wide red sash three times around her diminutive waist to hold the sagging breeches up and could feel the bulky folds of excess fabric bulging beneath the band.

Discreetly she lifted her hand to check that all her curls had been completely tucked away under the red knitted cap they had given her. To make her more convincing, they had also given her a sword to hold. Most of her companions also held pistols, cutlasses, or daggers to help make their disguises more complete, although Charlotte feared such accessories might only make their shortcomings the more evident.

The captain had promised the nuns that at the first sign of battle he would send the girls below out of the line of fire, but Charlotte knew that if it should come to open warfare between the two vessels, she and her companions would be just as lost in their cabin as anywhere else on board.

She could feel the curious eyes of the nearby sailors fixed on her, and the blood rushed upwards through her body like a great hot wave to the roots of her hair. She was suddenly aware of the fact that although she was dressed the same as they, they were busy contemplating how she looked in their clothes. Their open appraisal made her uncomfortable, especially the gaze of the one who was easing in closer to her. The bright sunlight picked up a glint from the gold earring in his right earlobe. He flashed her a grin from his pockmarked face. He was not that tall, but she felt dwarfed beside him.

"Well, I'll be damned if I ever seen my breeches look so good!" he exclaimed, sweeping her up and down with bold black eyes. "Yes, little lady, them's my pants you're wearing, but you're welcome to them. You can get into my breeches anytime you like!"

He gave a sly wink to the other seamen and they chuckled, their eyes following the same course over her body. Although the second captain was not within earshot, Charlotte was thankful that at least he was in view, for she was sure they would have undressed her with more than their eyes, had none of the officers been close at hand.

Anger and shame welled up within her. She resented their making sport at her expense. She shot another glance anxiously in the direction of the second captain, but at that moment he was engrossed in conversation with another officer, so she just stood there, wishing desperately to escape that circle of probing eyes or at least to be able to think of something appropriate to reply to their insinuations.

The mariner, however, moved still nearer, deliberately blocking her from the officers' line of view. She could see the black tangle of hairs on his bronzed chest, where his coarsely woven blouse gaped open at the neck.

"Once we get them jackals out there off our tails, you can see a lot more of my breeches, if you like, little lady," he continued, motioning meanwhile to his shipmates to back off and give him a little privacy to pursue what he hoped would be an easy conquest.

They returned his signals with another round of guffaws but complied readily enough, for they were well aware of the fact that their shipmate was heading for trouble and told him as much. But the persistent crewman continued to be more interested in his breeches than their warnings.

Ignoring a parting word from one of his companions that there would be the devil to pay if the captain or one of the officers saw him trifling with one of the women at such a moment, the mariner immediately began to elaborate on his proposition.

"You may not fill out those pants as well as you do that blouse, my dear," he continued, dropping his voice so that only she could hear him, "but then that means there's all the more room for the two of us, *non*? What you say you give those nuns of yours the slip tonight and meet me for a little fun? If we're lucky enough to be alive then, that is."

"Please, monsieur, you're either very insolent or stark raving mad—"

"Come now, dearie, don't be afraid," he urged her. "There are lots of places on board where a clever pair can snuggle up and nobody'd be the wiser. If I'm not at the bottom of the ocean before the day is over, and you're not warming some pirate's bunk, meet me over there behind those barrels at twenty-three bells, and I promise I'll learn you something you'll like more than just prayers and hymn singing!"

He gave a playful pinch at her buttocks, but the breeches hung so loosely around her that he misjudged exactly where she was beneath them and missed his aim. Charlotte drew back quickly, her eyes flashing defiantly at him from her flushed face.

"Lay a hand on me again, monsieur, and I'll run you through!" she exclaimed, clumsily waving her sword at him.

The seaman burst out laughing as he dodged her easily. *"Voilà!* I see the bee in my breeches has a sting!" he ex-

41

claimed with delight. *"Sacre bleu!* What I wouldn't give to climb in there with you right now!"

Charlotte thrust her sword out threateningly at him a second time, and he gave another hearty laugh. Nevertheless, he cast a hasty glance in the direction of the second captain, who was looking curiously at them.

"Bien, bien," the crewman soothed her. "Now don't go getting all ruffled up, little lady. I don't mean no harm. Just joshing a bit, that's all."

The officer seemed about to come over to investigate.

"Remember, I might be dying to protect you and your friends before this day is done," the mariner hurriedly reminded her. "When a man ain't had a woman for months on end, he goes a little overboard, you know. I was only trying to have a little fun while waiting to meet my Maker—surely you can understand that?" he whined coaxingly.

"Ahoy there!" the second captain called out to them. "What's going on? Is everything all right?"

"Aye, aye, sir, all's well," the crewman hastily called back before Charlotte could find her voice to reply. "I'm just trying to learn the young one here how to hold a sword."

The officer shot a quizzical glance at Charlotte's silent figure and took several more steps toward them.

"Are you sure everything is all right?" he asked, directing his question more to Charlotte than to the seaman. She could feel the mariner's panic-stricken eyes desperately pleading with her.

"I—I—*oui*, monsieur . . ." she nodded meekly.

"Très bien," sighed the second captain, although there was a faint trace of doubt in his tone. He turned toward the sailor. "Let me remind you there'll be no wenching aboard this ship," he added sternly. "Any man who dares to cause trouble on that score will be severely flogged and clapped in irons. Is that understood?"

"Aye, aye, sir. Of course, sir," replied the crewman quickly, pulling himself up to a stiff salute.

"Then get to work and let the wench alone, or I'll stripe your hide, so help me God!" snapped the second captain. Then, without even waiting for the mariner's second salute, he spun round on his heel and returned to the officer with whom he had been conversing. He had more urgent matters to worry about at that moment than wasting time with some fool sailor for hankering after a pretty wench. The enemy ship was still circling them, and with each reconnaisance it was gradually working its way nearer.

As for the seaman, he cast a sheepish but grateful glance at Charlotte and then slinked away rather self-consciously to join his shipmates at the railing, who were having a good laugh at his expense now, although he shrugged his shoulders and tried to make light of the whole episode in an effort to save face.

Now that the pirate vessel had drawn up closer to them and Charlotte's eyes had grown more accustomed to the bright sunlight, she began to catch fleeting glimpses of the enemy—glimpses she would have preferred not to have had. The sight of that band of half-naked men lined up on the deck of the opposing vessel froze the blood in her veins, despite the warmth of the midday sun beating down on her. Armed to the teeth and brandishing their weapons menacingly, the pirates shouted obscenities at them, their loud, boisterous laughter and deliberate taunts wafting eerily across the calm, mirrorlike ocean that sparkled between the ships.

Charlotte could hear the gunners in the waist of the ship grumbling and cursing under their breaths as they hurried to finish loading the cannons, their naked torsos glistening with grime and sweat, while those standing by the railing stood at attention now with weapons unsheathed, taut like bow strings waiting to spring into action at the slightest provocation.

Meanwhile, on the poop-deck, Captain Hébert bit his tongue and held back the order to fire, refusing to be goaded into any rash action that might lead only to disaster. He suspected that his adversary was of the same disposition. Neither side, it seemed, wanted to begin a fight until it was sure of winning. Each one knew there would be no drawing back once that first shot was fired.

Charlotte had no way of knowing how long they stood there with the pirates circling them, drawing close for a better view and then pulling away quickly, as a cat plays with a mouse. As the danger of attack increased, the sailors' interest in the novelty of having so many young girls among them lessened. A pretty wench was always good sport, but when an enemy was breathing down one's neck, other things had to take priority.

By midafternoon it had become evident that the pirates had no intention of withdrawing, so Captain Hébert decided it was best to order the girls below. They had served their purpose. The buccaneers had had time enough to count heads, and keeping the women up on deck too long might only increase the risk of detection. Besides, the fact that the enemy had not withdrawn suggested that attack was imminent.

Charlotte and the other girls were welcomed back to the cabin below by their anxiously waiting companions, but there was little optimism in the air, for everyone knew that the reason why they had returned was because the pirates would probably be attacking the ship at any moment.

The women huddled together, listening with mounting apprehension to the activities taking place on the upper deck, starting at every unusual sound that drifted down to them through the heavy beams vibrating over their heads.

As the day wore on, however, and the hours continued to pass painfully by, the ship fell into a strange, expectant silence. Even the anguished prayers subsided. The women continued to cling to one another in the gradually darkening cabin, straining their ears to catch the sound of the first shot, which seemed overlong in coming.

It was as if the whole world had suddenly been suspended in time. Only the creaking of the boat's timbers as it rocked gently beneath them reminded the women that the minutes were still ticking away. Charlotte felt herself yielding to the hypnotic effect, almost forgetting the stark reality of their impending danger. It was as if they were swinging rhythmically with the mighty pendulum of time itself . . . a part of it now, and their separate identities were melting away.

Twilight fell, and they continued their vigil, sitting there motionless in breathless silence. It didn't even occur to anyone to light the lantern.

Suddenly the whole ship shook with renewed life. It began to sway more rapidly. Shouts and pounding feet set the boards over their heads resounding again. In that split second the startled women were aroused from their stupor, and they clutched frantically at one another in the dusk, as exclamations of terror escaped uncontrollably from their lips.

Heavy footsteps were coming in their direction, In one great chorus of despair they moaned and crossed themselves in unison. Sister Mathilde took her beads in hand and began to recite her *In Manus*, but Sister Marie took a deep breath. Her face was ashen in the dim light that filtered in through the porthole. She rose and walked deliberately towards the hatchway, where all eyes were focused now in dread anticipation. It was as if the nun hoped to put her frail body between her charges and whoever came through those portals.

When Captain Hébert's familiar voice accompanied the knock, Sister Marie swayed for a moment as if her knees were going to give way under her but, recovering quickly, she moved joyfully to let him in, while two other nuns rushed to help her with the heavy bar they had placed across the entrance. A wave of relief swept over the crowded room, and although the women were not certain what tidings the captain might be bringing, the pent-up terror they had held in check for so many hours welcomed that unexpected moment of respite.

Hébert's face was tired but jubilant as he entered, and the reddish glow of his lantern heightened the flush of excitement on his countenance.

"Don't be afraid, ladies," he greeted them, his three-cornered hat tucked under his arm. "I bear good tidings."

"Ah, *Capitaine*, you don't know how overjoyed we are to see you standing there!" exclaimed Sister Marie. "We didn't know whom to expect!"

"Aye, madame, I know," nodded Hébert. "But here, if you close the portholes, you can have a light. There's no need now to stay in the dark."

Then, while the captain lit their lantern from his own, he went on to assure them that the danger had passed. At first, he admitted, he had been convinced they would have to fight it out.

"But then another mast suddenly appeared on the horizon," he continued, the emotion of the day's events clearly visible in his dark, squirrellike eyes. "It was evident the pirates had seen it too, for they immediately swung round to get a better look at the newcomer."

"God be praised!" exclaimed Sister Marie.

"From what we could see, the other ship was a Spanish galleon, probably on its way home from its colonies in Mexico, so you can well imagine how the scent of gold sent those seadogs off in hot pursuit of what they hoped would be even greater spoils."

Hébert passed the sleeve of his jacket over his round face and heaved a sigh. "Not that I wouldn't've minded a go with them black-livered bas—I mean, we could've given them a good fight, mind you, but with you ladies aboard—*Sacre Bleu!* Your pardon, mesdames . . . that is, I—I'm glad just to turn tail and cut out of these waters as fast as we can go, under the circumstances, I mean . . ."

His voice trailed off, as he hesitated for fear of forgetting himself and letting slip something that might offend. It was rough going trying to talk of such matters to women, much less *religieuses.*

"God has heard our prayers!" declared Sister Marie, kissing the cross of her rosary reverently. "Come, everyone, let us send up our thanks to our merciful Lord and Savior!" and she led them in a prayer of thanksgiving, which everyone repeated with more fervor than usual, for they felt a new lease on life had suddenly been bestowed upon them.

But even as their voices mingled in joyous oration, the sounds of distant gunfire between the Spanish galleon and their recent adversaries echoed across the dark expanse of ocean, reminding them that they were leaving behind a grim reality that well might have been their own.

46

Chapter VIII

They were under strict orders now to close their portholes at night so no lights would betray their presence to unwanted marauders. Captain Hébert warned them that the closer they got to their destination, the greater the danger of meeting such freebooters would be, for the Caribbean was infested with outlaws who roamed up and down those waterlanes in search of victims. Charlotte recalled her aunt's dire predictions and wondered whether they had really been as exaggerated as she had thought at the time.

On October 6, one month to the day after they had crossed the Tropic and several experiences the wiser, they dropped anchor at Quay St. Louis, an island in Santo Domingo, where they spent a delightful week resting from their arduous voyage, while Hébert and his crew gave the ship a careful going over and made necessary repairs. Additional food and water were stocked, especially welcome after the recent weeks of daily servings of greasy, tasteless gruel.

The women were overjoyed at being back on dry land and happily accepted the hospitality offered them by the two gentlemen who represented the Company of the Indies there, as well as the governor of the island, who graciously held a banquet in their honor.

It was almost with regret that they boarded the *Deux Frères* once more to resume their voyage, but the week's respite had at least served to revive their spirits as well as their energies, and the good weather, along with the improved rations, freshly whitened linens, and meticulously scrubbed living quarters, helped make the next few days back at sea almost enjoyable.

They did encounter another squall, about three days out of Quay St. Louis, and once again some damage was done to the ship's rigging, but after the bad storm they had previously weathered, the girls laughingly declared themselves "seasoned mariners."

It came as a double surprise, therefore, when one sunny day in the first week of November the lookout called down from his perch that he had sighted an unidentified ship on the horizon. Since it flew no colors, it was immediately assumed to be another pirate ship.

Numbly the women hurried to their quarters, unable to believe the sudden turn of events. The overcrowded cabin was strangely subdued, as they sat there listening once more to the racing feet overhead, while Captain Hébert's familiar voice shouted out orders above a chorus of grunts and curses and the relayed commands of his subordinates. It seemed highly doubtful that another Spanish galleon would be appearing suddenly on the horizon to distract the enemy from them.

Their fears were short-lived, however, for the captain gave orders to let out the ship's canvas to full capacity. Thanks to the recent repairs done at Santo Domingo, they were able to outrun what had been probably another band of roving sea bandits. By midmorning the pirate vessel had disappeared below the horizon, and the *Deux Frères* found a favorable wind to speed it on to its destination.

Sister Marie proclaimed that the Holy Mother and St. Francis Xavier were indeed smiling down on them, and for days afterwards the women walked about with the elated feeling that God had truly sent his angels to watch over them on their perilous voyage across the ocean.

As for Captain Hébert, although not a very religious man by nature, he had to admit that the prayers of so many virtuous women certainly seemed to have brought him some luck on more than one occasion, but he knew better than to cry victory so soon.

Finally, on a chilly, cloud-laden day in late November, the long-awaited moment arrived. They had reached the mouth of the mighty Mississippi River, entrance to His Majesty's Louisiana Colony. Although the wind had taken on a biting edge, the women excitedly drew their wraps

48

around them and went up on deck to see the welcome sight of the land that was to be their new home.

Etched against inclement skies, the small islands dotting the Gulf at this point did not seem very different from the many others they had been seeing on their way across the Caribbean, but those dismal outposts with their tall, twisted trees, battered by wind and waves until hardly a leaf remained on their misshapen branches, heralded to the weary travelers the end of their long, arduous journey.

Charlotte suddenly found herself thinking how far away France and Aunt Germaine and M. Blégot were at that moment. The first eighteen years of her life seemed to have evaporated into that vast ocean she had so laboriously crossed. Nothing in the past mattered any more. Only the reality of the present and the pressure of the unknown future were important now. It was a frightening feeling, yet an exhilarating one. Unlike Madelón and so many of her companions, Charlotte could not focus her thoughts around the vague image of some unknown husband-to-be. Instead, she kept wondering how it was going to feel to be settled down in a new land and, for the first time in her life, make her own decisions.

Chapter IX

Their landing in the New World was not quite the way Charlotte and her companions had envisioned it. Even as they stood on deck trying to get their first glimpse of the Mississippi, a clap of thunder and a sudden downpour of rain sent them scurrying back below.

Shortly afterwards, in the midst of the brief but violent storm, they ran aground on a sandbar and spent a sleepless night trying to get loose. Although the rain finally slackened to a light drizzle, it seemed for a while as if the captain and his crew would not be able to save their floundering vessel. Deep in the bowels of the ship the bilge pumps worked frantically, while the captain sent out the ship's launch and dinghy with anchors to try to pull the vessel backwards, but the *Deux Frères* remained caught in the fatal grip of those treacherous, shifting sands that held it prisoner.

The women were asked to go topside with their luggage in the hopes of shifting the vessel's weight. They sat huddled together on their small trunks toward the rear of the ship, expecting at any moment to be asked to sacrifice their only worldly belongings to the dark, choppy sea lapping hungrily up at them. They watched the men throwing more and more barrels and ballast overboard in an effort to eliminate excess weight.

Charlotte drew her blue woolen cape closer around her aching body and pulled the hood down as far over her face as she could, not knowing whether her shivering was caused by the cold, misty wind blowing relentlessly against her or by the even greater chill of icy fear that gripped her from within. She looked off to where she knew the mouth of the Mississippi lay beckoning on the horizon, but all she could see was the yawning abyss of the black, relentless water around her. What irony it would be to have come such a long way, only to end their voyage there, with their destination in sight yet too far away to give them refuge. If they had to abandon ship, it was doubtful they would be able to get very far in such angry waters without capsizing.

The men strained and cursed, as their sweat mingled with the raindrops bathing their faces, while the women, cold and rain-drenched softly sent their prayers up to the dark, starless night above them. The captain was trying to decide whether to sacrifice one of his cannons or ask the women to throw their luggage overboard, when a French brigantine suddenly appeared, silhouetted by the early morning light as it exited from the yawning mouth of the river.

Captain Hébert and his crew let out a resounding cheer of welcome, and Charlotte and her companions suddenly forgot the weariness of their long overnight vigil on deck and also began to shout with joy. They embraced one another and gave thanks to *le bon Dieu* for having delivered them once more from the jaws of death.

With the additional help and equipment sent over by the brigantine, the grounded vessel was finally pulled free from what might have been its sandy grave and escorted to a small island located at the mouth of the river, where it finally came to rest like a wounded giant licking its wounds.

One of the first things Hébert did after weighing anchor was to send his second captain ahead up the river in the ship's dinghy to advise the Company of the Indies at the port of Balize that they had arrived but were delayed because of urgently needed repairs.

By the second day, which marked the first of December, the second captain had returned with three more small boats, as well as Monsieur de Verges, Commander for the *Compagnie* at Balize, who brought with him a number of workmen and additional equipment to help Hébert with his emergency reparations.

Sieur de Verges was a tall, pleasant-mannered young man in his early thirties who greeted the nuns and their charges with genuine warmth, assuring them that they had been anxiously awaited all those months and that a messenger had already been dispatched upriver to New Orleans to announce their arrival.

Captain Hébert was anxious to get his vessel in good enough condition to be able to make dock at Balize, where he could give the craft a general overhauling before undertaking the long voyage back to France. It was decided that it would be best if de Verges would escort the women immediately to Balize in the smaller boats. The captain would be able to finish his urgent repairs more quickly and follow them later.

As Charlotte stood alone in the empty cabin, looking with mixed emotions at the bare bunks, stripped now of their bedding and starkly silhouetted in the sunlight streaming in through the open portholes, a wave of loneliness momentarily swept over her. Once again she was saying goodbye. The convent in Marseilles, Aunt Germaine, now the ship that had been her home for so many months . . . Life, it seemed, was a succession of good-byes. She wondered if she would ever feel she really belonged anywhere or to anyone . . . really have a home of her own.

The weather had cleared up during their two-day wait at the mouth of the river, so the sun was still shining when they arrived at Balize later that same day. On their way upriver they had passed another small island, barely half an acre, called Island of the Cannons, where workers were busy completing a fort to guard that entrance to the river, for although the mouth of the Mississippi forked out into several different arteries as it made its tortuous way through the low marshlands to empty into the Gulf, the one used by Hébert was the most traversed.

The settlers at Balize welcomed the weary travelers as graciously as Sieur de Verges had done. They brought food and wine to the *Compagnie* lodgings, which had been immediately placed at the women's disposal. The tiny port was rather primitive by Old World standards, yet de Verges had managed to make his home quite comfortable with many imported luxuries, despite the fact that he was still a bachelor and lived in basically simple, unpretentious surroundings.

The three days that followed were pleasant, peaceful ones for Charlotte and her companions, who were filled with renewed vigor by the mere fact that they had actually reached the New World and were only thirty leagues from New Orleans. They were warned, however, that a five- or six-day trip still lay ahead of them, which would be slow going, since not only would they have to reckon with the treacherous currents of the Mississippi, but also the many dangers of the swamplands around them.

Beyond Balize the river was seldom navigable for ships the size of the *Deux Frères*. Occasionally a more maneuverable vessel might go on all the way into New Orleans, but most of the time they went no farther than Balize. Passengers and cargo were usually taken the rest of the way in smaller boats, escorted by experts who knew the terrain and its pitfalls. It would only be possible to travel by day, they were told, since they would have to camp at night on the banks of the wilderness that bordered the river on its winding path up to New Orleans.

Around noon of the third day in Balize, Captain Charles Dubair and his *coureurs de bois*—"runners of the woods," as they were called—arrived at the settlement to escort them on the final lap of their journey. This captain and his scouts looked like an unruly lot to Charlotte, as she and Madelón peeped out of a window at the band of nine or ten men making their boisterous entrance into the settlement. With their bearded, suntanned faces and strange leather garments they looked as if they had been spawned by the swamplands from which they were so noisily emerging. What manner of soldiers were these, wondered Charlotte. She had expected a king's officer and the men under him to dress more appropriately. These wore no impressive uniforms or ruffled jabots and cuffs, only strange deerskin outfits with coarse, open-necked shirts finished off with loosely knotted kerchiefs.

Granted the captain and a few of his men at least kept their hair tied neatly back at the napes of their necks, as was expected among gentlemen, and cropped their beards with some attempt at neatness, but most of the others simply wore their hair and beards hanging loose and unkempt about their shoulders. By all that's holy! Were these the brave young men of the New World she and her companions were expected to consider as future husbands?

The following morning, at the dawn of what promised to be a rather cold, dismal day, the women assembled on the dock with their cloaks wrapped closely around them against the damp air and their luggage stacked in a pile beside them.

Sieur de Verges made the brief introductions between the nuns and Captain Dubair, who was to lead the expedition. Although the tall, lean, powerfully built young captain was on the underside of thirty, the years of inclement weather and constant struggle for survival in the wilderness had left their mark, and he gave the appearance of being slightly older than he really was. Also, it was difficult for him to hide that this mission was not to his liking.

He acknowledged the nuns' greetings politely enough, but inwardly he despaired as he swept an apprehensive eye over the group that had fallen under his charge. Far better a bout with a hundred Indians than an assignment like this one! It was hard enough to keep his men disciplined without a bunch of petticoats to distract them all the more. His *coureurs de bois* were mercenaries and had to be led with a loose rein. After years of scouting, he felt he could handle them fairly well. But the women were another story. *Au diable!* Didn't he have enough to worry about with those recent Indian skirmishes north of New Orleans, without having to chaperon twenty-odd females who didn't have the remotest idea of what a trek through the swamplands was like?

Dubair supposed the first thing he should do was put the fear of God in them, at least enough to make them toe the mark and not get too far out of hand during the hazardous journey ahead. Putting on his sternest face, therefore, he drew himself up to the full height of his imposing stature and proceeded to lay down the rules of their forthcoming expedition in no uncertain terms.

"Ladies, please . . . *s'il vous plait,* may I have your attention?" The commanding ring to his voice immediately cut through the excited babble of the women and the townspeople who had gathered on the dock to see the travelers off. "The journey we are about to undertake is a perilous one, and it's best we understand one another from the beginning." As a hush fell over the group, he continued, "I'm afraid the boats are going to be quite crowded and overloaded, so please, ladies, no hoops or excessive underskirts. Bear in mind that your slightest movement could capsize the craft and send the whole boatload into the depths of the Mississippi. The current we'll face going upriver is fortunately very light during this season in comparison to what it would be say, in the spring, but don't be deceived. The river is quite wide and deep in many spots and there are often treacherous currents beneath its tranquil surface.

"Also, while camping on shore, please stay close together at all times. These swamps are no place to wander off. Besides the presence of wild animals and poisonous snakes, there is the added danger of the terrain itself, which is often not as solid as it looks. One false step and you might suddenly sink into a bottomless pit of quicksand. Remember, ladies, my men and I are here to protect and guide you on this expedition, so you must trust our judgment in all things and obey whatever orders I give without hesitation or question. Is that understood?"

The sea of hooded heads nodded as though controlled by a master puppeteer. Dubair could feel their wide, frightened eyes boring through him, and for a moment he felt rather guilty about alarming them so much, yet it was for their own good. They had to realize they were not going on a pleasure excursion.

"There are some things in our favor, of course," he added, trying to soften his menacing speech a little. "At this time of year you will at least be spared a few of those additional discomforts encountered in our swamplands during the summer months, such as the intense heat and our notorious friends the *Maringouins*. Once you've made the acquaintance of our mosquitoes, you'll understand what I mean when I say we're indeed fortunate to be making our journey in December and not in July or August!"

Thus it was a very subdued, apprehensive group that set out upriver from Balize, suddenly aware of the fact that the journey was not yet over and that many unknown dangers still lay ahead.

They were assigned to three large dugouts—strange, hollowed-out cypress trunks of enormous length and breadth, tapered off into points at both ends, which could normally hold from sixteen to twenty people apiece, but because of the additional room required for the traveling chests and mattresses, as well as the scouts' equipment, they could hold only a dozen passengers each.

To conserve space, each woman sat on top of her luggage, while the bedding and camping equipment were made into bundles and pushed into every nook and cranny of the giant *pirogues*, as the men sometimes referred to their craft. Although most of the girls did not own anything as elegant as a hoop, and they had long since abandoned stiffening their petticoats since they had set out on their voyage from Marseilles, they still had difficulty fitting in the boats with their long flowing layers of skirts, which overlapped so much that they felt they were practically sitting on top of each other.

Dubair had distributed three of his scouts to each dugout, fore, middle, and aft, so that when they finally got underway, there was not a free inch aboard any of the crafts.

Charlotte found herself sitting next to a small barrel in the middle of the lead boat, with the captain directly behind her and Madelón and Cecile seated together in front of her. The group from Marseilles had rounded out that first *pirogue*, which was slightly larger, so Sister Marie and Sister Anne accompanied them at the fore, while the remaining four girls paired off behind Dubair, with Sister Ernestine finishing off the group in the rear, amid several rolled-up mattresses. The rest of the girls and Sisters of Charity from Paris followed them in the other two boats.

The day remained cold and cloudy. Charlotte, like most of her companions, sat motionless, wrapped from head to foot in her hooded cloak, not daring to flex so much as a muscle for fear of falling from her precarious perch atop her *cassette*. It was a frightening feeling to be so near the water, to look down and see it right there beside her with only the side of the dugout separating her from the murky depths below. The fact that she could reach down and touch it, dip her fingers into the water if she wanted to, seemed to make her doubly conscious of the reality of the peril that lay all around them.

On the *Deux Frères* she had been reminded of the possible dangers facing them often enough, but even so, she had always felt a certain aloofness from the sea, viewing it from a lofty deck or through a small porthole. She had not experienced the sensation of actually being *in* the water, almost a part of it, as she felt now, sitting in the delicately balanced dugout, with the water lapping so close to her.

The brown waters opened up before them as their escorts cut into the surface rhythmically with their paddles. The man up front stood probing constantly into the depths with a long polelike paddle, while he cautiously sounded his way before proceeding forward or pushed the bark away from sudden sandbars or floating debris. There was a duet of

56

singsong signals frequently exchanged between him and the man seated in the rear steering with a shorter paddle.

In the middle of the boat, helping to sustain its delicate balance, was Dubair. whose double-bladed paddle steadied the dugout as well as lending extra paddling power when all was clear to go full speed ahead.

The tall reeds and cane, growing along the banks fifteen or twenty feet high, soon gave way to dense forests that came down to the very edges of the river and even into the water itself. Although the broad expanse of the Father of the Waters, as the captain said the Indians called the Mississippi, seemed tranquil enough, evidence of the strong currents beneath its deceivingly calm surface could be seen on both sides, where huge trees lay like fallen giants, torn up by the roots or twisted into tormented spectres by the relentless force that constantly rushed against them. They had so many narrow escapes that after a while Charlotte lost count and began to take them as a matter of course, as the *coureurs de bois* evidently did.

Seated as Charlotte was in front of Dubair, she could often hear his heavy rhythmic breathing as he paddled behind her. She felt sorry for him and his men. They were straining every muscle to make progress with such overloaded boats. Now that she had had an opportunity to get a closer look at the captain, he seemed less foreboding than he had at first. There was something in the crinkle around his eyes that belied the sternness of his countenance. But his nearness made her uneasy. This tall bronzed man of the swamps, swathed in buckskins, with his coonskin cap and clear light eyes that seemed so startlingly blue in contrast to his suntaned face, continued to frighten her a little. The firm set of his generous mouth suggested that here was a man who could inspire fear if provoked. Charlotte wondered what had brought him to Louisiana in the first place and why he had chosen so dangerous a job as running back and forth in the wilderness like this.

These men in the New World were a strange lot, so different from any she had seen in Marseilles. Those who had frequented her aunt's manor had usually been clean-shaven and perfumed with curled wigs and white lace furbelows peeping out from their elaborate frock coats. Although the sailors on board the *Deux Frères* had been a coarser breed, she still had been able to relate them to a world she could understand. These scouts, however, bewildered her, dressed as they were from head to foot in animal skins with muskets and powder horns slung over their shoulders and knives and tomahawks stuck in their belts. They made her all the more aware of how foreign she was to this strange new world in which she found herself, and she wondered whether she ever would be able to fit into it.

Chapter X

Around four o'clock in the afternoon they went ashore to make camp before an early nightfall. Although the grey sky never made good its threat to rain, the sun had failed to appear, making the atmosphere all the more damp and chilly. It was not easy to find a patch of solid dry land at the river's edge, but the experienced eye of the captain, who seemed familiar with every tree and blade of grass along the route, soon spotted a *chéniére*, as he called it—a point where the silt of the river had built up sufficiently to offer the weary travelers a temporary haven along that illusive shoreline, so often hidden behind a wall of high reeds and grass or tight rows of prong-rooted cypress growing down into the water itself.

Once the boats were made fast, the men helped the women ashore and unloaded the equipment they would be needing for the night. Charlotte's limbs ached after the long hours of being crammed in the boat. She pulled her hooded cloak more closely around her and made her way stiffly to where her equally exhausted companions were assembling beneath the sweeping branches of a huge oak tree fringed with hanging moss.

As soon as everyone was ashore, the captain and his men set about clearing the site for camp, razing the tall grass and vegetation to the ground with quick sweeps of their sharp tomahawks and machetes. Meanwhile the women were ordered to stay close to the vicinity of the oak, which the captain had carefully checked out for safety before discreetly withdrawing with his men in order to give them as much privacy as possible.

Extending their long capes along the length of their arms, like giant bat wings, the women tried to screen their more intimate activities as best they could, while the men went about building fires and preparing for the evening meal.

Once two good campfires were blazing cheerfully, everyone gathered around the inviting warmth to enjoy a primitive but hearty meal, their first since the breakfast they had eaten in Balize before starting out on their journey early that morning.

With the exception of some nuts, apples, and grapes, which they had been given to nibble around midmorning during the trek upriver, the group had not eaten anything all day, so they tore into the roast venison that two of the scouts had killed in the woods while the others had been clearing the campsite.

The crackling of the campfires and the tangy taste of the wild deer meat, washed down with a few sips of wine, seemed to warm their spirits as well as their tired bodies, and the awkward reserve that had existed until then between the women and their escorts dissolved a little, even as the strangeness of their surroundings began to melt into the dusky shadows around them. With the coming of night, the group became more aware of its isolation in the wilderness, as they sat huddled together in the twin islands of light made by their campfires.

The captain and several of his men took out their pipes and enjoyed a refreshing smoke, relaxing for the first time since they had set out on their journey.

Charlotte sat quietly beside Madelón and Cecile, her

face hidden in the shadow of her hood, as she listened to the murmur of her friends' conversations.

The tall, striking figure of the captain drawing on the long stem of his pipe held her attention. Perhaps because he represented the only authority, the only tangible protection for them in the midst of so many perils and uncertainties, Charlotte found herself observing him more than the others. She wondered what he thought of the *filles à la cassette*. He was always courteous and seemed genuinely concerned for their comfort as well as their safety, yet she sensed a certain aloofness about him that would have set him apart from his men even if he had not been their commander—or perhaps that was what had warranted him that position in the first place. It was hard to tell.

The other men made no secret of their delight over such an extraordinary abundance of female company. But the captain didn't seem to have the slightest interest. Of course, it was proper that he be discreet and set an example of restraint to his men, but there was something in his eyes that suggested his reserve wasn't feigned.

Charles Dubair fell into a pensive silence. No, he certainly was not as pleased with his mission as the majority of his ogling men were. He had tried to hand-pick the men for this trip, for he didn't want some woman-starved man complicating an already difficult assignment. Being responsible for seeing these giddy girls through the swamplands was not his idea of pleasure. He liked his women one at a time and at his leisure.

Since he had come to the colony, approximately ten years ago, he had seen one or two shipments of women coming from France, but most of them had been sorry candidates for blushing brides. But then, almost anything was better than his men running in the woods after those Indian squaws with their blackened teeth and grease-coated bodies. Scouring the streets and correctionals of Paris for their refuse, however, had hardly been a solution to the problem.

Although some of the women who had gotten caught in the merciless nets of the so-called justice of the glorious homeland had not really been prostitutes or criminals but, rather, innocent victims of circumstances, most of those who had come to these shores until now had been "undesirables," stirring up more trouble than they were worth, as they pitted one man against the other for their favors and then robbed the winners of their hard-earned pay. And how busy they had kept that midwife the Duke of Orleans had sent over! *La Sans-Regret*, they had nicknamed her. She had certainly earned the salary of 400 livres the government had paid her in those early years.

All that had changed now. Sterner measures were being taken against women of ill repute these days. In a land like this there was no in-between for a woman. She was either closeted and protected or trampled into the mud.

But he was glad he was in the Scouting Division and not of the regular army. He could go along with punishing troublemakers in the pillory, but he drew the line at flogging a woman. It didn't bother some, though, for he had seen one or two who had lain with a wench the night before laying the lash on her back the hardest as every man in the regiment took his turn publicly whipping her the following morning.

Only this past summer the council had resurrected that old edict of Henry II that made it a capital crime for an unmarried woman to conceal her pregnancy. The king had better send over more than just twenty little convent girls to keep the men of Louisiana happy. With such laws and so few women to go around, the council might be provoking exactly the kind of trouble it was trying to avoid. After all, many of the men in the colony had backgrounds just as bad or worse than the women who had previously been sent here, so they couldn't simply pass a few laws and expect morality suddenly to flourish. Even the decent men of the colony were only human and had needs. He himself had not always been immune to such *filles de joie*. He didn't brag about it, but he was only a man. Sometimes he had even felt a passing fondness for one or two of them, but marrying was something else. He wanted a better mother for his children.

As for the few respectable ladies of the colony, they were mostly the wives and daughters of officials who had come from France to join their menfolk at their new posts. There were a couple of young girls of marriageable age who had been all too obviously pushed into his company lately at social functions, but he had not seen anyone yet who had really piqued his fancy.

The coming of the Ursulines last year to the settlement had been one of the best moves the *Compagnie* had made in a long time. The presence of those hardworking nuns gave a stabilizing atmosphere to the colony. Now, thanks to them, decent women could come to New Orleans at last. Although they were all too few, it was easy to see that these Casquette Girls were of a different category than those who had been shipped to Louisiana in the past. They probably were the "girls of good character" that the King and the Church had endorsed them as being. At least they were an improvement over the ones who had arrived thus far. Personally, however, he couldn't work up much enthusiasm for them. The majority were hardly more than children. He doubted they really knew what life was all about, much less what the New World would demand of them in order to survive. Poor naïve little girls, so full of hopes that would probably never be realized! Bad enough for a man to have to struggle in a wilderness like this, but little convent girls?

Dubair remembered his own disillusion when he had come to the colonies in his late teens. With the impulsiveness of youth, he had run away from the monastery in Rouen where his well-to-do but domineering father had sent him to study to become a priest. He had been eager then to find the fame and fortune that had been promised in propaganda put out by men like that Scotch promoter John Law, who, backed up by the irresponsible Duke of Orleans, had said and done anything to get people to come to Louisiana and populate it. But all Dubair had found when he finally arrived was a rain-soaked wilderness. The "eight hundred beautiful mansions" on Law's posters proved to be twenty thatched huts and the streets "paved with gold and silver" were only muddy lanes run over with weeds.

Dubair had had little choice except to join the Sieur de Bienville, who was doggedly digging ditches and clearing canebrakes to make way for his dream city of Nouvelle Orléans, the port its founder insisted would someday dominate the mighty Mississippi Valley. But hardly had the little settlement begun to crawl up out of the muck of the marshlands when it was razed to the ground by the great hurricane of '23. There had also been some pretty bloody skirmishes with the Natchez that same year, and as time wore on, he had weathered his share of disease-ridden summers. Yes, at twenty-eight, he had long since relinquished whatever boyhood dreams he had had of finding adventure and a readymade fortune in the New World.

But there was no turning back now. He was a part of this land now and had come not only to accept it for what it was, but actually to feel something akin to affection for it. John Law's "Mississippi Bubble" might long since have burst, but the more he had come to know this place, the more it fascinated him. The soil of the Delta was fertile and therein could be found the real wealth of this region. He was looking forward to developing the piece of land that had been granted him a few years back into a prosperous plantation. Land was rising in value and before this month was out an ordinance was going into effect that would oblige every landholder to show the superior council of the colony that his property was under cultivation or he would forfeit it. Fortunately he had found himself a good administrator and a competent overseer, so he would soon have the place producing. A good thing, too, for taxes were going up so high these days that it wouldn't pay to keep the land without working it.

A man could do well in the New World if he set his mind and his back to it. The primary reason why he had chosen scouting was because it paid so well. No one knew the Mississippi territory as thoroughly as he did, so his services were at a premium. It wasn't his intention to spend the rest of his life running up and down the river as a *coureur de bois*. But he knew that resigning from his present post wasn't going to be easy. In all conscience, he could not refuse to serve when he knew he was still so sorely needed.

Although things seemed relatively peaceful in the colony at the moment, Dubair, probably more than anyone else in Louisiana, was only too aware of just how precarious the Indian situation still was. The new governor had a fine military record behind him and seemed genuinely conscientious about making much needed improvements around New Orleans, but his naval background had not given him the practical knowledge that his predecessor Bienville had had. Unfortunately the founder and former commander of New Orleans had been recalled to France, a victim of petty jealousy and backbiting within the *Compagnie*. Now, while the government played internal politics, its *politique indienne* was suffering, and unfortunately there were always avaricious men with no consciences around, ready to put muskets and firewater into savage hands just for a little extra profit. Years of scouting had taught Dubair that one could get a lot further with the redskins by using tact instead of force. If only he could make Governor Perier understand that.

Night had fallen now, and it was time to rest in the marshlands, where life was governed by the rising and setting of the sun. Dubair roused himself from his meditations and gave the order for the group to bed down for the night.

While the women watched curiously, the scouts spread out their bedding for them as close together as possible between the two campfires, so that all twenty-six of them could lie on the dozen mattresses. Over every two mattresses, placed side by side on top of a sweet-smelling carpet of freshly cut reeds, an impromptu four-cornered canopy was made by suspending a thin white meshlike material that the men called *baires* across the tall poles they had stuck into the ground. When all was ready, the women crawled into those tentlike structures, which would provide not only some warmth and privacy but offer protection from the numerous insects that always abounded in the swamplands, although fortunately the dread mosquito was not as abundant in the winter as during the hot summer months.

The women slept with their clothes on, several to each canopied pair of mattresses.

At first Charlotte had difficulty falling asleep. Those who shared her tent, Madelón. Cecile, and Sister Marie, went off as soon as they settled down, but she lay there for a while unable to relax completely. Actually, their crowded alcove was not too uncomfortable, since the nearness of her companions gave her a greater sense of security, while the

64

warmth of their bodies huddled together beneath the *baire* helped counteract the damp chill of the night air. But now that the camp was silent, she was even more aware of the sounds of the swamp around her—the drone of hundreds of crickets, the croaking of countless frogs, and the shrill calls of animals she couldn't even identify. The flickering fires, which the captain had ordered left burning throughout the night in order to ward off any night-prowling creatures, cast changing shadows against the nearly transparent covering that spanned the poles around her pallet.

The weary scouts had also stretched out on their fur pelts, enjoying a well-earned rest after the taxing labors of the day, but Charlotte could make out the silhouette of a sentry with his musket posted near their tent. It was comforting to know the men would be taking turns guarding the camp during the night. She looked closer and recognized the first on watch as the captain himself. The capricious light of the flames elongated and distorted his silhouette a little, but she knew it was Dubair by the set of his shoulders and the long-stemmed pipe she had seen him smoking earlier that evening. Somehow it made her feel more secure to know that he was there watching over them.

Chapter XI

The cold grey light of dawn crept up on them like a misty spectre stealing across the dark expanse of the Mississippi. Filtering in through the overhanging moss and the thin linen coverings of their pallets, it roused Charlotte and her companions to their second day on the river. Stirring sluggishly, the women rose to find that their escorts were already afoot, preparing for the next lap of their journey.

By the time their bedding had been snugly packed away in the dugouts and they had finished eating an unimaginative but practical breakfast of leftover venison, the sun had managed to come out enough to dispel the lingering wisps of early-morning mist and give promise of a bright cheerful day. Although the air was still crisp enough for the women to keep the hoods up on their capes, there was a delightful tingle in the air that made everyone face the return to the crowded *pirogues* with renewed vigor.

As the day wore on, the sun came out with even greater boldness, and although the breeze on the river had enough of a bite in it to keep them wrapped in their capes, the day warmed up considerably.

By noon the weather was so pleasant that the captain decided to accede to Sister Marie's suggestion that they disembark for a short rest.

The captain had just helped them out of their boat and Charlotte was making her way to higher ground, having been one of the first to disembark, when suddenly she was caught from behind by both arms and held fast.

A tense masculine voice whispered in her ear. "Don't move—stay as you are!"

A needless command, thought Charlotte, since she couldn't have moved even if she had wanted to, so tightly did those hands grip her arms through the folds of her woolen cape.

The voice rose. "Stay where you are, everyone! Don't anybody move!" Only then did Charlotte recognize that it was the captain who was detaining her.

She instinctively made a feeble effort to break away, but the fingers dug deeper into her arms as he held her pinioned firmly against him. "*Nom de Dieu*, mademoiselle, I said don't move!"

Then, between clenched teeth, as though weighing every word, he called out, "All right, Etienne—shoot—*now!*"

Charlotte half expected to be blasted down on the spot. Closing her eyes, she trembled and waited for the worst.

At the sound of the musket ball whizzing past her ear, she flinched and felt her knees buckling under her. If it hadn't been for the captain's grip, she would have surely fallen to the ground.

At that moment a long, dark, ropelike creature fell abruptly at her feet from the low branch immediately in front of her.

"Are you all right, mademoiselle?" she heard the captain asking anxiously, as he turned her around to face him. The hood of her cloak had fallen back from her tawny hair and she stood looking up at him in wide-eyed dismay, unable to reply.

For a moment Dubair was taken aback by her unexpected beauty.

"I—I'm sorry, mademoiselle," he stammered, letting his hands drop from her shoulders. "There was no time . . ."

Despite the fear Charlotte still felt over her narrow escape, her eyes shot gold flecks of annoyance at him, as she rubbed her arms where he had held her so tightly.

Sister Marie came up at that moment and caught the trembling girl to her excitedly. "God be praised, child!" she cried. "The good captain and his lieutenant have saved your life!"

Everyone was gathering around exclaiming over the incident. Even as Charlotte darted a final confused glance into the equally bewildered eyes of the captain, she was whisked away by her solicitous companions.

For a moment Dubair continued to stand there, seeming almost stunned by the events as Charlotte had been. Then, with a shrug of his shoulders, he went back to the business of getting the group under control again.

After they were in the boat again, Dubair pointed to what seemed to be just another log lying near the exposed roots of a towering cypress growing at the edge of the water.

"You see that log over there? It looks like just another trunk of a fallen tree, *non*? But it's not. It's a full-grown alligator. The warm sun has invited him to ease out of his niche for a few hours, but he's drowsy and isn't looking for a fight. If you awaken him, though, he might be meaner than ever for the disturbance. Perhaps now you can understand why I made that little speech to you ladies before we left Balize."

Charlotte sat atop her *cassette* with folded arms. The

noonday sun was so warm now that she had thrown her cloak and hood back. She reached into the wide bell-shaped sleeves that fell to her elbows, trying to get to the spots where her arms were smarting. She was going to be bruised, of that she was sure!

They were so crowded in the *pirogue* that as Dubair bent over his paddle behind her, he was sometimes almost as close as he had been when he had saved her from the reptile.

He looked at the head of tousled curls in front of him blazing like burnished gold in the sunlight and felt the urge to offer a few more words of apology. From the way she sat there rubbing her forearms, he knew he must have hurt her. She was only a slip of a girl and was probably terrified over the whole experience. He found himself remembering how she had trembled like a startled doe as he had held her against him. *Mon Dieu!* He had forgotten there were women like her in the world—he'd been in the wilderness too long.

"Please believe me, mademoiselle, I didn't mean to hurt you," he ventured, as he bent closer to her over his paddle.

She turned her saucy profile to him and replied over her shoulder in a voice that was a bit unsteady in spite of her efforts to give it haughtiness.

"I thank you for saving my life, *Capitaine*, but I do feel you were unnecessarily rough in the doing!"

"For that I'm truly sorry, but I had to act quickly before the moccasin struck."

"I hope you are as resourceful with the enemy as you were with me!"

"I admit I wasn't measuring my strength at that moment," he confessed rather sheepishly. "All I could think of was stopping you in your tracks."

"Wouldn't it have been simpler if you had just asked me to stop?" she chided.

"I couldn't take any chances," he replied, as he continued to keep the rhythm of his paddling unbroken. "You see, any movement on your part, even the flex of a muscle, would have made the snake strike. There was not a minute to spare."

"Well, I agree you were very effective," sighed Charlotte as she forlornly nursed her forearms. "I'll be black and blue for weeks."

"I hope you won't bear me any ill-will because of any overzealousness on my part."

She caught such a look of genuine consternation on the captain's countenance, as she glanced back at him out of the tail of her eye, that she relented a little in her scolding and replied, "*Mais non, Capitaine.* I would be very ungrateful if I were to bear you rancor for having saved my life!"

Charlotte fell silent, although she continued to be aware of the captain's proximity. Having him so near disturbed her. The only other male who had ever been so close to her had been Blégot. He, too, had hurt her. She realized her reaction to the captain's having seized her so forcefully, although justified, had been overcast by memories of that other more violent experience in Marseilles with Blégot. Of course, there was no comparing the two men. The captain really wasn't that repulsive. . . .

That evening proved to be a crisp, clear one, and as they sat around the campfire overlooking the river from a high rise of ground, after a watered down but filling rabbit stew, the dark mirror of the Mississippi reflected a sky aglow with a bright full moon attended by a glittering court of countless stars stretched out as far as the eye could see. As Charlotte looked up past the lofty trees to that vast tableau of celestial splendor, she thought how beautiful this New World was. But it was so big and lonely, too. . . .

The captain and some of his men pulled out their pipes and sat back to enjoy their final smoke before retiring. After a few puffs, however, Dubair rose, pipe in hand, and walked over to where Charlotte sat on a fallen tree trunk beside Madelón and Cecile. The women had thrown their cloaks around their shoulders again against the chill of the oncoming night, and were just commenting that, although it was not so cold in Louisiana as it usually was in Marseilles at that time of the year, the cold seemed more penetrating in the swamplands, since the atmosphere was so damp.

"And how are you ladies this evening?" asked Dubair in a surprisingly congenial voice. "Is everything all right?"

As the women nodded their heads rather self-consciously and thanked him for his interest, the captain fixed his eyes on Charlotte, noting how the amber in her eyes had turned to a liquid brown in the dim light, like clear maple syrup.

"And you, Mademoiselle, how are you feeling?" he continued. "I hope you've completely recovered from your fright earlier today?"

But it was Cecile, with her usual readiness to speak up, who quickly replied. "Oh, *Capitaine*, you should see her arms!" she exclaimed, her dark eyes flashing merrily. "There's a big bruise on each one!"

Dubair's flush could be seen even beneath his suntan, as he shifted his weight uneasily from one moccasined foot to another.

"*Chut*, Cissy!" scolded Madelón, nudging the small brunette impatiently, while Charlotte tried to cover her embarrassment.

"There's a certain leaf that grows here in the marshlands that might help the discoloration," suggested the captain. "I've learned about such things from the Indians. They believe that for every ill in the world the Great Spirit has provided a plant to remedy it. If you like, mademoiselle, I'll have my men try to find some for you."

"Please don't worry yourself over me, *Capitaine*," replied Charlotte, finding her voice at last. "I'm sure the bruises will clear up very quickly. In a few days the whole matter will be forgotten."

"And I hope also forgiven," added Dubair quickly.

"You don't have to wait another moment for that, monsieur *Capitaine*. You already are."

"What really frightens me is that there may be other snakes around us, even now as we talk," interrupted Cecile. "*Mon Dieu!* I'd die of fright just to see one crossing my path!"

"Don't alarm yourselves unduly, ladies," replied Dubair. "All vipers are not poisonous, you know. Out of some three dozen species I know of, only five or six are venomous. Of course, that doesn't mean you should not be alert, but there's no need to be unnecessarily frightened, either."

"But how can you tell which are dangerous and which are harmless?" asked Charlotte, still trying to get out of her mind the image of that giant snake falling with a thud to the ground at her feet.

"Oh, there are many ways. Their coloring, their type of eyes, or the number of tiny holes in their heads . . . after a little experience it's usually not too difficult to spot the bad ones."

"How much longer will it be before we get to New Orleans?" asked Charlotte, lifting the hood of her cape up over her head as she felt a shiver go through her. She was not sure whether it had been from the cold or those ghastly cries in the night.

"With no unforeseen mishaps to delay us, probably in three more days," he replied. "But I hope the weather holds out for us."

"I'm afraid we've been subjecting you to quite an inquisition, *Capitaine*," smiled Charlotte. "But at least you have helped lay some of our fears to rest, and we thank you."

"If I've been able to make you feel a little better, I'm content, Mademoiselle," replied Dubair. "But now we must think about retiring so we can get an early start in the morning. *Bonne nuit*, ladies. Have a good night's rest."

The captain touched his coonskin cap politely and sauntered off, his moccasin-clad feet belying the weight of his sturdy frame, as he treaded across the ground noiselessly.

"*Quel homme!* What a fine figure of a man that *Capitaine* Dubair is!" murmured Cecile. "I'd give anything if he'd only look at me the way he looks at you, Charlotte!"

"What a silly goose you are, Cissy! The captain was only making polite conversation," retorted Charlotte, taken aback by her friend's insinuations.

"*Vraiment?* Well, all I can say is I wouldn't mind having his fingermarks on *my* arms any time he wanted to put them there!"

"Really, Cissy, you rattle on like a *ra-ra!* scolded Madelón, shaking her blonde curls in disapproval. Then she turned to Charlotte, whose face had flushed bright red, and added consolingly. "Don't pay any attention to Cecile, dear. You know how she is. But she just might be right. The captain would make quite a catch for any girl, and you're the only one he seems to have paid any attention to."

"Don't be ridiculous!" exclaimed Charlotte. "What

71

would I want with a—an uncouth woodsman? To get more black and blue marks on me?"

"He can't be that much of a brute," insisted Cecile. "After all, he's an officer, and his manner is quite refined for all his buckskins. I'd throw my glove for him myself, if I thought I had a chance. But I'm afraid he prefers your type, as luck would have it."

"You don't know what you're talking about, harebrain!" snapped Charlotte, annoyed by her friend's foolish chatter. "The captain hasn't shown any interest whatsoever in me or any one of us. Just because he came over to say a few courteous words and inquire about how I was feeling doesn't make him a suitor. And even if he was—which he isn't—I wouldn't consider him for a moment, so let's say no more on the subject."

That night, lying on her pallet beneath the sheltering *baire*, Charlotte's annoyance over Cecile's comments began to turn to apprehension, as some of the things her friends had said began to take on added meaning. They were wrong about the captain, of course, but what they had said made her realize that the time was fast approaching when she would have to face the prospect of marrying someone. Somehow the thought did not appeal to her.

Aunt Germaine had said marriage should be a business arrangement, but it was also for life. Charlotte still couldn't imagine what it would be like to lie with a man, to give herself body and soul to him. The thought was more frightening than appealing.

Chapter XII

They awakened to another beautiful day. The cold, damp morning mist that hung over the marshlands soon dissolved in the warm rays of the rising sun, as they gathered around to eat generous servings of hominy—a coarsely ground corn boiled in water with a few pieces of salted pork to flavor it—which they were told was a popular Indian dish that had become a staple of the colonists' diets, as well. Although it was rather dull and tasteless to Charlotte, at least it "stuck to her ribs and warmed up her innards," as she heard one of the men describe it.

They had just finished and were beginning to break camp when the captain's lieutenant called out that they had visitors. Even as he came hurriedly over to speak to Dubair, three tall redskinned warriors emerged from the woods that bordered the encampment and made their way across the clearing toward them.

"Longhairs!" murmured Dubair's young officer.

"*Au diable!* That's all we need!" grumbled Dubair under his breath. Then he raised his voice, but only loud enough for those around him to hear. "Don't be afraid, ladies. The Choctaws are usually friendly. Just be quiet and let me do the talking. But whatever I do or say, you must go along with me, you understand, and don't let them see you're frightened."

He turned to Sister Marie, who stood nearby, her blanched face as white as her wimple.

"Madame, please keep the girls quiet, no matter what happens."

The trio of Indians advanced slowly but deliberately to where the captain stood, their sharp black eyes scrutinizing the group all the while. Their smooth, hairless, mahogany-colored bodies glistened in the sunlight, as the muscles in their long bare legs rippled to the rhythm of their stride. When they raised their hands in a gesture of greeting to Dubair, Charlotte could see they wore nothing beneath their bearskin mantles except loincloths. Colorful beads and feathers adorned the narrow headbands that held their long, straight black hair in place, and strange tattoos could be glimpsed through the multiple necklaces dangling from their necks. Charlotte and her companions stood watching in speechless wonder.

The tallest man, who equalled Dubair in stature, began to talk in a strange mixture of French and native dialect, most of which did not make any sense to the women, although the captain seemed to understand and was replying in the same manner.

From what Charlotte could gather, Dubair was inviting the trio to partake of what remained of their breakfast, for the Indians nodded their acceptance and, sitting down by the fire, they gulped down the hominy while the group stood by watching in fascinated silence. Out of courtesy to their unexpected guests, or perhaps to inspire trust, Dubair and his lieutenant joined them in the impromptu repast.

Then Dubair pulled out his pipe and, after taking a few puffs, passed it around to each of his guests.

The five men—Dubair, his lieutenant, and the three Choctaws—seemed to be exchanging polite pleasantries and, what was probably of greater importance to Dubair, the latest gossip of the region. Charlotte remembered she had heard the captain say just the day before that, with Indians, you cannot hurry anything, and now she could see what he meant.

Obeying their commander's orders, the women did not dare move or speak. Actually, there was little else they could have done, since there was nowhere to go except to the boats, and thus far, a hasty retreat did not seem to be indicated.

As Dubair rose with his guests, however, it was evident that the conversation had taken a turn he didn't like. He continued to talk with the one who seemed to be the leader, but Charlotte had come to know the captain well enough to

74

recognize, by the set of his closely bearded jawline, that he was either worried or annoyed.

Suddenly she felt an intangible fear beginning to stir within her, as she saw the chief warrior pointing toward where she and the rest of the women stood. The hollow in the pit of her stomach made her feel so weak and dizzy that she feared she was going to be physically ill, as she saw the men walking in their direction, although she could see Dubair talking rapidly to the redskins and still shaking his head.

The Indian leader paused only a couple of feet from where Charlotte was standing with Madelón and some of the other girls from Marseilles and pointed to them again. Sister Marie made a quick step forward but Dubair, who had come up from behind, discreetly restrained her and, instead, placed himself next to the women, his bearing still calm and seemingly unruffled. Yet Charlotte could sense the tension bottled up inside him.

"*Non, non*, they are *filles du roi* . . . they belong to our king . . . promised . . ." he was saying, interspersing his words with other phrases that only he and the Choctaw seemed to understand, as he tried to keep a patient tone in his voice.

The warrior, however, reached out a bronzed hand and with childish curiosity touched a few strands of Madelón's pale gold hair. The girl let out a low gasp and stared back at him with wide, terror-stricken eyes, like a helpless bird caught in the hypnotic spell of a serpent, waiting helplessly for him to strike.

"*Non, non* . . . not for you," insisted Dubair, taking Madelón's tiny hand quickly in his. Lifting her trembling arm, he pulled back her bell-like sleeve to expose the fragile arm beneath it. "Look—too weak, not make good woman for warrior like you."

The Indian stared at the delicate white arm for a moment and then glanced once more at the lock of spun gold he still held in his hand. Reluctantly he let it slip through his fingers and turned away, but his black penetrating eyes continued to scan the women. A strong odor of fish emanated from him and his companions, and suddenly Char-

75

lotte realized it was because they were covered with fish oil from head to foot.

Just then she was conscious of the fact that one of the Indians was pointing to her and saying something in his language to his leader, whereupon the latter turned back in her direction, and nodding in agreement, reached out towards her, as if to sample one of her curls or push back the cape to see her better. Whatever his intentions, Charlotte's mounting indignation over having to submit to such a humiliating perusal momentarily made her forget precaution. But as she was about to ward off the savage's curious hand on her breast in no uncertain terms, Dubair quickly stepped over beside her and put a protective, restraining arm about her.

The captain's presence seemed to steady her somewhat, and retreating even further into the welcome shelter he offered, she remained motionless, listening with pounding heart while Dubair once again tried to discourage the redskin from his notions of selecting a wife for himself from among the Casquette Girls.

"Your king, he has many women. He not miss one," the Choctaw argued. "I give you pelts for this one. We make good trade. Your king be pleased."

"*Non,* this one, she's . . ." Dubair's mind raced desperately, as he groped for new arguments to discourage the stubborn Choctaw. "This one is mine, *pour moi, ma femme.* I cannot insult my king, he gave me for wife . . . my woman . . . all these women taken, promised."

"A good friend give even his woman." A flood of more strange sounds followed, while Charlotte felt the muscles in the captain's arm increase their tension.

"I tell you no—*ma femme.* You not want woman with other man's seed, *vraiment*?"

There were other phrases she could not understand, but Charlotte had caught enough to bring a deep flush to her cheeks, and she stirred uncomfortably at the implications. Dubair tightened his arm about her just enough to remind her of his orders to be quiet no matter what he might say or do.

The Indian leader stood hesitating for a moment longer, mulling over the captain's words, undecided whether to in-

sist further or not. Seizing the opportunity to steer his persistent guests away from the women, Dubair hastily turned
Charlotte over to Sister Marie, as he murmured to the nun
and his lieutenant to get the girls into the boats as discreetly as possible.

The Indians were about to move toward one of the girls
with bright, carrot-colored hair, who had also caught their
attention, but Dubair continued to insist that he had given
his word to his king and could not sell any of them, that
unfortunately the ones that had especially struck their
fancy were already married and probably *enciente*, that he
had better gifts for them to demonstrate the friendship he
felt, far better gifts than just a mere woman.

While he spoke, Dubair motioned to one of his men to
bring them a jug of corn liquor and some beads and mir-
rors they had brought along for just such emergencies. As
the lieutenant led the women toward the boats, Charlotte
could see the captain still conversing with the warriors and
exchanging his wares for some of the pelts the Indians had
offered him earlier while bartering for her.

Chapter XIII

By the time the captain had rid himself of his uninvited
guests and joined them to shove off, the dugouts were already loaded and everyone in their places waiting to get
underway.

For the rest of the day, the women thought and talked of
little else. Near collisions with driftwood and half-
submerged sandbars took second place now to their impressions of that overwhelming first encounter with the New
World's native inhabitants. Although they had not under-

stood half of the strange sounds that had been exchanged between Dubair and the warriors, they had caught enough to realize that it had been thanks only to the captain's skillful handling of the situation that bloodshed had been avoided.

Of course, their party had greatly outnumbered the Choctaws, and it was doubtful the three redskins would have left the encampment alive, had they tried to take any of the women by force, but as Dubair pointed out to them, when they paused along the bank of the river once more later that day to have a light repast and refresh themselves, it was not just a question of three Indians against nine scouts. Any harm or insult done to one of those warriors would have had far-reaching repercussions, not only on their immediate safety during the rest of their journey upriver (for the Choctaws occupied much of the territory through which they were passing) but on the delicate balance the French settlers were striving to keep with the Indian nations of that region.

"The Choctaws are among the few tribes in the colony to date who have remained loyal to the French," explained Dubair. "If it weren't for their friendship, hostile tribes like the Natchez and Chickasaws would have banded together against us long ago."

"I certainly wouldn't call the way they acted so friendly," ventured Charlotte. "They looked us over like so much cattle up for barter. It was positively insulting!"

"I can understand your feelings, Mademoiselle," the captain agreed, "but actually, the Indians meant no offense. It's their way. They do the same when they choose wives from among their own women. The more they offer, the greater the compliment to the maid in question."

"Compliment? Buying a wife as if she were a cow? *Mon Dieu!* What savages!" protested Charlotte indignantly.

"And the way they examined us! How disgusting!" agreed Madelón with a shudder.

"It was your hair, ladies," explained Dubair. "They're always attracted to women with light hair, since they so seldom see any color except black among their own." He tactfully didn't add that the redskins seemed to have such a fetish for hair that they even collected it in the form of scalps. No need to frighten the women more than they already were.

Back in the boat, as they glided over the sunlit water, Charlotte renewed the theme with the captain. It embarrassed her to do so, but her curiosity was getting the best of her. She kept her face straight ahead as she spoke, glad that she didn't have to look into his eyes at that moment.

"*Capitaine,* I—I caught certain phrases while you were talking to those Indians . . . that is, I think I did. Didn't you tell them I was your—your wife? Or did I misunderstand?"

Dubair was taken aback for a moment. He wondered just how much the girl had understood of all that he had said to the Choctaws. He had babbled on for a while, playing the situation by ear, as he had groped for some way to discourage the Indians. He couldn't remember now what he had said in French and what he had said in the smattering of Muskogee he knew, but he hoped the girl hadn't understood *everything* that had been said!

"Yes, mademoiselle," he confessed rather sheepishly. "It seemed like a good idea to say that at the time. I hoped it might make them hesitate even more if they thought you were already married. They'd expect an even harder fight on their hands if they tried to take a man's wife and perhaps unborn child from him. But the truth is, I think the argument that probably convinced them most was that I'd be betraying my king if I let them take any of you. That's something an Indian can understand and accept, for he usually puts a high value on a man's word."

"I must say, *Capitaine,* you seem to give those Indians a lot more credit for morals than I'd have thought," quipped Charlotte. "From what I could see, they were nothing more than half-naked savages reeking of fish oil and—and with pictures painted all over their bodies!"

Dubair smiled as he dipped his paddle into the water. "I admit they are rather impressive the first time one sees them. But you see, mademoiselle, they rub themselves with oil or grease to keep warm in the winter and to ward off insects in the summer. As for the tattoos, I guess you might say they wear those symbols in much the same way as we do our medals or images of saints for protection."

79

Charlotte turned toward him in an effort to see his face.

"If I didn't know better, I'd think you were defending them," she said in surprise.

"I wouldn't go so far as to say that, for they are, as you say, savages, and can often be incredibly cruel. But I've come to understand them a little over the years and, although they may have many customs I deplore, I've come to respect their ways in certain things."

"*Vraiment?* And perhaps one of the things you approve of is the way they treat women?" She was somewhat vexed over the fact that the captain had had anything whatsoever to say in favor of those barbarians after the manner in which they had treated her and her companions.

"I'm sorry, mademoiselle. I didn't mean to give you that impression. It seems I have a knack for unwittingly incurring your displeasure."

"It really doesn't matter," replied Charlotte, annoyed by the slight tone of reproach she detected in his voice. "Fortunately I'm not really your wife, *mon Capitaine*, so there's no reason why you should worry about pleasing me!"

"Frankly, mademoiselle, if I may be so bold, I find it hard to understand why a girl like you had to come all the way to the New World to find a husband. Are the men in France so blind these days? Or perhaps it's because mademoiselle is by nature hard to please?"

Although she couldn't risk upsetting the boat to turn around and see his face, Charlotte had the uneasy feeling he was smiling behind his beard at her expense.

"You're very insolent, monsieur *Capitaine!*" she retorted angrily.

"And you, *ma petite*, are—are very young, *très jolie*, and have so very much to learn. But I'm truly sorry if I've offended you. A girl as pretty as you can most certainly give herself the luxury of being hard to please."

They fell silent while the captain occupied himself with his paddling, and she in keeping her equilibrium atop her luggage.

Dubair continued to smile a moment longer, as he looked at the saucy tilt of the head in front of him. He shouldn't have spoken to her as he had. After all, what brought her to the New World was no affair of his. But it did puzzle him. She was indeed very young and impressionable, perhaps even oversensitive at times. But, like a wayward child, there was a certain charm to her petulance.

He wondered where she had acquired that touch of *raffinement* that set her apart from the rest of her companions. She obviously was one of the girls who had been educated privately by the Ursulines, but that didn't explain everything. Despite her naiveté, there was a noticeable air of elegance about her that homespun clothing couldn't demean. He suspected she had had at least some brief exposure to the social graces of the upper class in France, for her knowledge of such things came too easily and was not simply the clever imitation of a chambermaid aping her mistress. Most certainly he could more readily picture her walking the halls of Versailles than slushing through the muck of Louisiana's swamplands!

And she was a beauty, too . . . not one of those painted courtesans with so much powder and rouge you couldn't appreciate the contents for the package. It simply didn't make sense, a girl like that traveling all the way to this wilderness to find a husband! He couldn't imagine her wed to any of those honest but illiterate farmers to the north of the settlement or to the roughneck trappers and *coureurs de bois* like the men under him. Of course, the single officers of the colonial militia would probably be given first choice. One thing was sure, she'd be snatched up the very first day.

He looked again at the proud little figure, so full of spirit, sitting there on top of her *cassette*, and a surge of tenderness welled up in him at the thought of how a girl like that could suffer in a land such as this. But he caught himself quickly and decided then and there to put her out of his mind. He wasn't ready to marry yet. As long as he was scouting, he wanted to remain single. A man could hardly keep his wits about him out here in the wilderness juggling Indians and 'gators while worrying about a wife and children back in the city! He'd seen too many of his men torn between their families and the service, hating more and more with each passing day those long expeditions that separated them from their homes and loved ones. No, he'd think about marrying the day he could settle

81

down on that plantation he was planning to build upriver. But that was at least a couple of years off yet. Protecting pretty young girls was his duty at the moment, but he was in no position yet to take on one as a daily commitment.

Although Charlotte and the captain did not exchange another word for the rest of that day, she still had to face considerable teasing from her companions that night. Cecile, who was never one to miss anything going on around her, had been close enough to Charlotte and Madelón that morning to catch most of the conversation between Dubair and the Indians. Much to Charlotte's chagrin, the girl had related the entire episode in detail to those who hadn't heard it, so by the time evening fell, she was being addressed as "*Madame Capitaine*" and congratulated for having landed the catch of the journey. It did no good for her to deny any interest on her part or the captain's. The girls were convinced that Charlotte and Dubair would be married the day they arrived in New Orleans.

They had also seen the pair conversing once or twice as they had traveled upriver, and the women were certain the two had been whispering sweet nothings to each other. Even Sister Marie was inclined to think there might be something between her favorite and the captain, but she remained discreetly silent, since it was a match she would probably approve of if it happened.

Another target of the girls' teasing was the freckle-faced redhead in the Paris group who had also attracted the Choctaws' attention that morning. She was openly accepting the approaches of one of the scouts assigned to her boat, so the girls were making merry at her expense as well, but she only lowered her eyes with a smile and said nothing. Charlotte, however, was indignant and, although she blushed at their heckling, she vehemently insisted there was no attraction whatsoever between her and the captain.

"You can't tell me you don't like the *capitaine*," insisted Cecile, shaking a knowing finger at Charlotte. "I saw the way you snuggled up to him when he put his arm around you, and I can see how you both look at each other whenever you think no one's watching."

"Oh, Cissy, stop exaggerating!" scolded Madelón, who

could see how uncomfortable her friend was whenever any-one alluded to Dubair.

"Then you swear there's nothing between you and the *capitaine?*" Cecile asked Charlotte with a sly twinkle in her impish black eyes.

"Nothing at all!"

Cecile clapped her dimpled hands with glee. "Then you won't mind if I set my cap for him myself? Do you give him to me?"

"Silly! The captain isn't mine to give!" retorted Charlotte crossly, weary of the theme. "Go ahead and throw your glove, and good luck to you!"

The girls fell silent as Sister Marie joined them and they crawled beneath the netting to lie down on their pallets. Charlotte was grateful for the nun's presence, since it stopped the probing questions and embarrassing insinuations. It was difficult for her to make the girls understand that she was not as eager to wed as most of them were. Certainly she wasn't going to get engaged to anyone before she even arrived at her destination! Besides, she was sure the captain didn't care for her at all. If the girls could have heard his last conversation with her they would have realized just how far from the truth they really were.

Chapter XIV

The morning was surprisingly warm for December, but although the sun came out, the day had a damp, sticky feeling about it, and the scouts frequently cast worried glances up at the sky, fearful that the rainclouds would soon be catching up with them.

As they had a hasty breakfast of hominy, Cecile made good her threat to Charlotte the night before. Pinching her cheeks to give them more color and inserting a few extra wads of cloth inside her tight-fitting bodice to make her already generous bosom even more conspicuous, she proceeded to lay her campaign for the captain.

Placing herself demurely next to him as often as she could, she made several attempts to strike up a conversation with him, but Dubair was in no mood for idle chatter. He was preoccupied with breaking camp as quickly as possible in the hopes of covering what distance they could before bad weather would slow them up again. He replied to Cecile's coy questions politely but briefly, sometimes with just an absent-minded monosyllable, and as soon as they had finished eating, he gave the order to check the boats and begin loading them.

Disappointed but undaunted, Cecile continued to stay as near the captain as discretion permitted, while he hurried back and forth across the clearing making last-minute revisions.

"She looks like a puppy dog following at his heels like that!" whispered Charlotte disapprovingly to Madelón, while her friend stifled a giggle and nodded in agreement.

Finally they were told it was time to embark, and the group moved toward the boats.

Seizing the opportunity for what she hoped would finally be a way to get the captain's attention, Cecile ran ahead and jumped up on top of a fallen log by the lead boat, calling out urgently to Dubair, who was coming up behind her with Charlotte, Madelón, and Sister Marie beside him.

"Oh, help me, *mon capitaine*! I thought I could do it alone, but now I think I'm going to fall!" she exclaimed, her slim figure swaying in feigned disequilibrium. Dubair shot a surprised glance at her and then moved with such rapidity towards the spot where she stood that Cecile was delighted by the response she had finally won from him.

But even as she was eagerly awaiting the moment when he would be near enough for her to be able to trip and fall directly into his arms, as she had calculated, Cecile suddenly felt the log beneath her feet begin to move, and before she realized what was happening, she found herself actually toppling off her unsteady perch into the muddy water that partially covered the site where the boats were moored. Her billowing skirts puffed up around her, and for a moment her tiny figure floated buoyantly above the water. Then she sank down past her waist, screaming in authentic alarm.

Dubair shouted to Cecile to grab hold of the side of the boat, which was still tied fast to shore, and to remain perfectly still.

Charlotte arrived at the water's edge a few seconds behind him. Before Dubair could warn her to stay back, however, she saw the log moving toward her and, as she watched in horror, realized it was opening heavy-lidded eyes and lifting a long, jagged-toothed snout from the mud, where it had lain half buried until Cecile had disturbed it. It was a swamp monster like the one Germaine had predicted would devour her in one gulp!

With a cry of terror, Charlotte turned and ran screaming past Sister Marie's detaining hand, back across the empty clearing and blindly on to she knew not where. Only one thing mattered now. She had to get away from that diabolical creature following at her heels. In her hysteria she plunged into the interior, away from the river.

Dubair's men had already begun to try to distract the alligator with their long poles and were holding their muskets and unsheathed knives in readiness, just in case their efforts failed to keep it at bay, while one of the scouts waded out into the water to rescue the weeping Cecile.

Meanwhile, with a sharp command to the women to stay back, Dubair called out to his lieutenant to take over and dashed off after Charlotte's retreating figure, which was disappearing into the surrounding marshes. Sister Marie had already begun to move across the clearing after her, but the captain ordered her back with the rest of the party.

"Please, Sister, don't complicate things more than they already are," he begged. "I'll bring her back, I promise."

The nun stooped slowly and recovered the white cap Charlotte had been wearing from where it had fallen to the ground after a brush with an overhanging branch during her frantic flight. Clutching that tiny bit of ruffles and lace, she began to mumble a fervent prayer over it.

Charlotte's feet, winged with the certainty that the moment had come at last for her aunt's dire predictions to be fulfilled, carried her doggedly on, past the tangled brush

85

that clawed at her skirts and hair and the sharp unyielding branches that lashed out at her despite her feeble efforts to ward them off.

Small animals scurried to get out of her path, while startled birds shrieked and flew away in a flurry of flapping wings. She had all she could do to keep herself afoot. Giant roots and sudden ravines began to slow her down. The deeper she penetrated into the swamps, the more she was confronted by walls of rampant vegetation and row after row of towering trees set so close together that the sun had probably not shone in some of those niches for centuries. Soon the terrain became so irregular that she stumbled and fell sobbing to the ground, unable to go farther.

She lay there exhausted and gasping for breath, expecting at any moment to feel the claws of that slimy, thick-skinned creature tearing away at her, those huge jaws opening and gulping her down. She wondered if it would be like Jonah and the whale in one of those Bible stories that had given her nightmares as a child at the convent.

When Dubair found her huddled there, murmuring disconnected phrases from prayers and whimpering like a frightened child, he didn't have the heart to give her the tongue-lashing he had been preparing to greet her with. His anger melted as he realized the poor girl was truly in a state of shock. The dragon had finally appeared in her fairy tale, thought Dubair, as he gently helped her to her feet.

On recognizing the captain's familiar figure and realizing there was no monster anywhere in sight, Charlotte felt such an overwhelming wave of relief sweep over her that she fell against him, weeping uncontrollably.

Dubair drew her closer, a little bewildered by the turn of events, but trying his best to calm her. Crying women always made him feel awkward and inadequate.

"There, there, *ma petite*, it's all right," he kept repeating softly, as he stroked her hair rather clumsily with his large, suntanned hand. "There's no danger now."

She lifted her disheveled head and looked up at him through her tears, trying to reassure herself that he was really telling her the truth. For a moment they looked openly at each other for the first time. The sounds of the wilderness around them seemed to fade away. The only reality was pulsating between them.

Like a magnet, her upturned face seemed to be drawing the captain's down towards her. She could feel the hardness of his body beneath the soft buckskins as his arms tightened around her. His beard was brushing her cheek before the sound of Sister Marie's voice calling out to them from the edge of the clearing brought them sharply back to reality. The warm brown of Charlotte's eyes was the color of smoky topaz, as she opened them once more.

Dubair was as startled as she was. Devil take it! What was he doing? He was amazed, even a little annoyed with himself. Quickly he stepped back, but even as he did, he was aware of how she instinctively clung to him for a second longer before she, too, broke away.

"Mademoiselle, I . . . We'd best be getting back," he stammered. "Are you all right now?"

Charlotte lowered her eyes quickly to hide her confusion. In an effort to steady her churning emotions, she occupied herself with smoothing out her tangled hair and rumpled skirts while Dubair cupped his hand and called back to the waiting group that all was well. Now that the terror had passed and the captain was by her side, Charlotte suddenly felt ashamed of her hysteria.

"But the monster . . . has he gone?" she asked in disbelief.

"The alligator? Oh, yes, my men will know how to handle him. Fortunately 'gators are rather sluggish at this time of the year. They're still dangerous if provoked, of course, but right now most of them would rather sleep than fight. Your friend would have been in trouble, however, had she continued to splash around in the water right by him. But you were never in any real danger, mademoiselle. The alligator was not pursuing you at all."

He took her by the arm and helped her keep her footing as they picked their way carefully over the sharp rise and fall of the muddy terrain on their way back to the river bank. Charlotte was surprised at how deeply she had gone into the marshes.

The silence that fell between them became awkward as they continued to wend their way back to the others, for when there were no words to fill the void, the memory of that moment when they had been so close loomed all the more vividly between them.

Dubair's countenance slowly resumed a sterner expression as they neared the clearing. "I don't like to scold you, mademoiselle." he said softly but firmly, trying to reestablish some semblance of formality between them, "but I hope this will teach you a lesson. All this wouldn't have happened had your friend and then you not disobeyed my orders. I warned all of you about leaving the group and going off on your own."

Charlotte's head drooped, a sorry mass of tangled curls entwined with broken twigs and random burrs. "But the monster—that creature—was coming straight at me," she protested lamely. "All I could think of was turning and running."

"Yes, and you probably would have run right into the even greater danger of some hungry wildcat or a bottomless pit of quicksand, if I hadn't come along when I did," chided Dubair.

"I—I know now how foolish I was," she admitted, "and I'm truly sorry. It seems I'm always causing you trouble."

Dubair's sense of humor nearly made him lose his aplomb. By all the saints, the girl had certainly said a mouthful there! She probably had no idea of just how much trouble her very presence was causing him right at that moment!

In all his years of scouting he had never come so close to losing his head as he had with this little convent girl. Even that time six or seven years ago when that voluptuous little minx—what was her name? ah, yes, Nanette—had flirted outrageously with him during the whole trek upriver, he had held himself in check. Not that he hadn't been tempted, but he knew that if he wanted to keep his men out of the canebrakes with that shipment of flighty females he had to set a good example.

Now he was letting an attraction for a naïve slip of a girl with six nuns for chaperons stir him into doing something foolhardy. Whatever had he been thinking of back there? One stolen kiss with such a girl and he'd have the Church and the king himself to answer to if he didn't seal the act with a marriage vow. If things were different he might not reject the idea. In the right hands a girl like this could mature into a jewel of a woman, but he couldn't indulge in such fancies now. He had a lot to do first.

Charlotte ran to the waiting arms of Sister Marie, as they entered the clearing, and she began to weep anew while the nun tried to smooth her tangled hair and gently scolded her for having given them such a fright.

The men were already cutting the alligator up into stew meat for future meals, while the women had gathered in a knot on the bank once more, chattering excitedly over the recent events. Cecile was conspicuous for her unusual silence, as she sat sullenly on a tree stump trying to dry her dripping hair and mud-streaked dress.

They had lost so much time now and the day was so cloudy that Dubair decided thay had best get going and make no stops until it was time to make camp for the night.

He called the group together and gave the women one of his most harrowing speeches about the dire results that lack of discipline on such a trip could bring.

"If you want to live to reach your future husbands in New Orleans, ladies, you had better calm down and do as you're told," he concluded. "My men and I are here to guide and protect you. Please cooperate and let us do our jobs."

Back in the boat again, Charlotte was painfully conscious of Dubair's presence immediately behind her, and she sensed he was rather uneasy, too, as the memory of their embrace in the marshes lingered between them. The breeze was stronger that day on the river, and every time the captain inclined towards her, with each dip of his paddle, she could catch the faint scent of his leather jacket and tobacco pouch. It was not a disagreeable odor. To the contrary, it seemed to evoke a flood of emotions that were warm and pleasant. She had discovered that day that it could feel nice to be in a man's arms, that the firmness of his body could arouse passion as well as fear, that the same hands that could bruise could also be gentle as goosedown when stroking her hair. . . .

The nuns had taught her it was a sin for a man to touch

89

her unless he was her husband. She had worried at first that Blégot had doomed her immortal soul to perpetual damnation by having made such advances on her person, but Sister Marie had assured her she had not sinned, since she had not desired in her heart that Blégot touch her.

In the case of the captain, however, Charlotte wasn't sure. She wondered whether she was still without guilt in the eyes of the Blessed Virgin, for she could not honestly say she had not wished, deep down in her heart, that he had kissed her.

Chapter XV

Their last night on the river was uneventful, and the next morning, there was a rush to set out again.

They had only been in the boats a few hours when they turned a bend in the river and, for the first time since they had left Balize, began to see signs of human habitation on the banks. The palmetto huts and log cabins soon increased in number, and people often came running out to wave and shout friendly greetings.

Around noon the captain decided to make a final stop at one of the more populated sites along the bank in order to let the ladies refresh themselves so they could make a more dignified entrance into New Orleans. After all, they only had about eight leagues more to go and could make that by sunset.

The people, mostly French or Canadians, vied with one another for the honor of having the travelers as their guests. Some said the Ursulines were already teaching their daughters at the new school for girls that the nuns had established in New Orleans since their arrival there a little over a year ago.

The owners of one of the larger plantations, Monsieur and

Madame Saunders, invited the party to their two-story home for *potpourri*. Although they called it pot-luck, it seemed like a banquet to the tired, half-frozen travelers.

The lady of the house invited the women to retire upstairs where they could refresh themselves and even change their clothes if they wished. She and her husband urged Dubair to accept the hospitality of their roof for the night, but he declined. The closer they got to New Orleans, the sterner and more short-tempered the captain seemed to become. He was anxious to get the journey over without any further delays.

When he saw Charlotte coming down the staircase with her honey-colored halo and bright blue woolen dress topped by the froth of a fresh white fichu crossed demurely over her bosom, he knew it was best he deposit his charges at their destination as soon as possible. He had to admit to himself that he would have liked to have gone on seeing her once their journey was over, but he knew that couldn't be. He had his orders to continue on upriver to the Illinois country just as soon as he returned to New Orleans. The expedition would take months, and she would probably be getting married right away. That's what she had come for, hadn't she? A woman like that would be among the first to wed, and she should. In a wild, lawless land like this she would need a man to protect her. He wondered who would be watching over her now that he wouldn't be around to do it. But why worry his head over it? There would be candidates galore for the job. He remembered how she had momentarily clung to him, even as they had broken their embrace . . . Damn this scouting job that had him living like a vagabond from post to post! Damn the man who got her!

Madelón had noticed the look on Charlotte's face when Dubair had spoken of his coming mission to their host and hostess, and gently drew her friend aside to a corner where they could sit and talk for a moment.

"Charlotte, dear, please don't be angry with me. You know I love you as if you were my own sister, but . . . I can't help wondering . . . are you certain, really certain, that there is nothing between you and the *capitaine*? I mean, are you sure he doesn't interest you just a little . . . *un petit peu?*"

"Of course not—that is . . . I'm not sure," Charlotte faltered. "If he asked me to marry him at this moment I don't think I'd accept . . . yet I confess I hate to think I won't be seeing him again. I—I don't know—he fascinates and frightens me all at the same time. But what does it matter? He's never spoken of love or marriage to me, so why talk about things that don't even exist?"

"But perhaps he feels something for you, too," insisted Madelón, "and is only waiting for a sign from you that he wouldn't be rejected if he were to speak up."

"The captain isn't the type of man to be timid with a woman," disagreed Charlotte. She blushed a little as she recalled how his face had brushed hers when he had held her in his arms for that one brief moment in the swamps.

Madelón guarded her silence after that, not wishing to be accused of prying, but as she sat observing Dubair very carefully, she could have sworn there was something in his eyes every time he looked at Charlotte that not even the grim set of his bearded jaw could completely disguise.

With a grateful farewell to their newly made friends, the group, refreshed in body and spirit, climbed aboard the pirogues for the last time to finish the short distance that remained of their journey upriver.

As Dubair helped her climb aboard the dugout, Charlotte dared not look up at him, but she could feel his eyes so fixed upon her that she nearly tripped getting into her place. He steadied her quickly with his arm, but she thought she could feel a slight reluctance on his part to touch her. It had all happened so quickly, however, that she wondered whether it hadn't been her own tremor she had felt and not his.

Word of their coming had gone on before them, and it looked as if the whole town had come to the docks to see their arrival. The cannons fired a thundering salute and the people cheered, while some of the young men danced with joy at the sight of the women and began to wave wildly at them. A few of the more impatient ones went so far as to dive into the river, heedless of the icy waters, and swim out to meet them. Some of the bolder girls, swept up in the excitement of the festivities, waved back merrily, until the nuns scolded and reminded them that they should

92

act like well-bred young ladies and not create a wrong impression.

One of the men swam up to where Charlotte sat and began calling up to her repeatedly in hopes of getting her attention. Somewhat bewildered by the exuberance of the reception, however, she simply sat there blushing and quickly retreated behind the hood of her cloak, while Dubair gruffly gave the overanxious suitor a light push with his paddle and told him to be off before he upset the boat. Finally, with a curse over his shoulder, for the captain, the man went on to see what the other two boats might have to offer.

No less than Governor Etienne de Perier, commander of His Majesty's colonies in Louisiana, was there in his best *perruque*, with his hoop-skirted wife on his arm, waiting to give the nuns and their long-awaited charges his official greeting. The militia was lined up behind him in full regalia, not only to make the occasion more pompous, but also to insure that the bachelors of the town would not get too far out of hand in the presence of so many marriageable women at one time.

As Dubair had calculated, by paddling at all possible speed, they had beaten the sunset with time to spare, and although it was not an exceptionally bright day, the sun even made a feeble attempt to come out in honor of the occasion. The biting wind had subsided somewhat, and despite the cold snap to the air the atmosphere was not too disagreeable as the weary passengers disembarked from their cramped places in the dugouts.

More men came running up to help the women as they climbed ashore, but Charlotte instinctively pulled her wrap more tightly around her and drew back from the strange hands reaching out toward her. Dubair saw her reticence and quickly extended his arm to her. She caught hold of it immediately and raised grateful eyes to him. So many unspoken words hung suspended between them. For that one long moment they looked at each other and said a silent farewell.

Chapter XVI

A hush fell over the boisterous townspeople as the women fell to their knees in a prayer of thanksgiving. It was exactly four months and eight days since they had knelt on the deck of *Les Deux Frères* in Marseilles to ask God's blessing on their perilous voyage to the New World. Now that vague, intangible destination had become a reality.

The historic overtones of the occasion were further brought home by the florid speeches of M. de la Chaise, director general of the *Compagnie* in La Nouvelle Orléans and Governor Perier, *commandant-general* of that official seat of His Majesty's province of Louisiana, who took turns welcoming the "good nuns and those virtuous flowers of France that they had brought with them" to be the "future mothers of that brave New World to the glory of God, their King and country . . ."

Charlotte's mind wandered, and she missed many of the things they were saying, for her eyes were instinctively following Dubair's tall, buckskinned figure as it melted into the crowd of officers standing behind the governor.

The mother superior of the New Orleans convent, accompanied by three other black-robed Ursulines, was on hand to greet them, as well as several Jesuit priests and Capuchin friars, who had temporarily laid aside their rivalry over the religious jurisdiction of the colonists' souls long enough to lend their mutual support to such an important event.

Immediately after the formal welcome, some of the more impetuous young men began to press forward to get a better look at the prospective brides and perhaps even begin to pay them court, but the nuns circled their charges like mother hens defending their chicks, and insisted the girls could not see anyone except at specified hours within the walls of the convent, with all the rules of propriety strictly observed.

Thus, with constant reminders to keep their hoods up and their eyes down, Charlotte and her companions were whisked off, bag and baggage, to the refuge of their new home, which proved to be one of the most imposing buildings in New Orleans—a large, two-story wooden structure near the edge of town not far from ex-Governor Bienville's plantation. The Company of the Indies was already constructing an even finer convent for them, of brick with glass-paned windows, on the other side of town, explained Sister Marie Madeleine of St. Stanislas, a spritely young novice around the same age as Charlotte, who had come to New Orleans the year before with the original group of Ursulines from Rouen and was soon to make her final vows. As the mother superior's secretary, she led the newcomers to their allotted rooms, chattering merrily all the way, while they wearily climbed the huge staircase behind her.

It was obvious the tiny nun was proud of all that the Ursulines had accomplished in the short time they had been in New Orleans, and she went on to tell them how the *Compagnie* had even had to build additional rooms on to their temporary dwelling to accommodate the overflow of young girls that were already being sent to them for instruction from not only the city but neighboring settlements as well.

There were a few Negro and Indian servants at the convent to help them with their luggage, and an inviting fire was burning in the chimney to bid them welcome and take the damp chill out of the large room that had been prepared for them. Since mattresses were at a premium and the ones the travelers had brought with them were still muddy and damp from that last night on the river Charlotte and her companions doubled up on the few cots that were complete in the dormitory. After the conditions under which they had been sleeping for so many months, how-

95

ever, the girls felt they were at a luxury inn and even joked about not having to stay there that long, anyway, judging from the reception the yong bachelors of New Orleans had given them at the docks.

The girls also felt less inhibited now that Sister Marie and the other nuns had been given separate accommodations, and Charlotte was amazed to hear some of her friends talking about the men they had seen on the landing. She couldn't remember a single one of them; their faces had all been a confused blur to her. Only the captain's kept coming back clearly to her mind.

The next day Charlotte and her companions immediately set about cleaning and mending their traveling clothes and bedding and investigating more closely their new home. There were large windows everywhere, but since glass panes were still not easily available in the colony, finely woven pieces of white cloth similar to the mesh *baires* had been spread tautly over the inside of the frames so that the light could come in, but not insects from the nearby marshes.

They had a small garden and barnyard with cows, sows and different kinds of fowl. Sister St. Stanislas told them the convent also had been provided with a large plantation upriver, which sustained the bulk of their needs. And generous townsfolk, who were grateful to have the Ursulines there, constantly brought them additional food and offered to help in any way they could.

The Rev. Mother Superior, Mary of St. Augustine Tranchepain, whose surname of "sliced bread" caused some twittering among Charlotte and her companions, had arranged with the governor to have sentries posted around the convent for as long as the women were domiciled there, so the place resembled a fortress with a guard at each of its doors.

Excitement ran high when the girls were informed they would be receiving the eager bachelors of the town in the main parlor of the convent beginning the very next day. It was decided that the men would be allowed to visit between the hours of three and five in the afternoon, which was convenient for the nuns, since they would be free to chaperone the girls once the special classes they offered daily from 1:00 to 2:30 to the Indian and Negro girls of the vicinity were over.

Madelón and two other girls, as well as Sister Ernestine, had caught bad colds from the damp chill of their last night in the swamps, so Sister Marie thought it best they not attend that first open-house. Charlotte asked if she too could be excused, but the nuns laughed and told her not to be shy about the forthcoming meeting and insisted she present herself.

Rather reluctantly, therefore, Charlotte sat in the large, whitewashed parlor with the rest of the girls, dressed in her bright blue woolen dress with a freshly whitened kerchief and cap, her eyes demurely fixed on the floorboards, awaiting the onslaught of suitors who had been clamoring outside the doors since noon.

Their entrance was greatly subdued, however, once they got past the sentries and were met by the stoic-faced greetings of Sisters Marie and Mathilde. Somewhat abashed, they followed the nuns into the main parlor and then stood sheepishly in the center of the room, blinking at the equally apprehensive girls lining its walls.

There was a long awkward moment, and then the ice broke. The men began to move toward the girls of their liking. Some of the more forward women even rose to meet them, although they did try to remember to keep their eyes lowered with proper maidenly modesty, as they had been warned to do time and again by the nuns.

Like bees drawn to honey, at least a third of the fifty-odd men swarmed down upon Charlotte, all talking at once, pushing and shoving to capture her attention. She pressed back against the wall, wishing it would open up and let her in, not knowing what to do or say.

Fortunately Sister Marie had anticipated such a possibility. With her calm presence, she immediately imposed some order on that overenthusiastic siege of admirers.

"*Mon Dieu, messieurs!* Give the poor young lady air to breathe! You won't impress her very favorably with your manners if you act this way!"

The nun ordered chairs brought in and suggested that the men be seated. After that, the room quieted down a little, especially since some of the women had already walked off to a second large parlor with one or two suitors and the press of the reception room had become less intense.

Cecile, obviously enjoying the whole procedure immensely, went off merrily with four smitten young men following frantically at her heels. If the men expected to be more alone in the second parlor, however, they were sorely disappointed, for they were greeted by another group of placid-faced nuns there, as well.

Meanwhile, Charlotte had resigned herself to sitting back quietly and simply listening to each would-be suitor pour out to her his life story, his list of qualifications, and a bevy of pretty phrases meant to please and win her favor. She had never seen such an assorted lot of human beings gathered in one spot as those who sat there before her at that moment—sturdy, poor but honest farmers from the German colony upriver, well-dressed merchants and tradesmen of the town, uniformed men of the colonial guard, and bearded woodsmen and trappers dressed in leather.

They were of all ages, some stammering and shy, afraid they would be found inadequate even before pleading their suits, others bold and bragging, trying to impress her with their many fine qualities. But they had one thing in common—their desperate loneliness, a burning desire to find someone with whom they could share a future in this wild new land.

Since she had no idea how to answer them, Charlotte said nothing, which seemed to be more or less what a well-bred young lady was expected to do, anyway.

Charlotte was relieved when the nuns announced it was time for the visitors to leave. At first the men protested, but they accepted the curfew when they were assured they could return the next day at the same hour.

That night the girls sat whispering to each other in their moonlit dormitory long after the lanterns had been dimmed, comparing *prétendants* and confiding their preferences to one another.

Madelón and her two companions, who had been in bed since early that afternoon with hot grease on their chests and herb teas and broth in their stomachs, were anxious to know how the others had fared. Cecile rattled on about her many suitors and admitted that, although she liked them all, she would probably decide for the one with the most money.

One or two other girls said they had already made their selection, but another reminded them they might be meeting a whole new batch of suitors on the morrow, so perhaps they should wait at least another day or so before announcing anything definite.

Marguerite, the carrot-topped girl from Paris, confessed she still preferred the scout who had been with her on the boat coming up from Balize, but added sadly that he had not presented himself that afternoon as she had hoped he would.

"Perhaps he's gone on upriver with the captain," suggested Charlotte, although she regretted her interjection almost at once, since her mention of Dubair invited a new round of teasing from the girls.

"Too bad the *capitaine* wasn't able to show up this afternoon," sighed Cecile with mock compassion, still smarting a little from her own frustrated attempt to win him for herself. "But, of course, if he had been *really* interested in you, I'm sure he'd have said something about his intentions to the nuns before leaving, *non?*"

Marguerite sprang to Charlotte's defense. "With all the admirers our friend had flocking around her today, I'm sure the captain was the last person in her thoughts!" she retorted quickly, making no secret of the fact that she didn't approve of Cecile's sharp tongue.

The room quieted down after that, but Charlotte lay there for a while longer, still unable to sleep.

She looked down at where the drawstring of her coarsely woven nightgown had loosened and bared her shoulder in the bright moonlight filtering in through the shutters. She could just barely see the bruise on her forearm. It was slowly fading to a faint yellowish green now. The memory of Dubair flooded back to her. They had really only known each other five days—less time than it takes even for bruises to disappear! But they had been through so much, lived so intensely the twenty-four hours of each of those days, that it seemed she had known him longer.

She wondered where he was now. Probably rowing up the Mississippi to that distant Illinois territory on the other end of the river. Or was he taking a rest here in New Orleans for a night or two before going on? Perhaps he had a woman . . . a mistress somewhere . . . after all, what could a near-kiss mean to a man like him? She was a fool to let her thoughts dwell on a soldier of fortune! With all the dozens of women he'd probably known, why should she expect he would even remember her five minutes after he had deposited her on the dock with the rest?

Perhaps she should have saved herself all this trouble and simply stayed in Marseilles and taken the veil. She might just do that yet. . . .

Chapter XVII

Even as one of the girls had predicted, many new suitors did appear at the convent the following afternoon.

Madelón and her two companions, who were recuperating from their *grippe*, were permitted to join the group for an hour, under the condition that they return upstairs at the very first signs of fatigue.

The golden-haired girl, already naturally fair, fretted over how pale and hollow-eyed she looked, as she pinched her cheeks to give them more color and took a place on one of the sofas beside Charlotte.

"They won't pay any attention to me, anyway," she smiled wistfully. "Not with you sitting next to me!"

"I wish I didn't have to be here at all!" confessed Charlotte between clenched teeth, dreading the ordeal of those regimented courtships. "I think I'm destined to take the veil."

Madelón shot her friend a quizzical look, but could say

no more, for the men were entering the room. Suddenly she nudged her friend and whispered, "Oh, Charlotte, look! That tall dark one over there . . . what a handsome man he is, and how elegant!"

Charlotte halfheartedly followed Madelón's gaze. The man indeed cut a fine figure. He made those around him shabby by comparison, both in dress and bearing. She hadn't seen anyone like him since she had left Germaine's manor. Although it was evident he wore no wig, his thick dark hair, which he wore neatly tied back, was more abundant than any *perruque* would have been. There was vitality in those equally dark eyes, and although his tall, lean figure might have been an inch or two less than Dubair's and not quite as broad shouldered, it still dominated the room.

There was an elegance in his dress that came not only from the cut of his clothes, but their good taste, as well. The russet-brown riding habit showed off to advantage his slender silhouette, and the white lace cravat and cuffs were impeccable. His high black boots and trim riding crop all added to the picture of a highborn gentleman taking an afternoon saunter. He seemed out of place in that room full of sombre-clad nuns and lowly convent girls with their equally unpretentious suitors. Charlotte wondered what he was doing there. He looked like a Parisian who had lost his way.

Pierre Treval stood to one side of the parlor, nonchalantly surveying the scene. He was rather annoyed with his friend Gustave for having dragged him there in the first place. But it had been a boring afternoon, and Gustave had cajoled him into stopping off at the convent to take a closer look at the *filles à la cassette* who had arrived a couple of days ago. It was a lark, of course, and nothing more, although his mother had been nagging him lately about settling down and marrying "some nice girl." It had become a litany this past year, especially since he had celebrated his twenty-fifth birthday and his mother had gotten it into her head that Mlle. Ninon Planchard, a distant relative of the governor's wife, ought to be that "nice girl"!

He was about to turn on his heel and drag Gustave back outside with him when his eyes fell on Charlotte. She was getting to her feet and begging the group of men gathered around her not to crowd in so closely. Now there was a sight that made the trip worthwhile! Who would have expected to find such an Aphrodite rising out of a sea of drabness like this? She must have some hidden deformity or a foul disposition to have come all the way to the New World to find a husband, looking the way she did.

There was something about her that suggested quality. If this shipment of girls had been like the others, he would have supposed her to be some exiled aristocrat who had gotten into trouble in France, but the town crier had been announcing for days now that these were women of good character who had been gathered from the orphanages and convents of Paris and Marseilles, and although one assumed they had been educated mostly by the nuns and, therefore, had a certain refinement along with their virtue, it didn't seem likely any of them would be highborn. Perhaps she was the illegitimate child of some nobleman. Fascinated, he made his way toward her.

The little knot of eager admirers around Charlotte fell back instinctively as Treval's imposing figure joined them. There was resentment in some of their eyes, but they stepped aside as if already acknowledging defeat in the presence of such overwhelming odds.

"Forgive my intrusion, mademoiselle," he began, bowing with a courtliness that would have been acceptable even in Versailles. "Permit me to introduce myself. I'm Pierre Treval, your humble servant and admirer. May I say your beauty lights up this whole room!"

Charlotte didn't have to remember to lower her gaze as she had been schooled. She did so instinctively as she felt the intensity of those dark, lustrous eyes.

"You're very kind, monsieur," she murmured, feeling uncomfortable under the impact of that penetrating gaze. "But I'm sure a man of your obvious position in society has admired many women of far greater wit and beauty than myself. I would hate to think you're simply amusing yourself at my expense."

The young man was taken aback. He hadn't expected such a reply to his compliment. Now he was more certain than ever that the girl was an unexpected find.

"*Mon Dieu, mademoiselle*! Why would you think such a thing? I assure you I mean every word. I—I wouldn't dream of offending you! Surely you must know you're a remarkably pretty young woman—and with a wit equal to your beauty, I see. I confess you've already placed me at a disadvantage."

"Surely you haven't come here to propose matrimony to me or one of my companions," insisted Charlotte.

"I'll not trifle with your affections, mademoiselle," replied Treval, flushing beneath his smooth olive complexion. It was clear to see his gallantry had seldom been questioned before. "I confess I came here out of curiosity. Like any bachelor my age, I'm drawn to feminine company. Although I can't say I'm looking to marry someone before the week is out, I don't see why that should stop me from wanting to feast my eyes on beauty and admire it."

Charlotte pushed back a golden-brown curl from her forehead and tucked it under her cap again. She liked his honesty. Her first impression of him had softened considerably, now that she knew he had not come there to make fun of her and her companions. Here at last was one man who wasn't talking of getting married by sundown tomorrow!

He was asking her to accompany him to the second parlor where the groups were more intimate and the atmosphere less pressing.

Accepting the arm he offered, she murmured her apologies to those around her and allowed him to lead her away from the circle of would-be suitors, who watched in dismay as they saw her being snatched away from them.

Charlotte spent the rest of the afternoon with Treval. Talking to someone like him made her feel she was back in Marseilles again at one of her aunt's *soirées*. In that first meeting they found themselves sharing little details that surprised them both. There was a carefree manner about the dark-haired young man that put her at ease. Also, the fact that neither she nor the Creole had any urgency to enter wedlock eliminated much of the strain that might have been put on their budding relationship.

Pierre Treval, she learned, had been born in the neighboring Spanish colonies, where his father had been an important dignitary of his king for many years, until his death approximately five years ago. Although the senior Treval had left his wife and only son well provided for, Pierre's French-born mother had always yearned to return to French soil, so she finally prevailed upon her young son to take her to New Orleans, where she could "spend the last years of her life among her own kind." Despite the fact that there were times when Pierre felt he would have preferred the more sedate colonial life of New Spain, which already had two centuries of exposure to European culture behind it, he soon took to the less restrained atmosphere of this raw new land. He and his mother now had a large plantation upriver, while they spent most of their time in their fine brick townhouse in the heart of the settlement.

Since Señora Treval was the sister of one of the officials of the *Compagnie* in New Orleans, she and her son had been immediately welcomed into the town's most select circles, where elegance and etiquette were as much the order of the day as in the court of Versailles. It all depended upon the heights from which one viewed New Orleans, whether one called it "Little Paris" or a "hellhole of mud and mosquitoes!"

With his aquiline features and dark hair and eyes, Pierre resembled his Spanish father, and having spent most of his life in the Spanish colonies, he tended to sprinkle his speech with occasional Castilian phrases. Although he spoke French with equal fluency, there were moments when the influence of his formative years would momentarily surface.

As Charlotte told him of her own background in France, the Creole's handsome face broke into a broad smile. He exclaimed, "I knew it! Good breeding always tells! From the moment I laid eyes on you I knew you had to be well born."

Charlotte remembered the locket Germaine had given her, which she had carefully laid away in her *cassette* during the voyage for fear of losing it, since the catch on the brooch from which it hung was old and not too reliable. Pierre seemed so genuinely interested in seeing it that she finally excused herself for a moment and brought it down from her dormitory for him to see.

Discreetly avoiding the more embarrassing details, Charlotte told him how she had decided to join the consignment of Casquette Girls in order to avoid a marriage her aunt had wanted to arrange for her with a detestable old man almost old enough to be her grandfather.

"I hoped I might do better here," she concluded, "for at least I was assured by the *Compagnie* I could marry someone of my own choice, and I intend to hold them to that promise, although sometimes I think I might end up taking the veil instead."

"Now that would be a pity indeed!" exclaimed Treval. "What a waste of beauty if you locked yourself behind convent walls forever!" And what a loss to some man, he thought, for if ever a woman was made for love, this one was.

"There's a certain peace here that's very appealing to a woman alone like myself," she continued. "Sometimes the world outside these walls can be very frightening . . . at least I have found it so."

"Yes, I can understand your *temor*," agreed the Creole, his dark eyes softening as he thought how feminine and helpless she looked at that moment. "And that's why you must marry, of course. But you are wise to approach so important a step with calm and prudence. Few women have the opportunity to choose their own mates. It's a pity your guardian wasn't more considerate of your feelings in her handling of your affairs, but then I would have never met you if she had, and that, too, would have been *una lástima!*"

The ease with which she had been talking about herself to this charming stranger surprised Charlotte. When the nuns announced that the hour was late and the visitors had to leave, she couldn't believe so much time had passed.

Treval, too, was reluctant to take his leave, and only did so after Charlotte consented to see him again the following afternoon.

"Without any commitments?" she asked hesitantly.

"*Sin compromiso,*" he agreed with a smile.

As she watched him join his friend, another well dressed youth, less impressive but obviously also of the upper class, Charlotte wondered whether she would ever see her new admirer again. After all, why should an elegant gentleman like that waste his time with a simple convent girl like herself with her homespun dress and lack of courtly manners? Although he had assured her he was not just having fun at her expense, and had seemed sincere enough, he had all but admitted he had gone there on a lark just to ogle the girls. Perhaps she had been a fool to believe him and chatter away as she had. He was probably having a good laugh about her with his friend right now!

But the next day Pierre Treval was there again. And the day after that as well, until Charlotte found herself looking forward to those visits, each one a welcome oasis in the dull routine of convent life. Some of her fainter-hearted suitors began to turn reluctantly to more receptive girls, but a goodly number persisted, hoping that some miracle might yet occur to make her choose one of them over her more highborn admirer.

Cecile jealously observed that, for someone who was always insisting she was not in a hurry to get married, Charlotte certainly knew how to attract the best "catches" every time!

Sister Marie watched the young Creole's successive visits with a cautious eye. Although her policy was to interfere as little as possible with the girls and their selections, she was growing increasingly preoccupied with the thought that perhaps this latest admirer of Charlotte's was only wasting the girl's time and distracting her from the more likely prospects around her.

Of course, if the young Creole's intentions were serious, then Charlotte had indeed made an enviable match, but if not, her sensitive young charge might suddenly find herself nursing a broken heart. It wouldn't be the first time a dashing aristocrat had amused himself for a while with a naïve young girl until he wearied of the game and then went on to newer conquests. Although Charlotte was highborn enough to be acceptable in Treval's class, her background was so foreign to the aristocratic world that had given her birth that she knew little of its ways and even less about how to defend herself from the subtle yet very real pitfalls it could hold for her.

The nun suspected the girl had already suffered her first disillusion with Dubair. She might be mistaken, but it seemed to her Charlotte had looked piqued and wistful ever since the captain had left them on the docks and gone his way.

Meanwhile the nun held her silence, deciding to bide her time a little longer until she could see some sign of what Treval's true intentions were. The young man's continuing visits seemed to denote interest on his part. Sister Marie didn't want to say or do anything that might upset the cart before it got to market!

By the beginning of their second week in New Orleans, it looked as if at least half of the Casquette Girls would be married before the year was out. So the nuns arranged with Father de Beaubois for the couples to wed *en masse* at a special mass on Christmas day, which would also celebrate the first anniversary of the colony's new church, dedicated just the year before.

Among the first to decide was Cecile, who for all her talk of marrying the wealthiest man she could find finally decided in favor of a young *sergent* of the colonial militia. Like most of those serving in the regular army, he was rather poorly paid, but as Cecile pointed out, the king, in an effort to encourage matrimony in the colonies, had promised to give any soldier who married "a plot of land, an ox, a cow, a pair of swine, a pair of fowl, two barrels of salted meat and a bit of cash." She kept an itemized list to refer to when the time came to collect, just to be sure nothing would be overlooked. Besides, as she further pointed out, her *sergent* had his whole career ahead of him, and he really did look dashing in his uniform! With her usual unbounded enthusiasm for what she could accomplish once she set her mind to it, Cecile concluded, "Who knows? He might be a general by the time he's thirty-five! After all, a man can go far with an ambitious wife to urge him on, *n'est-ce pas?*"

Another girl in the first group planning to marry on Christmas day was Madelón. From that first afternoon she had gone to meet the hopeful bachelors, the tiny blonde had taken to a sandy-haired young man, whose shyness in

107

the presence of women had appealed to her almost at once, probably because it struck a responsive chord in her own innate timidity.

The twenty-one-year-old trader was an industrious young man who had been educated for a few years by the Capuchins after the Indian attack on New Orleans in 1723 had left him an orphan, but in the past three years Jacques Ansleau had begun making trips up and down the Mississippi and now had almost enough money saved to set himself up in a small business. After one or two more trips upriver, he hoped to be able to settle down to his own little shop in New Orleans, where his customers could come to him, instead of his having to seek them out.

At first the nuns were worried about giving their consent, since it was evident Madelón would be left alone a great deal during that first year. They tried to convince the young couple to wait until Ansleau had made his last trips upriver before embarking on matrimony, but the youngsters had looked at each other with such starry eyes and pleaded so touchingly that they be allowed to begin their married life at once, that Sister Marie and the nuns had finally relented. They agreed with even more enthusiasm once Ansleau assured them he had arranged with M. and Mme. Pichou, who rented him a room over their general store in the heart of town, not only to let Madelón continue living there whenever he had to leave the settlement, but to watch over her for him during his absence, as well. Since the Pichous had a long-standing reputation around New Orleans as an honest, God-fearing couple, the nuns felt relieved to know that Madelón would be living under their roof. Although Sister Marie had also offered Madelón the refuge of the convent whenever her husband was away, the young couple had declined. Not that they hadn't appreciated the offer, but as they pointed out, they wanted to feel they had a place they could call their own, even if it was only one room for the time being.

Charlotte was a little sad to think her dearest friend would no longer be living at the convent with her, but was comforted by the fact that Madelón would be close by in the town. They promised each other to make frequent visits, and when Madelón asked her with a knowing smile whether she too might not be marrying very soon, Charlotte ignored the insinuation and hastily assured her friend she was sure she would be staying at the convent for quite a while yet.

Chapter XVIII

The afternoon of Christmas Eve, *la nuit de noël*, saw a beehive of activity at the convent. The mother superior had gone with three of the Ursulines to visit the sick, but upstairs on the second floor, the prospective brides were excitedly preparing for their joint weddings the following day with the help of their laughing, teasing companions and Sisters Marie, Anne, and Mathilde.

Meanwhile the other nuns were on the first floor with Sister St. Stanislas, giving a little party for the schoolgirls at the convent who, for one reason or another, were unable to spend the holidays in their homes or, as orphans, had no homes to go to at all.

Each child sat with a cookie in one hand and a glass of lemonade in the other, listening to the young novice repeat the familiar story of the Christ Child, when Pierre Treval arrived, radiating holiday cheer and laden with a huge clay potbellied jar decorated with multicolored paper cutouts and filled to the brim with bonbons and sugar candies.

In the Spanish colonies where he had spent his childhood, the Creole explained, children would hang such a pot up by a string in the parlor at Christmas and one by one, blindfolded, try to break it.

Sister St. Stanislas was delighted with the gift and accepted Pierre's offer to hang the *piñata* from one of the beams of the ceiling, while she sent a servant upstairs to tell Charlotte she had a visitor.

Pierre had blindfolded one of the little girls and was explaining to her how to try to hit the *piñata* with the stick in her hand when Charlotte arrived.

For a moment she paused at the bottom of the staircase and looked at him standing in the parlor surrounded by the happy children. She thought how this ingratiating young man had come to be such a pleasant part of her life since she had landed in New Orleans only a few weeks before. Things happened fast, it seemed, in this wild New World where there were no borders on the horizon to limit one's dreams and one could live a lifetime in only a few hours or days.

Leaving the laughing, shouting children to their game with the nuns, Pierre drew Charlotte aside to the privacy of the dimly lighted second parlor. They chose the sofa by the inviting warmth of the fire.

"That was good of you to bring a gift to the children," she told him. "They have so little. Something like that will live in their memories for many years. I remember my own lonely Christmas Eves as a child at the convent back in Marseilles."

"Charlotte, *linda*, those days are behind you," he said gently. "As long as I'm here, I promise you'll never be alone again. That's what I want to talk to you about." He moved closer to her. "Something has come up at my plantation upriver," he continued hurriedly, "and I have to go there for a few weeks to check on its management, so I'll be gone for New Year's Eve and probably into the next month. But I'll be back by the end of January, and I want you to promise not to make any decision about your future until I've returned and we can talk at length together. Do you promise to wait for me?"

Charlotte sat there wide-eyed, feeling as if she had been struck in the pit of her stomach. "You—you're going away?" she repeated dazedly.

"Yes, my dear, but I'll be back soon, I promise."

"You don't have to invent excuses," she said numbly. "If you have to stop coming to see me, it's all right."

Treval laughed and caught her hand impulsively. "Ah,

110

my *linda niña*—my lovely child! It pleases me that you don't like the idea of my going away. But it will only be for a few weeks."

There was a lump in her throat. The captain had gone up the river and out of her life. Now her new friend was telling her he was going upriver, too. *Mon Dieu!* How she hated that word! It evoked an image of crossing over into the Great Beyond. She had heard the nuns talking of how men had gone up the Mississippi into that vast untamed territory above New Orleans and never returned.

Pierre was repeating her name. "Charlotte . . . look, silly girl, I've brought you a little gift—*un regalito* just for you." He put a tiny jewel box in her hand and pressed her fingers over it. "It's a gold chain for your locket, so you can wear it without fear of losing it now, and at the same time have something that's mine around that pretty neck of yours to remind you of me."

She looked down at the delicate gold chain set against black velvet and smiled wistfully. "It's lovely, Pierre," she said. "It's very thoughtful of you to give me a farewell gift."

"I wouldn't exactly call it that," he protested. "It's for the New Year. I got it for you before I even knew I'd have to be leaving town. It's simply a holiday gift, that's all."

She took off her brooch and tried to remove the locket from it in order to place it on the chain, but her fingers fumbled so that Pierre finally took it and tried to fix it for her.

"It's a lovely gift," she murmured, as she sat watching his dark head bent intently over the delicate task of removing the locket from the brooch and putting it on the chain. "I'll always treasure it."

He helped her put it around her neck and clasp it. The children in the next room were letting out little squeals of delight as someone broke the *piñata* and they scrambled for the shower of candies that had fallen from it.

Pierre let the necklace fall into its place within the soft folds of the fichu crossed over her bosom and, bending his head forward, quickly brushed her cheek with a furtive kiss.

"Mi linda mujercita, te quiero!" he murmured in her

111

ear. "I love you, do you understand? *Je t'adore.* I'll be back. I promise."

Charlotte jumped up quickly, confused by the sudden turn of events. *"Non, non,"* she cautioned him, pushing him away as he moved close to her once more, hoping to find her lips. "Please don't! The nuns . . ." She groped lamely for some excuse to stay him, more afraid of the turmoil she felt rising within her than the discreet advances of her admirer.

"All right . . . *está bien,*" he soothed, drawing her down beside him on the sofa once more. "Forgive me, little Charlotte, if I've startled you. It wasn't my intention to take liberties with you, believe me. But I can't hold back any longer. These past two weeks, day after day—I've come to care for you very much. I hope you feel something for me, too. Please say you do."

The children's high-pitched voices wafted into the room as the nuns began to lead them in a familiar Christmas carol. Sister Ernestine's imposing black-robed figure could be seen silhouetted in the doorway, where she had taken her post as a discreet but very visible reminder that they were not without vigilance.

Pierre was asking her again softly whether she cared for him or not.

"I—I don't know," she replied, and in all honesty she didn't know what she felt at that moment. "I can only say I shall miss you."

"Then you'll wait until I return before making any decisions?" he begged, his dark penetrating eyes never once leaving her. "You won't marry anyone else while I'm gone, will you? Please wait until I come back and we can talk further. Promise me at least that much."

Charlotte lowered her golden-brown head. "I—I won't be marrying anyone in the immediate future," she murmured. "Later on, only *le bon Dieu* knows."

"But do I have a good chance to be the one who is accepted?" he pressed. "Please don't be coy with me, Charlotte. Your answer is very important to me."

"All I can answer is that there's no one nearer my heart at this moment than you, Pierre. But marriage . . . We'll

112

have to wait and see when the moment comes. I honestly don't know."

"That's enough for me now," he smiled, catching her tiny hand in his and kissing it passionately. "I know I can win you if you give me the chance to court you when I return."

As Charlotte stood in the open doorway watching Treval's tall, elegant figure walking away from the convent, she was aware of the late afternoon chill setting in. The sentry on guard stood discreetly at attention, his eyes peering out blankly from above the coarse woolen muffler with which he had wrapped the lower half of his face.

Closing the door with a sigh, Charlotte returned to the warmth of the fireplace in the parlor where she and Pierre had been sitting. A sudden feeling of loneliness overwhelmed her. Would Pierre really come back? She was afraid to dream, to be hurt again. Dubair had gone away just when she had begun to feel something stirring within her. Now Pierre had begun to arouse similar feelings, and he, too, was leaving her.

Chapter XIX

The mass wedding Christmas morning was a moving ceremony. The ten couples, dressed in their finest attire, stood solemnly before the altar, while Father de Beaubois united them in holy wedlock and made an eloquent speech about the great adventure those fortunate young men and women were embarking upon to the glory of the church, their king and the Louisiana Colony.

Everyone of any importance was there, beginning with the governor, members of the council, and the officials of the Company of the Indies, all accompanied by their families. In a special part of the church the black-robed Ursulines and Grey Sisters of Charity sat complacently with the remaining ten Casquette Girls and twenty young schoolgirls and orphans, who were also under their care at the convent. In another section of the church, the Capuchin friars sat with their boy orphans and a few of their Indian converts.

Rounding out the congregation were the rest of the townspeople, dressed in their holiday best, who filled to overflowing the large wooden framed church, elaborately decorated, with blazing candles in the best candelabra and a colorful *crêche* to one side of the main altar, composed of beautifully carved and painted wooden figurines depicting the Nativity scene.

Charlotte and her companions wept openly as they went up to their newly married friends to wish them Godspeed, once the Mass was over and the couples were leaving the church to go their separate ways.

Charlotte felt doubly lonely in the weeks that followed. With Madelón and so many of her other companions from the voyage to New Orleans gone now, the convent seemed suddenly empty. It was especially quiet after all the hustle and bustle of those last few days just before Christmas.

As Charlotte watched her friends, proclaiming their intentions to wed, she began to wonder whether there was something wrong with her. Why couldn't she just accept one of those strangers and take a chance with him? Her companions were doing it. Why couldn't she? It wasn't that she didn't find some of her *prétendants* likeable as she chatted with them. She felt she could have probably become friends with several of them. But when it came to trying to pick out a possible husband from among them, they became a sea of blank faces.

After the second mass wedding on *le Jour de l'An*, Charlotte decided to talk to Sister Marie about her feelings. The Ursuline had wisely held her silence and waited until the young girl had come to her. After all, Charlotte was there in the New World because someone had tried to make her marry against her will. It was only natural she would not

114

be in as big a hurry as the others to put her head into the yoke.

"Please, *Soeur* Marie, don't make me marry anyone yet," she began rather clumsily.

"Why, child, I have no intention of forcing you to choose anyone," protested the nun. "Whatever makes you think I'd do such a thing?"

"Because there are only three of us left now," replied Charlotte, "and I fear the *Compagnie* will want us to make up our minds soon, too."

"They cannot force you to wed anyone against your will," the nun assured her, "so you can rest easy on that score."

"But what happens if I can't make up my mind . . . ever?"

"I don't know, child. I suppose you'd have to return your dowry and reimburse the *Compagnie* for the money it spent to bring you to New Orleans. But that wouldn't be very nice, would it? You did sign a contract with them to get married here in the colonies."

"Sometimes I think I might like to get married, but then there are other times when I don't."

"But you're of marriageable age now. Is it possible that out of all the suitors you've had—and you've had more than any of the other girls—you haven't seen at least one who has interested you at least a little? What about Pierre Treval who was coming here to visit you almost every day until *la Nuit de Noël*? You seemed to like him well enough."

"He—he told me he had to go to his plantation for a few weeks."

"But what are his intentions? Has he ever spoken of marriage to you?"

"He said he—he loved me and wanted to talk with me when he returned."

"Well, there you have it. If you want to wait for him to return, child, you may do so with no fears that anyone will force you to wed anyone else."

"But I haven't really made up my mind yet what I'll say if and when he returns," confessed Charlotte. "A part of me is tempted to accept, but then again, something inside

115

of me still holds back. I don't know what's the matter with me, *Soeur* Marie. Sometimes I wonder whether I shouldn't take the veil—that is, if I'm worthy enough for such a calling."

The nun smiled and patted Charlotte's drooping head.

"I don't think you should make such a decision yet, my dear," she replied cautiously. "Let's wait a little longer and see what happens, *non*?"

But the weeks wore on, and as Charlotte feared, the end of January came and Pierre did not make an appearance. Now that the first week of February had gone by, she began to wonder whether she had not been right, after all, when she had suspected that his gift might have been in reality a farewell one. But then she would remember the warmth of his voice, the tender look in his dark eyes and the urgency of his embrace as he told her he loved her, and she would begin to worry that perhaps he might not have returned because he had been hurt or, worse yet, had even been killed in that wild country upriver. When such horrible thoughts occurred to her, she would cross herself quickly and beg the Virgin to protect him wherever he might be. She would wonder then whether she might really be in love with Pierre.

Her concern for him was genuine, yet if he walked in the door at that moment, she knew she might still refuse his proposal of matrimony—at least at this time. She yearned for love. She recognized that much now in herself. But she also knew her loneliness put her in an extremely vulnerable position. It would be so easy to say yes to an attractive young man when he had his arms around her and his lips so close to hers. Her flesh was so weak! If it weren't for the good nuns, she would have probably ended up a shameful hussy like those who had come to the New World before her. Nor could she contemplate taking the veil with such thoughts in her head. She wasn't worthy.

Charlotte fingered the gold chain around her neck and tried to analyze her true feelings about Pierre. If he didn't come back, she would miss him, at least for a while, even as she had missed Dubair at first more than she had cared to admit, and still did sometimes . . . but memories tend to fade, even as bruises do . . .

116

Besides keeping busy around the convent, helping the nuns with their classes, especially those with the younger girls who were learning the alphabet and needlepoint, Charlotte prevailed upon Sister Marie to give her permission to visit Madelón. Charlotte and the two remaining girls of her group were finally allowed to go in the convent's private coach, driven by a trusted old Negro slave, with strict orders to go directly to their destination and back again within two hours.

The girls donned their freshly bleached caps and threw their cloaks lightly over their shoulders as they went merrily off, not only delighted over the prospect of seeing their friend, but glad to have an opportunity to get away from the convent for a little while and have a look at the city, which they had hardly seen at all since their arrival.

From what they could see, as they giggled and tried to peep out of the draped windows of the coach, the town was carefully laid out into neat squares lined with picturesque whitewashed houses of brick and mortar or fashioned from wood, topped by shingled or palmetto-thatched roofs.

The Pichou building was located in the heart of New Orleans, just a block and a half from the Place d'Armes, the town's public square, which faced the river at the point where it cut deepest into the city's crescent-shaped shoreline. A large, white, two-story structure, made of cypress logs, it had been converted into a general store on the ground floor, with the front part open to the public and a storeroom and kitchen to the back. The private living quarters were upstairs.

Monsieur and Madame Pichou's only daughter had recently married and lived on the fringes of town, so it was the latter's former bedroom that the elderly couple was renting to Madelón and her husband. It was a large, cheerful habitation with a wide window that let in considerable light through its thin net covering. Madelón was delighted that her friends had come to see her, for her husband had just left on one of his trips upriver, and it was the first time the newlyweds had been separated since they had wed approximately six or seven weeks before. The young bride was feeling very lonely, despite the efforts of the kindly Pichous to make her feel at home with them.

"Besides, I have good news to tell you," beamed the fair-haired girl. "I think I'm *enciente*."

Her visitors looked at her with round-eyed curiosity.

"Silly *bêtasses!*" laughed Madelón, flushing beneath their scrutiny. "You can't tell anything yet! It's too soon. But I must have gotten pregnant from that first night . . ." Her grey eyes momentarily softened at the recollection of her passionate young husband, and her blush deepened all the more. Then she went on hurriedly, "These past two mornings I've awakened with the morning sickness. Of course, my stomach has always been rather squeamish, as you well know after that horrid voyage we had, but I'm sure this time it's for a different reason. But that's enough about me. Tell me about you and the rest of the girls. I'm eager to know all the latest news!"

The time allotted for their visit flew by so quickly that they barely had time to bring Madelón up to date.

Madelón was surprised when Charlotte told her she had not seen Pierre since Christmas Eve. Although Charlotte had hastily shown her friend the gold chain her suitor had given her, she hadn't had an opportunity to relate all that had transpired in that last conversation with Pierre. Now that he hadn't returned, Charlotte kept her silence for fear of being ridiculed by the other girls. She simply replied that he had probably been delayed, but in her heart she was beginning to suspect he had simply gone and wouldn't be back. As an orphan, she had learned not to expect too much from life, especially from personal attachments.

Angelique gave a long, tearful account of how she had been about to accept a suitor when she had discovered him holding hands with another girl in the second parlor, just as soon as her back was turned.

As for Felicité, she sighed and said she wasn't attracted at all by the *prétendants* she had had. "The ones I like don't seem to care for me, while the ones that like me, aren't to my liking!" she lamented. "*C'est la vie, non, mes amies?*"

They promised to return soon, as they hastily bade Madelón goodbye, for they had already overstayed their time.

Sister Marie was standing in the doorway of the convent waiting to receive them, and they hung their heads sheep-

ishly as they breathlessly got out of the carriage, ready for
the tirade of reproaches due them for having overstayed
themselves on their outing. But they were spared any reproaches just then, for they soon saw the nun was not
alone. Standing beside her was a familiar figure which,
with a sudden acceleration of heartbeat, Charlotte recognized as Pierre's.

Chapter XX

Charlotte gave Pierre's passionate clasp of her hand a
chilly reception, as he bent his dark head over it in greeting. Her companions quickly withdrew to their dormitory,
whispering and suppressing a giggle or two on the way up
the staircase.

Sister Marie poked up the fire in the second parlor,
where she had led the young couple. Then she discreetly
retired to a high-winged armchair in a far corner of the
room in an effort to give them as much privacy as possible.
She felt the forthcoming interview between Charlotte and
her handsome admirer would be an important one, perhaps
decisive for the girl's future, so she wished to give them as
much freedom as possible within the limits of propriety.

"Charlotte, my dear, please don't be angry," the Creole
pleaded with her. "Believe me, *mi cielo*, I've come as soon
as I could. There was so much to be done when I arrived at
the plantation that I couldn't get back as soon as I had
hoped. But I'm here now, *verdad*? Look *niña mia*, I've
come back as I told you I would."

"*Oui*, monsieur, so I see," she replied coolly.

"Please, I'd like to talk to you," he said, gently pulling
her down beside him on the sofa by the blazing fireplace.

He continued, dropping his voice so it would not carry over to where Sister Marie sat busily knitting at the other end of the room. "You have no idea how I've missed you, my sweet Charlotte. You've filled my thoughts all these weeks, and I've been impatient to return to your side."

"Your impatience has been very noticeable," she retorted, trying to speak with a sophistication she hoped might veil the tremulous uncertainty she felt at that moment.

"*Por favor*, Charlotte, let me speak my heart!" he pleaded once more, a pained expression on his face. "I know I stayed away longer than I'd promised, but that was due to circumstances beyond my control. My feelings for you haven't changed, *niña*. To the contrary, the added time away from you has only made me realize how much I really care for you. I hope it's done the same for you . . . that you've missed me a little . . . I'd like to think your annoyance over my delay in coming back to you stems from the fact that you feel something for me, too. You do, don't you, Charlotte? Please say you do."

"I can't say I'm indifferent to you," she admitted in a weak voice that, try as she might, she couldn't keep steady.

"I confess that when I came here to the convent that first day, I did so on a lark. Although I had no intentions of making fun of anyone, I did come out of curiosity, with a very human desire to see some pretty girls, to flirt a little perhaps, and that would be it. But then I saw you, *mi dulce Charlotte*, and everything—my whole world changed."

He took her hand from where it lay among the folds of her wine-colored skirt and was surprised at how icy it was. He stroked it gently as he continued speaking.

"By the time I came here on Christmas Eve, I could deny it no longer. I knew I was hopelessly in love with you, and I would have long since made my formal request for your hand in marriage, if I hadn't had to leave immediately for my plantation. But there was a problem there that couldn't wait. My mother and I had uncovered evidence of theft in its management, and it had to be investigated and stopped at once. The truth is, the matter still requires further attention, and I must return there for another few weeks to be sure the new overseer I've placed in charge can really do the job. But I didn't want to be away from you a day longer, so I came to New Orleans today just to see you. I know how skittish you are, *niña mía*, and was afraid you'd think I wasn't coming back and might decide in favor of some other suitor."

"I confess I'd reached the conclusion you weren't coming back," Charlotte replied, "and I was somewhat hurt, since I do consider you a very dear friend."

"Friend? I'd hoped for more than that! I want you for my wife, Charlotte, not a friend!"

"I—I don't know yet . . . I'm not sure . . ."

"But surely you've had more than enough time to clarify your feelings about me during the time I've been gone?"

"Since I didn't know what to think, I was really in no position to clarify anything. Actually I was more confused than ever!"

"Charlotte, *linda*, if you consent to be my wife, I'll speak to the nuns to formalize our relationship this very day, so you can be making your plans for the wedding while I finish my business at the plantation. Then we can be married immediately on my return, which should be by the end of this month, right before Lent, God willing."

"Please, not so fast!" exclaimed Charlotte, suddenly withdrawing her hand from his. "You men of the New World! Who can understand you? One minute you're off to that vague land of yours called 'upriver' and disappear for weeks, even months, as if time stood still there. Then the next minute you're pressing a woman to marry you in a quarter of that time, as if the hours of your life were numbered! Is the selection of a mate so much less important than your precious business upriver? Does it merit so little of your attention?"

Pierre laughed and playfully tweaked the unruly curl peeping out from her white ruffled cap. "You really are a delightful child!" he exclaimed.

"Be that as it may," retorted Charlotte, not to be cajoled into accepting a hurried proposal, "I refuse to make so important a decision, one that will affect not only the rest of my life but yours as well, in such a rapid manner."

Treval was taken aback. "Then . . . then you're rejecting my proposal?" he asked incredulously.

121

"I'm neither rejecting nor accepting it," she replied. "If you have made it in all sincerity, I don't think you'll mind giving me more time to consider it further."

A wave of relief swept over his face. "Of course, my dear. I don't want you to feel rushed, but . . . but I'd hoped to get your answer before returning to the plantation so that, in the meanwhile, we could go ahead with the plans for the wedding. I don't want any mass-marriage or cap and apron outfit for my bride. If you consent, I'll present you to my mother, and she can help you choose a fitting gown and everything else that is appropriate for the nuptials of someone in our position in the colony. You understand, of course?"

Charlotte was overwhelmed. "I—I'm sorry, Pierre," she murmured. "I can't give you a final answer at this moment. But I'm very glad you've returned, for it would have hurt me deeply to have discovered I'd placed my trust in someone not deserving of it. I'm also extremely flattered that you've asked me to become your wife, and I promise I'll take your proposal to heart and consider it very carefully. Perhaps when you return I'll be able to give you a decision."

"Is there anyone else?" Pierre asked anxiously. "I know you have many admirers. Are you perhaps seriously considering someone else?"

Charlotte smiled at his boyish eagerness. "I'll be candid with you, Pierre," she replied gently. "There's no one I prefer to you at this moment. But I still don't feel sure enough of my sentiments right now to be able to give you a definite answer without giving it more thought."

Pierre would have liked to press his suit further and get some definite commitment from her then and there, but he feared he would only lessen his chances for acceptance if he annoyed her with his haste, after having already invited her displeasure by his delay in returning. At least she had assured him he was the most likely candidate among her suitors.

He bade her a reluctant goodbye, bending quickly to brush the wayward curl on her forehead with his lips, while the wings of the huge armchair still partially blocked them from Sister Marie's view.

As they stood in the doorway taking final leave of each other, and Charlotte suddenly realized she wouldn't be seeing him again for another two or three weeks, she impulsively reached out to touch him shyly on the sleeve.

"Please, Pierre . . . be careful," she murmured. "As you say in the land of your childhood, *vaya con Dios* . . . go with God."

His eyes filled with tenderness. He caught her hand quickly and lifted it to his lips. "And God watch over you, my sweet Charlotte. I hope when next we meet it will be to plan our wedding."

Sister Marie was surprised that Pierre had left without any formal declaration to her about Charlotte. However, when the girl told her he had indeed asked her to marry him and had wanted to formalize their relationship before leaving, the nun couldn't help but show some impatience with her charge.

"Really, Charlotte, I don't understand! A man like Treval offers you his name and place in the community, and you hesitate! *Mon Dieu!* What more could you possibly want, child?"

"I—I'm not sure," she replied. "I felt I needed more time to consider."

"But consider what? You certainly can't expect a finer candidate. Perhaps you're letting foolish romanticisms turn your head!"

"I—I want to be sure we have enough to build a life on . . ." stammered the girl.

"Most people have built on much less than what you are being offered," chided the Ursuline. "You're indeed fortunate to have so much to consider."

"Am I wrong in being so cautious, then?"

"Perhaps not," admitted the nun, "but sometimes I'm afraid you're going to reason yourself out of a truly fine match and will come to regret it later."

"I'll probably accept him," confessed Charlotte. "I do like him. He's the only one of all my *prétendants* I think I could really consider seriously."

With that Sister Marie said no more. She was fairly certain Charlotte would be marrying Treval in the near future, so she turned her attention to helping her other charges resolve their futures. She convinced Angelique to agree to see her ex-*prétendant,* who had been presenting himself at the convent every afternoon since the day of their disagreement, in the hopes of begging his former fiancée's forgiveness, and as the Ursuline anticipated, it didn't take much for the estranged couple to patch up their differences once they could talk things out. The banns for their wedding were announced immediately, and they were wed the following week.

Felicité, however, would not be swayed. She was firm in her decision to take the veil, so after long, soul-searching interviews with the girl, Sister Marie was convinced the latter was sincere in her resolve to enter the religious life, and set about obtaining the girl's acceptance in the Ursuline order as a postulant, as well as arranging restitution for her dowry with the *Compagnie.* Since the girl was to become a part of the much needed personnel at the convent, which the Company was also interested in developing to its fullest in the colony, the officials were content to waiver the expenses of having brought her to New Orleans and only asked that she return her dowry.

Meanwhile the three Sisters of Charity who had come to New Orleans with their group of Casquette Girls from Paris took their leave and embarked for France to take up their duties there once more. They spoke of perhaps returning that following year with more marriageable girls for the settlers, now that they had seen how sorely needed such women were in Louisiana.

When the *Compagnie* asked about the last girl on the list, Mlle. Charlotte Montier, Sister Marie assured them there should be no problem there, since she not only had many suitors to choose from, but seemed to be on the verge of accepting a very fine proposal.

Toward the end of February Charlotte went again to see Madelón. She was worried about her friend's health, especially now that the girl was *enciente.* Sister Marie was also concerned. Madelón had never been very strong and the hard voyage had left her in a considerably weakened condition. The Ursuline would have preferred the girl to have waited at least a few months longer before taking on the

124

extra burdens of marriage and childbearing. If only the child had taken a little more time to build up her resistance first. But the young couple had been so eager to begin their life together.

When Charlotte and Sister Marie arrived, they found Madelón in bed. The Pichous were glad someone from the convent had come, since they said they were beginning to worry about the girl being alone so much while they were downstairs tending the store. It seemed she couldn't keep anything down, and the midwife had warned that, although Madelón was only two months pregnant, she was giving evidence of facing a difficult pregnancy and was in danger of losing the baby at any moment if she exerted herself in any way. The *accoucheuse* had ordered the girl to bed and warned that, if her orders were disobeyed, she would not be responsible for the survival of either the expectant mother or the child.

Sister Marie's first reaction was to bundle the girl up and take her back to the convent with them, but Madelón began to weep and insist she wanted to stay in her new home so her husband would find her there when he returned. The Pichous, however, were worried, since they were not only unable to give the young girl the attention she needed, but actually were looking for help themselves, now that their daughter had married and was no longer there to aid them as before. They confessed they had originally hoped Madelón would be able to lend a hand sometimes in the store in return for her food and lodging, and the girl had also liked the idea when such an arrangement had first been suggested. Now, however, Madelón was in need of help herself.

There were poignant signs in the room of how the young bride had made enthusiastic efforts to give the habitation those intimate touches that change a place from just another room to a home. Ruffled curtains framed the window, a matching canopy covered the bed, a large hook-rug lay by the fireplace. Madelón was so upset at the very thought of having to leave that Sister Marie deemed it prudent not to press her any further for the moment. But she was still very much concerned over what could be done to make the situation more comfortable for all those involved.

125

"Perhaps I could come and stay with Madelón for a while," Charlotte suddenly suggested, "and at the same time I might be able to help M. and Mme. Pichou out a little in their store, at least until Madelón's husband returns or she gets better."

"But you'll probably be getting married yourself within just a couple of weeks," replied Sister Marie, "so what good would that do?"

"I haven't really made up my mind yet," replied Charlotte. "I've just about decided to tell Pierre I'd like to wait a little longer before marrying anyone. I feel I need more time to get used to the idea."

"You'll probably lose him if you put him off again," warned Sister Marie.

"Then he wouldn't have loved me that much, anyway," observed Charlotte. "Six months or so isn't that long to wait when one's whole future is in the scales, is it? After all, we took almost that long just to get here, *n'est-ce pas?*"

The Ursuline nun was utterly bewildered.

"But what is it that you want then in life, Charlotte? Surely by postponing your marriage to M. Treval—and I assume that, if you marry anyone, it'll be to someone like him—no practical purpose will be served. And if you don't take a husband, what is left for you? A woman cannot survive here in this wilderness alone. Surely you realize that?"

"I could always follow in Felicité's footsteps and take the veil . . . that is, if I'm worthy enough."

"It's not just a question of worthiness, child. It's simply, as I told you before, I don't think that is your calling in life."

"Couldn't we just wait a few more months then and let the matter rest in God's hands?" the girl insisted. "Meanwhile I could be of service here with my friend who needs me and help the Pichous, as well."

"Mlle. Charlotte would be well taken care of here," interspersed Madame Pichou, her broad countenance lighting up as she saw the possibility of solving their immediate dilemma in the person of this delightful young girl who reminded her so much of her own daughter.

"Charlotte is under the protection of the church, and we must answer to the *Compagnie* and the king himself for

126

her safety and well-being until she is wed," Sister Marie reminded them.

"We'll chaperon her as though she were our own daughter," promised Madame Pichou. "If you could convince the authorities to let her stay here with us, at least until Madelón can be up and around again, we'd be eternally grateful, and I'm sure I speak for Madelón as well as myself, don't I, child?"

She turned to Madelón for confirmation, and the young girl nodded with tear-filled eyes. "Oh, yes, *Soeur* Marie. It would make such a difference if Charlotte could stay with me. We've always been like sisters, you know."

Sister Marie recognized that Madelón's emotional state was almost as important as her delicate physical condition at that moment.

"All I can do is promise to speak to the mother superior and the *Compagnie* about the matter and see how they receive such an unusual request," declared the nun. "I can't say anything definite at this time, nor am I making any promises, you understand? Meanwhile, I'll let Charlotte come back tomorrow to help you for a few hours and will send you some herbs I think might help settle Madelón's stomach a little."

Sister Marie didn't know whether relaxing the reins on Charlotte might stop her from chaffing so much against them. For all her docility in most things, the girl had an independent streak in her and could resist stubbornly when she felt she was being pressured into something she hadn't fully accepted yet in her heart. The Pichous were good, God-fearing people and should be acceptable chaperons for Charlotte. As for poor little Madelón, Charlotte's presence might indeed make all the difference to the girl at this difficult time. If Treval loved Charlotte, he would have to learn sooner or later how to handle that rebellious spirit of hers.

From all evidence, Charlotte had already decided in her heart to accept the Creole, but only wanted a little more time to enjoy her newly found freedom—to savor just a little longer the feeling of being her own mistress and able to choose as she pleased. It was a chimera, of course, as the child would soon learn, for none of us can ever really completely control that tangle of threads that make up our destinies. But in one thing Charlotte was right—it was probably best to leave her future in the hands of the master weaver, *le Bon Dieu.*

Chapter XXI

Charlotte stood behind the counter of the Pichous' general store, absent-mindedly straightening the bolts of linen and bobbinet stacked on display. Saturday mornings were usually busy, and she was glad to have a few minutes to collect her thoughts.

She had enjoyed the independence of that past week. It was good to feel needed and earn her own keep. Sister Marie had had a difficult time at first convincing the mother superior and the *Compagnie* to let her leave the confines of the convent. The Rev. Mother Mary of St. Augustine and the company authorities were all amazed that Mlle. Montier still hadn't made her choice. A pretty girl had a right to be finicky, they supposed, but she certainly had enough suitors to pick from. So much hemming and hawing was absurb. The girl was giving herself too many airs, they said, and needed a good talking to.

Sister Marie tried to defend her favorite, pointing out it would only be a temporary arrangement until Madelón's baby was born. After all, the girl wasn't refusing to marry. She was only asking for a little more time, nothing more.

Such an attitude, however, still seemed highly irregular. A representative of the *Compagnie* spoke to Charlotte, trying to find out if she was dissatisfied with anything in particular. The mother superior also interviewed her at length. They all wanted to know what the problem was.

Charlotte found it difficult to put into words. She couldn't tell them, of course, that she had not come to Nouvelle Orléans just to get married, that actually she had come fleeing from matrimony, that she had hoped to find some measure of freedom from a past in which she had only known subjection.

Although she was eighteen now, Charlotte was the first to admit she was still very much a child where men were concerned. Until only a year and a half ago, when she had gone to live with her aunt, she had really not come in contact with anyone of the opposite sex. Behind the cloistered walls of the convent, men had seemed mysterious creatures to be avoided at all costs until the moment of wedlock. The selection of a future husband had been equally vague. She had not given it much thought and might have accepted the customary procedure of letting her guardian do the choosing for her, if the man her aunt had selected had not been so completely repulsive.

Sooner or later she must choose, of course. A woman needed a man to protect her, especially here in the New World, but would it be fair to wed a man while there was still doubt in her heart? How could she get through life tied to someone she didn't love? What about that long chain of minutes and hours that make up each day of ordinary living?

Her friends didn't seem to have such thoughts. Was she so different from them?

Madelón's constant nausea had improved somewhat, now that Charlotte was giving her Sister Marie's herb teas. The *accoucheuse*, a widow with a tangled mop of silver-grey hair that resembled the moss Charlotte had seen hanging from trees in the swamplands, had stopped by to check on her patient and found her better, but she still cautioned that, under no circumstances, was Madelón to get up and move around, for it would surely provoke a miscarriage. The old woman also left more herbs for the girl to take in small doses every few hours, so Charlotte was kept busy running up and down the stairs most of the day tending to her friend's needs, while still trying to help the Pichous in their store.

The elderly couple was not only grateful to have the

129

young girl there to lighten their load, but welcomed her company as well. Charlotte, with her ready smile and winning ways, had won them over completely. There were times when she reminded them of their own girl.

Charlotte was given a small room on the upper floor between the Pichous' large bedroom and Madelon's room, but it was finally decided it would be best to put her cot in her friends's room, at least as long as Ansleau was not in town, since it would be easier to attend Madelón that way, if she should call out for something during the night.

Charlotte's presence had done much to lift Madelón's spirits. Her lighthearted manner had always had a positive effect on her more timorous friend. Now that the latter was alone and in such delicate health, she was even more prone to spend the long hours of her confinement fretting over the fact that her young husband was off wandering around the waterways of Louisiana while rumors of Indian unrest were increasing with each passing day. Charlotte and the Pichous tried to keep any upsetting news from her, but the girl had already heard enough during the first two months she had been living there, before her pregnancy had confined her to her room, to make her worry about young Ansleau's safety. It was only thanks to Charlotte's reassurances and constant efforts to keep Madelón's mind off her husband's possible danger that the poor girl was not more ill than she was.

Of course, business had picked up considerably since Charlotte had begun to help out in the store. And why not, with the town's last eligible Casquette Girl to be found there? Some of the suitors who had first approached her at the convent had followed her to her new domicile; other new ones had come, as well. The Pichous were very strict, however, about no loitering, so the young men would go in rather timidly, browse around, and then buy some trifling thing, just to have an excuse to say a few words to her. She had heard so many proposals of marriage now that she knew what was going to be said before the words were spoken. They had lost much of their meaning for her. As some hopeful admirer would press his suit, she would find herself only half listening, while she tried to visualize how it might be to spend the rest of her life with that near stranger standing there before her.

Out of all those who had actively courted her, there was still only one who really interested her. Her pulse quickened when she thought of Pierre. He should be returning soon, and she would be glad to see him, but she dreaded his reaction when he found her at the Pichous and learned of her plans to stay there until Madelón could be up and around again. There was an intensity about him she liked, yet at the same time feared.

Of course, if money and position were to be considered, as Aunt Germaine had always preached, Pierre would easily win over just about any male in the colony. Most of her admirers were good, hardworking planters, merchants, or woodsmen. Pierre, on the other hand, was an aristocrat. The prospect of living the elegant life of a lady of high standing in the community was tempting in itself, but Charlotte could honestly say that what appealed to her most was Pierre himself. It was not easy to say no to someone like him.

A tall, uniformed officer stood silhouetted in the sunlit doorway. Almost filling the low-beamed entrance, his striking figure set off to advantage the black leather boots that reached past his knees and the blue coat with its red and gold trimming that spanned his well-developed frame. He walked towards her with an easy gait, suggesting agility as well as self-assurance.

"*Bon jour,* mademoiselle," he greeted her. "What a pleasure it is to see that pretty face of yours again!"

There was the hint of a smile in the friendly blue eyes that looked down at her.

"I—I'm sorry, monsieur, but you have me at a disadvantage," stammered Charlotte, feeling suddenly self-conscious beneath the openness of his gaze. "Have we met before?"

"I had flattered myself that you might remember me, mademoiselle."

"Forgive me, monsieur, perhaps at the convent . . . there were so many . . ."

The smile in his eyes began to spread oper his countenance. "Yes, I'm sure there were! But in the swamplands . . ."

Charlotte lifted her hazel eyes and dared to look more closely at the clean-shaven, suntanned face above her. There was something familiar about that handsome, bold-featured countenance.

"Oh, *non*! It's Captain Dubair!" she exclaimed, unable to relate this image with the one she had held of him until that moment.

"But yes, it is, Captain Charles Dubair, *sans* beard and *sans* buckskins, but still ready to serve you in whatever way I can."

Charlotte couldn't take her eyes off his smiling face, and he seemed to be enjoying her amazement immensely.

"But you—you look so different," she faltered. "I—I didn't recognize you!"

He laughed at her confusion. "I admit that as soon as I returned to town this morning and heard you were still un-married, I took pains to shave off my beard and put on my best finery in a desire to make myself as presentable as possible before coming here to see you, but I must say I didn't expect you wouldn't even recognize me!"

"I'm sorry, *Capitaine*. Of course I remember you! It was only the surprise of seeing you dressed so differently that momentarily stunned me." She hoped her voice would not betray just how much she had remembered him . . . the many nights she had lain awake recalling the feel of his arms around her, the brush of his beard against her cheek . . . How many times she had looked at the bruises on her arms, watching them fade away, almost with sadness!

"I've thought of you often since we parted on the docks some three months ago," Dubair confessed, noting how her simple, golden-brown gown with its tightly laced bodice and modest froth of white lace at its neckline set off her magnificent honey-colored hair and eyes. To say he had thought of her during those past months was quite an un-derstatement. All the way up the Mississippi to the Illinois country, he had not been able to get her out of his mind. This little slip of a girl with her enormous golden eyes and bouncing brown curls had wormed her way into his thoughts until she had reached the core of him. Everything had seemed to remind him of her. He would be parleying with the Indians and would suddenly find himself recalling

132

how he had held her close to him and told the Choctaw she belonged to him. And as he had made his way up the river, the memory of those other days, when he had sat so close to her in the *pirogue* kept coming back to haunt him. Sometimes he could even recall the odor of the sachet she must have kept in that little *cassette* of hers . . . Most of all, he had relived time and again that moment when they had stood alone in the swamps, almost as one. The thought of how sweet and lingering that unfinished kiss would have been, if the nun hadn't called at that moment, had not let him sleep for many a night.

At first he told himself he had been without a woman too long. When he arrived at the Illinois settlement, he had deliberately taken up with the most tempting armful he could find. A few tumbles with a willing wench skilled in the arts of love should have knocked out all memories of a silly little convent girl who still believed in dragons and trembled like a leaf if you so much as touched her.

But when he had awakend that next morning, the emptiness inside him had been all the greater. His yearning, if anything, had only increased. He had to recognize that he wanted something more now than just an occasional night of carousing with a woman who meant nothing to him. He hadn't realized, however, just how true that was until he had met this girl. All the way back to New Orleans, as he poled down the river, he had continued to think of her, but a part of him had dreaded seeing her again, for he was certain she had married by now.

When he had arrived in New Orleans that morning and asked his friends about the *filles à la cassette*, hoping to learn what had happened to her, Dubair couldn't believe his ears when they told him that, except for one who had decided to take the veil, the prettiest Casquette Girl was the only one who had not made her decision yet. The little coquette—feeling her oats and then taking over the reins! But thank God she had!

Without stopping to think, he had hurriedly washed and shaven and put on his city clothes in order to seek her out at once. He wouldn't be a fool this time. *Le bon Dieu* had given him this second chance, and he wasn't going to run the risk of losing her again. Now here she was, standing

133

before him, even more lovely than he had been picturing her all those months. The lilt of that oft-remembered voice was music to his ears.

"I hope you didn't have a bad trip upriver, *Capitaine*," she was saying. "That is, I hope you had no dangerous encounters with Indians or any snakes or monsters and the like?"

He was pleased over her concern. "Oh, I guess you could say I had a few narrow escapes, *ma petite*, but here I am, thank God, and none the worse for it."

"They say the Indians to the north of the city are showing more signs of hostility. I—I was afraid you might have had trouble with them."

"Frankly, that was one of the motives of my mission," admitted Dubair. "Fortunately I'm rather well known by most of the tribes that live along the Mississippi, and the majority of them seem to trust me a little more than they do most white men. At least they are usually willing to talk to me, although I'm not always sure what they say is the whole truth or simply what they wish me to know at that moment. But enough of *politique indienne!* I've had my fill of that these past three months! I'm glad to be back now and would prefer to hear about you, mademoiselle. They tell me you haven't married yet. I hope I haven't been misinformed."

While they had been talking, Madame Pichou had come out from the storeroom in the back, and Charlotte could feel the grey-haired woman's eyes staring curiously at her and the captain. She feared her chaperon would soon be coming over to cut their conversation short.

"There's nothing much to tell," she replied rather timidly. "I simply haven't been able to make up my mind yet. I know I'm probably foolish to feel as I do, but I think such a decision shouldn't be made in haste."

"And you're right, of course, mademoiselle," agreed Dubair, "although you must admit such an attitude among those of your sex is unfortunately not very common, especially in these parts. From what I could glean around town this morning, you're well on the way to becoming a legend in the short time you've graced our colony."

The captain noted with secret pleasure how she was

brushing back with an impatient hand that rebellious curl of hers, which every now and again had a way of escaping from her cap. How often he had recalled that gesture of hers, as he had made his way through the lonely wilderness.

"You give my silly vacillations too much importance, *Capitaine*," Charlotte protested.

"Then you're not married. But—but perhaps you're engaged?" He tried to keep his voice light and conversational, hoping to conceal just how important her replies really were to him.

"I'm considering . . . no, not really . . . not yet."

"It's hard to understand how you weren't the first to wed," confessed Dubair. "Surely you're the prettiest girl to have landed in these parts in many a year. Don't you want to get married?" He checked himself hastily and added, "I'm sorry, little one, I don't mean to pry. I have no right—I'm sorry."

"Oh, I'll be marrying soon, I guess," she replied. "It's just so difficult to choose. I'm sure I'm much too particular!"

"And well you might be. But then, so much the better for me that you haven't wed yet, for if I may be so bold—I'd like to throw my hat into the ring along with those of your countless other admirers."

Charlotte was taken aback. This was a development she hadn't anticipated. The captain's bid for her acceptance of him as a suitor left her at a loss for words. The emotions within her were churning wildly. Suddenly thoughts of Pierre loomed up before her.

At that moment Madmae Pichou waddled up to them. What the latter lacked in height was more than compensated for by her imposing width. The congenial storekeeper and her husband knew Dubair and liked him, but she remembered her promise to Sister Marie always to keep an aura of propriety around the young girl who had been placed in her charge.

"Ah, *Capitaine*," she greeted him with a broad smile on her round face. "It's good to see you in town. We're glad you've come back safely to us again. And what can we do for you? Is there something you want?"

135

Her sharp eyes had already told her the answer to her last question, but she had to remind him as discreetly as possible that Charlotte was still as well chaperoned under this roof as she had been at the convent, so he would not get the wrong impression and think he could take liberties with the girl.

"Bon jour, Madame," smiled Dubair, secretly lamenting the interruption, but understanding the good woman's position. "I came here to see Mlle. Montier, whom you may remember I had the pleasure of escorting to New Orleans from Balize a few months ago. I was eager to know how she had fared since her arrival here. I haven't been in town, you know, since that day I left her and her companions on the docks."

"Ah, yes, *Capitaine,* and we have missed you. I hope you had a good trip and bring us good news from up north."

"More or less, at least for the moment."

"Thank God for that!" exclaimed Madame Pichou, crossing herself fervently. "And may it remain so!"

"Now that I'm here," continued Dubair, "I'd like to get a little more tobacco for my pipe, if it isn't too much trouble."

"Of course, *Capitaine.* Give me your pouch and I'll fill it for you." She withdrew for a moment, and Dubair took it as a sign of her favor that she hadn't sent Charlotte to go instead. Quickly he seized that brief moment to press his suit further.

"You haven't answered me, Mademoiselle. Could I hope for some opportunity to see you again in the near future?"

"You know where to find me, *Capitaine,*" she faltered. "I'm here all the time now, at least for the moment, since I'm taking care of my friend Madelón—you may remember her, the pale blonde girl? She—she's not well and her husband is out of town. The Pichous need help, too, so the nuns have given their permission for me to stay here for a few months."

"Now don't play possum with me, *ma petite,*" chided Dubair. "You know very well what I'm asking. I don't know how to be a bashful suitor. Like you, I may take a little more time than some in coming to a decision when I think something is important enough to merit careful deliberation, but once I've made up my mind, I'm not one to hang around in corners. What I'm saying is I'd like to court you, *ma petite* . . . that is, if you'll let me."

She was so flustered that he feared his approach had perhaps been too bold, or worse yet, that she was not interested and didn't know how to tell him so.

"Of course, I realize you have to know me a lot better," he added quickly. "I'm not presuming to ask you to marry me yet. All I want is for an *entrée de la maison*—an opportunity to see you, to court you. We can talk about the future later. But rest assured, mademoiselle, my intentions are serious."

"I—I don't quite know what to say, *Capitaine*. You have taken me completely by surprise!" protested Charlotte. Even as she toyed with the idea of what it might be like to have the captain as a *prétendant*, she could feel the gold chain around her neck burning into her flesh, as Pierre's dark passionate eyes seemed to be glaring accusingly at her in the midst of her confusion.

"I had hoped the Pichous might give me permission to call on you," continued the captain. "If it's agreeable to you, I'd like to begin by requesting the honor of your company at the governor's reception this Tuesday night. As you probably know, Commander Perier plans to give a Mardi Gras Ball the day before *Carême* begins, and I'd consider it an honor to be able to escort you once more—but this time to a social affair instead of through the marshes of Louisiana. I'd like an opportunity to show you that there's another side to that brutish *coureur de bois* you've known until now."

When he saw how she still hesitated, he drew back and exclaimed suddenly in dismay, "*Mon Dieu!* Don't tell me I'm too late! Are you already spoken for?"

"No . . . I . . ."

"Then have you already accepted someone else's invitation to the ball?" he pressed anxiously.

"Not really," she had to admit, trying to sort out the thoughts that were rushing through her mind. Pierre hadn't asked her yet. He wasn't even in the city. But he would probably be returning any day now and would naturally expect her to go with him. Until now he knew she preferred him to all the others, so his attitude had become one of self-assurance . . . perhaps possessive would be a better word. He had already concluded she would sooner or later be his. If she continued to let him monopolize her completely, he would take it as confirmation that she had definitely decided to marry him, and she wasn't ready for that—at least not yet.

She heard Dubair pleading with her again to let him take her to the ball. This man was no stranger to her. To the contrary, he had been in her thoughts often enough since they had met. On more than one occasion he had saved her life. He had even held her in his arms, and she had liked it. Something inside her wouldn't let her refuse him.

"Perhaps, *Capitaine*," she heard herself replying in a voice she scarcely recognized as her own, as Madame Pichou joined them with the filled tobacco pouch in her plump hand.

Dubair immediately seized the moment to ask the storekeeper if she would grant Charlotte permission to go to the ball with him.

"Charlotte is still under the protection of the Ursulines," replied Madame Pichou, as she handed him his fresh supply of tobacco. "If you wish to have any formal relations with her, I suggest you speak to the nuns about it. For my part, I have no objections."

The captain turned back to Charlotte, who was still bewildered by the force of the tide that had suddenly swept her up and was carrying her along to she knew not where. She couldn't even understand her own feelings at that moment. She had just about decided to accept Pierre when he returned, yet here she was saying yes to Dubair! Of course, the captain was only asking her to go to a ball this Tuesday, and not to make an appointment with a priest to be married. She looked down at the deep waves of his thick chestnut-brown hair, neatly tied at the nape of his neck, as he bent over her hand and took his leave, promising to speak to the nuns about the ball before the day was over. The moment seemed unreal. It was difficult to relate this tall, uniformed officer with the bearded scout she had known in the marshlands.

Chapter XXII

It was a bright Sunday morning, typical of the first days of March, with the warmth of the coming spring already creeping into the chill of the dying winter. Sister Marie came by in the simple black coach of the Ursulines to take Charlotte to mass. The nun had brought with her one of the Negro slaves from the convent to lend Charlotte and her friends a welcome hand for a few hours, so the Pichous were delighted to be able to accompany them to mass without fear of leaving Madelón unattended.

After church, the Ursuline returned to the Pichous to check the ailing girl more carefully. The herbs seemed to be having their effect, and Sister Marie found her much improved, able to eat some solid food now, and much stronger than only a few days before.

The Pichous insisted that the nun stay and partake of the noonday meal with them, and the latter accepted, for after having spoken to Dubair that previous afternoon, she felt Charlotte might well feel the need of some counseling.

As Sister Marie had told Dubair, when he had asked for permission to court Charlotte, the final decision would have to lie in Charlotte's hands, and she had discreetly tried to warn him that there were other candidates in the picture, including one of extreme wealth and position in the colony.

The captain, of course, could hold his own with any of the girl's suitors, even Treval. He was well received in all levels of the community; had a good background and the colony owed him a great deal. With his heroic exploits over the years to lend color to his already imposing good looks and reputation for straightforwardness, he was regarded as quite a catch among the ladies of New Orleans.

Sister Marie had been even more impressed with the captain's qualifications when he had also confided to her his plans to build a plantation on the outskirts of town, with the idea of settling down there just as soon as the Indian situation had become more stable and he could turn leadership of the *coureurs de bois* over to someone else.

Although Dubair hadn't thought it prudent to go into the details of why he had run away from France as a boy, since he could hardly have expected the Ursuline nun to sympathize with his innate distaste for monastery life, he had gone on to explain how he had come from a well-to-do family in Rouen and, despite the fact that his boyhood rebellion had incurred his father's wrath for several years afterwards, he had eventually received the senior Dubair's blessing and, in time, even a small inheritance upon the latter's death. Although Dubair's oldest brother, as was the custom, had received the bulk of the family estate, the captain had managed to save some of his own earnings from his scouting services, which were in great demand in the territory, so, as he pointed out discreetly to Sister Marie, if all his assets were considered together, he really had a sizeable amount of money and property to his name and could look forward to what should be a very prosperous future. Under the circumstances, the nun felt she could hardly forbid him to court Charlotte, although Treval could probably offer the girl more immediate luxuries.

Then, too, Sister Marie recognized that, besides Dubair's ample financial qualifications, he also had another point in his favor, for she had not been blind to the fact that he had been one of the few men who had managed to awaken some visible signs of interest in Charlotte. The nun had noted the attraction that had existed between the two on their trip upriver from Balize, and she recalled how wistful Charlotte had been those first few weeks after she and the captain had parted on the docks. Of course, Treval might have won an even firmer hold on the young girl's sentiments, but the Ursuline felt it only fair to let the captain

140

put in his bid for Charlotte's hand in marriage, now that he had declared his intentions were serious.

Sister Marie was doubly glad she had decided to stay on at the Pichous that afternoon, when Treval suddenly made his appearance. From the look of dismay on his face, it was quite evident he and Charlotte were going to have a lot to talk about. He had just come from the convent where he had immediately gone to visit her upon returning from his plantation, and could not hide his disapproval of the move she had made during his absence.

Poor Charlotte, thought Sister Marie. The child still had much to learn about men! The very qualities that had probably attracted her to Treval and Dubair in the first place could be dangerous when ignited. Neither the Creole nor the captain were men who could be aroused without sparks beginning to fly.

When Pierre asked permission to take Charlotte out for a promenade down the Rue Royal, which was only two blocks away from the Pichou dwelling, Sister Marie felt she could hardly refuse him. She could see how the young Creole, struggling to contain himself in their presence, was anxious to speak to Charlotte, so when he invited her to accompany them, as both courtesy and propriety dictated, the nun discreetly begged off, feigning more weariness than she actually felt. She sent the old Negro woman to accompany them instead, knowing the young couple would feel freer to talk to each other if the nun didn't go along.

Still dressed in her Sunday best, Charlotte tied a tiny white lace hood around her head and walked out rather nervously into the delightful afternoon with Pierre. The soft curls of her hair took on a golden sheen in the bright sunlight where they peeped out around the sides of her face. It felt good to be promenading through the heart of the city on the handsome Creole's arm, with her pink and blue flowered silk flowing loosely down her back in a long sweep of graceful folds, as it rustled gaily to the rhythm of her steps and the sway of the fashionable paniers and ruffled petticoats beneath it. For now that she was helping the Pichous in their business, the grateful storekeepers had insisted she choose whatever she needed from their stocks, and this ensemble had been her first selection.

141

People stared when she passed, for as Captain Dubair had said, she was fast becoming a legend in New Orleans.

Since it hadn't rained recently the street beneath the boarded *banquettes* where they walked were dry. The houses in that section of the city were well built, especially on Royal Street, one of the most aristocratic thoroughfares of New Orleans. Pierre's own townhouse was only a block away on Chartres. The dwellings here were either brick or a combination of upright joists filled between with mortar and then whitewashed. Their green shutters and doors were open to the bright afternoon warmth, and the pitched roofs of tile with their dormer-windowed attics added a certain charm to the street, which in some ways reminded Charlotte of Marseilles.

The people who sauntered by were as elegantly dressed as she and her escort. As always, Pierre cut a striking figure. His jewel-handled sword, seen through the slits of the stiffened skirts of his dark green velvet coat, swung jauntily at his side. The large black bow on the queue at the nape of his neck and the white jabot beneath his chin rounded out the angles of his face becomingly.

Except for a few polite phrases of no real consequence they walked in silence, saying nothing until they were seated in an exclusive little coffee shop and the waiter had brought them their order.

The old Negress, Deedee, who had followed directly behind them, sat off to one side, staring tactfully into space with placid, unseeing eyes.

"Charlotte, I must say I cannot approve of this new arrangement of yours," Treval blurted out. "I don't know what the good nuns could have been thinking of to have permitted you to take up residence away from the convent."

"Surely you can see I am helping a very dear friend who needs me very much at this moment," replied Charlotte.

"Your motives are to be commended, my dear, but couldn't you just go there a few hours a day and continue to live at the convent?"

"Madelón needs attention at all hours. Often the Pichous are downstairs and busy and can't even hear her when she calls. Then, at night, they're sleeping off in another room.

Also, they're old and need their rest. Madame Pichou isn't really too well herself sometimes."

"Then let them hire someone. They could even buy themselves a slave."

Charlotte smiled at her impetuous suitor's reasoning. "You don't realize what it is to be poor and alone, Pierre. Madelón and Jacques are just starting out. Even the Pichous are not in a position to take on anyone at the moment. Actually they had rented their daughter's old room to boarders in the hopes of not only getting a little extra money but some help around the place, as well."

Pierre sighed and tried to stifle the countless other arguments that occurred to him. He decided it might be better to go on to more important matters.

"*Está bien.* Helping your sick friend is one thing, but this tending store like a common shop girl! *Qué barbaridad!* You're gently born, Charlotte. There's nothing wrong with your coming to me as my wife out of a convent, but out of a general store! *Nunca!* This is madness! Whatever is *Soeur* Marie thinking of to let you lower yourself that way?"

"I can't see where doing a kindness to people in need could be criticized by anyone," protested Charlotte.

"A well-born lady simply doesn't do such things!" insisted her *prétendant.* "Let's look at this matter sensibly. If you wish, we can go ahead and be married and I'll send one of my servants over to care for your friends. *Voilà!* What do you say to that? It's all solved, *non?*"

"Pierre, please don't pressure me. Perhaps in a few months . . ."

"But you promised to give me your answer when I returned. I'd hoped we could begin making plans for the wedding today."

"I thought I could—I honestly did, but I find I can't. I really need a little more time."

The Creole's dark eyes flashed impatiently, but he tried to hold his temper in check in the hopes of perhaps gaining ground with her in the long run. "All right, then. Have it your way, Charlotte. We'll wait a little longer, if you're so set on it. But let's at least fix some definite date. We could still be formally engaged, *comprometidos.*"

"You—you don't understand," she replied, finding it even more difficult to convince him than she had anticipated. "I don't feel I'm ready to make any decision at all yet about my future. I need time, Pierre. After all, we really have only known each other a little over two weeks. I simply don't feel that's enough."

Charlotte took another sip of her hot chocolate as she tried to avoid the scrutiny of those dark, probing eyes. There was a moment's silence. Then Pierre sighed and his look softened. "I realize I haven't attended you as well as I should have these past two months," he conceded. "But I promise you, *mi cielo*, I won't go off any more now. We'll let the matter drop for today. This Tuesday we can talk more. Governor Perier is having a ball, and it will be one of the biggest social events of the season. You'll go with me, of course?"

Charlotte set her cup down and dared not lift her eyes.

"I—I'm sorry, but I can't."

"Don't worry, I'll talk to *Soeur* Marie. I'm sure she'll give her permission."

"It's not that. It's just that I already have an invitation to go."

Treval had placed some coins on the table to cover the bill and was beginning to rise, but at Charlotte's unexpected words, he sat back down, his eyes wide with disbelief.

"You *what*?"

"I—I accepted an invitation to go just yesterday," she confessed, feeling like a child caught out of school.

"Aha! Now I see it all! At last the truth comes out! There's someone else, *non*? That's what's at the bottom of all these evasions of yours!" His hand went instinctively to the hilt of his sword. "And who is this newcomer? How long have you known him?"

"He—he's not really a newcomer," murmured Charlotte. "I've known him as long—longer than you. He's the captain of the scouts who escorted me and my companions from Balize to New Orleans."

"That mercenary? Do you mean to tell me my rival is a backwoodsman?"

"You're being deliberately unkind, Pierre! Captain Du-

144

bair is as well born as you are!" chided Charlotte. "And the work he does in protecting us here in the colony is to be commended, not belittled!"

"*Vaya!* How you defend him! You love this *capitaine*, then?"

"I'd hardly consider an invitation to a ball a proposal of marriage."

"But he *has* proposed?"

"I'll not lie to you. He speaks as if he's contemplating it."

"And are *you* contemplating it, as well?" His whole being bristled with rage. Charlotte had never seen him in such a state before. His reaction was even more passionate than she had anticipated. Pierre had been jealous enough over a few of her other suitors, but this hostility toward Dubair was so fierce it frightened her, perhaps because the Creole sensed that in the captain he had a more formidable rival than the others.

"I told him what I told you. I need time to consider such an important step and cannot promise myself to anyone at the moment. I'd like to know both of you better . . . and myself, as well. I must say, however, that Captain Dubair seemed a lot more understanding."

Pierre suddenly went limp. He was a picture of dejection, his proud shoulders sagging, his chest sunken. He could feel her slipping through his fingers.

"I've lost you!" he groaned, and there was such pain in his face that Charlotte's heart went out to him. "I curse the day I had to leave you! Only a few weeks and I've lost you! *Dios mío!*"

She reached out impulsively and touched his arm. "My feelings for you haven't changed, Pierre," she said gently. "The fact that I also esteem Captain Dubair takes nothing from you. Please try to understand. He saved my life on more than one occasion—"

"And for that I'm grateful to him," admitted Treval grudgingly. "But surely you realize, Charlotte, he was only doing his duty. After all, he was being paid to protect you. Don't forget that."

"It would be very ungrateful of me to dismiss his gallantry with such callous reasoning," retorted Charlotte.

"Tell me the truth, Charlotte, what do you feel for this *capitaine*?"

"I'm not sure. I—I suppose you might say that . . . at this moment I look upon him as a very dear friend . . . even as I do you, Pierre."

"Friend? *Dios Mío*! Friend! That's all I am to you?"

"Perhaps more," Charlotte admitted. "But please don't continue to press me this way, Pierre. When you act so violently you confuse me more than ever."

"But how long do you expect to keep me dangling this way? You're driving me wild, Charlotte!"

"I've told you . . . a few months, perhaps. I don't want to be unfair or hurt you, Pierre. If you feel you cannot wait . . ."

He sighed in resignation, accepting the inevitable as they finally rose and left the coffee shop. "I don't like any of this, Charlotte. You're making things very difficult for me and, I dare say, others as well, by dragging things out like this."

She lowered her head uneasily. "I'm really thinking of you, too," she said softly. "Would you want me to marry you while I still had doubts?"

For a moment she thought he was going to seize her in his arms right there on the street.

"God is my witness, Charlotte, yes! I'd marry you even if you hated me! I love you that much! Can't you see we could be happy? You love me, too, I think, only you're too young and inexperienced to realize it, that's all. Say yes, and I promise you'll never regret your decision."

She toyed with the lace furbelows filling in the flare of the pagoda sleeve covering her elbow. "Please, Pierre, don't begin again . . ."

He heaved a sigh of exasperation, and they began to walk down the street once more. Her heart was suddenly filled with a wave of affection for him. She felt a little guilty now about having accepted Dubair's invitation. It had hurt Pierre so.

"I suppose you will continue to show yourself in that store, too," he mumbled, as they headed back in the direction of the Pichous'. "I'm sure half of the men who go

146

there these days only do so to gape at you. I don't like all those ruffians ogling you like that!"

Charlotte smiled. "Don't exaggerate, Pierre!"

"But if you're to marry me . . ."

Now it was Charlotte who was losing her patience.

"I haven't definitely said I will yet."

"Sometimes I think you're deliberately trying to torment me!" he exclaimed.

"You're not being fair, Pierre. After all, I—we're not really betrothed. I'm still free to come and go as I please, and you'll certainly not win me by trying to dictate to me this way."

"All this is a game to you, isn't it? I dare say it flatters you to see how miserable you can make a man. Tell me, do you play such games with your hero Dubair as well?"

Charlotte's hazel eyes deepened, and she stepped back as if he had struck her.

"You have no right to talk to me that way!" she protested angrily, resentment suddenly replacing the tenderness she had felt for him a few moments earlier.

"And you have no right to play with a man's affections the way you're doing with mine!" he retorted, the rage and frustration that he felt welling up within him.

"You don't have to tolerate me one more minute then," she assured him, weary of the bickering. "Please take me home at once." She turned on her heel and began to walk hurriedly on.

Pierre caught her arm anxiously, realizing he had let his temper carry him beyond the point of discretion. Even in his anger, he knew he didn't want to lose her.

"Charlotte, wait," he pleaded. "I didn't mean to offend you. It's only that I love you so . . ."

A man was coming toward them along the boardwalk, but she paid little heed, scarcely lifting her eyes from the crudely hewn planks beneath her feet. Pierre followed behind her, desperate now, pulling at the lace cuffs on her bell-like sleeves, as he tried to detain her a moment longer. At last she paused and turned her head back over her shoulder.

"Either escort me properly or I shall go on alone," she told him icily.

Before Pierre could reply, a voice asked, "Is this man annoying you, mademoiselle?"

She looked up in amazement to see Dubair standing before her, his suntanned hand poised expectantly on his sword.

"May I be of assistance?" he asked her again.

Charlotte saw Pierre's dark eyes glower threateningly, but she drew her arm away from his grip and addressed Dubair.

"Please, *Capitaine*, I'd appreciate it if you'd see me home."

"Has this gentleman offended you?" The captain's hand was restless on the hilt of his sword, as he swept an appraising glance at Pierre. So this was the rival Sister Marie had warned him about when he had spoken with her at the convent yesterday.

Charlotte shook her head firmly.

"Please, *Capitaine*, I ask only that you escort me home," she repeated. Then she turned to where Pierre stood taut and quivering like a bowstring ready to spring into action at any second. "Please, Pierre, thank you for the little outing, but I think we should end it here. Perhaps when you're in a better mood we can take up our conversation again."

Dubair offered her his arm, but Pierre stayed him.

"Monsieur . . ."

The captain stood his ground and put his hand over Charlotte's where she had laid it on his arm. The two men glared at each other across her lace-covered head, their knuckles whitening over their respective rapiers.

"Messieurs, please," she implored. "Don't make a scene!"

The Creole paused yet another moment, then let his detaining hand drop and bowed stiffly.

"*Está bien*. If that's the way you want it, Charlotte, I bid leave of you both. Mademoiselle . . . *Capitaine*."

Enveloped in cold formality, he turned on his heel and walked sullenly away.

148

Chapter XXIII

Charlotte stood watching Pierre's tall, straight back retreating from her until he turned the corner. For a moment she had the urge to call him back. Pierre was so proud, so intense about everything! She hadn't meant to humiliate him. But that was the danger of bickering. A tide of words can often sweep you up into a tumultuous sea of confusion and suddenly dash you against some unexpected rock before you even realize where you have been going.

"Are you all right, *ma petite*?" she heard the captain asking her a second time.

Charlotte turned apologetically to Dubair. "I—I'm sorry I've imposed myself upon you, *Capitaine*," she murmured, feeling embarrassed now by the whole incident.

"Think nothing of it, mademoiselle. I'm glad I came along when I did. I only wish you had permitted me to teach the fellow a lesson."

"Ah, *non, Capitaine*, you don't understand. Treval is—is really quite a gentleman. It's only that he—he's so very jealous."

A smile flickered in Dubair's blue eyes.

"Then I can sympathize with him, mademoiselle," he declared meaningly.

They began walking once more in the direction of the store.

"He—he was very upset because I'd just told him about the Governor's Ball . . . that I was going with you."

"Ah, I see."

"M. Treval has a quick temper. I doubt he meant what he said."

Charlotte was already regretting her dismissal of Pierre. He was so proud . . . perhaps he might never try to see her again!

"Are you his intended?" asked Dubair.

"No—he would like—no."

"Then what right does he have to be so possessive? I'd say you are too easy on him, mademoiselle."

Charlotte smiled a little sadly and shrugged her shoulders. "He says he loves me, and I've heard it said that love excuses many things."

"I hope mademoiselle is as well disposed toward all those who chance to fall in love with her," murmured Dubair, and she cast a curious glance up at him to see whether his face matched the tone of his voice.

"The truth is, I was on my way to see you," continued the captain. "I spoke with Sister Marie yesterday after I left you, and she gave me permission to take you to the ball."

"Yes, I know," replied Charlotte, as she lifted her skirts slightly to cross over to the other *banquette*, while Dubair held her arm to steady her. "Sister Marie is at the Pichous' now. That's her servant who's with me," and she gestured towards the Negress who continued to walk discreetly behind them, her ebony face as expressionless as ever, as if she hadn't even noticed that Charlotte had changed escorts along the way.

"M. Treval isn't always that way," she assured Dubair. "Today was the first time I've ever had cause to be annoyed with him. I've never seen him so upset before."

"Perhaps because it's the first time you've had occasion to cross him," suggested the captain.

"Actually, I suppose he's been quite patient with me until now," sighed Charlotte, dangling her head like a repentant child.

Dubair smiled down at her. She was so refreshingly open and without wiles. It worried him, however, to see such signs of genuine affection whenever she spoke of the Creole.

"I'd say you're doing a very fine job of defending him, mademoiselle," he remarked. "You almost make me wish I were in his shoes."

"It's strange you should say that," observed Charlotte, "since he was just accusing me of defending you too much to him!"

The captain laughed.

When Charlotte's friends saw her returning on the captain's arm, they could scarcely hide their amazement. Although Sister Marie gave Dubair a friendly greeting, she immediately turned to Charlotte with raised eyebrows and asked, "And Pierre?"

"I don't know," replied Charlotte rather sheepishly. "We argued, and the captain happened along, so I asked him to take me home."

The nun put her hand bewilderedly to her coifed head. "Really, Charlotte, sometimes you overwhelm me! I never know what to expect next from you."

Nevertheless, she turned again to the captain and thanked him for having seen the girl safely home.

Dubair felt a little uneasy beneath so many curious stares, so he only lingered long enough to have a final word with Charlotte. Although the Pichous urged him to join them for a cup of *café au lait* or *chocolat*, he politely declined, saying he still had to stop off at the governor's mansion before returning to the barracks, since he didn't feel it was the moment to extend his call. It was evident they were eager to get Charlotte alone to question her about what happened that afternoon.

As they descended the stairs to the street door and walked through the closed store, Charlotte added her own thanks to those of Sister Marie's.

"It was a privilege, mademoiselle," the captain assured her. "I was glad to happen by just when you needed me. But I wish I could be seeing you again soon."

"The ball is only two days away," she reminded him. "You'll see me then."

"But that seems so far away. Perhaps I could come by for you tomorrow morning or afternoon and show you some of the city . . . our new levee, the palisades . . . ?"

Charlotte smiled at the captain's boyish eagerness. It was an aspect of him she hadn't suspected. "I'm afraid I'll be rather busy tomorrow, *Capitaine*," she replied.

"Then perhaps you might care to go to the theatre tonight? There's still time. I could arrange to return for you later on this evening. I'll wager you haven't seen the troupe that came over on the boat from Paris last month. They'll be giving their last performance before Lent tonight."

Charlotte laughed and held up her hand to stop his onslaught.

"Mon Dieu, Capitaine! I see you're indeed a campaigner!" she interrupted him merrily. Dubair paused, somewhat abashed, and then he, too, began to laugh.

"I'm sorry, *ma petite.* I didn't mean to surround you," he apologized, "but all these months away from you have made me hungry for the sight of you!"

"You'll be seeing me soon enough," she smiled. "I've had enough outings and excitement for one day, and tomorrow I really do have a lot to do. Monday is a busy day in the store, and I'll have to prepare for the ball."

The disappointment in Dubair's suntanned face was so evident that she hastened to add, "But I might accept your invitation to see more of the town later on . . . perhaps after the ball."

Their eyes met, and for a moment that same overwhelming current that had raced between them that day long ago in the swamplands began to stir once more.

Charlotte tore herself away from the intense gaze of Dubair's eyes and quickly opened the street door for him to leave. "Until—until the ball, then," she murmured, extending a rather shaky hand to him as a gesture of farewell.

Although there was as much fire melting the captain's ice-blue eyes at that moment as there had been in Pierre's darker, smoldering ones earlier that afternoon, the years of self-control that soldiering had required of Dubair stood him in good stead, as he took the tiny hand proffered him and kissed it with a little more fervor than etiquette would have requried.

"I'll call for you then around 7:30 Tuesday evening," he said, "if that's convenient?"

"Yes, *Capitaine,*" she agreed softly. "I—I'll be looking forward to seeing you again. And once more, thank you for your many attentions to me this afternoon."

She watched the captain walk down the street toward the

Place d'Armes. *Mon Dieu!* What was happening to her? First she hadn't wanted to think about marrying anyone, and now she was falling in love with *two* men! That independence she had longed for had brought with it far more complications that she had bargained for. It was good to have freedom of choice, but what use would that be if she couldn't make up her mind?

Sister Marie shook her hooded head in disapproval when Charlotte returned upstairs and related the events of that day. "*Mon Dieu*, Charlotte! You're so impulsive sometimes it frightens me. You'd better decide quickly between those two young men of yours, or you're going to have more trouble than you can handle. It's a pity, too, for they're both good men. Prolonging this situation can only lead to bitter rivalry between them."

"I'm afraid it's already too late," admitted Charlotte. "No matter whom I choose now one is going to be hurt. I realized that today. But I don't want to hurt either one of them! Oh, *Soeur* Marie, what shall I do? I wish I were twins!"

"You must prefer one a little more than the other, *non?*" asked Madelón, who had been listening with a sympathetic ear to the girl's tale.

"When I'm with one I feel I belong with him. Then along comes the other, and it's the same thing all over again! Every time I think I might be able to make a decision, I end up changing my mind because I can't bring myself to hurt the other. I'm so confused! You can see why I feel I need more time. I certainly can't marry one feeling the way I do about the other, now can I?"

The Ursuline's head was spinning. Such romantic entanglements were not her specialty. "No one can choose for you, child," she said. "But I warn you, Treval and Dubair aren't men to lead on. Neither one is accustomed to losing, and I'm afraid you're going to have a powder keg of emotions exploding in your face one of these days, if you're not careful."

"That's the trouble with marriages for love," volunteered Madame Pichou with a sigh. "There's something to be said for quiet, businesslike matrimony."

153

Charlotte sat wide-eyed and bewildered, feeling suddenly inadequate to cope with the situation in which she found herself.

Sister Marie's heart went out to her, and she patted the young girl's hand in an effort to comfort her. "At least you're right about one thing, child. You shouldn't marry either one of them until you can do so without the other still clouding your thoughts."

Chapter XXIV

The next two days it was Charles Dubair who brightened Charlotte's thoughts.

By the time Tuesday arrived, she had surrendered herself to the festive mood of the Carnival celebrations all around her and was eagerly looking forward to the thrill of going to the governor's ball. There had been singing and dancing and feasting in the streets all day long, and since the Pichou dwelling was so near the main square, Charlotte and her friends found themselves in the heart of the merriment. The music and laughter wafted up to the second-story window while Charlotte, with the zealous help of Madame Pichou and Madelón, had gone through the complicated ritual involved in preparing for such an important social event.

Now the moment had come at last, but Charlotte still couldn't believe it. She literally floated into the ballroom on Dubair's arm.

The merrymaking of the revelers outside in the Place d'Armes, which the governor's mansion faced, faded as the strains of the orchestra in the salon drowned everything else out. With all the festivities going on around them, Charlotte hadn't expected their arrival to attract much attention, but as soon as the doorman announced them, every eye in the place turned in their direction.

A wave of curious whispers buzzed around the room as they saw her on the captain's arm. Just when everyone had about decided Treval would be the one, here she was with a new *prétendant*!

Charlotte felt the blood rushing hotly to her face as she felt their open scrutiny. She was glad now that Madame Pichou had taken her in hand and helped dress her for the occasion. As the only unmarried Casquette Girl left in the colony, Charlotte invited not only the admiring glances of every male in the room, but the critical eyes of the women as well, for she had the two most eligible bachelors in New Orleans vying for her favors!

How fortunate it had been, too, that Germaine had insisted on her packing one of the latter's Parisian gowns in her *cassette*. At the time, she couldn't imagine what she would be doing with so elegant a dress in the wilderness, but tonight she suddenly realized New Orleans had another, more luxurious side to it that she hadn't dreamed existed. A governor's ball in Nouvelle Orleáns, it seemed, could rival a court function at Versailles.

The pale green satin skirt of her gown flowed gracefully over the extra wide paniers that Madame Pichou had given her to wear under her petticoats, setting off to even greater advantage the diminutive pointed waist, while a large corsage of lace and tulle, matching the tufts on her short puff-sleeves, made a discreet but not entirely successful attempt to cover the bareness of the stylishly low-cut neckline.

Charlotte had fashioned a collarette of green velvet ribbon and lace to wear around her throat with the gold brooch her aunt had given her nestled in its center, but when Madelón had eagerly offered to contribute her one and only prized family possession—a long pearl necklace—Charlotte hadn't wished to offend her friend by refusing, so the women had finally hit upon the idea of gracefully draping the string of pearls from shoulder to shoulder across the front of her decolletage, catching the strands up in the center beneath the corsage of tulle, so that they gently followed the curve of her bosom, so well marked beneath the tight-fitting boned bodice.

155

Madame Pichou had also insisted on powdering the young girl's hair especially for the occasion, for as she explained, everyone was sure to be wearing their formal full-dress wigs. But those who knew Charlotte could tell at a glance she was wearing her own abundant hair. That unruly lock of hers still persisted in dipping over her forehead despite the rice powder and paste she had so energetically applied to it, and all the way to the governor's mansion, she had fretted over it, much to Dubair's amusement, for he secretly hoped she would never find a way to keep that adorable curl in its place. Personally, he didn't like the idea of covering such lovely hair with powder at all, but he realized that the formality of the occasion demanded it.

A fan was indispensable, and once again the Pichous' general store had come to the rescue with a tortoise-shell-handled one that showed a lovely garden scene painted in pastels on a silken background.

The captain led her proudly into the ballroom, somewhat surprised at himself, as he realized he was enjoying the stir they were creating. As a rule, he hated notoriety and social functions even more. But tonight he was showing off the woman he hoped would be his wife.

Strikingly handsome in his colorful uniform, the captain was a far cry from the bearded *coureur de bois* in his worn buckskins whom Charlotte had met on her arrival in the New World. His long black red-lined cape was thrown over his shoulders to reveal the royal blue knee-length coat with its *basques* folded back to allow his sword to hang more freely at his side and show off the white tight-fitting breeches and vest beneath. His high black boots shone brightly from the extra buffing he had had the boy at the barracks give them, and even the small crescent-shaped gorget of silver hanging on its chain amid his ruffled jabot had been given an additional polishing for the occasion.

Determined to show Charlotte he could be as elegant as that Creole aristocrat Treval, Dubair had even gone so far as to wear his hair fashionably powdered and caught back into a black *appendage* at the nape of his neck, so that his high gold-edged collar wouldn't be soiled. He hated the mess of all that rice powder and paste in his hair, but he didn't own a *perruque* and had no desire to invest in one, so he carried his black gold-trimmed tricorne under one arm in order not to disturb the "pigeon's wings" the barber had insisted on combing for him.

Although it was not his usual style to flaunt his decorations, he had decided at the last minute to wear two of the more important medals that had been bestowed upon him by the colonial government over the years. Women, he had noted, always seemed to be impressed by such accessories, and he knew he would have to play every card he had in his favor if he hoped to win Charlotte from her more ostentatious suitor.

Charlotte found it difficult to believe she was in a settlement only a little over a decade old. The gathering could have rivaled any of her aunt's elaborate parties back in Marseilles. A profusion of glittering jewels echoed the sparkle of the magnificent chandeliers ablaze with candles above them, and the generous skirts of the women, billowing over enormous paniers, had an undulating movement whenever they moved.

Beauty-patches were boldly displayed everywhere. Those tiny black stars and crescents, deliberately affixed in carefully studied locations, ran the gamut of feminine coquetry, from the "galant" on the cheek or the "impassioned" at the corner of the eye, to "la silencieuse" on the chin. Some of them even found their way into the cleavage of a bosom so bared that Charlotte had to look away to cover the embarrassment she felt. She was sorry, however, that she hadn't let Madame Pichou convince her to wear at least one such patch. How foolish she had been to be afraid of being conspicuous. The only woman at the ball without one, she was even more obvious now.

The men, not to be outdone, also wore their share of jewels, velvets, cloth of gold and brocades, with the tails of their fashionable frock coats stiffened out to balance the bell-shaped skirts of their companions. They, too, wore white wigs or had powdered their own hair, and some of the beaux of the town sported patches and carried bamboo or ivory canes topped by weirdly carved heads or tufts of lace to finish off their outfits.

Red-heeled shoes, that affectation used to denote nobil-

157

ity, were everywhere, and the odor of snuff and exotic perfumes hung heavily in the air.

Perier was a gracious host, and came up to greet Dubair personally as soon as he heard the captain's arrival announced. Despite the reputation the governor had earned as a stern commander, he was very amiable socially. In the brief time since he had taken office, he had done much not only to improve the city itself but to establish some semblance of law and order, as well. There was a police force now and vice was being punished severely. The slightest misdemeanor could lead to a hanging these days, but in a raw wilderness like this, men would run wild if not strongly curbed.

Madame Perier was especially charming as she flitted in and out among her guests, seeing to it that the servants kept everyone supplied with refreshments and that those who wished to dance were kept happy by the small orchestra that had been organized from among the town's musicians for the occasion.

Although the ball was being held in honor of the traditional Mardi Gras celebration—the Carnival that the colonists continued to observe annually on Shrove Tuesday, despite the distance from their mother country—the only thing that distinguished it from any other social affair was the distribution of colorful velvet or lace masks to the guests on their arrival. Soon the atmosphere became one of a masquerade ball.

Charlotte and the captain had just finished a quadrille and now, as many of the guests went into the adjoining salons to sit and chat or partake of refreshments, while others continued to dance a *courante,* Dubair drew her aside to a quiet corner where a large potted palmetto offered some measure of privacy.

The old Negress, whom Sister Marie had sent from the convent to chaperon Charlotte that night, was seated with the other slaves off in a corner of the large ballroom near the door that led to the kitchen, so although there were people on all sides of them, the captain hoped he might at least have a few minutes with her relatively out of earshot from the others.

They were in a light-hearted mood and, perhaps because

158

of the added sense of privacy that the masks afforded them, they had spoken openly of many things as the evening progressed. Dubair had told her of his boyhood rebellion against entering the priesthood and his daring escape to the New World, and even found himself confiding some of his dreams for the future. Finally, however, he had refused to go on until she had told him something more about herself, so as they sat together on the red velvet settee, Charlotte related to him briefly her principal reasons for having come to New Orleans and even showed him the locket with the miniatures of her mother and aunt in it.

Dubair had listened, fascinated, to her story, and now as she snapped the locket shut again, he smiled and caught her hand before she could lower it from her throat. His eyes couldn't help following the delicate lines of her neck down to the gentle swell of her partially bared bosom, and he was thankful at that moment to have the aid of his mask to hide the effect that the sight of those lovely young breasts were having upon him. He had never suspected how delightfully developed she was beneath those frothy white fichus she usually kept crossed so demurely over her necklines.

"So, like me, you're a little rebel, *non?*" he laughed, trying to keep under light rein the surge of emotions that she always seemed to arouse in him whenever she was near. "Frankly, *ma petite*, the fact that you're well born doesn't surprise me. There were certain signs that made me suspect . . . an innate refinement that made me wonder . . . But tell me, little one, what of your future? Do you really mean to live up to your legend?"

Her eyes widened in surprise. "What do you mean?"

"Well, do you intend to hold your title of being the only unmarried Casquette Girl in the colony forever?"

Charlotte smiled. "That's not entirely my fault, *Capitaine*," she replied, hoping to dismiss the question lightly, for she knew full well where he wished to lead her. "Blame it on you charming gentlemen who have made it so difficult for me to choose!"

But Dubair's eyes, made more intense by the blue of his uniform and the contrasting black velvet that framed them, became suddenly serious.

159

"Please, Charlotte, don't hedge. If I ask you something, will you answer me truthfully?"

"But of course."

"Then—then, do I have a chance? Will you consider me when you make your decision? For I'm in the chase too. You must know that."

She tried to keep the mood light, but her heart was beginning to beat more quickly. "If—if you wish, *Capitaine*, you will naturally be considered."

He tightened his grip anxiously on her hand as he felt it begin to slip away from his. "I don't want to be merely considered, little one. I want to be chosen."

"My!"

"I'm serious. Please, don't mock me. I couldn't take that from you, *ma petite*!"

Her smile faded. "I could never mock you, *Capitaine*."

"This Treval—you're considering him too, I suppose?"

"Of course. Very much so."

"Bah! You don't love him!"

"And what makes you so certain?"

"If you did, you'd have married him by now."

"Indeed? Simply because I hesitate doesn't mean I don't like him."

"*Like* him, perhaps, but *love* him, no."

She tossed him a coquettish glance through her mask as she toyed with her fan. "Don't be too certain of that, *mon capitaine*!"

"He's not for you, Charlotte," he insisted. "You're so full of life and unpretentious, while dandies like him are so austere and affected."

"I haven't found him so. To the contrary, he's anything but that most of the time!" she teased with a laugh.

Dubair sighed. "I see you're discovering the power you can wield over a man and enjoying it, *vraiment?*"

At that moment the unmistakable figure of Pierre Treval, impeccably dressed in wine-colored velvet with a mask to match, made a tardy entrance into the ballroom. After a few words of greeting to the governor and his wife, the Creole strode across the salon directly to where they were sitting.

Chapter XXV

It was plain that Treval didn't like the setting in which he found the couple. His dark eyes flashed shafts of annoyance through the twin holes of his mask as he made his way toward them.

Like Dubair, he wore his dark hair powdered and caught back in a black satin bag at the nape of his neck. His red heels clicked formally as he bowed a stiff greeting to them.

Despite their masks, Charlotte was quick to catch the exchange of hostile glances between the two men.

"Ah, mademoiselle, I see you're in bad company again."

Dubair, equally annoyed by the intrusion, was quick to reply. "Since you've arrived, monsieur, yes."

Charlotte tried to laugh away the ominous atmosphere. "Ah, *mes amis*, what jesters you are!"

Pierre turned to her. "I'd like to see you alone for a few minutes, if I may, Charlotte," he said, trying to ignore the disturbing presence of the captain.

"I—I don't know, Pierre. After the way you behaved the last time . . ."

"I want to apologize for that, my dear. You did say we could continue our conversation when I was in a better mood. I promise I won't do or say anything to offend you again."

Dubair stood, eyeing the two with mounting apprehension, fearful that Treval might win back some of the ground the latter had lost at their previous meeting. He observed Charlotte carefully.

She opened and closed her fan nervously, not knowing what to answer. The captain didn't deserve that she aban-

161

don him at that moment to talk to Pierre, yet she knew how difficult it was for a proud man like Treval to plead forgiveness, especially in the presence of a rival. She hated to send him off angry again.

"I thought you might honor me with the next dance," he suggested.

"I'm sorry, Pierre, but I've already promised the next minuet to the *capitaine*."

The fury Treval was trying desperately to keep under control bubbled dangerously near the surface once more. This Dubair wasn't going to edge him out again!

"Does that matter?" he replied tartly. "He took you from me the last time. Why cannot I take you for one dance tonight?"

"You seem to forget, monsieur," Dubair broke in, "I'm Mlle. Montier's escort to this ball." His hand had dropped to his sword hilt.

"You didn't remember such technicalities this past Sunday afternoon!" the Creole reminded him tartly.

"Mademoiselle herself asked me to see her home," retorted Dubair. "It wasn't my fault, *monsieur*, if you didn't know how to escort her properly."

The Creole stepped back, livid with rage, his hand also on his sword.

"Pierre! Charles!" Charlotte pleaded desperately, feeling they were suddenly being borne away on a current they could no longer control.

"I don't need the likes of you, Captain, telling me how to escort a lady!"

Charlotte repeated their names, trying to stop the momentum of their increasing hostility. But they were lost in a complicated world of inflexible honor and unbounded pride.

"Perhaps a man the likes of me could teach you a few things, monsieur—beginning with good manners."

"Captain Dubair, I take your words as an insult I cannot overlook."

Treval ripped off his mask angrily, and Dubair was removing his, but the latter was calmer, more controlled. The masquerade of manners between the two men was over.

"Do you demand satisfaction, monsieur?"

"I do."

"Then I shall be only too glad to accommodate you. There is also the matter of your offense to mademoiselle the other day to settle. My seconds will see you in the morning."

At that moment, however, the governor came up behind them. Madame Perier, an alert hostess, had anticipated trouble from the minute she had seen Treval making his way toward Charlotte and the captain. It didn't take a seer to predict that angry words might pass between the two *prétendants,* and when she had seen them facing each other with their hands on their swords, she had immediately sought out her husband and warned him of the impending storm between the two men.

Charlotte was relieved to see Perier and turned anxiously toward him.

"Please stop them! Don't let them go on arguing."

"I certainly won't, mademoiselle," agreed the governor, his voice stern behind his black velvet and lace mask. Turning to Pierre and the captain, he continued even more sharply, "Messieurs, whatever dispute there is between you must end right here and now. I'll not tolerate any dueling over a woman. Captain Dubair, such hotheadedness isn't like you, but I suppose love makes fools of us all. And you, Treval, don't make a scandal you and your esteemed mother might come to regret."

Perier could see, however, that he was not making much headway with either of them. "Mademoiselle," he said, turning again to Charlotte, who stared through her mask in wide-eyed dismay at her two suitors. "Can't you choose between these schoolboys and put an end to their bickering once and for all? Either one would make you an excellent husband. You can't find two finer men in all the colony, I assure you."

Charlotte's eyes went blank behind her mask as she shyly lowered her lids.

"I know, *Commandant,*" she replied meekly. "And therein lies the problem. Each one has so much to recommend him that I can't bring myself to choose between them."

"Then let me suggest they draw lots," ventured the governor. "We can't have them killing themselves over you, can we? So there you have it, messieurs. Draw lots for the lady. That should settle it to the satisfaction of all, *non*?"

Dubair and Treval had calmed down considerably by now and were already beginning to lament their outbursts of temper.

"You're right, of course, *Commandant*," agreed Dubair, relaxing his hold on his sword. "What's more, we shouldn't be subjecting Mlle. Montier to this distasteful scene of jealousy."

"For once I agree with you, *Capitaine*," echoed Treval. "You may rest assured, your Excellency, we will not settle our difference on the dueling grounds. We will try to do it in a less violent manner."

"Good, good," smiled Perier. "Then let's get on with the ball, and no more fighting, right?"

They nodded rather sheepishly. "Would you like to draw lots for the lady right now?" he offered. "I'd be glad to officiate in the proceedings."

But here Charlotte interrupted, her white face suddenly flushing to a bright red beneath her half-mask.

"Please, your Excellency, I appreciate your intervention, but I'll not have lots drawn for me!"

"I mean no offense, mademoiselle," the governor assured her. "It's only that some way must be found to settle this situation, don't you agree?"

"I'm the first to agree with you, *M. le Commandant*," she replied, her timidity giving way to the indignation she felt welling up within her, "but I refuse to be lotteried off like a chattel. I was promised the privilege of choosing my husband, and I don't wish to relinquish that right."

The governor was taken aback by the girl's sudden display of spirit. And she was a beauty, too! Women of her calibre were few and far between. No wonder the captain and Treval had lost their heads over her.

"*Bien, mademoiselle*. I'll not press you," he acquiesced. "But mind you, make your decision speedily before there's a tragedy. I don't want the blood of two fine young men flowing simply because you couldn't make up your mind.

Go on now and enjoy the ball, and no more of this matter tonight, *s'il vous plait*, messieurs."

He turned then and walked off to rejoin his other guests, leaving the three of them considerably subdued.

Once he had gone, however, it was Charlotte's turn to admonish her errant suitors, as they both began to offer her their apologies.

"Don't either of you say another word!" she exclaimed angrily. It was her turn now to tear off her mask with indignation. "You've not only embarrassed me before the governor, but have completely ignored my feelings throughout all of this!"

"You're right, of course," admitted Dubair, "and I'm truly sorry to have let things go as far as they did."

"And I confess I let my temper get the best of me again," lamented Pierre. "Just when I had promised myself not to let it happen any more!"

"*Bien*, messieurs, I'll tell you both," continued Charlotte, relieved to have the situation under control again. "If you two dare to fight a duel or presume to draw lots for me, I swear by all the saints I'll never speak to either one of you again! If you resort to such measures, there will be no winner, for you'll both lose my respect and affection."

The two men stood there before her, tall and elegant in their finery, but hanging their powdered heads like guilty schoolboys before an irate teacher. They had locked horns, but it had been Charlotte who had come out the victor, for now they had been forced to accept the fact that only she would decide her future—and theirs, as well.

Chapter XXVI

In the weeks and months that followed, Charlotte managed to keep her impetuous suitors fairly well in tow. The incident at the ball had served to put her in command of the situation once more, and although neither Pierre nor Charles liked each other any better than before, they kept the lids on their tempers as best they could and contented themselves trying to win her favor in earnest.

"If you are really interested in courting me," she told them with a firmness that now she felt capable of exerting, "you'll do so properly and stop pressuring me or insulting each other. I'd like very much to continue seeing both of you for these next few months so I can really get to know you better. When Madelón's baby is born, I'll have to make a decision or go back to the convent, so you can be assured my future will have to be resolved by that time or perhaps sooner. If you truly care for me, then show a little patience and court me with dignity. With a little peace of mind, I might be able to make a decision that none of us will regret."

With so lovely a taskmaster dictating the rules, her *prétendants* bowed their heads with no further word of protest.

About the only thing the men had in common, however, was their love for the same woman. Although they both had an air of self-assurance that appealed to Charlotte, the captain's was that of a man who had come to grips with life and mastered it, whereas Treval's was that of one who had always been its master.

166

Pierre, for all his love of formality and sobriety, was more fiery and possessive than his rival, who had learned self-discipline as a way of survival in the wilderness, although the twitch of the latter's jaw often betrayed what such a bridle on his emotions was really costing him.

The problem of keeping a chaperon also presented problems. Occasionally Sister Marie would go with Charlotte on her outings; other times she would send the old Negress Deedee, or Felicité, who was a postulant now at the convent. Sometimes Madame Pichou was able to go. But it kept Charlotte's elders busy trying to keep up with her and her attentive *prétendants*. Of course, Charlotte was not allowed to go cavorting about on an endless round of frivolity. Nor could her suitors spend all their time courting her. They each had duties that also required attention. As a rule, they were allowed to take her out only on weekends, when she was not needed in the store, and although they stopped at the Pichous' to see her for a few minutes during the week, they understood they could not abuse that privilege.

As Madelón's pregnancy progressed, her nausea improved, and she could sit up more and even take a few steps around the room, but she was warned that any violent exertion might cause her to abort the child.

Jacques Ansleau still had not returned, and as the months wore on, Madelón tearfully declared, with ever increasing anguish, that she feared she would never see her young husband again. Although everyone tried to reassure her to the contrary, the gnawing fear that perhaps the young woman's apprehensions were well founded began to grow in them as well.

With the coming of spring and warmer weather, the citizens of New Orleans began to prepare for summer as if they were getting ready for a mighty battle. In reality it was just that—their annual battle for surviving yet another year.

As the heat grew more intense, the very atmosphere seemed to hang heavy with expectancy. The swamplands took on new exuberance, encroaching all the more upon the city, the vegetation surging anew in the streets and the river rising so dangerously high that it threatened to flood what the wilderness could not completely reconquer. People spoke forebodingly of the hurricane season and stocked up with food and fuel against the coming storms, while there was a run at the Pichou store for the white netting that everyone used to make their *moustiquaires*, which were zealously stretched over every open window and suspended from the testers of every bed at night.

When Charlotte began to scratch at the stinging red welts left in the wake of those midges or gnatlike creatures that the colonists referred to as *Maringouins* and *Frappes d'abord*, she understood at last why Dubair and his scouts had told them they had been fortunate not to have made their excursion through the swamps during the summer months. Between the heat and such insects, snakes and alligators would have seemed the lesser of the evils they had to face!

Sometimes, after a few days of continuous rain, when the streets were flooded up to the *banquettes*, the mosquitoes would be so numerous that the white screens on their windows would become black with the pesky insects. At night it became quite a challenge to get into bed without one or two of those uninvited guests slipping under the *baires* at the same time.

When she wasn't making clothes for her expected baby, Madelón passed her time sewing tapes and metal rings on to yard after yard of those mosquito bars and weaving palmetto and bamboo fans for the Pichous to sell in the store, as well as swatters for the more aggressive souls who declared open warfare on the flies and mosquitoes that plagued them. Fortunately the mosquitoes at least left their victims more or less in peace during the day. As soon as dusk fell, however, they came out *en masse* to draw blood wherever they could find it.

Dubair suggested they burn sticks of citronella and take a lesson from the Indians and anoint themselves with a repellant, but Charlotte protested she didn't want to repel everyone else around her as well as the mosquitoes. With a chuckle, the captain assured her not to worry and on the following day presented her with a pleasantly scented mixture of citronella and lavender oils thinned out with alcohol, which he had concocted for her and her friends—a vast improvement, she had to admit, over the bear grease or fish oil she had seen the Indians using.

The captain urged her to use the lotion, for he was especially anxious that she protect herself from any type of insect bite, which his experience in the swamplands had led him to suspect might be the source of the malaria and pestilence that plagued the colony during the summer months.

Although her suitors had kept their word fairly well and not tried to exert undue pressure on her to reach an immediate decision during the months that followed, the Ursulines and the *Compagnie* continued to prod her discreetly to renounce her single state as soon as possible. From the letter she received from her aunt in early summer, it was evident the Company of the Indies had asked Germaine to try to influence her niece into fulfilling her commitment and contracting matrimony as soon as possible.

It had been the first news Charlotte had had from her aunt since she had left Marseilles the year before. She had written to Germaine on arriving in New Orleans, but even the faster, lighter ships took so long to cross the ocean to France and then make their way back again to the colonies that Charlotte really had not expected to hear from her aunt any sooner.

". . . You always have been such a contrary child!" Germaine chided, once she had gotten the usual greetings out of the way. "Personally I cannot see why you ever wanted to go to that barbaric land in the first place, but you were the one who wouldn't rest until I let you go. Now they tell me you're balking and refusing to honor your contract to take a husband there. You cannot disgrace your family this way. But if you have come to regret your foolhardy decision, I suppose I'll have to try to make a settlement with the *Compagnie* and arrange for your return. Frankly, that is what I think you should do. I'm sure we could find a far more suitable husband for you here. M. Blégot unfortunately suffered an accident in his carriage which has left him paralyzed from the waist down, but there are other good matches. Come back, I'm sure we can find someone. I wouldn't wait too long, however. You're going on nineteen now. Another year or two and people will be calling you an old maid."

Germaine then went on to write enthusiastically about the plans for her own coming marriage to a wealthy young nobleman only five years her junior, and relate a few more bits of gossip about different people in Marseilles whom Charlotte could hardly remember now. Why couldn't her aunt and the others understand? As if just marrying—marrying anyone, no matter whom—was the solution to everything!

She had to admit, however, that those past few months had not brought her any closer to a decision. She had hoped that time would have shown her the answer, but the more she knew Pierre and Charles, the more she had come to care for both of them. They were always so gentle and considerate with her. She wondered how she could ever tell either one she was rejecting him. She almost preferred not to choose at all than have to face that moment.

Pierre had taken her to meet his mother before the hot weather set in enough to send the more wealthy colonists to the cooler verandas of their plantations on the outskirts of town. As Sister Marie remarked, such a presentation was always the final proof of a man's intentions towards a girl.

Sra. Treval was still an attractive woman, despite her fifty-some years. Her salt-and-pepper hair framed the perfect oval of an even-featured face, which was only beginning to show slight signs of sagging at the jawline and an occasional line on an otherwise flawless complexion. Although her eyes were not as dark as her son's, they had the same intensity, and Charlotte felt rather uncomfortable beneath their veiled scrutiny.

Sra. Treval was not really against her son's marrying the girl. She secretly would have preferred it if he had set his sights on Ninon, Madame Perier's cousin twice removed, but once he had assured her that Mlle. Montier was well born and had been educated by the Ursulines, she had accepted his choice more readily. Convent girls were known to make docile, virtuous wives and good, pious mothers. He could do worse.

Besides, she had to admit the child was much prettier than Ninon and had more innate grace. What she couldn't understand was why the girl was vacillating so with Pierre,

170

and hoped it didn't bode a frivolous nature. She had never seen her son so smitten by any woman before. So young as the girl was, she probably knew how to play her cards well. Pierre had always had a reputation among the ladies of both New Spain and Nouvelle Orleans as being a hard man to pin down, yet this unassuming little Casquette Girl seemed to know how to keep him at her beck and call! Despite the child's obvious lack of worldliness, she might not be quite as docile as expected, but if Pierre was so determined to have her, she would just have to accept the fact. After all, he was of age and head of the household.

Pierre's mother was especially interested in seeing Charlotte's locket and then went on to speak at great length of her own family history and their plantation upriver, where she planned to spend the summer. Her health left something to be desired, she confided, and her fondest wish was to see her son married and hold her first grandchild in her arms before she departed from this life. Although Charlotte had the feeling Sra. Treval had many more years ahead of her than she was predicting, she felt she might not be too hard to take as a mother-in-law.

There were other outings with Pierre, such as a musical *soirée* at the governor's mansion, which was especially memorable. That was the evening the Creole waxed especially romantic and tried to steal a quick kiss from her behind the same palmetto where he had confronted her and the captain a few months earlier at the Mardi Gras Ball.

"Please, Pierre, don't take liberties, or I won't be able to continue seeing you," she had scolded, as he slipped his arm around her slim waist and drew her quickly to him.

"Charlotte, my lovely little coquette, you're driving me wild!" he protested. "When will you be mine—*really* mine? The day we wed, I'll order the nuptial chamber strewn with petals and have an orchestra playing softly beneath our window all night long—"

"Hush, Pierre! It's not proper to talk of such things!" she chided, as she quickly hid behind her fan. But deep within her she could feel the blood suddenly rushing through her veins before terminating in a blush on her cheeks.

Reluctantly he relaxed his arm and let her go. "You're

171

right," he admitted, "and I'm sorry, but you don't know how I dream of you night after night. You're such a child. You don't realize what you do to a man!"

The guests were gathering around the harpsichordist and congratulating him for his inspired performance, so no one seemed to be paying much attention to them at that moment, not even Felicité, their chaperon for that day, who was talking to Madame Perier.

"Tell me, Charlotte," Pierre continued softly. "Has this—this Dubair ever tried to make advances to you? Don't be afraid to say something if he does. Remember, I'm here to defend you."

She couldn't help seeing the humor of the situation. "And to whom, pray tell, should I report *your* misdemeanors?" she asked with a merry laugh.

"Come now, my dear, a little hug and a quick brush of the lips can't be called a sin," he protested, but he flushed a little and didn't pursue the subject any further. The thought that Dubair might have touched her, however, was maddening.

Sometimes the weather was too rainy to go out, so they could sit above the Pichou store having *café au lait* or *chocolat* and chatting with the elderly couple and Madelón. The moment Pierre looked forward to the most, however, was when she accompanied him downstairs to see him to the door, and they had a few precious minutes alone. He didn't dare kiss her for fear of incurring her anger or, worse yet, being caught by her chaperones and sent packing. But he would try to steal a little *besito* if he could, on a curl, her cheek, and once ever so lightly near her lips.

He had had women enough in his life, even one or two mistresses over the years—what man hadn't? But Charlotte was different. She was to be his wife. He would despise himself if he destroyed the purity he so worshipped in her.

Captain Dubair spent similar rainy days with Charlotte and her friends. In those rare moments when they were alone, he had similar problems in keeping his desire for her in check, but he didn't try to assuage it with stolen kisses. He knew he couldn't trust himself with this girl. If he touched her, he was afraid he might lose control and unwittingly offend her. She was like one of those lovely birds he had seen so often in the marshlands. The moment you tried to get too near it would start and fly off in a flutter of breathtaking color, lost forever.

He had doubled his efforts to get his plantation producing on a large scale and already had workmen constructing the main house. In an effort to show Charlotte and Sister Marie how serious his intentions were, he invited them to accompany him one Sunday to see how the work was progressing. It was a warm day in early June before the scorching summer heat had arrived in all its force, so they decided to make a pleasant outdoor affair of it.

Fortunately Dubair's land was closer to the city than most. He had been among the first in the settlement to choose his site, and as a favorite of Bienville's, had been given the grant in appreciation for his services to the colony. It had been only another piece of swampland then, and it had cost him a goodly sum to clear and drain it. Even so, it took them all morning to get there in a small boat and they did not return until sunset, which conveniently was not until late in the evening at that time of year.

Charlotte brought a basket lunch, and so did Sister Marie, who thought it best to take Deedee along, as well, since they were going to be gone for the day. At first Charlotte feared they might encounter Indians, but Dubair assured her there was little danger of meeting hostile Indians in the region.

As they sat under the shade of one of the giant oaks that adorned the site, the captain showed them the plans for the main house while the broad expanse of the river lay spread out before them with its usual deceiving tranquility. He explained how he and all the landowners of the region were building levees against floods, which would be tied in with the new embankments Perier had ordered constructed for the city only the year before.

Charlotte noted how his face glowed as he explained where each room was going to be and how the plantation would look when everything was finished. At the moment there were only three small log cabins on the land where the overseer and laborers were living with their families, but to the side of these, the wooden framework of what

173

was to be the imposing manor already stood etched sharply against the blue, cloudless sky.

"This lane of oaks where we're sitting will someday lead directly to the main entrance of our home," Dubair was saying, his eyes matching the vivid blue of the sky above him as he spoke. "It will be a place where our children will prosper."

Charlotte lowered her eyes modestly, and he suddenly remembered Sister Marie was sitting there beside them. With a flush that deepened his suntan, he quickly began talking about the crops. Suddenly he laughed and checked his enthusiasm, as he realized it was probably of little interest to women.

"But enough of that," he said, rising quickly and turning to Sister Marie. "May I take Charlotte over to see the construction for the big house more closely?" he asked. "I'd like to show her how it corresponds to the plans, so she can visualize it better. Perhaps you might like to come, too?"

The nun smiled and shook her head, knowing full well the young people were longing to have a few minutes out of earshot. "Go ahead and take Charlotte," she replied. "Meanwhile Deedee and I will be taking the food out of the baskets, so we can eat when you return."

Blueprints still in hand, the captain took Charlotte by the arm and led her up the lane of spreading moss-laden oaks that sheltered them from the noonday sun and funneled a cool breeze down its green carpeted corridor. He had worn his uniform as a concession to the ladies, but he really would have preferred to have been in his buckskins.

Charlotte, in keeping with the season, rivaled the spring in a rose-colored silk overdress that sported a white stomacher with tiny matching bows running down its center. The ruffled petticoats beneath it bounced merrily to her light step. She tied the matching ribbons of her straw hat under her chin and pushed back the rebellious curl from her forehead. Holding on to the captain's arm, she picked her way over the roots of one of the giant oaks. The trip on the river in the *pirogue* and the outdoor setting brought back memories to her of other moments they had spent together, when they had made their way upriver by day and camped under the stars by night . . . when they had been so close at times that she had known the feel of his taut muscles beneath the soft mold of his buckskins . . .

"Charlotte, *ma petite*," he said in a low voice, as they stood facing the huge shell of interlaced timbers from which he hoped their home would be born. "I'd like you to go over these plans with me. Tell me how you would like each room, everything you want, for this house will be yours. I'm building it for you. Surely you know that?"

It would be so easy to say yes just then, she thought. But there had been similar moments when she had stood like this beside Pierre and been tempted to accept him, too.

"There is time yet for all that," she replied, trying to put a lightness in her voice she didn't really feel at that moment. She moved away a little from his disturbing physical presence. "And what will your manor be made of?" she asked, stepping into the framework and standing on the foundations of what she assumed would someday be the entrance hall.

Dubair sighed, a little disappointed over her refusal to give him a more definite answer, but resigning himself to let the subject rest for the moment, he followed her into the maze of upright logs, carefully notched and fitted together as they squared off room after room according to the indications on the blueprint he carried in his hand. "It'll be built to last the years," he replied, not without a little pride. "All of this will soon be filled in with brick and mortar. Of course, there will be a lot of wood, too, good oak and cypress that can take the dampness and last for generations. The main staircase will be here. Right above this parlor will be our—the master bedroom."

He looked down at the gentle rise and fall of her bosom beneath the tightly laced bodice and could see how her breathing had increased despite her apparent nonchalance. It pleased him to see he could affect her more than she pretended to be.

Reaching out gently, he touched the dip of hair on her forehead and tilted her straw hat back from her face so he could see her better. Her hair blazed like burnished gold in the sun as the hat, sustained by its ribbons, fell back to the nape of her neck.

"How lovely you are, *ma petite*," he murmured, finger-

175

ing that fascinating lock of hair almost in reverence, as if afraid he might profane it with his large sunburned hand. "I want you, Charlotte," he said softly. "While we're talking about house building and crops, what I really want to do is take you in my arms and hold you again. I want you so much I ache inside. Don't make me wait too long, little one. My sweet little *fille* with her *cassette* . . . my bride . . ."

He bent closer to her lips and he knew she wouldn't fly away this time. He could see her eyes growing heavy-lidded and her lips instinctively parting as they waited for his kiss. She was so young, so vulnerable . . .

Suddenly he stepped back, a horrible thought nagging at him. He wanted to dismiss it, but he couldn't.

"*Mon Dieu*, Charlotte! Do you realize how you affect a man? That Creole—that Treval—I know the type. He wouldn't stop! Has he ever tried—Has he ever kissed you? *Mon Dieu*! At the thought of it, I could kill him!"

Charlotte blinked her eyes in the bright sunlight, bewildered by his sudden change of mood. She tried to regain her composure.

"You men!" she exclaimed indignantly. "What's right for one is a crime for the other!"

"Then he *has* tried!" His jaw was squaring off into a dangerously grim line. Sometimes there was an intensity about this *capitaine* that belied his seemingly calm exterior.

"Do you think I would continue to see him if he had lacked respect?" she asked with a flash of anger.

"I'm not talking about respect," replied Dubair. "I could have kissed you just now and still respected you."

"I wonder," she retorted. "You didn't even kiss me and here you are already accusing me of letting others, simply because I might have let you."

Dubair bent forward again eagerly. "Would you have let me, Charlotte? Does that mean . . . ?"

"It means, sir, that I find you extremely attractive," she replied, pushing him back with a smile, for she was in control of herself once more. "Now let's stop this foolishness. All I can say is that if anyone has come close to kissing me—*really* kissing me—it's been you, *Capitaine*. So if anyone had a right to be jealous at this moment it would be M. Treval!"

She stepped out of the forest of joists and studs into the bright sunlight once more. They were on the other side of the structure now. "I—I thought you might like your own private little garden here," stammered Dubair, deciding it best to follow her lead. He certainly didn't want to risk an argument. He had come too far, allowed himself to dream too much now . . .

Stooping to the ground near the edge of the clearing, he scooped up a dried ear of corn. With a sign to her to wait, he walked around until he finally found what he was looking for.

"If you were an Indian bride," he said, returning to her side with a boyish grin, "you'd bear an ear of corn in your right hand and a sprig of laurel in the other . . . like this."

As he spoke, he placed the dried cob in one of her hands and the green branch in the other. "The corn means she will know how to prepare it and take care of her husband as a dutiful and loving wife should," he explained, "but the twig . . . Ah, that's the part I like best! It's the symbol of her promise to stay as sweet and fair as she is at that moment. Smell the laurel leaf, little one . . . You see how fresh and sweet it is? That's the way you are to me. Don't let anyone, not even me, ever change you."

The corn had dropped from her hand, but she still held the sprig close to her nose, and the pleasant odor of the bruised leaves filled her nostrils.

Dubair's face broke into a broad grin. "That's what the Indian bride does in the marriage ceremony. She throws the corncob to the ground and extends her hand to the brave. Then he takes it . . . like this . . . and says, 'I am thy husband.' If she replies, 'I am thy wife,' they are married."

Charlotte stood with her hand in his, feeling her emotions beginning to get out of control again. "We—we'd better be getting back," she whispered. "Sister Marie must be waiting for us to have lunch . . ."

As they made their way to the shade of the trees where the nun and Deedee had laid out an inviting repast, Charlotte kept the laurel branch clutched tightly in her hand. Somehow she couldn't bring herself to throw it away.

177

That night she put it in the little pouch where she kept her most precious possessions: a small heart-shaped locket, a delicate gold chain, and now a tiny branch of bruised laurel leaves.

Chapter XXVII

The Indians of the region called July the Month of the Fifth Moon, the moon of peaches, and August was the Sixth, the moon of blackberries. Dubair told Charlotte how the natives offered baskets of each fruit as tributes to their gods of the sun and moon and held monthly festivals to honor them. The Indians were heathens, of course, but she could well understand how they had come to believe that something the sun was all powerful here in this land where the scorching heat dominated everyone and everything that fell under its spell during those long summer months.

One year ago Charlotte and her companions had set sail from Marseilles to come to the New World. So much had happened since then. Her life in France seemed so distant now . . . her aunt, Blégot, the old convent . . . Today a whole new future lay ahead of her—but with whom? Charles? Pierre? Both of them inspired such passion, such tenderness, in her that with each passing month she found it more and more difficult to choose between them. She was no closer to a decision now than she had been in March.

Madelón's time was approaching. The *accoucheuse* had warned her she must be more careful than ever, or she would bring the baby on before its time. Jacques Ansleau had been given up for dead. Like so many others before him, he had gone off into those mysterious swamplands of

Louisiana and never returned. Indian treachery was suspected, but no one was really sure. So many things could happen, even to an experienced man, in that unpredictable wilderness stretching for hundreds of miles between New Orleans and the Illinois territory at the other end of the river.

Madelón had reconciled herself to her loss now and was planning her future around the child she carried in her womb.

"I loved him, Charlotte," she told her friend with tears clouding her gentle grey eyes. "We had such a short time together, yet we truly loved each other."

She had the money Jacques had been saving to build their new home and set up the small business he had dreamed of someday owning, so there was no immediate problem. Also, the Pichous wanted her to stay on with them once the baby was born. They could help each other mutually, especially now that she had become like one of the family to them.

Meanwhile Charlotte was kept busy juggling her two *prétendants* so that neither would have cause to complain or accuse her of not giving him an equal opportunity to pay her court. Charlotte usually alternated Saturdays and Sundays between them, but when her birthday came on the last day of July, a new crisis arose.

Madame Pichou suggested they have a little party for Charlotte and invite them both to it, but the rivalry between the two men was such that the idea was discarded for fear of the celebration ending in another deadly argument between them.

The first gift that occurred to both *prétendants*, of course, was a wedding ring. But Charlotte warned them that would be the only present she could not accept yet from either one of them. Since her *anniversaire* fell on a weekday, and she could only spare a few hours off from the store anyway, her suitors were told they could come by for only an hour at separate specified times.

Pierre came first, bearing a lovely handpainted fan of ivory and Spanish lace, which he had asked a member of the *Compagnie* to bring over from Paris for him.

179

"You must have a fan worthy of a queen!" he had told her, pleased to see how delighted she was with it.

A little later, Charles came by with another unusual gift for her, a brooch he had asked the town goldsmith to fashion especially for her. He smiled as he watched her looking at it and saw she understood the significance of that delicate spray of laurel leaves frozen in solid gold with tiny topaz dewdrops sparkling from its depths.

"I wanted something very special," he told her, "something that would be very much you. The topaz stones match your eyes and hair, and the laurel leaves—you do remember, don't you, *ma petite*?"

She was touched. So much love! *Mon Dieu!* She had prayed so many times, in those long years that she had been growing up as an orphan and later as an unwanted member of her aunt's household, that she would someday find someone who would love and want her. Now she had found love here in the New World, but *le bon Dieu*, it seemed, had answered her prayers too well!

In those past few months the captain had fortunately not been asked to go on any lengthy expeditions. He had only been sent three times on short trips to Balize to meet passengers who had disembarked there and wanted to come upriver to New Orleans. Dubair hated the time that he had to spend away from the settlement, for it meant he couldn't see Charlotte. Also, he worried that Pierre might take advantage of his absence and try to see her more often. The captain made those journeys with more rapidity than hitherto would have been believed possible, squeezing the total trek to and from Balize into seven or eight days instead of the usual nine or ten. He would see Charlotte on a Saturday one weekend and come rushing back to New Orleans by the Sunday of the following.

The last time he had gone, he had been delayed a little longer than he had expected and had not arrived until late that Sunday afternoon instead of early in the morning as he had hoped. Not wishing to keep her waiting any longer, he had gone directly to the Pichous', still in his buckskins with the week's stubble on his face. He apologized profusely for his appearance, fearful she might be comparing him unfavorably with the more elegant Treval, but he had wanted to

180

stop by and at least explain the reason for the delay before going to the barracks to change.

Charlotte smiled at his obvious reluctance to let her see him again in his *coureur de bois* clothing. If he only knew how the outfit favored him, she thought, and how the sight of his unshaven face made the memory of his beard brushing against her cheek all the more vivid!

And there was Pierre, with his boyish eagerness, stopping by the store sometimes on the pretext of buying some trifling item, which she knew he neither needed nor wanted. He would be so very formal, while Madame Pichou glared at him for having come by on a day that had not been specified. Taking the package and paying for it very solemnly, he would leave like any other customer who had only wanted to make a purchase, but after he had gone, she would always find somewhere on the counter a nosegay of violets or a single long-stemmed rose with a note wrapped around it: "*Je t'adore.*"

Then, as they neared the last day of August, Charles announced he had to go again to Balize. He spent that Saturday with her at the Pichous', since the weather had been too bad for them to go out, but as he bade her goodbye, he promised he would be back by that following Sunday. It would be September by then, he said, and the moon of the new corn would be riding high in the heavens. Corncobs and laurel leaves . . . Charlotte fingered his brooch and smiled as she found herself already counting the days until his return.

Chapter XXVIII

The first Sunday in September was a dull, overcast day. The air hung hot and heavy over the long-suffering settlement. At least, when Sister Marie came by to take Charlotte to mass that morning, the sun was not beating down as mercilessly on them as it had been for all that past week.

The Ursuline found the Pichous in a state of agitation, for they had just received word from their daughter that her time had come to deliver her first-born. Although the girl, who had married only two months prior to Madelón, seemed to be healthy enough and no problems were anticipated, the prospective grandparents couldn't help but wish they could be with their daughter at that moment, especially since, as Madame Pichou observed, the midwife always took more interest in her work when someone from the mother-to-be's family was present.

Although it was Sunday and the store was closed, the Pichous felt they could not in all conscience leave their two young boarders alone, especially since Madelón was in such a delicate condition that she was running the risk of giving premature birth.

Sister Marie would have stayed with Charlotte and Madelón herself, but she had to make several sick calls after church, and she had even brought Deedee along with her to help on the errands. Under the circumstances, however, the nun decided she would try to manage without the Negress and offered to let the latter remain with the girls.

"But we can manage alone for a few hours," protested Charlotte. "You might need Deedee."

"I have the man who's driving the carriage," the nun

assured her. "Although he's not as ideal as Deedee, he's quite trustworthy and can be of some service if I really need help. Under no circumstances would I consent to let you stay here by yourself, especially with Madelón so helpless!"

"We'll only be gone for a few hours," promised Madame Pichou, her broad countenance shining with gratitude. "Besides, the *Capitaine* is due back any hour now, isn't he, Charlotte? He could always be of some assistance if an emergency should arise. Captain Dubair is not only an honorable man but a resourceful one, as well."

"We only want to see that everything goes well with our little girl," said M. Pichou apologetically. "I'll see to it we aren't gone too long, Sister."

"Then I'll go on to mass and make my rounds, which should take most of the afternoon," agreed the nun. "Once I've finished, I'll return for Deedee. If you leave now for your daughter's, you should have ample time to go see her and come back by then, don't you think? In the worst of cases, if you haven't gotten back by the time I've returned, I'll wait here for you. But I do think you should make every effort to be here before sundown, since I wouldn't like the idea of Charlotte and Madelón being here alone with just Deedee for too long a time."

"Nor would we," echoed Madame Pichou. "Rest assured we'll be back before nightfall. You're so good, Sister. May God bless you."

So with a recommendation to Charlotte that she join Madelón in the prayers that Father de Beaubois had left with her friend to read ever since the latter had not been able to attend Mass because of her confinement, Sister Marie went on her way.

Shortly afterwards, the Pichous also hurriedly departed, and Charlotte finally barred the front door and went upstairs to join Madelón and Deedee. While the two girls dutifully recited the special orations that the Ursuline had suggested they say to compensate for not having gone to church that day, the old Negress made them some tea.

Afterwards Charlotte took out her prized hand mirror, which the Pichous had given her for her birthday, and arranged her coiffure in anticipation of Charles's arrival. She

183

knew he especially liked her to wear her hair uncovered, although caps and hoods continued to be the fashion. Since it was so hot and sticky that day, she decided it would be very easy to please him on that score. Anyway, she doubted they would be going out that afternoon, since she didn't want to leave her friend alone with just Deedee. If any emergency should arise, Deedee would be a great help, but she needed direction.

Madelón's frail body was swollen with child now, and the poor girl was miserable with the added discomfort of the unbearable heat. She was sitting up in bed, her wheat-colored hair caught up off her neck with a ribbon, as she continued to read a special prayer for Jacques' soul, "wherever he might be at that moment," and at the same time trying to keep cool with one of the large round bamboo fans she had woven for the Pichous to sell in their store.

Charlotte arranged a fresh white linen fichu over the low-cut neckline of her simple blue linen gown and pinned it in place with the spray of gold leaves Charles had given her. The taut lacings over the white linen stomacher that ran down the center of her tight bodice terminated at her waist in a tiny point. She pulled the lacings a shade tighter, hoping she could take off half an inch more that way. Aunt Germaine had always preached that a young girl's waistline should never be larger than eighteen inches around, and hers measured eighteen and a half sometimes, especially after an extra helping at mealtime. She decided to have only a slice of cold chicken for her midday repast. It was too hot to eat much, anyway.

By noon the sky had blackened considerably, and it became evident a storm was brewing somewhere nearby, probably making its way up from the Gulf. She hoped Charles would get back to the settlement before it broke.

A strong breeze began to whip at the white linen coverings on the open windows. Although it brought welcome respite from the suffocating heat, they were finally forced to close the shutters, as huge drops of rain, heralded by rolls of distant thunder, began to penetrate the flimsy gauze screens. They had already lit the candelabra, for even before they had shut the windows it had grown so dark outside it might as well have been night.

Although Charlotte welcomed the long overdue break in the heat wave that had gripped the city, she hated to see a storm brewing, for the streets flooded so terribly when it rained and they would be muddy for days afterwards. Also, it would make immediate passage difficult and might delay Charles's arrival as well as the return of the Pichous. Somehow she felt that if Charles reached town he would come, even if he had to paddle his pirogue right up to her front door!

The timbers creaked and shutters rattled as the wind increased in momentum and blew its mighty breath against the walls around them.

"*Mon Dieu!* We're going to have a hurricane!" moaned Madelón sleepily, as she momentarily awakened from her afternoon nap.

"*Non, non, chérie*, it's only a little storm. We've been through a lot worse. Go back to sleep, dear. You need your rest," soothed Charlotte, while Deedee sat in the corner, her grey-streaked head nodding complacently over her bag of mending, oblivious to the storm breaking around her.

Through the deafening din of pounding wind and rain Charlotte thought she caught the sound of a banging shutter below. There was one with a bad latch, she knew, and the force of the wind had probably blown it loose. With an exasperated sigh, she rose, deciding to check it. If the rain poured into the storeroom, some of the stock would be damaged. She'd have to watch for flooding, too, although the Pichous, having learned their lesson from previous experiences, tried to keep very few perishables at floor level during that time of year.

"Madelón . . . Madelón, dear, do you hear me?" she said softly, bending over her friend. "I'm going downstairs to check that everything is all right. Do you want anything before I go?"

"*Non, merci, chérie*. I'm all right," Madelón replied drowsily. "Go on and do what you have to do. If I need anything, I'll ask Deedee. Don't worry about me. All I want to do is sleep right now . . ."

She lay back and closed her eyes, her lovely blond hair spilling over the pillow, as she gave in to the effects of the herb tea she had taken only a short time before. Charlotte was glad to see Madelón relaxing and hoped she would sleep through the storm, lulled by the monotonous pounding of the wind and rain without.

Lantern in hand, she descended the staircase into the well of darkness below. Although it was only midday, with the shutters closed and the sky black as midnight outside, the whole downstairs part of the house was cloaked in darkness. She knew her way around the place by heart now, however, and walked past the familiar silhouettes of counters and racks with little hesitation. She could definitely hear the shutter banging now and knew just the one it was. She went directly towards the back storeroom.

As soon as she opened the door of the room, a gust of angry, rain-laden wind lashed out defiantly at her and nearly knocked her to the floor. Setting her lantern down on a barrel out of the direct current of air, she fought her way over to where the gaping window stood with flapping shutters and struggled to close it once more. The white netting that had spanned the opening hung in shreds from the frame.

By the time she had managed to get the shutters closed and latched again, she was damp from the spray of the storm. Impatiently she dabbed her face and neck dry with the ends of her fichu, thinking with annoyance how she would have to put her hair up in a cap after all, now that it had gotten wet.

At that moment she heard the creak of a floorboard behind her, and even as she thought fearfully that a rat might have gotten into the stockroom, she was suddenly grabbed from behind and pulled backwards. A coarse hand was clapped over her mouth before she could utter a sound of protest, and she felt the sharp point of a knife pricking at her throat.

The odor of stale sweat and alcohol filled her nostrils as a voice whispered in her ear, "Not a peep, Missy, or I'll slit that pretty throat of yours, you understand?"

She was too petrified to answer, but he pulled her even closer and pressed the point of the knife against her flesh until it nearly drew blood.

"Did you hear what I said, Missy? Not a peep!" he insisted, until she nodded her head stiffly in acquiescence.

He swung her around so she faced him, but kept the knife close to her throat all the while. "Well, look what we have here now," he grinned, his dark, bloodshot eyes glistening in the flickering light of the lantern, as he looked down appraisingly at her from his lofty height. "If it isn't the last of those little Casquette Girls—the one that's so hard to please! Well, you can stop your looking now, Missy, for here's a real man to breech you. Been waiting for Gaston, *non*?"

He grabbed her by the hair and tilted her terrified face up to his swarthy one, peering out at her like a shaggy bear through a tangled mass of matted hair and beard hanging wildly about his shoulders. "I was just noseying around here taking my pick of the stock," he said, with a wave of his hand toward a large sack lying on the floor filled to the brim with articles, "and I wás in the middle of trying to decide if I shouldn't maybe go upstairs and take my pick from the higher-class merchandise up there, when as luck would have it, here you come marching down to me!"

She struggled to free herself. "You'd better go," she warned, trying to keep her voice steady so he wouldn't know how frightened she really was. "You'll be in trouble if you're found here. I'm not alone, you know."

"Now don't tease Gaston, little Missy. I know no one's here but you and that pregnant girl upstairs. As for that old crone, I could slit her throat faster than I could skin a rabbit. But then we don't need anymore company down here than just we two, right?"

Charlotte knew he was taking advantage of the fact that she wouldn't want to do anything that would alarm her friend. In Madelón's delicate condition, such a shock would more than likely kill both her and the baby. As for the hope of anyone outside hearing her, the intruder well knew that the rage of the storm would more than cover any cries she might utter. Suddenly she realized just how alone and helpless she was. Charles . . . Pierre . . . Inwardly she shouted their names, but she knew they would not be coming. No one would. She was isolated in the midst of a raging storm with a demon from hell.

"Come on, Missy, don't keep putting on your airs with me!" he whined coaxingly, as she instinctively began to retreat from him. "You came all the way over from France hot for a man, didn't you? That's what you wenches came here for, *non*?"

Her eyes flashed up defiantly at him, as she stepped back again, but he continued to move in closer, like an animal stalking its prey. Finally the shelf-lined wall was behind her and she could retreat no farther.

Outside the storm had broken in all its fury, and the building groaned and quivered under the relentless onslaught of spiraling wind and rain.

The stranger pressed closer, moving in for the kill.

"You're not going to hold off Gaston like I been seeing you do those fine *prétendants* of yours," he sneered. "You got a real man here now who's not in the mood to play your pretty parlor games!"

He reached out and ripped the gold pin off from her fichu. After an appraising glance, he smiled and dropped it greedily into the pocket of his baggy breeches.

Then, holding the knife poised for one long moment directly in front of her widening eyes, he slowly, deliberately lowered it. She followed its gleaming tip with hypnotic fascination, as he lifted the white linen scarf up with the blade and flicked it aside with a contemptuous chuckle. Then, with the deftness of one who had trapped and skinned animals for many a year, he began to slash her lacings, one by one, from the top to the bottom of her stomacher, all the while delighting in the terror he saw mounting in the girl's eyes.

Finally in one brusque sweep, he caught the loosened bodice and tore it impatiently away. For a moment he stood there staring in disbelief.

"Mon Dieu!" he murmured, his mouth agape. "But this old trapper's gone and caught hisself a real fine hide! Damned if I've ever seen a pair of *mamelles* the likes of yours before!"

A flash of lightening zigzagged across the room from between the shutters and a clap of thunder ripped open the sky as the torrents of rain came pouring down with such force that it seemed the very walls would give way. For a moment everything seemed unreal to Charlotte. The room spun crazily around her as giant shadows danced wildly in the lamplight to the howling of the wind and the incessant pounding of the rain. This couldn't be happening! She'd be awakening at any moment now to find it was all just a horrible nightmare . . .

She had seen a similar look in Blégot's eyes that day in the garden, but he had been just a foolish old man playing a childish game. Charlotte knew instinctively that this stranger standing before her now wasn't going to be content just to pet and fondle her.

"Look at you!" continued the trapper, running a rough, weatherbeaten hand over the smooth roundness of her breasts in awed fascination, while she cringed beneath his touch. "Just like satin! So you really are a little convent girl ready for her first man, *vraiment*? What you say we have a tumble and then you go home with Gaston in his *pirogue*? I'll take you to my cabin in the swamps and you be my woman, *non*? I treat you good. You'll see. You came to New Orleans to find a man, *n'est-ce pas*? *Bien*, you'll have *beaucoup homme* in Gaston, I promise you that!" He tweaked her nipple in rough playfulness, heedless of her protesting moan. "I'll give you plenty loving like you want and maybe you'll cook and sew for your Gaston, too, eh? I'm a good trapper . . . make you a good husband. What you say?"

He grinned through his broken teeth as he caught her chin in his large paw and peered down into her white, terrified face. The loathing with which she glared back surprised him. He reeled as if she had struck him and anger welled up in him at her open contempt.

"Never mind," he grumbled crossly. "You'll change your mind once I've rolled you a few times. Like any filly, you just need breaking in, that's all."

His hand began fumbling at her skirts, working its way to her thigh. The edges of the shelves bruised the flesh of her bare back as she tried to recoil from him.

"Come on, wench," he growled impatiently. "Stop being coy! Off with all those fluffs and frills! Let's get down to the rest of you and no more foolishness. Once I've breeched you, you'll come along willingly enough."

But she stood paralyzed, unable to obey.

The howling wind had subsided somewhat and she could

hear his heavy breathing even more clearly against the backdrop of the steady downpour, as he fumbled clumsily with the ties of her skirts.

"This *pelletier* is going to skin your hide good, Missy!" he chuckled in her ear.

Something deep inside of her snapped. In desperation she lunged sidewards, away from him, dashing wildly for the doorway to the outer room. Better to brave the storm without than stay and submit to the indignities within. If she could only make it to the front door . . .

But with an agility that was surprising in one so large he lunged after her and caught her before she could make more than a few steps. With an angry snarl he pulled her back again and threw her down to the floor against the sack of loot he had gathered to take with him. He was on top of her now, muttering obscenities and groping beneath the layers of underskirts, clawing at her buttocks.

Lashing out wildly in all directions, Charlotte suddenly brushed against the half-empty brandy bottle lying beside the sack where it had probably been left when she had interrupted the intruder in his sampling of the storeroom's wares. As the flask teetered, it splashed some of its contents over her hand. Without stopping to think what she was doing, she instinctively clutched the neck of the bottle, even as she felt his broken teeth grazing her flesh.

With a cry of pain she brought the bottle down with all her might on top of him. It broke in two, splashing what remained of the brandy over both of them.

Surprise flashed across the trapper's face, as he partially lifted his head from where he was bending over her. He was woozy, as a trickle of blood began to wend its way down his forehead, but he did not release his hold on her.

She brought the broken bottle down on his head again, and this time his eyes glazed as he toppled over unconscious on top of her.

For a moment she lay there stunned, crushed beneath his heavy weight, wondering what to do next. *Mon Dieu!* He might come to at any moment and it would start all over again!

Cautiously taking the knife out of his lax fingers, she worked herself slowly, painfully upwards and out from un-

190

der that massive hulk, pulling frantically at her skirts. Even in death he was trying to drag her down to hell with him! But no, he wasn't dead. She could see the rise and fall of his breathing in the midst of that grotesque mountain of flesh lying there almost doubled up in the flickering lamplight.

Getting to her feet unsteadily, she caught the lantern in a trembling hand and ran out of the storeroom as though the devil himself were after her. The key . . . the key . . . she had to find the key!

Although the Pichous seldom locked that inner door, she knew they usually kept a key for it on a peg behind the main counter. Fumbling about nervously among the shelves, she searched desperately, fearful that at any moment that enormous bulk would be towering above her again. After an eternity of minutes, her stiff, fumbling fingers finally closed over the large, rusty key she had been looking for.

With a sigh of relief, she returned to the storeroom and, after only a fleeting glance at the unconscious form on the floor, she quickly slammed the door shut and locked it.

The storm had died down now, but there was a steady rain, and she doubted the women above could hear her, even if she tried to call to Deedee to come help her. Clutching the torn remnants of her bodice about her, she dashed up the stairs, her legs feeling so weak and shaky that she feared they wouldn't last to carry her to the top.

Not wishing to enter Madelón's room and frighten her, she called out from the other side of the doorway to Deedee in as calm a voice as she could muster that she would like to see her in the hall. She had to call twice before the old Negress finally stirred from her dozing and came out. Charlotte was relieved to see Madelón still sleeping peacefully, oblivious to the storm and all else around her at that moment.

For the first time since Charlotte had known Deedee the old slave's ebony face registered some signs of surprise when she saw the girl standing in the hallway in her tattered, brandy-stained dress. But with that customary acceptance of whatever she was told, the old Negress followed Charlotte down the stairs without question and obeyed, as the

191

young girl asked her to help pile up whatever they could find in front of the door so the trapper could not get out of the storeroom when he regained consciousness.

"But not a word of this to Madame Madelón," she cautioned Deedee. "If she asks where I am, just tell her I'm tending to something downstairs and will be up shortly. Stay there with her as if everything were all right, but listen in case I need you. Come quickly if I should call. Do you understand?"

Then, throwing a loose peignoir over her nakedness, she pulled up a chair and sat facing the entrance of the storeroom. With a lantern at her side and the trapper's knife in her hand, she took up her lonely vigil.

Chapter XXIX

Although it had seemed like an eternity, actually only an hour or so had passed from the time Charlotte had gone below to check the banging shutter until she had called Deedee to help her barricade the intruder in the storeroom.

The storm continued for a while longer, but as the day wore on it gradually calmed down to a steady drizzle, until around three o'clock in the afternoon it finally moved on.

There was no sound from the storeroom, and Charlotte began to wonder whether she might have killed the man after all. Perhaps she had only imagined she had seen him breathing.

But always the nagging fear that he might come charging out of the doorway at any moment returned to terrify her. Would the counter and all the things she and Deedee had piled on top of it be enough to hold him off? He was such a giant of a man.

She didn't know what she would do if he came after her again. The inward trembling wouldn't stop. Perhaps if she could cry . . . but the tears wouldn't come. She didn't dare give in to her emotions. It was important that she keep her wits about her to face whatever was yet to come.

The Pichous were the first to arrive. Worried over the damage the storm might have done and afraid some emergency might have arisen with Madelón, they had rushed back as soon as the storm had subsided. Their daughter had had a quick and easy delivery and given birth to a fine, strapping son, so they had left her doing very well, although she had urged them to spend the night with her instead of trying to make their way back through the flooded streets. Everyone had told them it was foolish to go out again, but the elderly couple had remained firm in their resolve to return home. So their son-in-law had brought them across town in his small *pirogue*.

The water was up to the doorways, filled with debris blown about by the swift but destructive passage of the hurricane, although fortunately its eye had not passed directly over the city, so they had thus been spared some of the greater damage and loss of lives so often left in the wake of such tropical storms spawned by the turbulent Gulf. It was at times like this that the colonists were thankful the founders of New Orleans had decided to locate their city farther upriver.

The Pichous entered the store commenting on the fact that the sign above their door was gone, blown to they knew not where, but they stood frozen in their tracks when they saw Charlotte sitting disheveled in the middle of the empty store with a counter and a mountain of furniture and merchandise piled up against the stockroom door.

Charlotte's relief knew no bounds when she saw them, and she ran eagerly to greet them. They listened in wide-eyed amazement as she related all that had happened that afternoon.

While Madame Pichou tried to console her, her husband loaded his musket. They were busily pushing aside the obstacles to the storeroom door with the intention of confronting the intruder anew when Pierre arrived. Fortunately he had come from his townhouse only a few blocks away, but his boots and clothes were spattered with mud from slushing through the flooded streets. Despite the fact that he had supposed Dubair to be with them and disliked the thought of encountering his rival there, he wanted to be sure Charlotte and her friends had suffered no damage during the storm.

He hadn't expected, however, to find the scene that confronted him, and when Charlotte and the Pichous related all that had happened, he was so indignant that he insisted he be the one to enter the storeroom first to deal with the scoundrel.

He took the trembling gril in his arms and gently comforted her as she poured out the story to him. *"Dios mío!"* he exclaimed, his face contorted with rage. "I'll cut the villain to shreds! He'll pay dearly for what he's done!"

Charlotte began to relax a little as she felt the security of Pierre's arms around her and knew she was no longer alone.

Madame Pichou suggested they summon the police, but Pierre said they wouldn't need anyone but the undertaker when he got through with the man.

They moved the rest of the things off the counter and shoved it aside. Then, cautiously opening the door, Pichou aimed the musket into the dimly lit room while Pierre entered.

But the trapper and his sack were gone. The freshly washed air that penetrated the open window through which he had fled filled the room with a damp uneasy atmosphere, still charged with the impact of the recent hurricane. The ransacked merchandise and broken brandy bottle on the floor were all that remained now to give mute testimony to the storm that had raged within those walls.

Madelón was calling down to them, for she had awakened, and the sound of so many excited voices and shuffling around of furniture had aroused her curiosity. Madame Pichou went hurriedly upstairs to assure the girl that all was well.

She had no sooner gone when Dubair made a breathless entrance. His buckskins were caked with mud and soaking wet, for he and his party had been hit by the hurricane while still on the last lap of their journey upriver from Balize. His apology for having been delayed, however, hung half-finished on his lips, as he saw Charlotte's confused appearance and noted the drawn weapons in the hands of Treval and Pichou.

"*Mon Dieu!* But what's happening here?"

M. Pichou was the first to find his voice.

"Charlotte had an intruder," he answered, as he set his musket down at last. "The poor girl had to fight him off and managed to lock him in the storeroom until we got home. But it looks as if he got away."

The captain blanched beneath his tan, and his usual aplomb momentarily left him.

"Oh, my God!" he groaned, visibly shaken. "How could such a thing have happened?"

In three long strides he was beside her, gently drawing her into his arms, oblivious of anyone else at that moment. He sensed she was half-naked beneath the flowered silk peignoir she had thrown over her tattered gown, and the anguish that welled up within him nearly choked off his voice as he asked anxiously, "Are you all right, *ma petite?* My sweet little one, tell me you're all right!"

She didn't mind the mud and dampness of his clothes. The feel of those familiar arms, where she had known refuge from danger in the past, seemed to break the dam of her stifled emotions, and even as she assured him she was unharmed, she began to weep softly, clinging instinctively to him all the while.

Pierre watched with mounting rage as Dubair continued to hold her close and murmur tender phrases in her ear. To see Charlotte being comforted, even for a moment, in another man's arms was more than he could bear.

"*Capitaine,* I think you're forgetting yourself with mademoiselle!" he said, trying desperately to keep himself from lunging on Dubair and physically tearing him and the girl apart.

Charlotte felt the captain tensing, but before he could reply she held out her hand to Pierre, and retaining Charles's, as well, led them both over to a bench on one side of the store and made them sit beside her. They continued to glare at each other over her head.

"Please, *mes amis,* this isn't the time to engage in petty

jealousies," she said. "You don't know the comfort it is to have both of you here with me right now."

At that moment Madame Pichou came downstairs and joined them once more, announcing that Madelón hadn't suspected anything. "She thinks everyone is excited because of the storm. She has no idea anything else has happened."

Suddenly Dubair, who had fallen silent, spoke his thoughts aloud. "I'm sure I know who the man was," he muttered through clenched teeth. The stubble of a week's beard couldn't hide the twitching of his jaw as he spoke of the trapper. "I've been thinking . . . From the description you give, Charlotte, and the fact you say he calls himself Gaston, I'm sure we can track him down. If it's the one I'm thinking of, he's always been a troublemaker around town. He's one of those many convicts the Duke of Orleans, our fair city's one-time patron and benefactor, graced us with a few years back!"

"If you do find the scoundrel," interjected Pierre, his dark eyes as stormy as the hurricane that had just passed, "I want to deal with him, too."

"He'll be hanged," said Dubair tersely.

"But I feel I have a right to represent Charlotte in this matter, as well," protested Pierre.

"There's no need to make a scandal of this incident, for Charlotte's sake," retorted the captain. "The law is very strict on such matters and the man will pay for his villainy with his life, you may rest assured of that."

"All of this never would have happened," observed the Creole, "if I could have been here with her as I would have been, if it hadn't been that you'd asked for this Sunday with her and then didn't show up!"

Charles flushed, his blue eyes flashing out angrily from his suntanned face. "I'm the first to lament the fact that I couldn't come as soon as I'd hoped, but I assure you the circumstances were beyond my control."

Madame Pichou saw tempers mounting, so she quickly interrupted. "Actually, my husband and I feel terribly guilty about all of this. If it's anyone's fault it's ours for having left the girls alone just with Deedee as we did."

Pichou shook his balding head sadly and added, "I'm

afraid the fault is mine for not having fixed that latch on the storeroom window better. I knew it didn't catch that well. I'm the one to blame."

Charlotte threw her hands up in protest. "Please, all of you! It's no one's fault. I won't have any of you blaming yourselves. Only *le bon Dieu* knows why such things happen."

Pierre caught one of her uplifted hands impulsively in his. "Perhaps it was His way of letting you know you should be married, my dear, living in your own home with a husband to defend you. I want so much to protect you, but as long as you vacillate between me and the captain, you're really only half-protected."

"And what do you mean by that, monsieur?" asked Dubair quickly, already smarting from the Creole's previous attempt to place the blame for Charlotte's recent ordeal on his shoulders.

"No offense meant, *Capitaine*, but Charlotte needs a man who can respond for her at all times. As a soldier, you must admit your life is not your own to offer her at this moment."

The Creole had hit a sore spot with Dubair. It had been his own reason for not having pursued Charlotte from the very beginning. "I confess that originally I, too, had thought of waiting until I could resign from scouting before asking anyone to become my wife," he admitted, "but I realize now we cannot subject our personal lives forever to outside factors. Life goes on and we must try to adapt to the situation in which we find ourselves and continue living," He was really addressing Charlotte now, pleading his case with her, not just justifying himself to a rival. "Naturally I'd like to have everything perfect to lay at Charlotte's feet. She knows my plans. But in the meantime, if she'll have me, I'll go about getting what we need with her at my side. Besides, I won't be scouting after the end of this year."

"A pretty speech, monsieur," smiled Pierre," but the fact remains that, in spite of all your good intentions, Mlle. Charlotte needs a man now, at this very moment, and as long as you're a backwoodsman, how do you expect to protect her while you're off on your expeditions up and down the river?"

197

"If it weren't for backwoodsmen like me and my men, Charlotte and the rest of you would be in even greater danger," snapped Dubair, always sensitive to slurs about his *coureur de bois* activities.

"I'm not making light of your work, *Capitaine*. It's needed and greatly appreciated by all of us in the colony, but permit me to point out that, be that as it may, you cannot be in two places at the same time. On the other hand, if Charlotte were my wife, things would be different. I'd see to it she'd never be unattended."

"Oh, I'm sure you would," replied Dubair, sarcasm creeping into his voice. "You could always assign her to your mother or your servants. I've seen how you aristocrats mind your wives while you're off gambling or visiting your mistresses. My poor Charlotte would be well attended all right in her life of luxurious loneliness."

The blood rushed to the roots of Treval's dark hair as he drew himself up sharply. "You're simply making conjectures now to evade the crucial point of this discussion, which is which one of us could attend Mademoiselle Charlotte better. Married to me, she'd never be alone."

"*Bien,* and who said I'd leave her unattended if she were my wife? Even if she were to wed me before the year is out, I'm not that poor a man I couldn't hire a few trustworthy servants to watch over her when I couldn't be there myself. But one thing is certain, monsieur when I'm not at her side, she'll know it's because I'm off defending her and the colony and not for more frivolous reasons!"

"Charles . . . Pierre . . . please don't continue this quarreling," begged Charlotte, sensing they were heading toward a dangerous point of no return. But they rushed on, as though eager to lock horns at last.

"Surely, *Capitaine*, you cannot compare what you have to offer with what I could give her. If it's her welfare you really care about . . ."

"Oh, I know you live a fine life, monsieur," sneered Dubair, regretting that he had to stand facing this elegant beau with his lace-trimmed jabot and cuffs and embroidered frock coat, while he wore his dirty, mud-spattered buckskins and sported an unkempt beard. "It'll always be easy for you while *pauvres diables* like me slush around out there in the swamps spilling out our guts in the muck so popinjays like you can go on living your life of leisure here in the city!"

Treval's hand flew to his sword. "*Capitaine*, you tread on dangerous ground when you put my honor in question. If the town were in real peril, I'd be the first to defend it with my life."

"I don't doubt it," conceded Dubair. "Once the shoe pinched you and yours, you'd be forced to do something about it. But meanwhile you *fainéants*—you do-nothings—make merry and let others fight your battles, even as you belittle them, until you can no longer get out of doing it yourselves! Bah!"

Pierre's sword was halfway out of its sheathe, his face engulfed in fury. "You're calling me a coward, *Capitaine*, and that I cannot let pass."

"I'm only stating facts, monsieur. If the coat fits, put it on!"

Charlotte felt helpless to stop the flow of words. It was as if a dam of pent-up emotions had finally broken and a flood of long-standing resentments had suddenly burst forth. It was not just the rivalry between two *prétendants* now. It had suddenly become the clash of opposing ways of life, the contempt between classes. It had taken the tension of that afternoon's unnerving events to bring the conflict out into the open, but it had always been there, seething, waiting to surface at the slightest provocation. Their jealousy had been the spark to ignite the fire, but the kindling had always been there.

She jumped up quickly and stopped the Creole from drawing his rapier. "Pierre, please!" she pleaded. "I won't have you two fighting like this!"

She could feel him trembling with rage as she detained his hand.

Finally he let his sword slip back in place. "My seconds will see you in the morning, *Capitaine*," he said tersely.

In despair Charlotte turned to Charles, who, although he had a musket slung over his shoulder, wore no sword at that moment. He had raised his hand to the dagger in his belt, however, ready to defend himself if Treval had attacked him.

Dubair hesitated for a moment longer. Then he, too, let his hand drop. "Agreed. We'll discuss details tomorrow morning. There's no need to subject Charlotte to our differences. She's been through enough already."

She stood there helpless between them.

"Why can't you wait . . . just a little more time . . . let me decide for myself! You both agreed . . ." she begged, as tears welled up in her eyes.

"Little one, the time has come for us to settle things once and for all," said Dubair solemnly. "We can't go on like this any longer."

"Oh, no!" moaned Charlotte, looking tearfully from one set face to the other.

"It's really best this way," Pierre told her. "You're too young and inexperienced to make such a decision for yourself, my dear. We may as well do it for you."

"If either of you hurts the other, I'll never forgive you!"

"Unfortunately there's no way to know how a duel will end, *ma petite*. It's in the hands of God now."

They could not be cajoled this time. There was no governor to intercede, no more arguments they would listen to. So many words had been uttered on both sides. Jealousy and hurt pride could not be reasoned with. A challenge had been given and accepted, and neither one could withdraw at this point without shame and disgrace—and neither Charles nor Pierre was a man who could live without honor.

As she bade them goodbye, she felt it was for the last time. For there would be no victor. Charlotte knew she could never be happy with the one who survived, for the shadow of the other would always be between them.

Chapter XXX

Although Madame Pichou put her to bed after a good bath and cup of relaxing herb tea, Charlotte could not sleep. Nor could she eat anything. Although the Pichous insisted she not go downstairs to help them in the store that day, she still could not rest.

Through the thin netting of the upstairs windows she could glimpse the townspeople busily clearing the debris from the streets. The shouts of some boys playing with a water snake that had wandered in from the swamp rang out over the busy hum of voices drifting up from below.

The sun had come out again in all its force, and although customers told the Pichous that a few of the streets remained flooded, the water in the heart of the town, where they were, had already gone down completely, and if the sun continued to blaze down on them the rest of the day, the rain-soaked *banquettes* and dwellings would be steaming by noon and dry by nightfall. Soon the mud in the streets would turn to dust again.

Sister Marie came by early that morning to fetch Deedee. She had been forced to cut short her sick calls and return post-haste to the convent that previous afternoon when it had become evident that the storm was really going to be the tail end of a hurricane.

The nun listened to the succession of events that had taken place in bewilderment, trying to follow it all as best she could, as she exclaimed, *"Mon Dieu!"* every now and then and, shaking her wimpled head, crossed herself.

"The good Lord sometimes sends us ordeals to try us, child," she said, encircling the sobbing girl within the long, flowing sleeves of her habit. "At least, in His mercy, He spared you the worst. I should have never allowed you to talk me into letting you live away from the convent. None of this would have happened if you'd been there where you belong, or better yet, would be married and living in your own home under the protection that only a husband could give you in the community.

"As for the duel between Treval and the captain," she continued, "I've been afraid that was coming. I warned you, my dear, you couldn't keep men like that dangling on a string forever. It's a pity they had to reach this point, for I'm afraid there's nothing you or even they can do now without one of them losing face, which to men like them would be worse than losing life itself. I only hope and pray no tragedy will result from their encounter."

"Oh, *Soeur* Marie, if one of them is killed, I'll die, too!" exclaimed Charlotte. "I'll never stop blaming myself, for I will have brought one of them to his death simply because of my foolish indecision! But even now, I can't honestly say which one I'm praying for the most! If either one of them dies tomorrow . . ."

"Whatever happens, child, I think God has given you sufficient signs that you should wed as soon as possible. Of course, Madelón is too near her time now for you to leave, but you should return to the convent the moment she's delivered. That is, you should stay there at least until you're married."

"I don't think I'll ever marry now. If either Charles or Pierre doesn't survive that duel, I'll never be able to be happy with the one who does. Yet I'm sure I'll never be happy unless I marry one of them, for I dearly love them both. Oh, *Soeur* Marie, I'm so confused and miserable!"

"My poor child, you've suffered so much in these past twenty-four hours!"

"Even the memory of that horrible intruder fades before the vision of what tomorrow might bring," confessed Charlotte. "All I can think of at this moment is what will happen to Charles and Pierre. Do you think if I went to the governor . . . ?"

"They'd be furious if you did. Besides, it would solve nothing. It didn't at the ball, and would not today. I'm afraid there are things between them that even drawing lots for you wouldn't settle."

"Perhaps if I went to the dueling ground and pleaded again with them . . ."

"My dear, you must face the facts. It's too late now for anything else."

"I don't know how I'll be able to live until tomorrow, much less all the long years afterwards if one of them is killed because of me!"

"Have courage, child, and pray for guidance. Ask God to watch over them. They're both good men, a little too stubborn and proud perhaps, but good men. Put them in the hands of the Blessed Virgin."

Sister Marie left with Deedee, promising to return the following morning. "Meanwhile, pray, child . . . pray."

Madelón wasn't feeling too well that day, but she tried to put some finishing touches on the baby clothes and made one or two straw brooms for the Pichous. Unaware of the turmoil in her friend's heart at that moment, she could, nevertheless, see that something was wrong and asked her about it.

"I just don't feel well. It's probably just a touch of the vapors, that's all," was Charlotte's only reply.

Although she had not eaten since lunch the afternoon before, Charlotte still had no appetite and only agreed to take an occasional sip of tea or broth just to appease her friends. She spent most of her time on the cot in Madelón's, room, drained of energy, aching in spirit as well as body. Rising only when necessary to attend to her friend, she moved with leaden feet, her head swimming with confusion over the recent events, which had left a storm raging within her that made the one that had racked the town seem like a summer shower by comparison.

When Madelón finally dozed off around dusk, Charlotte rose quickly and groped her way over to the *priedieu* in a corner of the dimly lit room, illumined only by the feeble light of the votive candle flickering before a crudely fashioned image of the Virgin and two smaller figures of saints beside her.

"Oh, blessed mother of God," begged Charlotte, fixing her eyes upon the statue with desperate intensity, as she lifted her clenched hands in supplication. "Don't let Charles and Pierre hurt each other. Quench the fires of anger between them and let only love remain. Surely there cannot be evil in so much love! But if anyone must be punished, let it be me. The fault is mine, not theirs."

She had placed the gold chain Pierre had given her with her aunt's locket on it around her neck, but no longer having Charles's gift, she had gently laid the dried sprig of laurel leaves that had inspired the stolen brooch in her kerchief and slipped it between her breasts. Futile, foolish gestures now, she knew, but it comforted her to have those symbols of their love so close to her as she prayed for them. Perhaps they would move the Blessed Virgin's heart just a little . . .

Madelón began labor pains in the middle of the night. Her cries had awakened Charlotte from where she had fallen asleep, still on her knees at the *priedieu*. The room was hot and stifling. She lit a lantern and rushed to call the Pichous.

Although it was still two or three weeks before the calculated time, Madame Pichou was certain Madelón's hour had come, so she sent her husband shuffling off, still half-asleep, to find the midwife. Meanwhile the women dressed hurriedly and took up their vigil beside Madelón, who lay groaning and tossing about her bed in pain, her gown drenched with sweat.

Madame Pichou had Charlotte put on water to boil and gather together some of the things that would be needed.

"I don't know whether the *accoucheuse* will get here in time," lamented the older woman, as she fanned Madelón with one hand and dabbed a cool cloth on the wretched girl's feverish brow with the other. "She's had trouble keeping the baby in her this long!"

Charlotte lit another lantern and ran down the staircase to the kitchen in the back of the store opposite the storeroom. It was four o' clock in the morning. She wondered whether her *prétendants* were sleeping, or perhaps lying awake in anticipation of their duel only a few hours away. They might even be thinking of her . . . cursing her, perhaps, for having brought them to such a pass!

She lit the fire in the kitchen hearth and put a large

copper kettle of water to boil while she dashed about gathering the things Madame Pichou had told her would be needed. Scissors, twine, fresh linen . . . A pitcher and basin? A slop jar? No, there were already several in the commodes upstairs.

She slipped the scissors and cord in the pocket of her apron and piled the towels and a spare sheet in her arms, as she caught the lantern and made her way upstairs again. The blazing fire in the kitchen hearth only served to make the house even more unbearable.

As Charlotte entered the bedroom, Madelón was crying out again and instinctively clutching at her swollen belly. The dimly lit room was heavy with the anguish of pain and late summer heat. A breath of fresh air would have been welcome, but they dared not open the window completely, for the netting stretched across it was black with clusters of mosquitoes droning against it. As it was, two of the insects had somehow managed to get past the barrier and were buzzing with maddening persistence above Madelón's bed, while Madame Pichou tried impatiently to swat at them with the palmetto fan.

The elderly woman had put a leather strap in the moaning girl's mouth so the latter could bite on it instead of her bleeding lips, but as Charlotte went nearer, Madelón reached out and, catching her friend's hand, clung frantically to it, as she murmured incoherent phrases Charlotte could only half understand. "Please . . . don't leave me . . . my baby . . ."

"Don't worry, my dear," soothed Charlotte, stroking her friend's damp forehead lovingly. "We're here, and the *accoucheuse* is coming soon. Everything is going to be all right."

Madame Pichou made a sign to Charlotte with her plump hand to come over to the side of the bed where she was standing.

"The pains are coming quite frequently," she whispered. "We have to be ready. Go back now and get the water. It should be boiling by now. And you'd better put on another kettle before coming up. Fortunately the water barrel is almost full. We'll be needing a lot before this is over."

Downstairs the heat was even more intense. The kitchen

with the fire crackling in its hearth was like an inferno. Charlotte hurriedly took the kettle off the hook and put another freshly filled one on it. The sweat from her forehead rolled down into her eyes, blinding her, and she blinked, trying to clear her vision, as she struggled back up the stairs with the boiling water in one hand and the lantern in the other, hoping she could reach her destination without splashing any of the scalding water on herself.

Madame Pichou, her fat face glistening with sweat, met her at the door and caught the kettle out of her hand quickly. Madelón was twisting and turning in the bed, lashing out her arms and clutching at the empty air around her in a frantic effort to disperse the torment that racked her body.

"Help me, child," directed Madame Pichou. "Tie a corner of the sheet you brought me to the post at the foot of the bed and knot it on the free end. It'll be easier for the poor dear if she had something to hold on to."

"Oh, Charlotte . . . is that you?" came Madelón's voice, so weak it was barely audible.

"Yes, dear, I'm here. We won't leave you."

As soon as Charlotte had tied the sheet to the foot of the bed, Madame Pichou sent her off again to fetch more water.

"You'd better bring me another sheet, too, when you come back," Madame called out after her. "Get one from the storeroom if you can't find any more in the cupboard."

Charlotte went first to the kitchen. Charles and Pierre would be getting ready now . . . duels were usually at dawn. Had they chosen swords or pistols? She knew both her suitors were highly skilled at arms. Pierre had mentioned once that he had already experienced such an encounter when he had first come to New Orleans, and on that occasion he had emerged the victor. Among gentlemen of quality, until one could say *J'ai fait mes preuves*—"I have proven myself on the field of honor"—he could not be considered a man.

Although Charles had never had reason to duel in private before, he was a soldier and had had more than his share of combat, especially the desperate kind, hand to hand fighting against savage foes in the swamplands. Fighting to him had always been more than just a question of defending one's honor—it was usually a life or death matter.

Charlotte took the kettle off the hook before the water could boil away, and then checked what linens were left in the cupboard. Just the thought of going near the storeroom again had set her insides trembling.

There were no more sheets left, however, so she picked up the lantern and the steaming kettle and reluctantly walked out into the still dark store.

Leaving the boiling water to one side of the staircase, as she passed it, she proceeded along the same route she had taken that Sunday afternoon toward the stockroom, making her way with heavy steps to where she knew the dreaded door was.

Panic gripped her heart. She saw the familar portal looming up before her in the faltering glow of her lamp. A paralyzing fear was creeping over her, the feeling that danger lay behind that closed door. She couldn't shake off the sensation that all was not right. She realized now that she had probably been more affected by her harrowing experience with the thief than she had cared to admit.

Still hesitating, she reached out and touched the key in the door, but then pulled her hand back in amazement. How hot it was! And the odor of burning kindling . . . She realized now it was somehow stronger here than it had been in the kitchen.

Lifting the lantern high, she stepped back and let the circle of its light fall over the full span of the doorway. It was then she saw it. Small tufts of smoke were curling out from around the edges!

Fear giving wings to her feet, she dashed back toward the staircase, nearly tripping over the kettle of steaming water she had left there. Catching it up quickly, she raced up the steps, heedless of the water she was spilling along the way.

"Madame! Oh, Madame! I'm afraid the storeroom's on fire!" she exclaimed breathlessly, trying to keep her voice down enough so that Madelón would not hear.

But her friend was oblivious to anything but her own

all-consuming pain at that moment, as she stifled a scream through the leather belt in her mouth and tugged desperately on the knotted sheet tied to the bedpost.

"Madame! The storeroom is on fire! What shall we do?" repeated Charlotte anxiously.

Madame Pichou, however, had her hands full. She was bending over the tormented girl on the bed and couldn't even so much as lift her head at that moment.

"Go to the neighbors and try to get help," she said. "I can't leave her right now—the baby's coming!"

Charlotte raced back down the stairs. The odor of burning wood was strong now. She dashed across the store to the front door. From where she stood, she could see tiny tongues of flame beginning to work their way through the cracks of the storeroom door.

Fumbling nervously with the bolt on the street door, she finally drew it back and ran out onto the banquette. The sky was grey now, but it still lacked a little more time before actual sunrise.

"Fire! *Incendie! Au secours!* Help me, please!" Lifting her lantern high above her, she stood in the middle of the street shouting at the top of her lungs for any and all to hear. Then, desperation mounting with every passing moment, she ran from door to door, pounding against each one, as she continued to call out.

Windows began to open and night-capped heads peeped out at her through bewildered sleep-swollen eyes. As soon as they heard that dread word *incendie*, however, they sprang into action, well knowing that unchecked fires had been known to speed through a town like wildfire. There was no time to lose.

For Charlotte, the scene soon took on the aspects of a nightmare, with people rushing about in desperate confusion, trying to form a bucket brigade and at the same time carrying out as much of the merchandise as they could from the store to the street, in the hopes of saving something if their efforts should fail.

The stockroom was already a total loss, blazing away before the fire brigade could even be organized. Red-gold tongues were lashing out from beneath the staircase, where the storeroom wall backed up against the kitchen, and the rampant flames were meeting in fiery embrace with the ones that had been burning in the hearth.

Charlotte begged one of the men, a tall husky blacksmith with a dark bushy beard, to accompany her upstairs to carry Madelón down.

"Whoever is up there," he grunted, as he eyed the spreading fire with apprehensive eyes, "ought to get out of there but fast!"

She raced ahead, calling out to Madame Pichou that they had to abandon the premise. But suddenly, as she was about halfway up the staircase, the latter came running down towards her, her plump figure a mass of pulsating flesh, as she grabbed Charlotte by the arm and exclaimed tearfully, "They're dead, Charlotte! God knows I tried to save them, but they're both dead!"

"Come then," urged the blacksmith, taking Madame Pichou's arm and turning to go back down the stairs. "We have to get out of here fast, before the whole upstairs caves in over the storeroom."

Charlotte stood on the staircase, unable to believe what was happening.

"Dead? Oh, no! It can't be . . ." She continued wild-eyed up the steps. "*Non, non* . . . Madelón! Madelón! You must come with us!"

Madame Pichou reached out a plump hand to detain her. "No, child, it's no use. The poor girl's heart just suddenly gave out, and the baby—it never so much as drew a breath! I tell you they're dead!"

The blacksmith, who was already descending the staircase and pulling Madame Pichou with him, held out a hand to Charlotte as he urged her to come down with them.

But the girl had lost all reason. She knew only that she had to save Madelón and the baby.

Sparks were beginning to rise up through the cracks in the floorboards as she entered the dimly lit bedroom. It was as if she had suddenly stepped into the fiery realms of Hades itself. In the ghostly light creeping in through the white netting on the window, she could distinguish Madelón, her long pale hair streaming about her like a canopy

209

of spun gold. Her lovely face was quiet, all torment gone from it now. Beside her lay an equally still bundle.

Charlotte went over to the bed and touched her friend's shoulder in disbelief. "Madelón! Come, *chérie*, you must come! I'll help you!" she kept repeating. How could Madelón be dead? She was lying there so warm and lovely . . .

She took the girl's limp hand and urged her to try to get up and come with her. It was still warm but there was no pulse.

Off in the distance the church bell was sounding the alarm. People were shouting. Someone below was calling up to her, begging her to go down. But they were drowned out by the pounding of her heart and crackling of the flames beginning to shoot up around her. The heat was overwhelming. She could still hear Madelón's last words to her . . . "Save my baby . . ."

Grabbing her cloak from a peg where it hung on the wall and emptying a kettle of water over it, she wrapped its generous circumference around herself from head to foot. Then, catching the tiny bundle to her breast beneath the protective folds of the cape, she brushed a gentle kiss on Madelón's smooth brow, still damp with the sweat of her labor, and made the sign of the cross over her. Hot tears stung her eyes as she looked down for the last time on her friend's lovely, Madonna-like face. To leave her there alone in the midst of the consuming fire . . . to take her baby away like that from her side . . .

The floor trembled under her feet, and Charlotte turned quickly to make her way out of the room. Yet she paused to snatch up one more thing, a battered little box that contained the only worldly possessions left behind by Madelón Ansleau: the small sum of money that her husband had labored so long and hard to accumulate for a future that had never come, and a long string of pearls.

Looking down from the top of the staircase, all Charlotte could see was a blur of red. The flames were dancing everywhere. Her eyes burned and her lungs felt as if they would burst. She drew the damp hood down over her face and went blindly on, pressing the tiny bundle beneath the cape even closer against her body. For a fleeting second, she thought she felt a slight resistance. Oh, God! Was it only her imagination, her wishful thinking, or was the baby truly alive?

The stairs began to shake and rumble beneath her as she continued her dash downwards. I'm descending into the lower regions of hell, she thought numbly. The roar of the flames deafened her ears to all other sounds. Would she ever reach the bottom of the stairs? She could barely see the entrance door shimmering and undulating through the ruddy haze that partially veiled it from view. It seemed so far away. She would never make it in time . . .

Suddenly there was a mighty roar behind her as the bedroom began to cave in. The whole second floor was coming down, the staircase with it—Holy mother of God! Sweet Jesus! Madelón was dead . . . her baby lay lifeless in her arms . . . Charles and Pierre were probably illing each other at that very moment . . . her whole world was crashing about her.

Chapter XXXI

The early morning haze hung heavily over the clearing. Dawn was just breaking, and the sun still had not penetrated the spread of the mighty oaks that sheltered the spot with their huge moss-laden branches.

The two men, with a calm born of the assurance that only experience can give, faced each other near the wooden palisade that bounded the limits of the town.

They had chosen swords and stood in their tight-fitting breeches, buckled shoes and white ruffled shirtwaists with blades poised for the signal to begin. Their seconds, with large, delicately designed gold watches in their hands, stood to one side holding the opponents' wide-cuffed, gallooned coats over their arms. Pierre's man, a middle-aged, stoop-shouldered aristocrat, was a member of the *Compagnie*, who seemed rather accustomed to such affairs, but the other, Dubair's young lieutenant Etienne, looked flushed and excited over this, his first experience as a second in a duel.

Both Dubair and Treval were impatient to begin. They had reached the conclusion that such a confrontation was inevitable, so they might as well get it over with.

Dubair was prepared to fight to the death if need be. When a man decides to enter any kind of combat, he must foresee such a possibility. He hoped it wouldn't come to that, however. Not that he owed Treval any favors, but he knew Charlotte would never accept him if he killed the Creole. Treval, with his fine feathers and aristocratic airs, had wooed his inexperienced little Charlotte like the expert he was in affairs of the heart. To an impressionable young girl, he probably seemed like the Prince Charming of her fairy tales. She was dazzled by him, that was all. But he could tell by the way she vibrated whenever they were close to each other that her heart, her desire as a woman, called out to him . . . God was his witness! If ever he had wanted to live, it was now.

Treval knew his opponent was not to be taken lightly, but he felt he had a slight advantage in the choice of arms. The sword was a gentleman's weapon. Dubair would prob-ably be a direct fighter, less schooled in the subtleties of fencing by men of quality. Although Charlotte had been quick to tell him that the captain was highborn, the latter's years of scouting were bound to have left their mark. Well, Dubair would soon realize he was facing a more formidable foe than some redskin or renegade! He supposed a fighter such as Dubair would be inclined to go all the way, and that would be all right with him. *Mon Dieu!* The way he had felt ever since this meddling backwoodsman had thrust himself between him and Charlotte, he could run the man through with pleasure! But he knew he had to play it by ear. Make a martyr of this Dubair, and he might as well let him win the match. This *capitaine*, according to Charlotte, had saved her life on one or two occasions, and he must have seemed like a knight in shining armor to her as he strutted around out there in the muck of the marshlands. If the captain wanted to go all the way, however, he would be more than happy to do so. But he would have to be able to justify himself to Charlotte if he did.

The sun was beginning to disperse the mist.

"Are you ready, messieurs?"

"*Oui.*"

"*Tres bien . . . maintenant . . .* Begin!"

The blades flashed in the grey morning light, their sharply tapered points incisively slicing the dull, thick air. Charles's two-edged rapier was parried by Pierre's three-grooved *colichemarde,* but he was quick to retreat.

The Creole displayed such an amazing flexibility of movement that it was almost impossible to break his guard. Dubair was more aggressive, ever watchful for an opening, yet cautious of his opponent's lithe wrist and footwork.

They thrust and parried until their full white shirtwaists of lawn and lace hung in damp folds upon their perspiring backs.

The seconds watched, fascinated, wondering between themselves who would be the first to draw blood. Even the austere nobleman with his snuff-stained nostrils and red-heeled shoes had become aroused, and the young lieutenant's boyish face was tense with anticipation as he watched the duelers with mouth agape and saucerlike eyes.

Suddenly from off in the distance came the sound of the church bell ringing wildly and sharp cries drifted across the rooftops, past the palisade and into the moss-laden grove where they were fighting.

The seconds looked up from their vigil.

"*Nom de nom!* Fire! The town is afire! See there—that red light in the heart of the city!"

"*Mon Dieu! La ville . . . incendie!*"

The duelers' blades ceased clashing and hung limp at their sides. The red glow lighting up the grey sky above the palisade grew in intensity even as they looked.

"Fire?" repeated Pierre in bewilderment.

"In the heart of the city?" echoed the captain.

"Charlotte is there, isn't she?"

"*Mais oui*—Charlotte!"

In that instant they no longer thought of their rivalry. Their only concern was for her.

Black eyes met blue in mutual consent.

"May I suggest we take up this matter at another time, monsieur?"

Treval had already sheathed his sword.

"*De acuerdo*, and may I further suggest, *Capitaine*, that I leave my carriage at the disposition of our seconds and use, instead—with your permission, of course—one of the horses that you and your lieutenant came here with? We could go faster that way."

"Agreed."

With a few hasty words to their amazed seconds, the two men abandoned the field of honor at a fast gallop.

Chapter XXXII

So here she was, back in the convent again . . . and much the worse for her brief exodus out into the world.

Charlotte lay in her bed, trying to fight off the depression that had overwhelmed her since the fire. She realized she should be grateful to be alive at all. But to be unable to move her legs at all . . . was this the way she was destined to spend the rest of her life?

Although the bruises where the beam had fallen upon her had been big and painful in the beginning, at least the burns had been slight. There had been only a few singed spots where the flames had begun to penetrate her dampened cloak and skirts before the townspeople had managed to douse her with water and rescue her from the burning building.

Over the past two months since the fire, Sister Marie's

poultices of herbs had just about cleared up the worst of the burns and black and blue marks, but Charlotte's legs had remained numb. Although no bones had been broken, something had happened to her lower limbs. It was as if they were paralyzed. No one seemed to know exactly why or what else could be done to help her. The town doctor, the *sage-femme*, and even Madelón's midwife had been called in to examine her, but they all left shaking their heads. It was in God's hands now, they said.

Sister Marie insisted on massaging her legs every day, and Charlotte was touched by the nun's persistent efforts to help her, but sometimes she felt they were fighting a losing battle. Perhaps it was God's will that she never walk again.

At least her sacrifice had not been in vain. Madelón's baby, though premature and fragile like her mother, was alive. If her uncontrollable grief had not sent her, half-crazed, back upstairs, refusing to believe her friend and her newborn child were dead, Madelón's little girl would have perished in the flames! She shuddered at the thought. The blessed Virgin had guided her to that room and then down the stairs again through the fire. People said it had been a miracle that she and the child had survived.

As they had seen her cloaked figure coming through the fire, stumbling toward the front door with the backdrop of the fiery staircase and the second floor caving in behind her, they had immediately begun throwing buckets of water into the entrance to keep the way clear for her. She remembered the charred frame of the open doorway beckoning to her and the sea of anxious faces swimming in the grey light of the breaking day on the other side, even as she had tripped and fallen . . . At that same moment a hail of burning rafters had begun to shower down around her, and a heavy weight had suddenly pinned her down. Helpless and suffocating, she had lain only a few yards from the safety of the waiting doorway.

What happened afterwards came to her now only in fleeting flashes, like vivid tableaux etched in her memory forever by the sharp fingers of fear and pain. The intense heat . . . the stinging odor of acrid smoke burning her eyes, her nostrils, the very core of her being . . . And in the midst of the raging inferno, that joyful sound of the baby whimpering, telling her at last that it was really alive. . . . As the silhouette of a huge man made his way toward her, she remembered holding the child out to him from where she lay trapped beneath the rafter. Then everything had gone blank and she had let herself sink into the bottomless depths of oblivion.

She learned afterwards it had been the blacksmith and his son who had gone in and lifted the beam that had fallen on top of her legs and carried her out. She had no recollection of the fire after that. It had raged for hours, they said, and before it could finally be brought under control, the entire block had gone up in flames. It was a mass of charred ruins now.

The Pichous had gone to live with their daughter and her family. Although the stockroom had been the first to go, much of the merchandise in the store itself had been saved before the fire had spread too badly, so the elderly couple decided to sell it for a lump sum and retire to the more peaceful life of helping their son-in-law in his tailoring business.

Madame Pichou was beside herself when she learned Madelón's baby had not been born dead, as she had thought, and crossed herself every time she recalled the entire ordeal of poor Madelón's delivery and that dreadful moment when the frantic girl had tried to get up to leave the burning building and suddenly fallen back gasping her last breaths of life.

"At least the poor dear never knew her little girl gave all appearances of having been born dead," sighed Madame Pichou, as the tears spilled down her large round countenance. "I could have sworn that baby didn't have a drop of life in her! God forgive me! If it hadn't been for Charlotte, that dear child would have died there in the flames, and we'd have never known! *Mon Dieu!* The very thought of it sends shivers down my spine! If Charlotte hadn't insisted on going back . . ."

They had already rescued Charlotte from the building and Madame Pichou and another woman were trying their best to revive her and the baby at one side of the street, while the majority of the townspeople were still frantically trying to check the rapidly spreading fire, when M. Pichou made his belated arrival with the *accoucheuse* and Sister Marie. He had found the midwife in the midst of birthing a child in a home near the limits of the town, not too far from the Ursulines, so he had notified Sister Marie while he was at it, knowing the good nun would have wanted to be advised. The Ursuline had immediately placed the convent's coach at the disposal of Pichou and the midwife, as well as her own services and those of Deedee's. They had been approaching the Pichou dwelling at a fast trot when they neared the center of town and suddenly realized there was a fire in the vicinity.

On arriving, the *accoucheuse* had immediately taken charge of the baby, which had begun to give more vocal signs of life, while Sister Marie had joined Madame Pichou in trying to attend Charlotte, who was still gasping and choking from the smoke she had inhaled and struggling to get fresh air into her lungs.

Charlotte couldn't remember the exact moment that Charles and Pierre had arrived on the scene, but it must have been shortly afterwards, since they were the ones who had helped put her in the coach, and together with Sister Marie, the *accoucheuse* and the baby, had taken her to the refuge of the convent.

On hearing the familiar voices of Dubair and Treval, Charlotte had stirred and, in her delirium, reached out both hands towards them.

"Where are we?" she murmured confusedly. "Are—are we in heaven?"

"More likely Purgatory!" muttered Pierre, as he and Dubair gently lifted her into the coach, where Sister Marie's black-robed arms waited to support her.

"We're all alive, *ma petite*," soothed Dubair, "and you're safe from the fire now, thank God! Everything's going to be all right."

"Please . . . please don't fight . . . don't hurt each other . . . please . . ."

"That's all the poor girl has had on her mind these past two days," sighed Sister Marie, smoothing Charlotte's damp, tangled hair back from her soot-streaked forehead. "It would help if you could reassure her on that score."

217

Charles shot a quick glance at Pierre. "Under the circumstances, I think M. Treval will agree with me when I say we have postponed our duel, at least for the time being."

Pierre shook his dark head in assent and leaned closer to Charlotte's ear. "Yes, my sweet, don't fret your pretty head over us. You come first—even before honor itself!"

"Just get well, little one," said Dubair softly. "That's all that matters now."

But Charlotte no longer heard them. She had sunk into unconsciousness again.

The two men had stayed with her until she had been safely settled in the convent. They had paced anxiously in the downstairs parlor while the nuns and the *accoucheuse* examined her more carefully, and wouldn't leave until Sister Marie assured them that the young girl was out of danger. For although she had been badly bruised and slightly singed from the fire and would need time to mend, no broken bones had been found and at least, at that moment, no permanent injuries had been evident.

The captain and Pierre had returned then to help combat the fire, for they knew they were needed there and could not ignore their duty to the community. A fire was always a major calamity. Whenever the church bell rang, it was a call that disaster threatened, and next to Indians, a fire out of control was the young city's greatest peril. The bucket brigade needed every hand available to keep it going. As it was, it had taken the townspeople well into the night before they succeeded in completely extinguishing the fire. By that time the entire block where the Pichou dwelling had stood had been consumed by the raging flames.

Charles had not been able to return to the convent until early the following morning, but when he did, he had some very surprising details to tell them about the fire. It had been confirmed that the incendary had originated in the stockroom of the Pichous' general store, but the charred remains of a body found in that spot had also led them to believe that the fire had been accidentally or perhaps deliberately set by its victim. What's more, the captain was fairly certain that, although the man had been burned beyond recognition, he knew who it had been.

Drawing out a scorched leather pouch from his pocket, Dubair had taken another smaller packet from it and gently placed it in the palm of her hand. As the deerskin fell away from the object within it, the girl's eyes widened in disbelief.

"Why, it's the brooch, the one you gave me, with the laurel leaves! But it was—that horrible man took it from me . . ."

"Yes, little one, I'm sure the man who died in the fire was the same one who broke into the store last Sunday and attacked you. I spent most of Monday trying to track him down. My men and I even went to his cabin in the swamps looking for him, but he wasn't there. I think he must have hidden out somewhere here in town and then returned to the Pichous' that following night. My own guess is he was drunk and looking for more liquor. Treval says he might have wanted to get revenge and deliberately set the fire, but I'm inclined to think he set the place off by accident while in a drunken stupor.

"We'll probably never know for sure what happened or why, but he still had your brooch wrapped up and carefully tucked under his leather belt. It was only because it was protected by so many layers of leather that the fire didn't get to it. You see, *ma petite*, for all their delicate beauty, these laurel leaves managed to survive the ordeal . . . even as you did."

Charlotte looked down at the gold pin with the topaz stones adorning it and smiled. What would her *capitaine* say if he knew that the original leaves he had given her still existed too, and had been tucked in her bosom even as she had made her way through the fire?

Fortunately she also still had her aunt's locket and the gold chain Pierre had given her, for she had been wearing them at the time of the fire. Well, the Virgin, it seems, had heard her prayers. Charles and Pierre had not fought their duel—but at what a price! Of course, she had begged the blessed mother to punish her instead of her *prétendants*— perhaps she somehow deserved this cross and would have to bear it as best she could.

Since the fire Charles and Pierre had outdone themselves in seeing to it she lacked nothing. In their mutual concern for her, the two men had declared a truce. There was no more talk of dueling, at least for the moment.

They had even come to a gentleman's agreement concerning any help she might need to get well. Both had been very emphatic in their declaration that they wanted no expense spared in assuring that she receive the best attentions and comforts available during her recuperation.

At first it had looked as if they would fall to quarreling again, as each one insisted he be the one to pay her bills, but finally Sister Marie suggested they share equally in whatever expenses Charlotte might have, until she was well enough to choose between them, at which time the one who would be her husband could reimburse the other for whatever money he had spent. Although both Treval and Dubair were quick to declare they had little interest in reclaiming any money they gladly spent on her, they accepted the arrangement, since they recognized it was not only a fair way to resolve their argument, but also would leave the one whom Charlotte married free of any obligation to the other. Also, as Sister Marie pointed out to them, there would be less pressure on Charlotte if she did not feel obligated to one more than the other, since she might then be influenced more by gratitude than love when the time came for her to make a decision. Thus some semblance of peace had finally been established between her two suitors.

When Charlotte learned of their arrangement later, she reacted with mixed emotions. Her first thought had been that it was putting more pressure than ever on her to decide between them, since she could not be supported by the two of them indefinitely, but at least the arrangement was serving to keep a sort of truce between them, and they had promised her to control their rivalry and abide by her decision, no matter what that might be.

As time passed, however, and she didn't regain the use of her legs, Charlotte began to despair. How could she marry anyone while an invalid? Although Pierre and Charles each assured her that it didn't matter, she felt neither one deserved being burdened with a wife who could not even walk to the altar with him. What's more, the fact that each one had behaved so nobly and continued to be so loyal and loving throughout her illness only made the final choice even more difficult. How could she hurt either one of them after each had proven his love for her time and again, even under the most adverse of circumstances? What was to become of her? As it was now, she couldn't even consider taking the veil!

Sister Marie had arranged with the mother superior to let her have a small room just for herself on the upper floor, right off from the main dormitory, so she could have more privacy and rest. With the generous donations that both of the girl's suitors had made to the convent, the reverend mother could hardly object.

Charlotte reached down and, lifting her skirts, looked closely at her legs. The skin was smooth again and the discoloration was fading now. She swung her legs stiffly over the edge of the bed, but even as she did, panic gripped her. She had tried such movements so often in these past few weeks, and always she had ended up on the floor. Her legs were like lead, as if they belonged to someone else. Every time she tried to put her weight on them, they would collapse beneath her—even as her whole world had collapsed.

Holy mother of God! Have I been so wicked that I deserve this? she wondered. And Charles and Pierre—why must they suffer, too? She longed for love now more than ever. She was weary of facing the world alone. Her freedom, that right to choose for herself, was a responsibility that weighed heavily on her now. Sometimes it was more difficult to be independent than to let others make the decisions for her!

She clutched her rosary so tightly that her knuckles went white. "Blessed Virgin, have pity on me! Give me the strength to walk again. Let me find the wisdom to make the right choice. Send me a sign . . ."

Chapter XXXIII

They had wanted to wait to baptize Madelón's baby until Charlotte had completely recovered, but as time went by and she still could not walk, they finally decided to go ahead with the ceremony. Charles and Pierre took her to the church and carried her to the baptismal fount, where the tiny bundle was placed in her arms and christened in memory of its mother. Charlotte was *marraine,* and although both Charles and Pierre expressed a desire to be chosen as *parrain*, it was decided it would be better not to give further cause for rivalry between the two men, and to bestow the honor of godfather on M. Pichou.

As Charlotte held the sleeping child in her arms, clad in the long, flowing *robe de baptême* she had made for her, she looked down at the peaceful little face and thought how the child was an orphan now, even as she and Madelón had been. The nuns had taken the baby under their wing, and Sister St. Stanislas, the young novice who had greeted the Casquette Girls on their arrival at the convent and taken her final vows just before Easter, was especially fond of little Madelón. The gentle nun, who had a way with youngsters, was also watching over two other unfortunate toddlers, orphaned the year before when their parents had died of the *peste*.

Charlotte had already confided to Sister Marie and the mother superior that she hoped the day would come in the not too distant future when she would be in a position to take the child and rear her as her own. For although she wanted little Madelón to have the benefit of a good Christian education under the Ursulines, she did not want her ever to want for a real home or a mother's love.

"May you never know the loneliness of not having anyone to really belong to," thought Charlotte, as she smiled down at the tiny face in its lace-trimmed cap and felt a restless little foot kick against the blanket. During the long weeks of convalescence, Charlotte had worked almost constantly on the christening dress and a few other simple garments for the child. There was already something in that delicate-featured countenance that reminded Charlotte of her departed friend.

"Someday I'll give you your mother's pearls to wear to your first ball," she silently promised her tiny godchild. "And I'll tell you how your mother and I came to the New World and how she loved and wanted you. You'll never be without a home as we were, *ma petite*, I can assure you of that!"

Tears filled Charlotte's eyes, as she thought of her friend. Dear, sweet Madelón, dead at barely eighteen. All the dreams they had so often confided to each other for the future . . . Why, the poor girl hadn't even begun to live yet! It comforted Charlotte, however, to remember what Sister Ernestine had once said about there being a special place in heaven for women who die in childbirth.

After the baptism, they returned to the convent, and Charles and Pierre lingered for another hour or so with Charlotte, while Sister Marie served them some of her savory peppermint tea. The weather had been delightful those past few weeks, refreshingly cool and sunny ever since October had begun. New Orleans was enjoying one of the most delightful times of the year.

Since it was one of those rare occasions when the two *prétendants* were visiting her simultaneously, they were more formal than usual, and obviously rather ill at ease, so Charlotte did not urge them to stay when they finally rose to take their leave. Each one told her he would return the following day at a designated hour, and left with a reluctant kiss on the hand that was all too closely observed by the other.

On their way out, the two men took advantage of being

alone with Sister Marie to discuss Charlotte's progress or, rather, lack of it at that moment.

"*Dios mío!* But it grieves me to see my poor Charlotte so pale and helpless!" lamented Pierre, his dark eyes clouding as he spoke.

"Has Dr. Dupont or either of the women who have examined her given you any hope she'll regain the use of her legs?" asked Dubair, unable to hide his concern, now that they were out of Charlotte's presence.

"I regret to say there have been no new developments," replied the nun, shaking her veiled head sadly. "They don't seem to know what else to do for her."

"Then there's no need to go on waiting," said Pierre. "The sooner she marries the better. At least she'll have some stability . . . a home . . . someone to care for her . . ."

"I'm inclined to agree," said the captain. "I'm sure Charlotte will walk again, but she must get on with living in the meantime."

Sister Marie stood at the bottom of the staircase with them, her hands folded beneath the flowing sleeves of her black habit, her eyes shielded by the dark veil falling over her white coif.

"Charlotte must decide," declared Pierre. "This situation has gone on long enough. I confess I can't understand how a woman like Charlotte can possibly be in love with two men at the same time. She's so open and sincere . . ."

"And therein lies the crux of her problem," declared the nun softly. "Charlotte's trouble is that she loves too much."

"I'm sorry, *Soeur* Marie, but I can't go along with such an idea," insisted the Creole. "Charlotte is not a frivolous woman."

"Are you saying you honestly believe she's in love with both of us at the same time?" asked Dubair incredulously. "She may be confused, bedazzled perhaps . . . . but in love . . ." His voice trailed off, almost despairing at the thought.

Sister Marie smiled gently at their consternation. "You see, messieurs, there are many kinds of love," she continued. "Perhaps as a *religieuse*, I can understand that better than you can. Oh, I'm sure Charlotte really loves one of you in the way you would like her to, as a woman who would be your wife and mother of your children, but she also truly loves, sincerely cares for the other, and she cannot bring herself to hurt the one she must refuse. You're both fine men and have proven yourselves to be more than worthy of her love. So she keeps putting off that moment when she must give that final blow to someone who doesn't deserve to be rejected . . . someone she truly loves as a brother, perhaps even as a man who has at times also stirred her passions."

The two men were silent for a moment, pondering the nun's calm, well-chosen words. Finally Pierre's thoughts burst to his lips.

"But innocent as Charlotte is, surely she must realize she cannot keep us both dangling like this forever. We're men with human needs and passions—we cannot build our lives just on platonic love. Surely she knows that?"

"Charlotte may be young," observed Dubair, "but she's also very intelligent and has a frankness that is innate in her. If she knows which one of us she truly loves—"

"I doubt she has permitted herself to face the truth yet. She probably hasn't come to recognize the subtle differences in the love she feels for each of you," explained the nun, weighing her words carefully. "I think her refusal to make a decision, her reluctance to cause inevitable pain to one of you, is affecting her physical as well as emotional well being. Once again, as a person who has devoted so many years to the spiritual aspects of life, I have seen some of the many strange things that a mind in turmoil can do to the body. People have died for no physical reason at all, only because they had no further desire to live. I know a child who lost her sight at the moment she saw the Indians scalping her mother and father. There have been some incredible cases. God has given us a great power in our minds, but it can also be a dangerous one."

"If Charlotte is afraid to make a decision for fear of hurting me, I'd rather step aside," said Pierre. "Much as it would devastate me, I wouldn't want her pity."

"It's not just pity she feels," interrupted the nun quickly. "She really cares. That's what is tearing the poor girl apart."

"I certainly wouldn't want Charlotte to do harm to herself simply because she wants to spare me heartache," declared Dubair.

"But how can we help her make the decision that sooner or later she must reach, and bring this situation to an end?" asked Pierre.

Sister Marie paused, as though looking for just the right words before going further. Then, taking a deep breath, she went on. "To begin with, I don't think pressuring her at this moment is the answer. The more you do, the more she seems to retreat into her illness, perhaps unconsciously trying to avoid the disagreeable moment when she must hurt one of you. Remember, each of you keeps flooding her with passionate declarations of how your future happiness, your whole life, hangs on her decision. You have made her feel she will destroy one of you when she announces the one of her choice. I know you two aren't in an enviable position, but you're not the only ones suffering in this triangle. Perhaps it's Charlotte who has been the most affected."

"Then you feel our courting her, our insisting that she choose between us, might have a part in delaying her recovery?" asked Dubair.

"Perhaps. Mind you, I'm not saying Charlotte will ever walk again. That's in the hands of God. But I think you should relax your pressure on her a little. Let her see you can accept her decision, even if it means you might be the loser. It would require a lot of patience and sacrifice on your parts, I know, but it might restore some peace of mind to Charlotte, so she could at least resolve her emotional turmoil and go on living as happily as she can, within whatever capacities *le bon Dieu* chooses to give her. I've hesitated until now to speak so frankly, but you've asked for my opinion, and I feel the time has come for me to say what I think needs to be said."

"Then—then—what are you suggesting?" asked Pierre. "Must we stop coming to see her?"

"Oh, no, nothing that drastic. Charlotte needs to feel she's not alone. All I'm suggesting is that you try to maintain an atmosphere of tranquility around her. She has been through so much these past few months. Give the poor child an opportunity to collect her thoughts as well as re-cover her strength."

"It'll be difficult," despaired Pierre, "but if you think it will help Charlotte, we must at least try to do as you suggest."

"*Bien*, you're probably right, madame," agreed Charles. "I can see how the poor girl must be in a state of confusion after all that has happened."

The two men left greatly subdued, still pondering the wisdom of the nun's words. They suspected the Ursuline might even have her ideas as to which one Charlotte really loved but they knew the nun would never voice her opinions on that score. Her final words rang in their ears, as they walked down the path to the iron gate that led to the street.

"Just be a little patient, messieurs. God has a way a weaving our destinies within the framework of time."

Chapter XXXIV

True to their word, Dubair and Treval continued to see Charlotte frequently at the convent, yet tried to keep the tone of their visits pleasant and peaceful. They were tender and spoke of their love, yet did not press her with talk of marriage.

Since her daring rescue of Madelón's baby during the fire in early September, Charlotte had become a heroine to the townsfolk. Often people stopping off at the convent would inquire about her and bring little gifts of food or clothing for her and the baby.

Señora Treval's heart was touched by the tale of the young girl's bravery and her subsequent invalidism and not only

227

sent her a lovely hand-painted silk shawl but even went to see her shortly after the christening of little Madelón. She accompanied Pierre on one of his visits, and the three of them sat in the pleasant arbor behind the convent to enjoy the early November sunshine.

Although Pierre had warned his mother not to speak directly of marriage to Charlotte, Sra. Treval made it evident to Charlotte that she would be welcomed into the family if she chose to enter it. The attractive woman with her regal bearing still awed Charlotte a little, but after that visit, Sra. Treval seemed less austere and aloof to Charlotte than she had in their first interview.

By the third week of November Charlotte's color had greatly improved, and Sister Marie's persistent massages and applications of pomades and compresses seemed to be having some effect. At least she could stand for a moment unaided. But she still could not muster the strength needed to move her legs. They were like dead limbs on a tree, existing, but with no life within themselves.

There was an autumn snap in the air now, but since it had not rained in over a month, the disagreeable dampness so often present in the Mississippi Delta was not evident at that moment. Sister Marie had helped Charlotte dress in a lightweight woolen overskirt of burnished gold, gracefully caught back in front to reveal the contrasting ivory color of her quilted underskirt. A modest upstanding ruffle of blond lace finished off the low square neckline of her bodice and helped set off all the more her slender neck, prettily exposed by the upsweep of her close, smooth coiffure, topped by a charming cap of matching lace and lappets. Everything she was wearing was new, since the fire had left her without a stitch of clothing to call her own, but Charles and Pierre had given Sister Marie generous funds to buy her a complete wardrobe. Fortunately the nun had admitted her lack of knowledge in such worldly things and turned that assignment over to Madame Pichou, who had a greater sense of fashion than the Ursuline, who, left to her own inclinations, would have probably bought the young girl only an assortment of grey and black outfits and a few white aprons and caps to finish them off.

Charlotte knew Charles had arrived for she could hear

him talking to Sister Marie downstairs before coming up to carry her out to the fresh air and sunshine of the convent garden. She fingered the gold brooch of leaves and topaz stones pinned on her bodice and eagerly awaited the moment he would come up to fetch her. Dear Charles, putting Sister Marie through that usual inquisition as to the state of her health and current needs—as if he hadn't just seen her the day before yesterday!

Charlotte's heart suddenly froze as she looked up and saw him standing in the doorway in his *coureur de bois* outfit.

"Oh, *non*, Charles! You're going away again?" she exclaimed, the words bursting from her lips before she could stop them.

He smiled, a little pleased at her obvious disappointment.

"Yes, *ma petite*, I'm afraid so, but don't worry. I always come back, you know that."

A cold chill passed over her, and he noted the tremor.

"Do you find it too cool to go outside today?" he asked, coming close to where she was sitting on the side of the bed.

"*Non, non* . . . it's not that . . ." Then she reached up and, catching the arm of his buckskin jacket, looked at him with wide, frightened eyes. "—I just wish you wouldn't go. I—"

"Don't fret, little one. I'll be all right. Come, we'll talk about it downstairs. Let's get you out into the fresh air first."

He scooped her up with the ease that years of paddling up and down the Mississippi had given him. Despite the bulk of her flowing skirts, he could feel how she had lost weight during the past two and a half months since the fire, and it worried him.

She clung to the familiar feel of his leather jacket as he carried her down the stairs into the garden and finally set her down in the sun-speckled shade of the vine-covered arbor. Sister Marie followed with a basket on her arm and gardening tools in hand, deciding to take advantage of her chaperoning duties to do a little weeding and cutting in her herb garden, which was off to one side of the arbor. The young people needed some measure of privacy, and after the talk she had just had with the captain, she knew they would need it more than ever today.

"Will you be going to Balize?" she asked on the way down the staircase.

But before the answer came, she knew what it would be. "No, it will be upriver this time."

Upriver! The icy fingers gripped her heart once more. As soon as he had seated her on the bench beneath the colorful canopy of ivy entwined with autumn-tinted grape leaves, she pulled him down anxiously beside her.

"Oh, Charles, please—don't go. I'm frightened."

He was surprised by the intensity of her grip on his arm. "You'll be safe here, *ma petite*."

"I'm not afraid for myself. It's for you . . . that something might happen. I feel a premonition about this time."

He smiled. "Don't worry, *ma petite*. I know my way up and down the Mississippi very well. You know that."

"Yes, and all the other times you've gone on those horrid expeditions of yours, I've more or less always known you'd come back to me. I saw you out there, and I know you're well able to take care of yourself in the marshes, but . . . I don't know, this time I have a feeling . . . a bad feeling . . ." Her hazel eyes were filling with tears she couldn't control.

"Why, my sweet little one, you really are concerned, aren't you?"

"I'm so afraid . . . afraid you'll never come back . . . like Madelón's husband . . ."

He laughed then, but even as he did, cupped the tiny upturned chin in one of his large suntanned hands and gently wiped away the tear that was halfway down her pale cheek.

"Now that I see how much my safe return means to you, I promise I'll make an extra effort to come back safely to you! What's more, this will probably be the last time I'll leave you, *ma petite*. At the end of this year, I'll be resigning my command and settling down to being just a plantation owner. My lieutenant, Etienne, will be ready to take over my command by then. I've been training him for the job, and I think he's ready to handle it now."

She remained silent, but he could see she was still not convinced. He gently wiped away another tear from her cheek and tried to change the subject.

"The plantation has developed tremendously since you saw it earlier this year," he continued, enthusiasm beginning to sparkle in his clear blue eyes. "The main house is ready now for occupancy. It still needs to be decorated, of course, but we could—" He checked himself, remembering his promise to Sister Marie not to press her.

But Charlotte would not be distracted. The strange fear that had filled her from the moment she had seen Charles walk into her room in his scouting outfit would not leave her.

"I still have a bad feeling. Please, can't you let Etienne go on this expedition?"

"No, *ma petite*. Much as I'd like to, I can't. Governor Perier is sending me on a very delicate mission to Commander Chopart at Fort Rosalie, as well as to meet with certain Choctaw chieftains of that territory, whom I happen to know personally. No, little one, this trip will require all the experience I can muster, not only as a scout but a diplomat. Besides, Etienne will be needed here in the city while I'm gone. But don't worry, I'm taking two of my most trustworthy scouts with me, so I won't be alone. It pleases me, however, to see you care about what happens to me."

Charlotte reached out timidly and touched his suntanned cheek. "Oh yes, Charles, I do . . . very much."

He turned his face to meet the fingertips lightly tracing his clean-shaven jawline and brushed his lips eagerly against them.

"I'll be back, I promise, *ma petite*. Meanwhile you just finish getting well." He caught her hand in his and, bending nearer, ventured to add. "If I return, let it be to take you to the home I've built for you. We could finish furnishing it together the way you'd like it to be. I want so much to take care of you—"

He regretted his impetuosity as she drew back suddenly with a sigh.

"Oh, Charles, how can I marry you or anyone the way I am . . . a cripple."

He put his hand quickly over her lips.

"Hush, my sweet. Don't talk like that! Your legs will soon be strong again. Time will mend them."

"But if they don't . . ."

"They will! But for argument's sake, even if they don't, I still love you and that would only be all the more reason for me to want to take care of you."

"Whyever would you want to saddle yourself with a burden like me?"

He laughed. "Burden? Yes, a dear sweet burden that I've wanted to take on ever since I first laid eyes on you!"

"But you need a wife who can take care of you, too. Remember the Indian ceremony you told me about that day at the plantation? The laurel leaves were only a part of the vows. There was a corncob, too, and what it stood for—a wife should be able to tend to her husband, as well as please him."

Charles smiled at her earnestness. "And so you would, little one. Just being there would suffice. I could give you help, you know. You couldn't run a plantation all by yourself, anyway. All you'd have to do would be supervise and—just be there for me." He reached up and let the curl he loved so much free from the confines of her lace cap. What a vision of shimmering light she was in that burnished gold dress with the flickering rays of the sun dancing playfully about her, setting the golden glints in her amber colored hair and eyes aglow.

"If anything should happen to me," he continued softly, "I want you to be happy and not want for anything. I've told Sister Marie I've made legal arrangements—"

"Hush, Charles! I'll not have you talk that way! But I see you, too, have premonitions about this trip, even as I do!"

"*Non, non, ma petite.* It's not that. It's only that you may need more care and money for a while until you've completely recovered, and I want to be sure . . . If anything happens to me, I want whatever I have to be yours. Whether I live or die, I want you to have it, so all I've done is make it legal."

"My dear thoughtful Charles—always thinking of me, trying to protect me from harm . . ."

The tears were welling up in her eyes once more.

"I love you, Charlotte. That's it. There's no one else in my world but you. I've lived a solitary life for so many years, first in the seminary and then here in the wilderness. Until I met you, I never really felt lonely, but now I want something more, and it all centers around you."

"I—I don't think I deserve such a love," she faltered.

"When I first saw you, *ma petite*, I confess I feared someone as sensitive and gentle as you would never fit in a place like this," he continued. "Oh, it's true we Latins like our women fragile and relish nothing more than the challenge of protecting them, but this is a harsh land and, with the lawlessness of nature in the wilderness and the lawlessness of man within the city, I was afraid you'd soon be sucked into the muck around you. But I was wrong. You've proven your metal time and again. Although I've wanted so much to spare you the ordeals I knew would sooner or later come, unfortunately I haven't always been able to do so. Nevertheless, you've faced each trial not only with courage but a resourcefulness that has shown whatever you might lack in worldliness, you more than compensate for in spirit.

"My most fervent wish would be that you'd never have to suffer again, but no one knows what the future holds, so if I can't always be by your side to protect you, I'd at least like to know that whatever I'd leave behind would continue to serve you in some way. I really didn't want to speak to you about this, little one, because I didn't want to upset you thinking of things that will probably never happen. But I do want you to know how strongly I feel about the arrangements I've made, just in case something should—I wouldn't want you to refuse the money because of false pride or some misunderstanding of my motives. There are no strings attached to it. I realize that if I were no longer around you'd probably end up marrying Treval and whatever inheritance I might leave you would seem insignificant in comparison to what he could offer you. But I never want you to be in a position where you'd have to do or accept anything you didn't wish to simply because you didn't have the means to sustain or defend yourself. Then, there is little

Madelón to consider. I know you're concerned for her, too."

"Charles, dear . . . I'm overwhelmed. You're so unselfish."

"Don't give me qualities I don't have, *ma petite*. I plan to come back and have you and the fruits of my labor all for myself. My only regret is I didn't speak up from the very beginning. I like to think that if I had said something that last day before I left you on the docks, we would have long since been married by now and all the things you've had to suffer would perhaps have never come to pass. On the other hand, I don't know . . . sometimes I worry that it's been because of my selfishness in making a belated return into your life and persisting in my obsession to win you for myself that you've taken so long in deciding to settle down. I mean, I'm sure you were probably on the verge of accepting Treval and would have done so, if I hadn't returned when I did to muddy up the waters for you."

She suddenly realized that he, too, was racked by inner doubts and turmoil.

"All I know is I'm glad you did come into my life," she said softly, resting her hand gently on the deep waves of his rich brown hair, as he sat there with his head bowed in thought.

He lifted his face hopefully to hers.

"I've always wanted to believe it's been the two of us all along," he confessed. "That your reluctance to wed anyone was because you were, deep down, waiting for me. You see what a vain, selfish fool I really am!"

She smiled and let her hand drop to his arm.

"Just come back safe and sound to me," she told him gently. "As to the rest, I can't make any decision yet until I'm able to walk again."

"I have to leave now," he sighed, reluctant to tear himself away at that moment. He felt the link between them stronger than ever now and suspected that if he could stay longer he might win a definite promise from her regarding their future.

"All I ask, Charlotte, is that you get well while I'm gone. And if you really do care for me, wait for my return."

He rose and bent over her, slipping his arms about her to lift her up and carry her back into the convent. He could feel how soft and yielding she was to his touch. Her arm circled his neck to brace herself, and as she did so, there was that look in her eyes he had seen before. Impulsively his lips brushed her cheek, and she didn't draw away. Like a river bursting its dam, he moved hungrily to her waiting mouth. This time the kiss was long and lingering . . . the yearning had been there between them for so long.

Charlotte knew now she had been waiting for this moment ever since that first time they had embraced in the swamplands so many months ago . . . so many lifetimes ago . . .

"My sweet little one," she heard him murmuring in her ear, as he continued to brush her face with eager lips. "You're mine, *ma petite*, aren't you? Tell me it's so."

She clung to him, confused by the wave of emotion that was overpowering her. She felt she was caught up in the deep currents of the mighty Mississippi, rushing to she knew not where. All she knew was that she didn't want him to take his arms away from her. She didn't want him ever to leave her again.

Charles caught sight of Sister Marie's black-robed figure rising from where she had been kneeling over the bed of herbs, and the sight of the nun brought him suddenly back to reality. But his heart was singing wildly inside of him, as he swept Charlotte up into his arms and carried her out of the arbor towards the house.

"I'm sorry, madame, but I have to leave now," he said, wondering whether the sharp eyes of the Ursuline could detect the flush behind his suntan or sense how Charlotte was vibrating in his arms at that moment.

Sister Marie gathered up her trowel and scissors and calmly slipped them down the side of her basket, which was filled with freshly cut sprigs and leaves. Her face was as placid as ever, but the captain wondered.

"Go on ahead," she said. "I'll follow. I want to leave these things in the kitchen and wash my hands."

Dubair was grateful, for her failure to notice or her discretion in overlooking whatever she might have suspected.

As he carried Charlotte back up the stairs, his moccasined feet treading more lightly than ever despite his precious burden, the captain knew he had won a major victory. He didn't fool himself, however. The fact that she had reacted to his kisses didn't mean she really loved him, but it did mean her love for him was not platonic. There was certainly enough attraction between them to fan his hopes that she would indeed marry him when he returned.

Charlotte laid her head against the warm crook of his arm as he carefully took her back up the staircase to her room. The pounding of his heart sounded against her ears, and her face burned with the imprints of his lips. At that moment there was no one else in the world but Charles Dubair.

He seated her gently on the edge of the bed, but his arms lingered, loathe to release her. As he felt how she, too, still held on to him, he bent to kiss her again, but this time she drew back.

Reluctantly he contented himself with a final touch of his lips on her brow. Then, trying to regain his composure, he stood up once more and went over to the chair where he had left his musket and camping pack.

As she sat watching him sling his gun and equipment over his broad shoulders and set his fur cap on his head, a great sadness came over her. She tried to shake off the feeling that she was seeing him for the last time, that he wouldn't be coming back.

He returned to her side, ready to go on his way. How tall and straight he was, like the towering trees of the wilderness where he roamed! Oh, God, protect him . . . don't let anything happen to him in that enigmatic land upriver . . .

"Oh, Charles, please come back," she whispered. "I'll die if you don't come back."

He smiled and fingered the curl he had released from her cap while they had sat in the garden.

"Well, I'll just have to be sure I come back then, won't I?"

Sister Marie stood silhouetted in the doorway, waiting like a silent shadow to escort him down.

He bent over her hand to take his leave, but his eyes were fastened hungrily on her lips. "Remember I love you, little one." he whispered so that only she could hear. "I'll be back. I promise."

She watched his tall, lithe figure, unbowed beneath the heavy pack and musket, retreating from the room, and followed the sound of his voice conversing with Sister Marie down the stairs until the front door closed behind him. Already a feeling of loneliness was creeping over her. It would be months before she would see him again . . . perhaps never. She fell back upon the pillow and wept.

Chapter XXXV

The next two weeks dragged by for Charlotte. She couldn't get Charles out of her mind. Time and again she would relive that moment when their lips had finally met . . . the warm shelter of his arms around her . . . If letting him kiss her had been a sin, may God forgive her. She had desired it with all her heart!

She missed Madelón so much. At times like this her childhood friend would have been the one to whom she would have confided her innermost thoughts. There was Sister Marie, of course. The nun had always given her wise and compassionate counseling. But how could she expect Sister Marie to understand the way she felt whenever Charles put his arms around her?

Charlotte wondered whether it would be the same if Pierre kissed her the way Charles had. Somehow she seemed to be able to control herself more with Treval than she could with the captain. Whenever the latter was near her, she found it difficult just to push him away.

But if she chose Charles, how would she ever be able to tell Pierre? She couldn't bear to hurt him. How many times had he talked to her, his face aglow and his dark eyes shining with enthusiasm, of his plans for their wedding and happy future together?

But Charlotte had resolved she would never marry as long as she was unable to walk, so why even think of such things now? A listlessness fell over her as the days went by, and she could not shake off the premonition that Charles was in danger. The thought that she might not ever see him again hung heavily over her.

Pierre noticed the change in her, and sensed it was probably due to Dubair's absence. At first he had been glad when the captain had left on one of his expeditions, for he had hoped it would give him more time alone with Charlotte, but he was coming to the conclusion that it was easier to compete with the captain in person than as an absent hero.

The first three days of December had been cold but dry and sunny. Although it was too chilly now to sit out in the garden, it was comfortable enough in her small room to forego lighting the fireplace. Sister Marie had just finished massaging her legs and had helped her slip off the side of the bed to a nearby chair where she could sit for a while in the sunlight streaming in through the white linen screen on the window. The high shrill sing-song of the schoolgirls reciting their catechism in the classroom below mingled with the distant cries of a street vendor.

Sister Marie had promised to bring little Madelón up to her shortly, and she was looking forward to the daily contact she had with the child. During the three months that had passed since the fire, the baby seemed to have recovered from her tragic entry into the world and was thriving on the care that her godmother and the solicitous nuns were giving her.

As she sat, Charlotte tried to lift one of her legs and hold it straight out in front of her. Sometimes after one of Sister Marie's massages, she thought she could feel more sensation in her limbs. But it was short-lived. Perhaps it had only been her imagination in the first place. Her legs were as numb as ever, like lifeless logs. If it weren't for little Madelón, she would be tempted to say she might just as well have died in the fire than spend the rest of her life

238

like this. But she hastily pushed aside such morbid thoughts. It was a sin to wish something like that!

The chanting of the schoolchildren had stopped, and a buzz of excitement had replaced it. Off in the distance she thought she could hear the sound of the church bell. *Mon Dieu!* Could there be some kind of trouble in the town? Another fire perhaps?

Footsteps sounded on the staircase, and familiar voices. Pierre was coming up with Sister Marie. He was early. There must be something amiss.

At that moment the Creole and the Ursuline burst into the room breathlessly, the usual observances of protocol forgotten.

Pierre ran directly to her, while Sister Marie grabbed the cloak from her *armoire* and began to wrap it around her.

"Charlotte, *linda*, we must all go to the Place d'Armes," Treval told her. "Don't be frightened. There's no immediate danger, but it's best we go there."

"Yes, child," agreed the nun. "Don't be afraid. It's only a precaution."

"But what's the matter?" asked Charlotte bewilderedly, as Pierre caught her up into his arms and carried her out of the room and down the stairs, while Sister Marie raced ahead to see that all those in the convent were gathered at the entrance, ready to leave.

"It's the Indians," Pierre told her. "There has been a massacre upriver."

The blood drained from Charlotte's face as he placed her in his carriage which was drawn up to the front door of the convent.

"Upriver?" she echoed. Her throat had constricted so tightly she could hardly get out the next question. "Where upriver?"

Pierre hesitated. He exchanged worried glances with Sister Marie, who was handing little Madelón to Charlotte to hold, while Deedee was climbing in from the other side of the carriage with the other two young children from the nursery, who were rubbing their eyes sleepily and already settling down to continue their afternoon nap on the old Negress' lap.

Pierre sighed, trying to weigh his words more carefully,

as he saw the effect they were having on the girl. But there was no use trying to hide the facts. All the town would be speaking of nothing else once they got to the square.

"Fort Rosalie," he explained uneasily.

One look at the expression on Charlotte's face told him just how much she cared.

They sat waiting for a moment in the coach, while Sister St. Stanislas and Sister Ernestine squeezed the chattering schoolgirls into the two carriages behind them. Fortunately Pierre had had the foresight to bring along another coach with him, knowing that the one belonging to the convent would not be able to accommodate everyone there.

"How—how do you know it was Fort Rosalie?" he heard Charlotte asking him for a second time. He knew she was thinking of Dubair. *Dios mío!* Why did he have to be the one to break the news to her?

"Some of the survivors just came into town," he replied. "The first one really came in yesterday, but he was so incoherent that no one paid any attention to him. They thought he was either drunk or tetched. It wasn't until three more men arrived this afternoon with the same fantastic tale that the governor finally realized it was true."

"How—how bad was it?" persisted Charlotte, her hazel eyes widening as the terror within her increased.

"Those men say they were the only ones who got away. The whole fort was wiped out."

"*Mon Dieu!*" exclaimed Sister Marie, crossing herself in horror.

Charlotte sat there, her head reeling, unable to believe what she had heard.

"Are you saying everyone else there was killed?"

"Yes, *niña.* So it seems. But there's no way of knowing yet for sure. They may be exaggerating."

But after Pierre's first words, Charlotte was no longer listening. "Oh, my God! Charles! That's where he was going . . . he told me he had to go to Fort Rosalie to see the commander there. Holy mother of God! I knew something was going to happen! I had a premonition!"

It was like a knife twisting in Pierre's heart to sit and watch her anguish. Despite the presence of Sister Marie, he

240

drew Charlotte into his arms and tried to comfort her. But all the while the ache inside him was growing. It was plain to see now how much the girl loved Dubair. So the captain had won. He was probably dead, but he had won just the same.

With a heavy heart, he carried Charlotte into the church and left her with the rest of the women and children, while he went to join the other men gathering in front in the large public square, where weapons were being distributed to all able-bodied men and Governor Perier himself was giving orders for the defense of the city.

Inside the church, with the women and children of the town huddled fearfully around her, Charlotte sat quietly in one of the pews, her hooded face pale as death, as she listened in despair to the din of the bell still clanging its urgent summons above her in the steeple and to the frantic talk buzzing all about her. Sister Marie eyed the silent girl anxiously, as she sat holding little Madelón in the crook of her arm. The nun was especially worried, for the fragments of conversation that reached them only seemed to confirm the tragic news from upriver.

As soon as Cecile had seen the group from the convent entering the church, she had come over to sit by them, obviously eager to show off the two-month-old son she carried proudly in her arms. With that talkative effervescence so typical of her, she seemed to revel in the fact that as the wife of a military officer she had heard all the details of the massacre long before anyone else.

"When that first man, Ricard, came in yesterday, he was so out of his mind from the horrors that he had witnessed that my husband says no one believed him," she related, "but when Couillard and two others reached here today with the same story but in more detail, my husband and his men took them immediately to the governor."

Madame Pichou had joined the group with her daughter and grandchild and cooed lovingly over little Madelón, exclaiming over how the child was looking more and more like her late mother with each passing day.

"What a pity about poor Madelón," sighed Cecile, as she looked down sadly at the tiny sleeping face amid the folds of the blanket. "If it hadn't been for this poor *bébé*, she might still be alive today."

"I wouldn't blame this poor child for Madelón's death," chided Madame Pichou. "If anything killed the poor girl it was the voyage over. From what I could see, she'd never been able to fully get over that."

"Perhaps you're right," conceded Cecile. "I guess you could say that if she hadn't come to the New World, the poor dear would be alive today."

"I wouldn't be too sure of that, either," interrupted Sister Marie, with a shake of her wimpled head. "One never knows what the good Lord has decreed for us. After all, who knows what would have become of the dear girl in France? At least here she knew a small measure of happiness and now has left a part of herself to go on into the future of this brave new land."

"If the Indians attack us as they did Fort Rosalie, there won't be any future here for any of us!" lamented Cecile, hugging her tiny son closer to her breast as she loosened the lacings of her bodice and discreetly shoved the nipple of one of her milk-laden breasts into the child's hungry mouth to quiet his whimpering.

Madame Pichou agreed. "On the way here we heard the entire fort had been wiped out, burned to the ground," she declared, her plump hands gesturing excitedly as she spoke. "They're saying over two hundred and fifty men were probably killed and around two hundred and thirty women and children, as well as some two hundred Negro slaves, have been taken prisoner."

"That's what I heard, too," said Cecile, quick to take up the theme once more. "'They're saying the Indians do horrible things to their captives and then keep them as slaves," she continued, eager to share her superior knowledge with the group of wide-eyed women who had gathered around to hear what she had to say. "My husband told me the survivors related an incredible story of savage violence and treachery. The filthy heathen got into the fort early on the morning of November 29th, the eve of St. Andrew's Day, by pretending to be small isolated hunting parties. Each group stopped at a different home, as if it just wanted to

242

make a friendly visit—you know, the way the redskins sometimes do, asking for a sip of brandy or an opportunity to trade something. Then, at a prearranged signal, the savages fell on their unsuspecting hosts and, in a blast of firearms so close that it seemed to be but one volley, they started the slaughter."

Sister Marie crossed herself in horror. "May God have mercy on those poor innocent souls! I hope their martyrdom was short-lived!"

"Unfortunately that wasn't the case," continued Cecile, obviously relishing the privileged position of being the best informed of the circle. "You know how the Indians love to torture their victims first. That man Ricard says the bloody orgy lasted well on into the night and that from where he was hidden, he could see the savages piling up the heads of their victims in the public square as if they were pyramids of cannonballs, while they danced and drank themselves into a stupor until dawn!"

Madame Pichou blanched and gasped for breath, even as Sister Marie put up a detaining hand and exclaimed, "*Mon Dieu*, Cecile! Must you be so explicit?"

"I'm sorry, *Soeur* Marie," apologized the young girl, momentarily lowering her dark eyes. "I didn't mean to offend anyone's sensitivity. I'm only telling you the way they said it was. I could really give you a lot more details that I heard the men talking about—the unspeakable indignities that the poor women and children were subjected to—"

"Cecile, in God's name—*please!*" admonished the nun.

Charlotte had not uttered a single word, and from the deathly pallor of her face, Sister Marie feared the girl was about to faint away at any moment.

"Charlotte, you're so quiet," said Cecile suddenly. "In all the excitement. I've forgotten to ask you how you are. We heard about that brave dash of yours into the fire to save poor Madelón's *bébé*. They say you hurt your legs on the way out. I hope you're all right now."

"She's feeling a lot better now," replied Sister Marie, quickly coming to Charlotte's rescue. "She just needs a little more time for her legs to mend before she can get around again, that's all."

Suddenly Charlotte turned to Cecile, her hazel eyes burning like smoked topaz in the pale heart-shaped face that looked out from the shadow of her hood. "Did—did any of those men from Fort Rosalie say anything about—about having seen Charles Dubair there?"

"Merciful heavens! Are you talking about Captain Dubair—*our* Captain Dubair?" exclaimed the pretty brunette. "Don't tell me he was at the fort!"

Sister Marie saw how difficult it was for Charlotte to speak, so she took over the conversation for her. "Yes, we're all terribly worried about him. He went on a mission upriver around the twentieth of last month and said he would be going to the fort and perhaps meeting with the Indians in that territory."

"*Mon Dieu!*" exclaimed Madame Pichou. "No wonder poor Charlotte is so upset! I do hope the good *capitaine* wasn't caught in that massacre!"

Cecile shook her shining black curls, topped by a dainty cap of starched white muslin.

"Oh, Charlotte, I'm truly sorry! I liked the captain too, you know that! I didn't hear anyone mention his name, but the survivors say that the only white men who were captured and spared were a carpenter and a tailor, and those only because the heathens needed their services. It seems the Indians put the *tailleur* to altering the bloodstained uniforms of the dead soldiers to fit them! But then, even if the *capitaine* wasn't at the fort on that particular day, it's doubtful he's still alive. The Natchez have stationed warriors all along the Mississippi and are killing everyone in sight. They say the Natchez are trying to incite all the Indian nations of Louisiana to rise up against us. Governor Perier is taking immediate measures and has even asked the *Compagnie* to get reinforcements to protect us here in New Orleans. We have the palisades, of course, but they could be burned down so easily . . ."

Charlotte could no longer hear the girl's incessant chatter. She had toppled off the pew where she had been sitting and succumbed to the merciful relief of unconsciousness.

Chapter XXXVI

New Orleans was in a state of panic. Daily the church bells rang the alarm as stray fugitives from Natchez ambushes along the river found their way to the protection of the city, bringing more tales of horror and butchery. There were new stories to be heard every time the town was called to assembly at the Place d'Armes.

A few days after the massacre at Fort Rosalie, they said, five travelers coming downriver had been hailed by the Natchez and, not suspecting what had happened, came to a landing. Hardly had they touched the bank of the river when they received a discharge of musket fire in which three were killed and one was taken prisoner, to be tortured and put to death in public exhibition. Only the fifth had managed to flee to the woods, where he had been able to conceal himself until he could reach the friendly village of the Tunicas.

Meanwhile, the Yazoo tribe had joined the Natchez and, moving on further upriver, had started out the New Year of 1730 by attacking the small, understaffed fort of St. Claude, wiping out the garrison there of twenty men and the few families who had settled in that vicinity.

From the very first day that news had reached New Orleans of the tragedy at Fort Rosalie, the governor had sent an officer with a detachment of men by boat upriver to put the planters of the region on their guard. They were ordered to seek the refuge of New Orleans or construct redoubts at convenient distances along the banks so they could take refuge in them if need be with their families, goods, and cattle. Soon the entire coast from New Orleans to Natchez was in a state of alert and ready to defend itself against attack.

Perier had also ordered a rampart with moats and entrenchments constructed rapidly around the city. Calling together all the able-bodied men available, both in New Orleans and among the more prominent planters along the river, he issued arms and divided them into companies with a leader for each group. Since there was no love lost between the blacks and the Indians, even the loyal Negro slaves were given weapons and sent out against some of the Indian tribes in the vicinity.

But the greatest fear of the city was that the Choctaws, the largest Indian nation in that region, would be incited to join the Natchez. If this happened, they knew all would be lost.

The governor sent an urgent message to the king on a vessel that left for France the first week of January, begging for reinforcements to hold the colony against the Indian uprisings, and meanwhile word was dispatched to Point Coupée and Mobile ordering a concerted effort of all the French settlements to subdue the hostile tribes before the entire Mississippi Valley suffered the fate of Forts Rosalie and St. Claude.

In the midst of the sustained excitement of those following weeks, Charlotte seemed to withdraw more and more into herself. Everyone seemed convinced that Charles was dead and, although she continued to hope that he might have been spared by some miracle, the passing of time with no further news of him only seemed to confirm her worst fears. From the very beginning, there had been something about that dreaded word "upriver" that had sent a chill through her being—as if she had always known that Charles would someday disappear into that vast wilderness of the Mississippi Valley and, like so many others, never come back.

Pierre had tried to find out something more for her, but what he learned only seemed to suggest that Dubair had been present at Fort Rosalie or in its vicinity on November 29th. Couillard and another survivor remembered having seen the captain there about two days before the Natchez had attacked, but they couldn't say whether he had been there or not on the actual day of the massacre.

Treval tried to brighten their second Christmas together as best he could. He brought Charlotte a lovely hand-painted fan to replace the one she had lost in the fire and carried her downstairs to the warm glow of the fireplace in the second parlor, where they had sat—was it only a year ago? Sometimes it seemed as if it had been a lifetime ago.

The soft glow of the candelabra on the mantel mingled with the reddish gold of the flame snapping and crackling in the brick fireplace, giving Charlotte a touch of much needed color to her pale cheeks and highlighting the warm amber of her hair and eyes. Although she wore the gold chain he had given her the previous Noël, obviously with a desire to please him, he noted that, instead of her aunt's locket, she had attached to it the gold pin that Dubair had given her. Its gold leaves, tipped with twin topaz stones, stood out in stark relief against the dark velvet of her simple forest-green gown.

It grieved him to see her with such sadness in those lovely golden-brown eyes he had come to love so well.

"Charlotte, *mi linda niña*," he sighed, taking her limp hand in his. "What can I say or do to make you happy again?"

She tried to give him a wistful smile. "Poor dear Pierre, you've been so patient. I feel so guilty about you!"

"I'm not going to insist you tell me anything at this moment, but you should begin to think seriously of your future now that we're facing a new year. I realize now just how much you cared for Dubair, but I'd like to think that perhaps you feel a little something for me, too."

"I do, Pierre. Very much."

"I've wanted to win from the very beginning, you know that, but I confess I never wanted to win like this. I would have preferred, of course, that you would have chosen me outright, or that I might have won you in a fair duel on the field of honor. But to compete with a dead hero—*vaya!* That's something I don't know how to do."

"Pierre, I—"

"Wait, Charlotte, please . . . let me finish," he begged, putting a finger gently to her lips. "I'm sure if you married me I could make you happy. In time I might even make you love me enough to forget your captain."

"Pierre, dear Pierre, I'll tell you what I told Charles the last time I spoke to him and he urged me to marry him. I don't want to wed anyone unless I can walk again. It wouldn't be fair."

"I love you for yourself, not your legs!"

"But you cannot deny that as I am I'm so helpless and—"

"All the more reason why you should have a man to care for you. Surely you've learned by now that a woman cannot be alone here without a man to back her up with his name and his sword, if need be. Also, there's little Madelón. I know you'd like to give her a real home."

"Yes, Pierre. I'd like to give her the home that Madelón and I never had the good fortune to have when we were growing up. Of course, I could always have a place of my own and hire considerable protection if I wanted to, without the necessity of marrying, for Charles told me—he wanted his plantation to be mine if—if anything happened to him, so if I decide to marry anyone, you can rest assured it will be because I really want to and not just for convenience."

"Then—are you saying that if you marry me, it will be because you really love me?"

"You could say that. I really do care for you, Pierre, you know that. But I won't deceive you—the passion I feel—felt—for Charles was something very special . . ." Tears misted her eyes, and for a moment she couldn't go on. "I—I'm sorry, Pierre. I don't want to hurt you. But I just can't accept that Charles is gone. Perhaps I will in time. It's too soon yet, I guess."

Pierre gently drew her into his arms, and she lay her head on his shoulder like a forlorn child seeking solace from a world it could not understand. She rested there, weary of the tempest that had racked her those many months. It was good just to relax and feel the nearness of someone stronger than she, someone who loved her and whom she regarded as a dear, sweet friend.

Sister Marie had stepped into the other parlor to check on the refreshments for the children's party, and they were suddenly aware of the fact that they were alone. The fire crackled in the chimney, and the calm silence of the room was only occasionally disturbed by the ripple of a child's laughter from without. For a moment it seemed as if time had stood still, and a whole year with all its joys and heartbreak had suddenly faded away. She had just arrived in New Orleans, and Pierre was giving her the gold chain for her locket. . . .

Suddenly his lips were on hers, and she could feel the sweetness of his mouth, the tenderness of his love.

"Charlotte, let me love you," he was pleading softly in her ear. "I want you so much. Can't you love me just a little?"

His kisses became more ardent, more demanding, and she felt herself being swept along on a current of confusing emotions. She wanted so much to fill the void that Charles's loss had left in her, to love and be loved. If only she could stop hurting inside, even for just a little while!

As Pierre felt her resistance crumbling, he too was caught up in a wave of his own longing. The more than a year of wanting her, of aching to take her in his arms and love her to his heart's content . . .

His hands ran hungrily upwards from the tiny pointed waistline to the full curve of her tightly laced bodice, as he tilted her back gently against the sweeping arch of the sofa behind her.

Charlotte closed her eyes. She had ceased thinking. She was so tired of struggling with conflicting emotions. Little by little she began to abandon herself to the pleasant sensations of Pierre's caresses, the reassuring warmth of his nearness.

Suddenly the odor of leather and tobacco wafted across her memory and tears filled her eyes. *Oh, Charles, Charles . . . I want you so! These should be your lips kissing mine . . . your hands on my breast . . .*

Pierre sensed the sudden change in her mood, and even as he paused, the sob that escaped her lips, though barely audible, reverberated in his being and brought him back to reality with a start. *Mon Dieu!* What an impetuous fool he was! She wanted Dubair, not him!

For a moment he was tempted to go on, anyway. She

249

might be thinking of her captain, but *he* was the one who was there—he was the one making love to her. Perhaps she would be thinking only of him by the time he had finished. He bent to kiss the full white breast he had freed.

But the spell had been broken. He wanted her—Lord! How he wanted her! But not this way. He loved her too much to take advantage of her grief and confusion. She might even despise him afterwards.

Tearing himself away from her, he sat upright on the edge of the sofa, still atremble inside. The pulsating warmth of her breast lingered in the cup of his hand. He didn't trust his legs to hold him up if he tried to stand at that moment, yet he dared not remain there beside her if he hoped to control the passions he had finally allowed to surface. He buried his face in his hands, trying desperately to regain his composure.

"Forgive me, Charlotte," he murmured hoarsely. "I—I shouldn't have pressed you. This isn't the right time. I should have known."

She lay there somewhat bewildered by the turmoil suddenly welling up within her. Her pulse was pounding wildly, her body tingling from his caresses. There was a bond between them that could not be lightly brushed aside. As she saw his anguish, she felt an impulse to reach out and stroke his bowed head, yet dared not. All her instinct told her that if she touched him at that moment, she would not be able to trust him—or herself.

The fire continued to snap and blaze in the hearth, and the buzz of the children's chatter seemed so far away. The two taut figures on the divan were motionless.

Several minutes passed before Pierre finally rose and walked over to the mantel. Extending his hands as though to warm them, he stood looking pensively down into the restless flames, but even the ruddy glow that encircled him could not hide the pale intensity of his countenance.

Nervously Charlotte fumbled with her hair and bodice, trying to put everything right again, but there was nothing she could do about the disorder she continued to feel within.

It was not until Sister Marie's tardy entrance with a tray

of anisette and freshly baked bread pudding that the awkward silence between them was broken and they were able to look at each other once more. But even then, it took several days before they could do so without immediately lowering their eyes.

Chapter XXXVII

An air of tension continued to hang over the city. In the midst of all the terror and despair, however, the convent was buzzing with the news of the miraculous escape of a Jesuit missionary and a group of travelers, who had just arrived in New Orleans. It seemed that while coming downriver they had chanced upon the combined Yazoo-Natchez forces on their way to perpetuate their infamous deeds at Fort St. Claude.

"The travelers had stopped on the bank of the river in a shady spot to celebrate mass," Sister Marie told Charlotte, hoping the inspiring tale might help bolster the young girl's faltering faith. "But unknown to the group, the Indians had sneaked up on them and, even as the worshippers were dropping to their knees at the elevation of the Host, the savages fired a murderous volley into their midst.

"Yet in spite of the balls flying all round them, the priest and his flock were unharmed, and had time to make a dash back to their boat. The Indians, not to be cheated of their prey, reloaded and fired a second volley, but once more a miracle saved them. Although the group was clustered together in the boat, making a target that even the most inexperienced marksman could have hit, no one was wounded except the man who had been pushing the boat out from the bank, and even he succeeded in getting into the vessel safely. He's at the hospital now and is doing very nicely. The ball was extracted from his thigh this morning."

Here, Sister Marie thought, was the moment to bring home the moral of her tale. "The group attributes their providential escape to the presence of God among them at the elevation of the Host just at the moment the savages attacked them," she contined. "For surely it was the hand of *le bon Dieu* that saved them not once but twice from what should have been certain death. So you see, child, miracles do happen, and you should have more trust in the future that the good Lord has in store for you."

"It would take more than one miracle to bring me all I need," sighed Charlotte. "If only Charles could come back to me and I could walk to meet him! But who am I to ask for such favors?"

"Perhaps, if you believed enough . . . if you prayed to the Virgin . . ."

"I did in the beginning," admitted Charlotte, sighing sadly.

"And did she answer you?"

"Well, I guess you could say she did . . . but at what a price! I'm afraid to ask for anything now!"

"Perhaps you didn't pray long enough. You may have stopped too soon."

"My prayers haven't seemed to help those I've most dearly loved. Madelón . . . Charles . . . . and now I can't even help myself!" lamented Charlotte. "Tell me truthfully, *Soeur* Marie, do you think I should marry— even if I never walk again?"

The nun folded her hands within her long flowing sleeves. "You ask me, child, so I'll answer. Yes, I do, although I fervently pray that you will not only marry but walk again, as well."

"If only I had accepted Charles when he first proposed! Now that it's too late, I know he was really the one! From the very beginning, even on our way up from Balize, I was drawn to him . . . and then, as soon as he came back, it started all over again."

The nun smiled gently. "I suspected as much, my dear, but it was not my place to judge the workings of another's heart."

"Of course, I care for Pierre, too," admitted Charlotte blushing a little as she recalled how close she had come to succumbing to him on the eve of *Noël*. "If Charles doesn't come back, perhaps . . . But no, I still can't accept that I'll never see him again. Everyone keeps telling me he must be dead . . . lying somewhere out there in the swamplands . . ." Her voice broke.

Sister Marie patted the girl's hand consolingly. "There, there, child. It's only natural you should feel as you do. It's too soon to forget. You may never really forget, but you know very well the captain would not want you to grieve like this for him. He wanted you to be happy. Besides, there is more than one way to love. I think you could eventually find a deep, satisfying happiness with Pierre, if you'd just give him the opportunity. He loves you very much, too, you know."

"Yes, I know, and that's why I hate to hurt him as I have."

"It's not your fault or his that you love him in a different way than you did Dubair. We cannot deny the love that God puts in our hearts. We may control what we do about it but not the love we feel."

Charlotte looked at Sister Marie in surprise. "You—you speak so wisely, even about such worldly things."

The nun lowered her eyes and a faint smile momentarily flickered across her enigmatic countenance. "I wasn't always a nun, my child," she reminded her softly.

The young girl looked more closely at the dark veiled Ursuline, but the latter's face was tranquil once more.

Later that same day, M. Godard, whom Dubair had entrusted with his affairs during his absences, paid Charlotte a visit at the convent. A stocky, businesslike gentleman in his mid-fifties. Godard had been handling the captain's legal and financial matters efficiently for a number of years now, ever since the latter had received his inheritance and decided to combine it with his savings to develop the land that had been granted him while he had served under Bienville.

"The captain was a fine, upstanding young man," declared Godard, shaking his head sadly. "I liked the boy as if he were my own son, so I want to see to it that his wishes are carried out to the letter. He instructed me to turn everything over to you, mademoiselle, and to continue administrating the plantation and serving you in the same way as I had served him, unless, of course, you have someone else in mind?"

Charlotte was taken aback. "I—I really hadn't thought about it. I—But, of course, M. Godard, if Captain Dubair trusted you enough to handle his affairs for him, I most certainly would want you to continue doing so for me. The truth is, I know nothing about such matters and will have to rely greatly upon your counseling and guidance, as well as administration."

Godard drew out some documents, which were rolled up inside a large piece of leather for protection. "*Bien,* I'll do my utmost to live up to your faith in me, mademoiselle. I know the captain loved you very much. It was written all over him whenever he spoke of you. I'm sorry to have to bother you at this time, but if I'm to continue in my capacity as your administrator, I'll have to ask you to sign certain documents to make things legal."

"But aren't you being premature?" interrupted Charlotte in dismay. "There's still the possibility that Captain Dubair might return."

Godard lifted his greying head from the documents in surprise. "That's highly unlikely now. But perhaps you haven't heard. Can it be you don't know?"

"About the massacre at Fort Rosalie? Yes, but I've been hoping . . ."

"Ah, mademoiselle. Forgive me if I'm the one to bear ill tidings, but it's practically certain now that the captain was killed by the Natchez."

Charlotte felt so dizzy she feared she would fall from the chair where she was seated. Sister Marie, who had been sitting discreetly to one side, moved closer and put a steadying hand on the girl's shoulder.

"Then it has been confirmed that Captain Dubair was at the fort at the time of the attack?" asked the nun, also turning pale beneath her black veiled coif.

"On no, he wasn't at the fort on that morning," replied Godard, feeling increasingly uncomfortable as he saw the consternation mounting in the two women and realized he was going to be the one to give the death knell to those last vestiges of hope they had been so desperately clinging to. "He wasn't at Fort Rosalie, but he must have left there a day or so before the attack, for he was traveling on the river again when, from all evidence, he and the two men with him were ambushed by a Natchez war party. As you know, the Indians have been roaming the banks ever since the uprising."

"Then—then there's no doubt?" Charlotte's voice was so faint and strained that Godard had to bend forward to hear her.

"Very little, mademoiselle. They found the boat with two of the bodies still in it washed ashore at one of the plantations upriver."

"Bodies? *Mon Dieu!* They actually saw his—his—" she couldn't finish the sentence.

"The bodies were of the two scouts, but we must assume the captain was either killed and fell overboard into the river at the time of the attack, or was taken prisoner and killed later." Godard didn't want to say he hoped Dubair had died outright and not in some remote Natchez village, suffering the diabolical tortures that the savages reserved for enemies of special calibre, of which the captain would have unfortunately been considered. "Whichever way it happened, I'm sorry to say the captain must be dead by now, may God have mercy on his soul." He finished lamely, crossing himself solemnly, as Sister Marie repeated the gesture. But Charlotte was so weak she could not lift her hand to follow suit. She kept seeing Charles's face . . . the way he had looked as he had kissed her goodbye, his blue eyes filled with love, shining with intensity . . . begging her to wait for him. He had promised to come back . . . he had promised . . .

Chapter XXXVIII

Almost daily news would come filtering into New Orleans from upriver. Another Jesuit priest, Father Doutrelean arrived in the city with two wounds in his arm, telling how he had been attacked at the mouth of the Yazoo River and lost three men.

Governor Perier detached a group of twenty white men and six Negroes to carry ammunition to the Illinois settlement at the other end of the river and gave orders to the soldiers to pick up all French travelers they might meet on the way and escort them back safely to New Orleans.

The governor also sent a courier to two Choctaw chieftains who were shooting ducks not too far from the city on Lake Ponchartrain, asking them to come talk to him. He realized that much of the hope for resolving the precarious situation in which the colony found itself at that moment lay in the hands of the Choctaw nation. The side they chose would almost certainly be the victor.

Charlotte remembered how Charles had not wanted to offend the warriors of that tribe who had visited them in their camp that morning they had been coming upriver from Balize. She understood so many things now she hadn't then, so many things—but it was too late.

At last, in the end of January, the city began to receive encouraging news from upriver. The Avoyelles, Tunicas, and other small Indian nations had declared themselves against the Natchez and begun to harrass the latter by small attacks and marauding expeditions. Then, on January 27th, the commander of Point Coupée led approximately seven hundred Choctaws against the Natchez at St. Catherine's Creek, and fifty-four French women and children and over one hundred Negro slaves, who had been captured at Fort Rosalie, had been rescued. After having lost approximately eighty warriors, the routed Natchez had fled into the refuge of two forts they had built in anticipation of such retaliatory attacks, but within the week French reinforcements had arrived to swell the ranks of Choctaw allies, and the Natchez were now under siege.

The Choctaws, it seemed, had finally decided to stand by the French, and there was rejoicing in the colony. Hope surged again in the hearts of the settlers.

Although excitement continued to run high in New Orleans, the city relaxed a little from the daily alarms that had kept them in a constant state of anxiety for almost two months. Pierre had been assigned second command in the division of emergency militia that his uncle headed. The entire male population of the town walked about armed to the teeth, ready to defend themselves and their loved ones against attack at any moment. At least they would not be caught unawares, as Forts Rosalie and St. Claude were.

Despite his duties in the citizen's army, Pierre never failed to watch over Charlotte and her guardians. He kept two coaches at his constant disposal to dispatch to the convent at the first sign of an alarm and never let a day go by without at least stopping off for a few minutes to see Charlotte or inquire about her state of health.

Not that he was at any time unmindful of his mother's safety. Sra. Treval was surrounded by a bevy of servants in her townhouse, which was only a block away from the Place d'Armes, so she was well taken care of at all times and had easy access to the refuge of the church if an attack were to come.

Pierre had even thought of asking the nun's permission to let him take Charlotte to his mother for safekeeping in the Treval townhouse during those perilous times, but finally decided against the measure. Charlotte's overwhelming grief over Dubair's death at that moment would have made the situation awkward. His mother already found it difficult to understand why the girl had postponed marrying into their family for so long, anyway. He hoped, however, the day would come soon when Charlotte would finally accept the facts as they were and consent to be his wife. Then he could take her to the shelter of his home with no reservations. Meanwhile, he didn't want to run the risk of any hostile feelings arising between the two women. As long as he was not yet married, Pierre suspected his mother still harbored some faint hopes that he might reconsider matrimony with her original candidate for a daughter-in-law, Ninon Planchard, whose family was not only related to the governor's wife but good friends of his uncle's, as well.

Pierre was worried about Charlotte's general state of health. Not only didn't she show any signs of regaining the use of her limbs, but her depression had, if anything, increased in recent weeks, ever since she had spoken to M. Godard and learned that the dugout with the bodies of the two scouts who had been with Dubair had been discovered. She did not seem to want to face that final confirmation of his death.

"I feel so helpless, so frustrated," he told Sister Marie, as they stood in the parlor after having just descended the stairs from Charlotte's room. "What can I do to make her get up out of that chair and go on living? She's so young. She has all her life—our lives—ahead of her!"

"I agree with you, of course," sighed the nun sadly. "But the poor girl has had so many shocks in these past few months, one on top of the other. She needs time to adjust. But she will, I'm sure. Basically, Charlotte has a strong spirit and should react sooner or later. I'm thankful she has someone like you by her side to see her through this tragic period and give her hope for the future."

"If only she could walk! It cuts me to the quick to see my proud little Charlotte sitting there like that—like a little bird with its wings broken! I'd rather have seen her wed to Dubair than this way. Do you think she'll ever be able to walk again? A few months ago you had spoken as if you thought she might."

"And I still do. At least I think there's a possibility," replied the nun. "But not as long as she's in her present state of mind. You see, Charlotte has come to believe she can't walk. Now, with the added tragedy of the captain's death, she's lost even her motive to want to go on. Often one of the first requisites for a miracle is to desire one, to desire it fervently with all your heart. But I'm afraid Charlotte has stopped praying for one."

"But she's very religious. I'm sure she says her rosary every day and—"

"I don't mean that kind of praying. Of course, she does. And I happen to know she's saying special prayers night and day for the protection of the captain's soul wherever he might be—dead or alive—but that's not the kind of faith that works miracles. Charlotte must first really *want* to walk again and then have sufficient belief that it will come to pass."

"But we must also face the fact that perhaps she never will. If her legs were injured too badly—My poor *niña!*"

"From what I can see when I massage her, and from what those who have examined her have told me, the damage should have mended by now. Of course, there are things we can't see. We really know so little."

"But you said you had seen some cases before. You spoke of a blind girl who had had her sight miraculously restored."

"Yes, I keep thinking—hoping—that Charlotte's case might be similar to that child's."

"And what caused the girl to see again?"

"They told me she had gone blind at the moment she saw the Indians mutilating her father and mother, as she lay hidden with her young brother in some nearby bushes. We had placed the two orphaned children in the home of a childless couple, and only a few months afterwards, when I stopped off to see them, I was surprised to find the girl could see again.

"It seems the child had been outside playing with her younger brother, when the little boy wandered away and suddenly fell into a nearby creek. On hearing his cries for help, the girl began to grope around desperately to find him, and it was at that moment that her sight was restored. In her urgency, she had literally *willed* herself to see again. It was a miracle, of course, but brought on by shock, and emotion so strong that her prayer went out like a shaft of lightning straight to the ears of our Lord, who in his infinite mercy took pity on her and answered her great need."

"If only something like that could happen to Charlotte!" exclaimed Pierre, his dark eyes shining with renewed hope. "If only she cared enough about something—someone—that she would react that way."

"Of course, I'm not saying a miracle would *have* to happen in Charlotte's case, mind you," cautioned the Ursuline. "Remember, the majority of the blind never regain their sight and the lame seldom walk again. That's not the fault of *le bon Dieu*, of course. It's simply the lack of faith and understanding that we frail mortals have of his great wisdom and power. All I'm saying is that I have seen several instances where a strong desire or emotion can affect the body either favorably or unfavorably. In Charlotte's case, she's so *desolée* . . . the loss of her friend Madelón and then Dubair . . . her harrowing experience with the intruder at the store and then the trauma of the fire and injury to her legs . . . her battered spirit most certainly isn't helping her physical state. Of that much, at least, we can be sure."

The Creole left, pondering all the nun had said. Perhaps, if they could think of some way to make Charlotte *want* to get up and walk again—then he could take care of the rest himself. He was sure he could help her forget her *capitaine*, if she could just give him the opportunity. He loved her so much that some of it had to spill over into her heart, as well!

Chapter XXXIX

It was a bright sunny day, typical of early March, still cold and slightly windy, but with a promising warmth that foretold the coming of spring. Charlotte lay back on the sofa in the second parlor, enjoying the warmth of the fire and the cheerful sunlight that streamed in through the large front windows, making splashes of gold on the polished oak floor.

Pierre should be returning soon. He had come by earlier that morning, brimming over with good news. Almost three months to the day from the date of the Fort Rosalie massacre, the Natchez reign of terror had come to an end. After a months's siege by the combined forces of French and Choctaw warriors, on February 28th the Natchez had surrendered the remainder of their French prisoners to the Choctaws and stolen away into the night to seek refuge in the interior. From all appearances, the majority of that hostile Indian nation had abandoned their forts and lands along the banks of the Mississippi forever.

It was strange, thought Charlotte. Charles had once told her that the Indians celebrated March as the beginning of their New Year—the moon of the deer, they called it. The Natchez, then, had met their defeat during the thirteenth and last moon of their old year. Was that perhaps an omen?

More widows and orphans rescued from Indian massacres were streaming into New Orleans. Those women and girls who were not in need of attention at the Charity Hospital were welcomed with open arms by the Ursulines, while the young boys were sent to the Capuchins. Many of the French soldiers were also coming back, and the town was a beehive of activity. Pierre said the governor was promising the people they would never again find themselves in such a precarious position as they had been during those first panic-stricken days of the Natchez uprising, for he intended to complete the enclosure of the entire city and had already given orders to construct a chain of eight small forts between New Orleans and what had once been known as Natchez territory upriver in order to guarantee protection and places of refuge for the colonists in time of need.

Sister Marie and the other nuns were so occupied these days attending their new guests at the convent, as well as the wounded at the hospital, which the Ursulines also had under their charge, that Charlotte had asked to help out by at least rolling bandages.

The dormitory on the second floor, where Charlotte and her companions had spent their first days in New Orleans as *filles à la cassette*, was full again, this time with haggard-faced women and children, whose wide, terror-stricken eyes still mirrored the countless horrors they had witnessed during the slaughter of their loved ones and subsequent days of captivity.

Sister Marie had closed the door of the second parlor to keep some of the noise out, but Charlotte knew the well-meaning nun had probably also wanted to isolate her as much as possible from those constant reminders of the massacre and the memories it still held for her.

Charlotte felt a little ashamed of her own grief when she saw those unfortunate survivors. Each had lost a loved one, sometimes two or three—a father, brother, husband, lover—even as she had lost Charles, but at least she had been spared the agony of having seen him tortured and killed before her very eyes and then been subjected to unspeakable indignities at the hands of his murderers!

Mon Dieu! What a cruel, barbaric land this New World was! Only the other day she had heard Pierre and Sister Marie talking about the auto-de-fé the governor had ordered held on the levee facing the Place d'Armes, in which four captured Natchez warriors and two Indian women had been burned at the stake in retaliation for the butchery at Fort Rosalie. The town had turned out in great numbers to

262

see it. The people were in a vindictive mood, and that was understandable, but Charlotte was glad she hadn't been there. How could one horror wipe out another? As Sister Marie had commented, it was not a very good example of Christianity to the Indians they were trying to convert. Charles had always said that Bienville, the former governor and founder of New Orleans, had managed to keep peace with the Indians during his period in office because he had tried to win them over with friendship instead of force. And why shouldn't it be that way? After all, this new land was big enough to hold them all. Why couldn't they live in peace and mutual respect?

Pierre had asked her again to marry him, and she had finally agreed to discuss the possibility with him when he returned later that day. She had done so with reservations, for she felt it would be unfair to him. Not only would he be taking on the burden of an invalid wife, but he knew how she had loved—how she still loved Charles.

"I've always been a proud man, perhaps too proud sometimes," he had replied. "But when it comes to you, Charlotte, I have no pride. I want you on any terms. I admit it will be hard to have a dead hero as a rival, but I think I can make you happy if you marry me."

Perhaps he would. Most certainly if anyone could help her forget the pain of losing Charles, just when she had begun to realize how much she really loved him, it was Pierre.

She had laid the finished rolls of bandages to one side of the sofa and dozed off. The hustle and bustle of the convent had died down, now that most of the nuns had gone off to the hospital or were out in the back with the new boarders, trying to whittle down the mountains of dirty linen, while the children were at their studies in their classrooms and the babies taking their midday naps in the nursery.

Charlotte lay there, feeling delightfully warm and snug beneath the patchwork quilt Sister Marie had thrown over her, floating in the halfway world between reality and fantasy. She had been dreaming. Charles had carried her to the arbor and he was kissing her . . . no, they were in the swamps under a dark green canopy of trees . . . she could hear the low, vibrant timbre of his voice, feel his presence once more. It all seemed so real.

She heard footsteps coming softly across the room towards her, but she was reluctant to let her. dream go. It would be Pierre, wanting to awaken her with a kiss, but she kept her eyes closed, holding on to those last few seconds with Charles's phantom.

Mon Dieu! Would it always be like this? Pierre's lips on hers, but Charles in her thoughts? Poor dear Pierre! She must try to love him all the more. He must not know how much she still missed Charles.

A tear slipped out from beneath her closed lids. She dared not open her eyes at that moment, lest Pierre see she was crying.

The shaded clearing in the wilderness was still in her mind's eye. She could swear it was Charles bending over her. The very intensity of her longing had conjured his presence . . . the odor of his buckskins in her nostrils, the brush of his beard on her cheek . . . it all seemed so real.

She tried to see through her tears. Charles's suntanned face was shimmering there above her. She was still dreaming, then. Closing her eyes once more, she surrendered to the sweetness of the moment, not wanting ever to awaken again. At last she was dreaming the dream she had dared not dream until that moment. Charles was alive, vibrant and pulsating beside her. His presence filled the room, filled her being, and she let it envelop her. Eagerly she reached out and drew him to her, rejoicing in the hard urgency of his body, the taste of him.

Dream or reality, it didn't matter any more—she wanted him. *Mon dieu!* How she wanted him! The loneliness and anguish of all those bitter months rebelled within her, and she matched the increasing barrage of his kisses with her own. *Oh, God! Don't let me wake up now—let me be one with him, even if only in fantasy!* She clung to him desperately, loathe to let him sink back into the shadowy recesses of her dreams once more.

A finger traced the path of a furtive tear as it coursed down her cheek.

"My sweet little one, don't cry," came a familiar voice in her ear. "I never want to see you unhappy again."

Her eyes flew open a second time. She couldn't be dreaming. His beard had singed her lips and her mouth still smarted from the impact of their last kiss. Her phantom lover had suddenly materialized, but how or why he had come to be there didn't seem to matter just then. Nothing mattered any more except that he was there. At that moment even the black-robed nuns just beyond the parlor door were forgotten. All she could think of now were those endless months of yearning, those gnawing fears that they would never be able to be together again like this.

Charlotte reveled in the vivid reality of him, as his mouth cupped over her own and she parted her lips to receive him.

"*Ma petite*, I've waited so long," he whispered huskily as, spurred on by the passion he felt surging within her, he moved his lips downward to the white swell of her breasts where they rose impatiently to meet him from the dark confines of her black velvet gown.

For a fleeting moment she had a faint recollection of where they were. "Charles . . . not here . . . the nuns . . ." she protested weakly, but even as she spoke, she found herself instinctively helping him make his way through the tangled maze of her skirts. It was too late to stem the tide. They had called out to each other in their dreams for so long that now their flesh could not be denied. She knew it had to be. Her heart, her very being had made her decision for her.

"Oh, Charles, it's you . . . it's always been you, from the very beginning."

Chapter XL

A chorus of shrill young voices reciting their catechism suddenly reminded Charlotte that they were not really in a dream world. She disentangled herself from Charles's arms in a flurry of confusion and guilt. The years of convent training rose to the surface again.

"Mon Dieu! The nuns!" she gasped, trying hurriedly to rearrange her disheveled skirts and set the topsy-turvy white cap on her head straight again.

A little awed now by his impetuosity, Dubair rose and tried to regain his own composure as well. Seizing the quilt from where it had fallen to the floor in a colorful heap beside his musket, he quickly covered her again with it, flushing deeply beneath his tan as he tucked it gently about her limbs.

"Nom de nom! What have I done?" he exclaimed in dismay. He had always prided himself for his ability to control himself even under great duress. He would have killed any man who had taken her as he had just done!

"Charlotte, my sweet, sweet Charlotte . . . I—I didn't mean it to happen like this. There was no disrespect meant, but I've loved and wanted you for so long . . ."

Charlotte smiled, more composed than he, as the warmth of his love engulfed her and her body continued to vibrate as one with his. She seemed to draw strength and a sense of well being from the feeling.

"And I love and want you, too, Charles," she said softly. "I can't fight that truth any longer."

Taking his stricken face gently between her hands, she traced each familiar feature in joyous disbelief, still unable

266

to accept the testimony of her senses. "Oh, my dear, if this is a dream, let it go on forever!"

At her words, his eyes flashed and he drew her to him again, his lips eagerly seeking her out with renewed vigor, but this time she could no longer ignore the reality of where they were.

"*Mon Dieu*, Charles! Surely we're both mad! Imagine if one of the good nuns walked in on us just now!"

"They'd probably call in the priest and have him marry us on the spot," he laughed, "which is precisely what I've been trying to do for almost two years now!" Nevertheless, he made the effort to check himself, for the prospect of a *religieuse* suddenly appearing on the scene and passing judgment on him momentarily dampened his ardor.

It had been a stroke of luck that he had been able to enter the convent at a moment when the few nuns on duty had been occupied out back or in the classrooms. The sentry outside already knew him, so there had been no need to use his rank to get by. Then, on entering the building and seeing no one, he had gone to the second parlor hoping to find someone there to announce his arrival, when he had seen Charlotte dozing on the sofa.

How precious those intimate moments with her had been! He hadn't expected so much to have happened so quickly, but her passionate response to his kisses had been all that had been needed to set him off. After all, he had been burning with desire for her for so long.

"But they told me you were dead," she was saying excitedly. "I still can't believe it's really you!"

"*C'est moi, c'est moi*," he replied with a chuckle, "and very much alive, as I think you know by now, *n'est-ce pas, ma petite?*"

He kissed her playfully, but was tempted to linger again as her lips parted and he saw his desire, still unquenched, echoed in her eyes. How lovely she was at that moment, her pale face flushed with the glow of love! She was a beautiful, passionate woman now—no longer the timid, trembling child he had held in his arms in the swamplands, terrified of monsters and even more of her own awakening emotions.

"But—but they found your *pirogue* and the bodies of

your men—everyone said you'd been killed and fallen into the river or, worse yet, been taken prisoner. Oh, dear, dear Charles, you don't know how I've suffered thinking of you lying dead somewhere in the marshes, perhaps with your head cut off—"

He listened to her agitated recital with a gentle smile, thinking how occasional glimpses of the wide-eyed child could still be seen beneath that new womanly exterior of hers. The provocative combination appealed to him.

"And all the while I thought my prayers were falling on deaf ears? May God forgive me!" she continued. "But however did you manage to escape?"

He sat beside her on the edge of the sofa and, taking her hand in his, tried to find the right words to explain. But how could he tell her of all the horror and bloodshed he had seen in those months he had been away?

"It's true, little one. I was shot and fell into the river when the Natchez fired on me and my men. But I managed to stay hidden under the boat until they went on their way. Then I swam as best I could to the opposite shore and made my way to a nearby Choctaw camp."

"Then you were wounded? Oh, my dear!"

He smiled reassuringly. "It's all right now. It was here in my arm . . ."

She touched the singed hole in his sleeve and peered anxiously at it, as if trying to see what lay beneath it.

"Does it still hurt?"

"Really, it's all right now," he laughed. "I've had worse wounds, believe me."

"At first we feared you'd been caught in the massacre at Rosalie."

"I did go to the fort, but that Chopart, the commander there, was an arrogant jackass. He wouldn't listen to reason. The Natchez uprising was his fault to a great extent. His high-handed ways with the Indians and refusal to take warnings or advice from anyone helped bring on the attack.

"*Bien*, to make a long story sehort. I gave up trying to talk some sense into that fool head of his and decided to go on with the rest of my mission, which was to see some of the more important Choctaw chieftains of that region and

268

try to insure their collaboration with us against the Natchez, in case of an uprising, which I suspected was already brewing."

"Then you had a hand in helping convince the Choctaws to side with us?"

"Yes. After I patched up my wound at the Choctaw camp, I prevailed upon the chieftain there, who already knew me and was convinced of my sincerity, to take me to Alibamon Mano, one of the most powerful leaders of the Choctaw nation, so I could talk to him and enlist his aid for our side.

"Meanwhile Captain de Lassus had gone to see some of the other Choctaw leaders in the vicinity of Mobile and also won their support, so when Commander LeSueur led almost eight hundred of them in the first assault against the Natchez and later the Sieur de Loubois arrived with reinforcements from Tunica for the siege, the Choctaws were our major fighting force. Actually, without them as our allies, we could have never resolved the Indian crisis in Louisiana. But enough of warfare! We have a lifetime ahead for us to fill in all the details. Tell me of you, *ma petite*."

"There's nothing really to tell, except my anguish," replied Charlotte, holding tightly to his hand, as if afraid he might suddenly fade back again into her dreams as quickly as he had emerged from them. "All the time you were fighting and risking your life time and again, I thought you were already dead! How I prayed for the salvation of your soul."

"And your sweet prayers probably did their share in saving me from the hell I was in at that moment, little one. You have no idea how many times I thought of you as I scouted the enemy defenses or fought off some murdering savage. Sometimes it was only the memory of my promise and the vision of you waiting here for me that made me fight just a little harder to stay alive so I could come back to you."

He reached out and, removing the cap from her head, buried his fingers in that mass of tawny gold hair until it fell free about her shoulders.

"How many times I dreamed of this moment," he murmured.

"Oh, Charles, if you leave me again I'll die! I just couldn't go through such agony again!"

"Don't worry, little one. I don't plan to be going anywhere for a long time to come. When the governor spoke of decorating me for my services to the colony and making me a commander of one of the new forts, I told him all I wanted was to retire to my plantation and just be a member of the citizen's reserve."

"Then you're here to stay? You really won't be going up and down that dreadful river anymore?"

"I won't ever leave you again if I can help it, *ma petite*. But what is this? All dressed in black? *Mon Dieu!* Where is that spunky little girl I fell in love with?"

Charlotte hung her head sadly, as the more bitter aspects of reality came flooding back to remind her that all her sorrows had not dissolved into joy.

"I've been in mourning . . . first for Madelón, then when I thought you were gone, too, I—life had no interest for me without you, Charles . . ." she finished rather lamely.

"Well, I'm back now, *ma petite*, just as I promised you I'd be, so there's no need to dwell on the past any more. We'll be married and get on with living. We've a whole lifetime ahead of us."

"I—I still can't walk, you know. I may never be able to."

"No more excuses. I can't promise you we'll never again have difficulties in the future, or even that I can make you walk someday—although I'll certainly never give up trying—but from now on, whatever comes, we'll face it together."

"I'm yours now," she replied softly. "I stopped refusing you from the moment I awakened in your arms and knew you'd come back to me. I think my heart has always been yours—ever since that first time you held me close in the swamps, remember? Everytime I'd feel your arms around me after that, something in me seemed to sense it was where I belonged."

He tilted her head up to his, his hand still buried in her abundant hair, and kissed her gently. "My sweet, let me take you home, to the home I've built for you."

"It will be the first one I've ever really known," she confessed. "And to think I had to come halfway across the world to find it—and most of all you, Charles, for wherever you are, that's where home will be for me."

She clung to the warm firmness of him, still marveling at the miracle of his presence. But their brief interlude of intimacy was short-lived, for suddenly the door opened abruptly and Pierre strode in rapidly, with Sister Marie following anxiously at his heels. His dark eyes flashed like glowing coals in his ashen face.

Chapter XLI

Charlotte stared at Pierre and Sister Marie in bewilderment. For just a little while she had forgotten anyone else existed in the world except her and Charles.

"Oh, look, *mes amis!* It's Charles—it's a miracle—he's alive!" she greeted them rather confusedly, trying to hide how awkward she suddenly felt beneath the anguish she sensed in Pierre's gaze.

"Yes, I know—the sentry told me as I was coming in," replied the Creole. "I congratulate you, *Capitaine,* on your good fortune, which seems to abound in many things."

Dubair rose. At any other time he would have felt rather self-conscious standing there unshaven and in his tattered *coureur de bois* buckskins beside this elegantly dressed Creole in his brown velvet riding outfit. But Charlotte was truly his now, and he felt like a king.

"I agree, monsieur. I'm indeed fortunate," he replied.

"We all give thanks for your safe return, *Capitaine,*" interjected Sister Marie, who was all smiles, but a little apprehensive as she watched the tension mounting by the second in Treval's countenance.

"I'm naturally glad to see you're alive, after all, *Capitaine*," conceded the Creole, "But I see you still haven't lost your knack for bad timing."

Dubair smiled, the sweet warmth of Charlotte's surrender still enveloping his being. "It's strange you should say that, monsieur, since I was just thinking how inopportune your own entrance was at this moment. You see, Mlle. Charlotte has just consented to be my wife."

Treval looked as if he had been struck. He shot a questioning glance at Charlotte, but the sight of her glowing eyes and flushed cheeks told him all he needed to know, perhaps more than he cared to contemplate. If only he had seen her look that way just once for him!

"Charlotte, how could you?" he stammered accusingly. "When just this morning you told me . . ."

She felt as if the knife in his heart were in her own. "Oh, Pierre, dear Pierre . . . I—I don't want to hurt you. Please try to understand. This morning I thought Charles was dead—but he's alive now and—oh, Pierre, dear sweet Pierre, I'm so sorry. Please forgive me!"

She caught his hand and pressed it against her cheek, bathing it with her tears. For a moment he stood looking down silently at her. As he saw her anguish, the anger and hurt in his eyes softened a little. He knew this was probably the last time he would ever look so deeply into that piquant face he had come to love so much.

Drawing himself up suddenly to his full height, his countenance became an expressionless mask.

"Captain Dubair, I think we must settle this matter outside, away from mademoiselle. All this emotion is not good for her."

Charles's blue eyes narrowed apprehensively. "I don't think there's anything left to settle, monsieur. Mlle. Charlotte has made her choice."

Charlotte continued to cling to Treval's hand, her eyes trying desperately to fathom the dark depths of those enigmatic eyes, even while a great sense of foreboding began to stir within her.

272

"Pierre, please," she murmured weakly. "Please, no more fighting!"

The Creole cupped the tip of her chin gently with his free hand and looked long and lingeringly at her. "Don't cry, *niña*. This has to be done. You'll thank me someday."

He tore his hand free from hers and turned abruptly to Dubair. "Shall we go into the other room, *Capitaine?*"

Charles sighed. "Very well, monsieur. I'm at your disposition." He turned for a moment to Charlotte. "Don't worry, *ma petite*. I'll try to settle this peaceably."

Pierre stood waiting impatiently in the doorway, his hand resting on the pistol in his belt, which he had been wearing daily since the Indian uprisings had begun. Dubair followed him reluctantly.

Sister Marie, who had been silent until then, suddenly spoke up in a firm voice. "Need I remind you, messieurs, that you're in a religious house, and we'll not tolerate any fighting on this premise?"

"We're aware of that, madame," replied Pierre. "For that reason, I'd appreciate your accompanying us, so you can witness all that transpires between us."

"Oh, yes, *Soeur* Marie, please go with them," pleaded Charlotte anxiously from the sofa. "Try to keep peace between them!"

She watched them retreat from the room, the apprehension mounting within her. *Mon Dieu! Don't let anything happen to Charles now that I've just found him again! And Pierre—don't let Charles hurt him! How he must be suffering at this moment!* If anything happened to either of them, it would be her fault. She should have never raised Pierre's hopes so high that morning. He had a right to feel doubly cheated now. But Charles was alive—the joy of it had obliterated all else. Accepting him had seemed so right. She belonged to him completely now, and there were no regrets.

They had left the door slightly ajar, and she listened eagerly to the voices in the other room. The outside parlor was large and they must have gone to the farther side of it. She could hear them talking, but the words blurred just enough that she could not distinguish one from another. The tones were polite and suppressed. At first she could hear nothing more than a few formal exchanges and remarks. Slowly, however, those well-modulated tones became strained, and Charlotte despaired. If only she could go to them and stop their quarreling before . . .

"Charles! Pierre!" she called, but they didn't hear or refused to heed her.

Louder still came their voices. She could catch her name being repeated several times.

Once or twice Ssiter Marie's gentle voice interrupted, but it was like a drop of water caught up in a hurricane.

"Charles! Pierre!" she called out again. How could she make them hear her? They must not duel! They had promised her time and again her decision would be final.

A pistol shot broke the raging storm of words like a clap of thunder. Then there was only silence. Trembling from head to foot, Charlotte bolted forward on the sofa. Holy mother of God! What had happened? Had Pierre shot Charles? Or had the captain drawn first? Why were they so silent? Couldn't anyone reply?

"Sister Marie!" Her voice was so pitifully weak she could hardly hear it herself.

There was only one thought in her mind at that moment. Who lay out there on the oakwood floor? She slipped her feet mechanically over the edge of the sofa and stood with surprisingly little effort.

"Charles! Pierre!" she called again, tears of frustration pouring down her cheeks. Why didn't anyone answer her? Everything was so quiet!

As on the day of the fire, she suddenly became obsessed with just one thought. She had to know. She had to get to Charles . . . to Pierre. Unconscious of what was happening, she took a step forward. Pain shot up her legs as her paralyzed muscles rebelled against the frenzy that urged them on. She started to fall, but caught herself on the arm of the sofa. Tears blinded her eyes, and she could see the half-open doorway wavering, so far away . . . the acrid taste of smoke seemed to fill her mouth, stinging her eyes and suffocating her lungs . . . No, her memory was playing tricks on her! There was no fire now. Only the door there, that door she had to reach at all costs.

The numbness of her legs had turned to a mass of throbbing pain, but she staggered on. *Oh, God! Charles! Pierre!* She called out to them, but no sound came from her lips. It took every ounce of strength she could muster to move the leaden weight of her limbs.

She fell again and for a moment knelt sobbing in despair on the floor. But the door was so close now. Drawing deep down into her being for a last spurt of energy, she reached out and caught the carved leg of a huge oak console table and dragged herself laboriously over to it. She nearly knocked over the silver candelabrum that stood on its top as she pulled herself up once more and stood there for a moment swaying unsteadily on her screaming legs. Better they were numb than the sharp, jagged pain that had awakened in them now! She grabbed for the jamb of the door and stood there, perspiration drenching her from head to foot, as she tried to see through her hysterical tears.

The three were standing there, as if suspended in a tableau that had awaited her appearance to animate it. At the sight of her tottering in the doorway, Dubair made a step to go to her, but Sister Marie's hand detained him a moment longer. Pierre was standing in the main entrance, gun in hand, but at a glimpse of her he turned and, without a word, closed the door behind him.

Charlotte lunged forward toward Charles, dragging her aching limbs behind her. Unable to stand there any longer, he broke away from Sister Marie's grip and ran to catch her, just as she began to crumple to the floor.

Lifting the trembling girl up quickly into his arms, he carried her over to one of the sofas.

"Oh, Charles, I thought—I thought . . ." The tears of relief choked her words.

"But you're walking, little one! Do you realize what you've done?" he exclaimed as he stroked the damp tendrils lovingly from her brow, while Sister Marie knelt beside her and, reaching beneath the ruffled petticoats, began to knead and massage her shrieking limbs gently.

"You see, child, you *can* walk. It hurts now, I know, but that will pass," the nun was saying.

Charles was completely bewildered. Even in the midst of his joy at seeing Charlotte walk, he couldn't help casting a

275

look of disbelief at the door that had just closed behind Pierre.

"He—he simply drew his gun out and fired—fired point blank up into the air, and then left! Whatever possessed the man?" he asked in dismay.

"I heard the shot and kept calling out to you, but no one answered!" wept Charlotte.

"He provoked me," continued Dubair, his face wreathed in confusion. "I kept telling him I didn't want to fight, but suddenly he fired straight up into the air and walked away with a shrug of his shoulders—almost as if he'd planned it!"

Sister Marie gave a knowing smile from where she knelt on the floor beside Charlotte. "I didn't understand what had come over him either, at first," she admitted, "but then it suddenly dawned on me what he was trying to do. That's why I wouldn't let you answer or go to Charlotte right away when she called."

"But I still don't understand . . ." said Dubair.

"Nor I," echoed Charlotte.

"You will," smiled Sister Marie. "But miracles shouldn't be questioned too closely. They should just be accepted with gratitude. For that's the final gift Pierre wanted to give you, Charlotte, the miracle of love . . . his for you . . . and yours and your captain's for each other!"

But at that moment Charlotte and the captain no longer heard her. Their eyes were locked in an embrace that had transported them into their own private world.

Sister Marie rose discreetly to leave the young lovers alone for a moment. There was still so much for them to tell each other, so many plans to make. Let them have a little privacy. After all, they would be wed on the morrow. With a contented smile she went to dispatch a messenger to the *Compagnie* to tell them that the last Casquette Girl was no longer available.